Firelight Flickered over
Jorion's Skin and Hair,
Catching Taine in the Snare
of His Attraction . . .

At that moment Taine knew why he was called the Golden Dragon . . . a golden dragon of unspeakable beauty. Gazing at him, she failed to realize that the coverlet wrapped around her had slipped perilously low . . .

Jorion drank in the tantalizing view. Generous breasts rose from the constraints of the tightly wrapped cloth, so near to freedom that the smallest tug would see them liberated. Pulse pounding, a nearly ungovernable urge grew to loosen the barrier to his goal and see the bounty of pale ivory flesh draped only in the dark fire of her luxurious hair. But doubtless such action would raise her anger—and her defenses. To forestall the ill-conceived compulsion, he forced his head up and his eyes away from her unknowing enticement. The motion drew her gaze to his.

Lured by his dark eyes, Taine tumbled into the depths where golden fires burned. The gilded net of the dragon's attraction wrapped around her, pulling her toward him. In a gaze gone soft with desire's dense mists, Jorion read her fascination and, unbidden, his arms lifted to draw her near . . .

The
Dragon's
Fire

MARYLYLE
ROGERS

POCKET BOOKS

New York   London   Toronto   Sydney   Tokyo

Another *Original* publication of POCKET BOOKS

POCKET BOOKS, a division of Simon & Schuster, Inc.
1230 Avenue of the Americas, New York, N.Y. 10020

ISBN: 0-671-62695-7

First Pocket Books printing February 1988

10 9 8 7 6 5 4 3 2 1

POCKET and colophon are trademarks of Simon & Schuster, Inc.

Printed in the U.S.A.

To Linda Marrow
for that second mile once and once again

Author's Note

In 1270 Prince Edward, son of King Henry III, embarked on a crusade with French King Lewis. When he landed on the African coast where they were to meet, however, he found that Lewis was dead and all of his supporters had made peace with the unbelievers. Edward was indignant and refused to be party to it. Although his force was extremely small, he went on, a deed either very brave or the height of foolishness. During the next two years he won several important battles but came to realize he could gain no material success in Palestine. After suffering a stealthy attack by a member of the Assassin sect (source of our commonly used term), he made a ten-year truce with Sultan Bibars. By the time he arrived again in England, his father had died and he was King Edward I.

Over the next decade and a half, Edward subdued Wales while keeping a covetous eye on Scotland, where his sister Margaret was wife to King Alexander III. Margaret had gifted Alexander with three children who survived to adulthood: two fine, healthy sons and a daughter, also named Margaret, who was wed to King Eric of Norway. The second Margaret bore a third Margaret and soon died. Within a very few years, death took the whole of Alexander's immediate family, leaving him with neither wife nor child. It was a king's duty to leave an heir to his throne and Alexander remarried.

In the meantime, the lords of Scotland gathered and agreed to accept Alexander's infant granddaughter, Margaret (called the Maid of Norway), as heir until a child was born of his new marriage. Yet, even as they agreed, there were rumblings from the Scottish clan leaders, a pressing for the choosing of sovereign from amongst themselves, according to the ancient custom of Scotland, by right of blood. Despite the warnings of many, on a stormy night Alexander rode across a rocky coastline to where his young wife was lodged. His horse stumbled and fell. Alexander was dead, leaving only the Maid to succeed him.

Edward, seeing his chance, lost no time in arranging a betrothal between his young heir and the Maid. The guardians of Scotland reluctantly agreed to the union whose fruit would join the crowns of Scotland and England forever. Again there was discontent among the clan leaders and talk of choosing a sovereign by right of blood (League of Turnberry).

A luxuriously outfitted ship was sent to Norway to bring the small girl to Britain. It came no closer than the Orkney Isles. From there a message was sent: the Maid had succumbed to the hardships of the crossing and died. There were quiet questions and whispered rumors that the girl yet lived. But no proof.

Thirteen claimants to the Scottish crown rose. Three held close claims, but only two were in serious contention: John Baliol and Robert Bruce (thereafter known as the Competitor). All claimants agreed to accept Edward of England's decision on the matter. He ruled in favor of John Baliol. When the time came for Baliol to be crowned and to accept the homage of the other Scottish nobles, the Competitor resigned his position to his son, also Robert Bruce, who avoided the ceremony and homage by accompanying his daughter to Norway to see her wed to King Eric, the Maid's grieving father.

Within four years Baliol came into conflict with Edward, was easily subdued, forced to kneel before the English king, and exiled to France for the rest of his days. While most of

Baliol's supporters submitted to Edward and retained their lands, some refused and their lands were held forfeit. Edward then took Scottish rule into his own hands, but for the next ten years he fought the rebellious Scots, who struggled on under the name of Baliol and the leadership of Comyn and Wallace. During this time the Bruces fought at Edward's side against the supporters of their old Baliol opponent. In the fall of 1303, Edward engaged in many battles with the Scottish rebels. Throughout the following winter he held his court at Dunfermline in Scotland and was there attended by his wife and most of his nobles.

By the end of 1304, Robert Bruce (grandson of the Competitor) began to fight the English under his family's claim to the throne and eventually won the Scottish crown. Edward's son and heir, a great disappointment to his father, became a thoroughly unlikable man and, as King Edward II, was forced to abdicate and then murdered.

There are several other points important to note. First, it was a common medieval practice to give hostages as insurance for a negotiated peace or truce. Second, neither the abduction of a wealthy bride nor the marriage of children for the sake of their property were uncommon in the Middle Ages. Also, child mortality was very high and, despite large families, family names often died out for lack of a male heir.

The Dragon's Fire

❧ Prologue ❧

Orkney Isles
October of 1290

ROLLING HILLS, BARE AT the top but ringed in green, rose from a treacherous sea. Serene and innocent but an hour before, the briny water was quickly becoming a roiling maelstrom, as if an angry giant were stirring some great cauldron too slow to boil. Bravely cresting angry waves, a man seated in the prow of the small boat shifted a blanket-wrapped bundle to lie more warmly in his arms. While two others struggled at the oars, propelling them toward the isle, he cast an appraising eye between foam-tipped furrows of salt water and the proud ship behind, pitching with each onslaught. The quickly darkening sky, with its ominously building clouds, reaffirmed the need for haste in concluding his errand. The ship's captain wanted to be out on the open seas before full nightfall. Far better to ride out the storm there than risk being dashed against this harsh and rocky strand.

A mighty wall of water picked up the boat, toyed with it awhile, then tossed it aside to land, bottom abruptly scraping on a pebbled stretch of shore. The oarsmen jumped into the freezing water to pull the boat from the sea's greedy hold.

A stiff westerly wind whipped the man's dark cloak about

him as he stepped from the boat. Leaving the oarsmen behind, he walked toward a solitary horseman waiting silent and still. The importance of the gently lifted bundle was evident in the care with which it was received.

"You know the landing point?" the cloaked man questioned. The horseman nodded.

"Three nights hence a ship will arrive. Once on the mainland, without pause make haste to Castle Cregel. Return then to Carrick."

Again the horseman nodded.

With a wary glance toward the dark shadows of the isle's steeply rising hills, the cloaked man added, "Get now to your shelter. Who can know what hidden eyes may see?"

Wishing the rider godspeed, the man stepped back, watching as the horse whirled to leap forward and quickly fade into the growing gloom. He pulled two items free from his tunic before turning to the two carefully chosen oarsmen. A jagged flash of light rent the surface of black clouds and a heavy rain poured forth. Wind-driven, hard drops beat a steady patter against the leather covering of the packet one burly oarsman moved to accept, the packet that had been excuse for this stop before their mournful return to Norway.

The giant roared and the man waited until his thunder quieted. "With this"—he held up a soft pigskin bag—"you can convince a fisherman to see you safe across to Scotland." The contents of the bag he dropped in an outstretched palm clinked unmistakably, bringing a greedy gleam to the oarsman's eyes. Clearly as little as possible would be wasted in securing passage. "And one bag more of twice the weight will you earn," he continued, "when my friends at the English court assure me 'twas quickly placed in King Edward's hand—no other's." His slight smile had a cynical twist; this oarsman was loyal to the cause, but a little added incentive would lend wings to his feet. The oarsman tucked both the packet and the bag into his tunic and set off at a brisk pace for the village while the man stepped into the boat and lifted an oar.

Long before the small boat had battled its way back over violent water to the tall ship's protection, the horseman with his precious bundle had disappeared into the dark, stormy night. The steady rhythm of hooves pounding against wet stones and soggy earth continued its monotonous dirge until a sudden thwap drove breath from the rider. For an endless moment he froze, back arched and mouth open in a silent cry. Sagging slowly to the side, he fell from his still-moving steed, bundle tightly clasped to his chest.

Two shadows detached themselves from the dark shape of a rock outcropping and slid soundlessly to the fallen man. Crouching at his side, one rolled the body over and reached eagerly for the small bundle. The blanket stained with the blood of their victim was hastily unwound. A sudden bolt of light flamed on the dark-fire hair of a small girl-child and, before it faded as quickly away, revealed the war between fear and fury that raged in the deep green eyes. As the storm rolled its echo, a tall and thick-set man lifted the child and rose to his feet.

His companion eyed the burden, brows drawn. So fragile a creature to be both five-year-old queen and deadly threat to Baliol goals. Shaking his head to clear the thought, he moved to join the other even as the sky abruptly lit again.

Attention caught by a gleam, the tall man glanced down to catch the quick image of a delicate ring formed by entwined gold and silver strands, loose but held tightly on the child's thumb by the fist clenched about it.

❈ Chapter 1 ❈

Dunfermline, Scotland
November of 1303

PRICKLES OF TENSION STUNG Margaret's neck. She tossed a heavy tangle of dark auburn curls over her shoulder and cast a quick, apprehensive glance behind. Sunlight without heat glared on the fair's colorful tents and striped awnings. Merchants stood in the shade beneath, shrill voices piercing the crisp autumn air as they hawked their wares. Through the throng she saw them advancing relentlessly: The tall one, whose deceptive gauntness hid a surprising strength just as his perpetual sneer added deep grooves to a face in reality less than a decade older than her own eight-and-ten; and the other, dull hair flailing in greasy strands over thick-set shoulders. Aye, they were near to overtaking her. The vicious gleam in their eyes told her the price she'd pay for her escape from both their advances and the prison they guarded, an escape that had put them in the path of a punishment well to be feared. She could nearly feel their hot breath singeing her back.

Picking up her pace, nearly running, she weaved through crowded aisles. Still they followed, steadily, persistently. Seeking some unobtrusive means to elude them, her eyes desperately traveled over the noisy crowd gathered on the wide, winter-dying meadow—and knew her own folly. Here no mouth-watering aromas of edible treats, no laughing children, no musicians to offer joyful tunes in hopes of a thrown coin or two. Indeed, there were no welcome sounds, only the low discordant rumble of many men speaking at once, as they jostled one another in a crush of tangled humanity. With the despised English invaders wintering in the town a short distance away, filling it near to bursting, no local woman would venture abroad; and the attention Margaret drew, a lone female of striking loveliness, made blending with the crowd impossible.

A miswitted moonling you are, the girl berated herself. From Bertwald's descriptions of the varied delights to be found at country fairs she'd woven bright dreams to relieve monotonous grey days in her castle-prison. In coming here she'd risked much to give life to those cherished fantasies but in the seeking had found naught but disappointment— an all-too-familiar emotion.

Disheartened by the death of her illusions, she failed to realize immediately that this was no village fair. These merchants made their living by seeking the royal entourage wherever King Edward chose to establish a long-term camp. A king bent on conquering all had drawn these men of business in his wake, across England to Wales and now to Scotland. The gains to be earned in offering goods nearly depleted to men long engaged in battle and held from home and its comforts lent an avaricious gleam to their eyes. The quality of their long woolen tunics and silver-buckled, wide leather belts demonstrated the success of their plan. Each stood surrounded by goods, either draped from strong ropes strung between forked poles or laid across the front of makeshift stalls. More weapons and male accoutrements than rich cloths or spices.

Eyes opened to the true nature of the gathering she'd foolishly joined, her shoulders sagged and steps faltered in momentary defeat. Suddenly, rough hands twisted in the trail of her skirts, dragging her back over the meadow's uneven floor until she stumbled to a halt. Dark curly locks swirled out, catching fire from the sun as she whipped her head around to meet her thick-set foe, eye to eye. Although alarm turned her breathing to ragged gasps for air, his jeering triumph renewed her determination, and she reached behind to tug recklessly at the coarse woolsey fabric he gripped tightly. *Win free,* she silently commanded herself, *and there will be a way, there has to be a way!* Unexpectedly, the cloth held taut between them fell slack. Loose, she whirled—and landed hard against the second man's chest. Her startled gaze flew up into a smug smile. Attention held by his cruel enjoyment, she took two slow steps back and was unprepared when the second pair of hands once more fastened on her. Trapped between them, their hands on her again, bending her once more to their will, panic rose.

Glancing wildly about, she found herself surrounded by leering faces and despair opened its chasm at her feet. Men, all men. No hope for a woman here, whispered a small, bitter voice. The course of nearly her whole life had been proof that men would aid a woman only for their own goals, a dowry, an heir—or a crown. 'Twas plain that the fairgoers, mostly fighting men in the English king's army, found only coarse amusement in the sight of a girl garbed in the rough clothes of a serf struggling against two men in mail. What surprise in that? A well-bred maid would take care not to wander abroad in such company, unless—

"Stop, or my husband will see you dead." It was a daft threat, but the first that came to mind, and if she'd had an idle moment, she'd have thanked the saints for the inspiration. The bold words halted her attackers although they failed to win her release. Refusing to cower before these wretched toads, she straightened to her full height, lifted her chin, and proudly met their disbelieving gaze.

"Where is he?" the taller one questioned, suspicion narrowing close-set eyes as he tilted his head back to look down his long nose at the tender maid. She'd been free for a few weeks, no more—surely not time enough to form such an alliance.

The other lifted one hand from its cruel grip on her shoulder to rub the three-day growth of dirty brown beard covering his heavy jaw as he laughed his derision. "What is he that we should fear him?" he sneered, flinging his arm out in a wide arc. "The local swineherd?"

Sensing their growing impatience, her eyes closed for a

brief moment as she sent an urgent plea heavenward. Then, desperation flashing in her deep green eyes like lightning through the forest, again her gaze flew wildly over the crowd. Though the air was chill, the sun was bright and glowed a beacon light on a gilded head not far distant. Surely, she reasoned frantically, a man with hair that shone so pure must be good.

"There," she pointed. Gaze fixed firmly on the back of a golden head, she missed the shock on her two pursuers' faces and failed to note the sudden stillness of those standing near enough to hear her words and see her gesture.

She refused to give thought to their staring audience for fear of losing her mad courage, as she led her pursuers steadily to the man's side. Slipping her arm through his, she rested slender fingers on the rich cloth covering an iron-thewed arm. The feel of his strength sent a shiver of aprehension over her, but it was too late to hesitate now. She turned to her pursuers and announced, "Here is my husband."

A frown of puzzlement drew fine brows together as she looked at the two men now instinctively falling back. She had expected belligerence, questions for her claim from these men who had relentlessly tracked her, not this fearful awe, these faces drained of color. Her own face grew suddenly cold as the warmth faded away. Holy Mary, what she done?

Suddenly aware of his great height, for she could meet most men at nearly eye level, her eyes traveled slowly up the broad, muscular expanse of a black-velvet-covered chest broken only by a heavy gold chain. Thick lashes fell and she drew a deep fortifying breath before opening them again to gaze with false bravado into the face of the man whose protection she sought, a deeply bronzed face that seemed all the darker for its frame of golden-blond hair. A mask of control held it devoid of expression, allowing her searching gaze to measure the strength and masculine beauty in high cheekbones, straight nose, and firm jaw. There was little of the Englishman there.

Her stare was met and returned fourfold. An inbred pride tilted her chin, more clearly showing the smooth curve of her graceful throat, as she unwaveringly met the inspection of night-black eyes. Beneath the brave facade her heart sank to her toes in fear of the trampling this lord—for so he must be—could easily administer.

Although he in no way revealed his surprise, the claimed husband was stunned by this sudden apparition of beauty who named him hers. Seeking to prove himself right-witted and not conjuring up some tantalizing vision after months of fighting in an unwelcoming land, he looked to the other characters in this mummers' play.

When at last the dark power of his gaze shifted to her two pursuers, Margaret quickly scanned the men gathered about him, plainly all nobles. Avid curiosity lit their faces, and apprehension tightened her chest. Peering surreptitiously up to the bronzed face and blond hair gilded by the sun, she grew more firmly convinced of her error in judgment and cursed herself for falling, nay leaping, into a position dependent upon the whim of such a man.

The taller of her foes, yet nearly two handbreadths shorter than the lord at her side, nearly whined his apology. "Milord, be the maid truly yours, we crave pardon for the error, but—" The silence that fell demanded the lord's confirmation or denial.

A burning awareness of her shabby old gown next to this lord's rich garb plus her growing tension threatened to strangle all hope. With held breath she too awaited his response. Again his intent stare compelled her attention. Remembering her oath never to quail before a man, she forced herself to look directly into his face.

The tall man let his fathomless black eyes study this unexpected beauty, whose delicate features were a creamy contrast against hair the shade of autumn leaves, hovering between red and brown. The shining curls hung in a thick mass to her hips, free of constraint as no gently bred woman of his acquaintance would allow. Her garb was not of his class, yet hers was a sweetly patrician face of pure and lovely lines—dainty nose, small pointed chin, and brows arched over wide-spaced eyes.

Beneath his inspection, courage held Margaret steady but, despite her effort to hide it, eyes of silvery seafoam outlined by deep forest green quietly pleaded.

Rose lips trembled slightly and drew his close scrutiny.

They were the most appealing he'd ever seen: top short and gently bowed, bottom full and tempting. He allowed his gaze to drop and slowly examine the form imperfectly disguised beneath coarse and poorly sewn brown cloth—tall, with the elegant grace of a willow sapling, its lithe slenderness emphasized the allurement of a generous bosom. Every inch a beauty—and a lady. One with a spirit he admired. She had been courageous enough to blithely make a claim no woman he knew would dare. A slight smile curved his lips. Often had Uncle Thomas chided him that no wellborn woman, save the one he had chosen, would willingly accept him for mate. Famous for his ability to make quick and unerring decisions, he lifted his penetrating stare to the two waiting men.

"My bride she is," he affirmed with a voice low and rich. "A very recent alliance." Staring again into green eyes, he deliberately added, "but binding nonetheless."

She heard the intensity of his final words and knew them for a threat. Her eyes fell before his unswerving gaze to sightlessly study the heavy leather boots that molded the lean, muscular shape of his calves. What game did he mean to play? What price would he demand for his aid? Rose lips lost their tender curve as they firmed bitterly. She'd paid a price to learn the perfidy of men and would not easily allow advantage. Doubtless he, like all males, meant to use her for his own gain.

"I beg pardon, milady," he continued, tone softened to a near caress, "I had thought you meant to keep our union secret yet a while; but, ever ready to do my lady's will, I follow your lead."

Her suspicious eyes flew up in time to see one corner of his lips tilt with cynicism, a smile that gave the lie to his willingness ever to be led. He cast a cold glance at her pursuers, even as he gently wrapped his arm about her shoulders and pulled her around to rest against his chest, hard-muscled, powerful, and threatening. Shocked and unprepared for such an embrace, more so in the midst of a crowd, she silently gasped as he lowered his head for a kiss. Braced for a rough assault, her senses tilted awry when his mouth met hers with tantalizing pressure. While his lips lifted, brushing back and forth to gently coax hers into parting, she stood motionless in his arms. Although initially aware only of the need to fool their audience, as he deepened the contact, sparks of pleasure ignited the dry tinder of her senses. The others faded into the smoky haze of a kindling blaze as his hand swept down her back, urging her closer to his heat. Scorched by his fire, she yielded, melting against the long, hard length of him.

The raucous calls of his companions at last called the lord back. Though golden flames glowed in his dark eyes, he drew away to give them a mocking smile, while her cheeks burned with embarrassment. He had not meant to carry the embrace so far nor to shame the maid before others, but holding an enticing form so close after long months without such tender company, coupled with her innocently ardent response, had driven cool reason into hiding. However, he was not displeased to discover a passion he could willingly claim his and no other's. The proof of her inexperience had been clear in a body taut until overcome by unforeseen pleasure.

Still quaking with new and frightening sensations, Margaret berated herself for submitting so fully, for losing command of her own responses and offering such an amusing scene to these knowing strangers. At least when her two pursuers, past goalers, had come to her chamber for similar purpose, she'd struggled unceasingly and won free to flee from them. She was still fleeing from them and their masters and for that reason must stand steady with this tall lord. The man holding her spoke and his words called her thoughts back from bitter memories.

"Pray give me leave to lead my sweet bride to more— accommodating surroundings." The bawdy jests his words inspired from his companions deepened the mockery of his half-smile.

The suggestive words sent a tiny tremor through the girl. His arm about her shoulders shackled her as firmly as stout rope, and she bit her lip to still the urge to struggle ignominiously. They watched so closely, these crudely bantering nobles.

"Hold, Jorion," one teasing voice called out above the rest. "Well have you kept your secret and for that deed we claim a forfeit." The speaker, a heavy-set man garbed in garish hues, leaned forward and with mock severity demanded, "Reveal the full tale of your romance."

At this request Margaret's heart stood still. How could he tell a tale that wasn't? Did the man suspect its untruth? The mere prospect produced a loud thumping that pounded in her ears and proved her heart beating most efficiently.

"Aye, tell us where you met and where you wed," called another, pushing the first aside with rough comradery. "Mayhap Rhyming Richard will turn your tale to song, and then we can claim to have known it firstly."

At the reference to his cousin Richard, the tall man's slight smile gentled with an affection that the girl, staring determinedly down at trampled meadow grass, failed to catch. Tension near unbearable, she peered up through the thick shield of lowered lashes to see sun-gilded hair catch and trap cool daylight as he shook his head in denial of the demand.

"Leastways give us your lady's name," bargained the first speaker. He stepped forward to block their path, a not inconsiderable obstacle that grew when he was joined by others.

Although as curious to know her name as they, the claimed husband smiled his refusal. "I've shared one secret with you this day. I'll savor the others for yet a while longer." His smile faded until narrowed black eyes held a hard glimmer. The cold tone with which the next words were spoken made them more command than request. "Once we've bid farewell, I pray you will find sufficient discretion to lend us peace and privacy." His companions backed away, although their coarse remarks continued as he urged the maid through their midst.

Knowing he meant to take her away, she could nearly feel the jaws of a new trap close about her and peeked up to meet wary black eyes. Curse him! He knew she had no choice but to accompany him without argument or to risk ruining all and proving the lie of her claim to her still-watching pursuers. She possessed a temper that, though quickly doused, flared as suddenly as Greek fire. It flamed when the rough crowd who had previously cast her knowing smirks now dropped their eyes and retreated as the intimidating giant accompanied her through their ranks.

As they approached the edge of the fair, Margaret saw a young squire meticulously brushing invisible dust from the black-and-gold livery of which he was so obviously proud. Catching sight of his lord, he beamed and stepped forward to proffer the reins of a magnificent golden stallion. Margaret's attention turned to the animal and she failed to see the squire's surprise on first noticing her. She would certainly have been displeased had she caught the knowing grin that suddenly flashed across his broad young face. Even the slight negative shake of his lord's head would not have warmed her humor. She'd been held in seclusion, true, but between her gaolers and the castle-serfs she'd seen enough to know the implication.

Although she had very little experience of horseflesh, she recognized the steed as an exceptional animal, sleek grace and power in every line. Aye, powerful. Temper quashed by qualms for the unknown, hesitant, unsure of the way to approach it, she halted two paces away. The man came to a sudden stop behind her. When his hands settled on her shoulders, she went rigid, feeling herself trapped between two overpowering creatures. Determined to display fear to no man, soft rose lips compressed, suppressing the urge to run in terror. However, as strong hands shifted to her slender waist and lifted her, a soft gasp escaped.

In one stride he placed her across the great beast's broad back and stepped away to look up, head tilted to one side. A strange creature she, the man decided silently, studying eyes gone deep green and meeting his unwaveringly, although an unquenchable silver glow of fear flickered in their depths. Brave enough to claim a stranger as husband but fearful of his strength. No matter, 'twas an accomplished deed. With a quick, lithe grace surprising in a man of such size, he swung himself up behind her.

She straightened her spine as the horse moved forward, holding herself stiffly to maintain the small distance between her and his broad chest. An inadequate defense, for his warmth stole out to enfold her in the aura of his power. It threatened to suffocate her. She would get away, she must! She had sworn she would never allow herself to be held again under any man's control. Yet, without protest, she was allowing one of the most intimidating specimens to quietly carry her away from the broad open field where the fair was settled, toward the town barely visible through sparse autumn-toned trees flaming on the horizon.

Unsteady in her sideways position, when their steed swerved to avoid a small boulder, she swayed and a slender hand flew out to brace against the horse's strong neck. The animal took exception to her desperate hold of his luxurious mane and tossed his head to free himself. Her hand fell to the soft cloth bundled before her and grasped it tightly. Looking down, she found her fingers twined, a white contrast, in rich black velvet. His cloak? It must be.

While her mind was caught in such inane thoughts, he calmed the high-strung steed, then pulled her against him to end her fear of a precarious seat and forestall further dangerous actions. Apollo, his stallion, was unaccustomed and unwilling to carry any but his master on his back. Unlike his huge destrier who was trained to move fearlessly through the clashing sound and threatening actions of fierce battles, this spirited creature, despite his master's wishes, might well rear up in attempt to free himself of the nervous woman's annoyances.

Seated as she was and now held close, she felt like a babe cradled in its mother's arms. The silent, mocking voice of her conscience forced her to admit that the unbidden thrill of his embrace was nothing like the gentle security of mother for child, but rather a frightening, threatening pleasure. An alarming hint that even without force this man might well be capable of rendering her powerless, subjugated to him.

Fighting back her own apprehensions, she looked again to her surroundings, to the fair growing small in the distance. As she stared around a broad shoulder to the scene behind, Apollo's hooves began a new cadence pounding on a well-worn track. Turning back, she found their path meandering through a stand of trees. Although not thickly grown, against the deep shades of towering evergreens the bright colors of oak, elm, and birch tangled in a rich profusion that offered concealment.

"No one will notice if I'm released here." Forgetting the dangers of such close proximity, the girl seeking freedom looked up to meet a steady gaze that seemed all the darker for lowered golden brows. Breath caught in her throat. The physical contrasts of the man stunned her again as completely as on her first view of him, an arresting sight of power and masculine beauty unique, unequaled. Yet she silently mocked the thought in an effort to dispel his fascination, for her experience in such matters was severely limited. The quiet voice in her mind again forced her to accept a clear truth: There could be no other such as he.

Heavy lids half-lowered, he held the strong planes of his face in an emotionless mask, allowing her lengthy appraisal. She seemed more fascinated than repelled by his foreign visage, this woman, nay lady, he had claimed his before many. Had she not realized that once the claim was made and acknowledged, he would be honor bound to see it true?

Suddenly aware of the length of her stare, she shifted her gaze to a point midway between their steed's ears and spoke again. "I thank you for your generous aid, but must hastily return to my father else he will worry."

For long moments no response was forthcoming; instead he continued to hold her closely, the horse's steady motion unchecked. The maid had been fleeing from others, and he had no doubt that once out of his sight she would as hastily flee from him.

As Margaret waited for him to answer, her fingers wrapped more tightly in black folds, threatening the cloak with irreparable disorder.

At last he said, "We'll send for your father—later."

He had spoken but the words were unwelcome to her. From his implacable tone she knew arguments would be futile. Moreover, what further argument had she to make when the whole was an untruth? She willfully relaxed tense muscles in an effort to lull his suspicions while mentally searching for some means of escape. Devising, then discarding a multitude of wild plans, she failed to hear him speak.

"What are you called?" his low voice demanded, exasperation evident for this need to repeat his query a third time.

Startled by words distinct and loud, she looked up again and found a trace of amusement on his face. As a last resort to make himself heard, he'd bent to nearly yell in her ear.

"Mar—" she began without thought, then stopped. Si-

14

lence stretched while her mind raced. She'd nearly told this English noble her name—surely a serious misstep. Although common enough, it might aid him in learning more of her than she would willingly reveal. Having met no wellborn women in the past thirteen years, save Morag, she knew few women's names. Staring blankly at the vivid patchwork of fallen leaves below, and desperately searching through the void, back from the misty memories of a little girl came a smiling face and a name. "Taine."

"Martaine?" Golden brows knit in puzzlement. Her long pause was unnatural and the name unfamiliar.

"Aye," she quickly agreed, a small smile of newfound confidence growing on soft rose lips. Congratulating herself on the natural sound of her response, she added, "'Tis most often shortened to Taine." She liked the sound of the word and determined to call herself by it from then on, an added concealment of a truth she would deny.

"And your family name?" he questioned further.

Though a perfectly sensible next question, Taine was caught unprepared. Startled green eyes flew up, but met black steadily as she coldly informed him, "I have none."

His eyes narrowed on the lovely face below, studying the stubborn set of the small chin. That she lied he was certain, but was equally convinced that the information could not easily be forced nor won from her. More, he was loath to batter the spirit and pride that attracted him. From the trials of his life he had learned many lessons, of which one was the value of patience and the ultimate victory it offered. In a siege the victor was he who outwaited his foe or lingered until a weakness was revealed. Her citadel he'd surrounded and would now merely watch and wait.

They rode free of the trees' shelter and over an expanse of cleared land in silence. The dirt path broadened barely enough to allow town traffic as they entered Dunfermline. While she plotted a possible plan for escape, her nervous tension was broken only by the sounds of villagers moving about in their usual chores, sparing the English lord and his burden no more than a bitter glare.

She rode quietly in his arms, patiently waiting for the right moment. Studying their surroundings to find her bearings, she stared down shadowed alleys and at houses crowded on the narrow lanes they traversed. Lulled by her pliancy, he slowly relaxed his hold. At her sudden kick, the high-strung steed reared up. Sliding from between two muscular arms striving to control the beast, she fell free, his cloak tightly clasped in her hands. Swirling the rich cloth out and about her shoulders as she went, she dashed into the shielding gloom of a dark alley and weaved between piles of refuse and stacks of baskets waiting for market-day. The black velvet that would reach mid-calf on him, was nearly full-length on her. It dusted the ground once she reached the alley's far side, she snatched up a stick from the metal-smith's woodpile to lean on as if stooped under the weight of many years.

❧ Chapter 2 ❧

ROUGH LAUGHTER LACED THE words to the ribald song that
rolled out from the open door of a low, mean alehouse and
into the growing gloom of dusk. It had taken Taine some
time to find her way back through narrow alleys and squalid
streets to this sorry shelter. From beneath the edge of the
cloak's hood she eyed it with disfavor but, still bent with
false age, moved forward. She entered the dim room and
the stench of bitter ale and numerous unwashed bodies
cramped into the small building swept over her.

A strange quiet settled on the boisterous crowd as she
shuffled toward the stairs to the bedchambers above.
Nerves, already stretched tight under the day's strains,
threatened to break when the people stepped back from her
as if in fear. Unsettled by their odd behavior and unwilling
to learn its source, she kept her eyes trained first on the
packed dirt floor and then on the rickety plank steps she
ascended.

After what seemed an endless climb, the bedchamber
door snapped shut behind her. With a sigh of relief she
straightened from the strain of her uncomfortable hunch,

letting the cloak fall to the floor at her feet. A smile of uncommon sweetness warmed her lips and lightened her eyes to the gentle shade of sea foam as she saw a grizzled grey head bent and held in despair between two gnarled hands.

"Bertie," she called softly. "I'm here."

A face of sharp angles and deep crags lifted immediately and watery blue eyes quickly examined her. The man, short and brawny, jumped up and rushed forward to wrap her in a bone-crushing hug even as he began to scold.

"Ayie, lassie. Ye'll drive me witless, sneaking out alone and staying gone 'til the sun air dead. You musna do it again." He had leaned back to deliver his final words with a glare of command. It was met and defeated by the affection in her smile.

Bertwald had been the caretaker of her castle-prison and only friend for the long, dreary years of her captivity. Her savior from the vicious attack of her gaolers and companion in flight, he was the only man she trusted. All others had proven eminently unworthy.

"Niver mind, you're safe with me now." He wrapped her once more in a relieved embrace.

Taine returned his hug; but, secure again for the moment, reaction set in with small, persistent tremors. Safe? Hah! She had a strong premonition the bronze-skinned, bright-haired lord would find her and, because of her unforeseen response to him, she was more afraid of him than the other two. The others! She'd forgotten them, proof of the lord's unhealthy effect on her.

"Bertie"—she pulled free—"they found me. We must leave—now!" Clasping one strong forearm between her hands, she tugged, as if to haul him away immediately.

He stood steady, unmoving as the tors at Stonehenge, face grown grim. He knew the danger better than his noble lady. Her long imprisonment had been a fearful treachery, yet that evil deed had held her innocent to most of the world's perils. He shook his arm free to join the other in stilling her struggle.

"I'll go hitch the mule tae our cart. Bundle our things away tae be ready when I return." Moving toward the door, his attention was caught by the carelessly discarded cape he'd not noticed before. Seeing the quality of the cloth, he bent to lift it. Velvet. A rich cloth indeed. Brows drawn, he spread it out to reveal the coat-of-arms embroidered on the back of the black cloak with thread of gold—a mighty dragon rampant. His hands snapped open, dropping the garment as if it were poison. "The Golden Dragon!" His low exclamation came forth with the same sound as breath driven out by a gut-pounding blow.

Taine felt the weight of Bertwald's questioning eyes, a small added burden to the impact of his words. Tales of that powerful and fearsome half-Saracen lord had carried even to her remote prison. Extremely uncomfortable, she shrugged and mumbled the lie that she'd found it.

Bertwald's snort of disbelief was immediate. "Not likely, that. Still, we doona have time tae speak on it now, truly not if that fierce knight has a part of the doing." He turned again toward the door but glanced back to add, "Drop the bar and open tae none save me."

Once she had obeyed his order, Taine hastily began to roll her second gown and his spare tunic, gathered up a half-eaten loaf of rye bread and a hunk of strong yellow cheese and leaned the cudgel nearby, all the while giving wide berth to the fallen cloak. Eyes drawn unwillingly to the offending cloth, she glared at it as if 'twere the man himself. By some trick of weak and flickering candle flame, it almost seemed she could see him there, tall and broad. A fire-breathing dragon? Yes, that she could believe. A fierce knight? That, too. Saint's tears, what a sorry choice she had made in claiming him for husband, what false hope in hair as gold as the sun, when beneath lay a deeply bronzed face and eyes as black as night. Surely an example of the treachery in all men: bright hope on the surface with dark motives beneath.

She snatched up the cape and quickly rolled it into a tight bundle, burying the golden needlework from sight just as she buried in the depth of her soul the soft voice reminding her that he, at least, had not denied her claim. Indeed, he had saved her from a threatening evil. With disgust she added the tightly wound velvet to the stack of their pitifully small collection of possessions. The last of the lot, she folded the corners of the moth-mangled bed fur over them just as Bertwald called out from the far side of the barred door.

Taine rushed to let him in and shut the door fully behind him but left it unbarred, prepared for immediate departure. Bertwald shouldered their fur-bound possessions and took his cudgel in hand, while Taine bent over the uneven planks of the table to extinguish the single, foul-smelling tallow taper. A loud crash jerked her back from the unfinished task and she whirled to face the gaping door. Bertwald's burden thumped to the floor as he lifted his cudgel menacingly in both hands toward the tall man silhouetted against the hall's light, light that made the stranger's hair a golden halo for the face they could not clearly see.

Taine took a step back, biting her lip and wondering illogically if her fancies of minutes before had led him here.

"Who air you?" demanded Bertwald belligerently, although a sick feeling told him the answer.

No response was forthcoming as the stranger silently studied the tense maid.

"What you want here?" Bertwald questioned further and more to the purpose.

"I have come," came the calm, low answer, "to claim that which is mine."

Taine dropped to her knees and wildly rummaged through the fallen bundle until she located the tightly rolled ball of velvet. Rising again, she tossed it at the blocked doorway.

The stranger neatly caught the missile, shook out the rich fabric, and fastened it over his shoulders before turning his gaze to the slender maid. "This is not the full extent of my possessions, I claim more."

Taine's chin tilted and she snapped back, "I took no more."

Silence reigned for long moments while the man and the girl faced each other with unswerving attention. Driven to action, Bertwald suddenly moved forward, cudgel raised higher. The stranger's arm snapped out to jerk the weapon free. Bertwald gasped in surprise. The man must have eyes in odd places.

"Calm yourself," the stranger instructed Bertwald with quelling composure, holding the cudgel across his broad chest. "I offer no harm. I have come only to take my wife home."

With a sigh of relief, Bertwald's tense shoulders relaxed, although he stepped back to wrap a protective arm about Taine. "Then truly, milord," he smiled, "ye've come to the wrong door."

The stranger had no answering smile. Golden head bent to one side, he studied the two before him. The gentle roll in the girl's voice was intensified to a deep rumbling burr in the man's, revealing them both Scots-bred. "Is it not the law of this land," he asked quietly, eyes firmly fixed on Bertwald, "that when a man and maid declare themselves wed before witnesses, that then it is so?"

Dread began to build, but Bertwald responded firmly, "Aye, 'tis the right of it."

"Then in truth the maid is mine." His gaze shifted to Taine.

Taine's eyes had gone wide in shock. She'd heard nothing of this strange custom and her thoughts clashed together in a wild jumble of confusion, seeking some sensible explanation.

"Ah, lass." Bertwald turned to face the girl, lifting hands to sharply grip her shoulders. "What folly have ye done?"

In the muddle of her thoughts, she asked the same, calling for the aid of all the saints to see her free of this coil. "It canna be true," she said, disbelief still clouding the eyes she turned to the golden-haired stranger, "else it must be some long-forgotten custom."

"Aye." He nodded, a small smile of understanding, almost sorrow for her confusion warming his lips. "Old and seldom used but binding nonetheless, as I warned you when you named me husband and I claimed you mine."

"He speaks true, lass," Bertwald confirmed, stunned by this unexpected and incredible turn of events. "'Tis a binding deed."

Frustrated by her inability to find valid argument and confused by his apparent sympathy for her feelings, Taine scowled at the man blocking the only escape route.

"Is the cart at the inn's door yours?" he questioned.

Bertwald nodded while Taine glared.

"Then gather your things and follow me," he directed

Bertwald, motioning toward the discarded bundle. "The men who wait with your cart will ensure you don't lose the path as we go. Lady Taine?" He offered his arm for her to rest slender fingers atop as he spoke. She straightened and tightly clasped her arms about her middle in rejection, even as she darted a swift glance at Bertwald, silently warning him to accept the stranger's name for her.

The stranger leaned forward to take her arm, but she pulled free. Be it she must go, then 'twould be unshackled and unled. With another fierce stare, she marched stiffly past him through the door. Just outside she met again the eyes of the young squire. He held the firebrand that brightly lit the normally dim hall and gilded his lord's hair. Quelled by a temper that blazed near as vividly as the red sparks in her dark hair, the lad quickly turned to light her path down the steps. The amused lord followed their hasty route, a barely suppressed grin warming dark eyes that lingered with appreciation on the graceful back and gently rounded derrière descending before him.

The ride to the Golden Dragon's lair (Taine's belief that the title suited the lord had been reinforced) was accomplished in short time, although it seemed never-ending to Taine. The squire rode on the cart's seat with Bertwald, while she sat in lonely state in the back. Reined in to match the mule's plodding pace, the golden horse and rider traveled beside her. The long autumn evening was well begun and the narrow streets were nearly deserted. Two knights rode behind. For the full length of the trip, she sat perfectly still, staring unwaveringly into the gloom beyond the front of the cart. She had escaped him once, she reminded herself, she could escape him again. Refusing to allow further doubts, her thoughts turned to weighing the threats to success. How had he found her? How could she prevent him from finding her again? Bertwald would know, she reassured herself. Bertwald would get her safely free as he had done before. 'Twas a fine thing that the skirt of her homespun gown was already beyond hope, else the twisting of her nervous fingers would have made it so.

The dragon's lair was a two-story wooden structure on the town's outer boundary. Its importance was exhibited by the chimneys that rose on either end to offer warmth to the great hall and yet to the chambers above. Drawn up before the house, the powerful dragon lifted her from the wagon bed as easily as if she were a toddling. Desperately seeking some focus for her attention save the warmth of his strong arms, she trained her eyes on the patches of light stealing free of the house through hide-covered windows. She entered on dragging feet and paused just within to quickly examine the small hall. It was lit more than adequately by two blazing fires at opposite ends and by tall metal stands, each bearing a multitude of candles, all apparently of wax for the fetid tallow odor was absent. The dragon's people, mostly men-at-arms, lounged in groups about the fires but turned from talk and dice to stare at the new arrivals.

Feeling woefully conspicuous, Taine lifted her chin in defense as a woman dressed in the manner of one wellborn stepped from a cluster of men by the far fire to come forward. Hall absent any other lady, Taine realized that apparently she was acting as the dragon's chatelaine.

"Take my 'guest' above," he quietly directed the woman, "and return immediately. I have news of import to share."

For their lord to invite any to his home was unusual but to bring a lone woman of apparent quality, despite poor garb, was little less than shocking. It raised a strong curiosity in the young woman directed to lead the visitor to a chamber. Nonetheless, her natural warmth asserted itself and a wide smile broke across her lavishly freckled face as she cheerily motioned Taine to follow.

Though mistrustful of other's motives, Taine's parched soul welcomed the refreshing rain of an open friendliness she'd met neither in her dour prison nor on her furtive flight.

The woman led Taine up the stairs to a chamber on the upper level. As they went she called for warm water and a goblet of mulled wine and chattered brightly of mundane matters until they arrived. First looping back the huge bed's curtains and turning down its covers, though plainly wondering at the purpose of the stranger's presence, the woman wished her an enjoyable night and hastily departed. She was anxious to hear the earl's news.

Dropping her clothes to the floor, Taine gratefully dipped

the clean cloth provided into steaming water. Passing the cloth over creamy cheeks and down the long arch of her throat, she seemed to rinse away not the grit of the day alone but also the muddled fog in her thoughts. By the time she had wrung excess water out of the cloth and laid it to dry by the fire's heat, it was clear that the longer she tarried in the dragon's domain, the more difficult would be her escape. Haste was the answer to every query. Refreshed and filled with renewed determination, she turned, only to realize that the bundle containing her change of clothes was either still in the cart or in Bertwald's possession. To rest prepared for her best chance for freedom she had but one choice. She swallowed her distaste and lifted the bedraggled garments from the floor to slip them on once more. Placing her shoes where they could easily be found, she slid into bed fully clothed.

Even dressed, she could feel and savor the lush warmth above and soft ticking below. She'd slept for long years beneath coarse covers ever unequal to chill air and on mattresses filled with straw that pricked and poked. Yet, as she luxuriated in this sudden comfort, a niggling anxiety grew. 'Twas a large bed of fine quality—the lord's bed? He'd claimed her as wife in theory—did he mean to claim her in fact? Suddenly suspicious of the woman's wish for an enjoyable night, her fingers whitened in their grip on the edge of the fur she held tightly under her chin.

In the room across the hall from the apprehensive maid, her future was the subject of conversation between Bertwald and the lord who had led him there.

"I am Jorion de Brae," the golden-haired lord needlessly informed Bertwald, once they were seated at a small table before the chamber's roaring fire with tankards of ale in their hands. Jorion was certain that Bertwald, though assuredly not her father, was the man responsible for Taine. As such, honor demanded he explain his position, a favor seldom extended to any. The older man knew him by reputation at least but, mayhap more for that reason, he felt it necessary to speak of his heritage and his intentions for the maid. He swallowed a long draught of deep brown liquid and carefully replaced the vessel on the table's use-smoothed surface. Black eyes looking steadily into faded blue, Jorion spoke of facts well-known to his peers but never referred to by him.

"My father, third son of the Earl of Radwyn, accompanied Edward on crusade. To ensure the truce with Sultan Bibars he was left as hostage when Edward left the Holy Land."

Bertwald's bushy brows knit. He wondered why this great and feared lord chose to speak of such matters to him.

Deliberately misinterpreting Bertwald's frown, Jorion shrugged slightly, sending glints of firelight over the heavy golden chain stretched across the wide expanse of black velvet covering his chest. "His stay was not unpleasant. Not truly a prisoner, he was rather a visiting stranger whose bravery and physical prowess gained his host's respect. Indeed, he wed one of the Sultan's many daughters—a gift of honor from the Sultan. She died giving birth to their son—me."

Bertwald's frown grew deeper. He'd known as did nearly all that the man was half-Saracen, but was curious for the reasoning. Without pausing to consider the wisdom of questioning so powerful a noble, he said, "I doona ken how the bairn of a Moorish union can inherit an English fiefdom."

One side of Jorion's mouth curled into the cynical half-smile most common to him. He'd seen that curious look before, although few were either brave or foolish enough to ask. "They were married by both Moslem and Christian rites," he dryly explained. Pausing, he closely watched the other man's face for signs of distaste. Bertwald earned his respect by steadily meeting his eyes. "During a riding competition two years later," Jorion continued, "my father fell from his horse. But, before he died, the Sultan promised to raise his son a Christian."

As his voice died away, Jorion's gaze shifted to the orange and yellow flames weaving in an exotic dance against soot-grimed stones. The memories he'd long suppressed flowed again. There were many and few were pleasant. His Saracen relatives had been as repelled by the mingling of bloodlines as had his English kin.

In the quiet that stretched and lingered like twilight on a

summer evening, Bertwald waited patiently, idly wondering why the man spoke so distantly of "the Sultan" who was his grandfather.

A log crackled on the hearth and burst into a small storm of sparks, startling Jorion from his useless preoccupation. Embarrassed that he, the famed warrior, had allowed his attention to drift into senseless reveries—a fatal error for a fighting man—he sat up and turned toward his guest. When he spoke again, self-disgust made his tone more sarcastic than intended. "A decade later I was invited to this land, but only after my two English uncles died childless. Only then did my grandfather send for me so that he would not die without a De Brae heir to the Earldom of Radwyn. I am now the earl." Again he studied Bertwald for reaction.

"The Earl of Radwyn," Bertwald agreed solemnly, "and the Golden Dragon that Scotch mothers use to frighten naughty children." He grinned.

Jorion's smile lost some of its cynicism as he nodded. He liked this man who was unafraid to banter with him. He went on. "As I have said, I am a Christian and you have my oath that before taking her as wife, I will wed the maid by the laws of the church as well as by the ancient laws of Scotland."

Bertwald's eyes widened in surprise. For the purpose of inheritance, a Christian marriage was necessary, but that the earl would deny himself the undeniable temptations of her body until the rites were performed was a demonstration of honor few lords would show once victory was achieved. He lifted a hand to ruffle through his wiry grey hair as he openly examined this man who was both more and less than expected, more of honor and less of terror.

Jorion withstood the close scrutiny, amused by the man's continued nerve in facing him unflinching and unbowed. "Having revealed my heritage," Jorion added at last, "tell me now of your charge's." Pinning Bertwald with a penetrating gaze, he added, "Don't tell me that you are her sire." The maid's afternoon claim was plainly a falsehood, yet Jorion wondered if both would offer the preposterous lie. More, had they in earlier times passed themselves off as father and daughter?

Startled by the suggestion, Bertwald's jaw dropped.

Jorion was pleased with Bertwald's reaction. It proved the truth in the matter more clearly than words. Yet content became displeasure when Bertwald refused to respond to his request, refused to speak of her background at all.

"I could force you," Jorion stated with deceptive carelessness, while taking a small, wickedly curved dagger from the sheath at his waist. The blade flashed and the jeweled hilt gleamed as he idly spun the weapon before testing its sharpness against the pad of his thumb.

Unflinching, Bertwald met his narrowed gaze. "You kin kill me but still I willna break my oath, and by the killing you ensure the silence I have sworn." He had known the maid since she'd first been brought to the dreary castle, wide-eyed but stubbornly brave, and he was willing to risk much to see to her safety.

Jorion's full white smile broke across his bronzed face like dawn on the horizon. He admired Bertwald's strength of will—for not many would tempt his ire. Moreover, Bertwald's determination to hold Taine's background unknown lent a measure of proof to his belief that she was wellborn. Putting away his knife, he stood and motioned Bertwald to follow him down to the common room and gestured toward a pallet beside two of his sleeping knights. Wishing Bertwald a pleasant rest, Jorion turned back toward the stairs.

Bertwald stared after the tall figure in black, pondering this strange twist in his lady's life and weighing the conversation just ended. The Golden Dragon was a strong man, a powerful lord, a man much better equipped to defend the maid than he. Though he would never break his oath and speak of her birthright, if the earl were truly the man of honor he seemed, then Bertwald would willingly pass the responsibility for her safety to him. He bent to the bedfur wrapped bundle they'd brought. It had been left conveniently at the foot of his straw mattress. As he emptied its load, he determined to only watch closely for a time and not to seek their freedom until he had seen the truth of the man. Bedfur now emptied, he stretched out and wrapped it warmly about himself, content with his decision.

❧ Chapter 3 ❧

THE HEAVY DOOR SCRAPED ominously over plank flooring. Taine froze. Gripping the latch so tightly it creased the soft skin of her palm, she waited in the dark for some answering sound. Only the loud thumping of her own heart stirred the slumbering peace. With a sudden movement, she jerked the door wide. It took less bravery to act with quick confidence than to move with slow, nerve-destroying caution. After one swift glance, she stepped into the gloom of the deserted hall.

For what seemed like endless hours, she'd lain awake fearing the dragon's coming; but at length the nearly forgotten comfort of a down mattress had offered a temptation to slumber that was difficult to resist. She'd succumbed to its seduction more than once but had been driven back to wakefulness by a dragon formed of golden stitches, a beast of fierce beauty that came to life and stalked her dreams. She would; she *must* escape that unfamiliar and fascinating threat. Ambitious men had imprisoned her for more than twelve years but yet had not inspired the depth of fear this one man had. She'd vowed never again to be held within the ring of any man's power, and by the time a deep quiet settled on the house all question for the wisdom of her plan had flown like fog on the wind. She must steal away—now, not at some later time. No price was too dear.

Candles had long since guttered out and the windowless hall was a black void through which she must move. Laying one hand lightly against the wall on her right, she took several quick paces forward, then slowed. The stairway was close and dangerous in the dark if suddenly come upon. With caution she felt for each firm foothold but continued steadily to the stairs. As she descended she peered through the gloom seeking a familiar shape among the dim forms revealed by the faint glow of embers dying on both hearths. Taine hesitated, nibbling on a full lower lip with indecision. Several men lay stretched out on pallets, but she was unable to distinguish one from another. If she moved too close, she risked waking the dragon's men, a fact that forced an unhappy decision. She must leave without Bertwald, without even their meager supplies. Leave and flee alone. 'Twas a frightening thought, but not so frightening as staying under the dragon's dominion. She had often claimed she needed no man. Now was the time to prove it true.

The outside door made no sound as it swung open, and satisfaction curved soft lips. A good omen that. Taine hesitated on the steps only long enough to glance at the nearly full moon riding low on the horizon. Against its dull glow the rugged terrain rose in harsh silhouette, an eerie sight. Behind her lay a town filled with enemies, ahead lay a lonely and mayhap equally dangerous journey into forest and mountain. She had no specific destination, no knowledge of the countryside, and no notion of the direction to anywhere. Her lack of knowledge, she decided with a wry shake of hood-hidden auburn curls, offered complete freedom of choice.

Spurning the small knot of fear growing in her chest, she quelled the desire to glance apprehensively behind as she began her stealthy escape. The dragon was asleep within his lair and could not know his prey was slipping away. Hurrying toward the wild countryside beyond the stable, she slipped quietly from the long shadow it cast to the gloom provided by the nearest tree. Thank the saints she'd found her own dark cloak. Inadequate though it was against cold, the deep hue blended well with the shroud of night. Only the white plume of her breath floating on chill air threatened to reveal her path. Unwavering, she picked her way over stone-strewn ground, consciously steadying and lengthening the breathing that fear and haste had labored. Sparse trees provided a shield for her climb up the gentle first incline of the steep hills ahead. Refusing still to glance guiltily over her shoulder, she failed to see her silent stalkers.

Elation filled the two men who crept carefully behind. They'd lost her once and were determined that this time the maid would not know herself in danger 'til she was firmly caught in their snare. They'd been watching the earl's house since shortly after he'd taken their quarry from them. Waiting only for some lax moment, some hour when she was left unattended, they'd never dared hope she'd sneak out alone to offer herself so easily into their hands. Yet they must wait, follow a course of caution. Not before they were so far into the wilds that even a sharp scream would fail to call the Golden Dragon to her aid, would they risk an attempt at capture.

Taine was tired. She'd climbed the first range of hills and descended into a steep valley, picking her way carefully around the larger stones but tripping over too many half-buried in shallow soil. Her feet hurt and shoulders ached. She'd not slept since nearly this time yester-morn. Surely she'd put enough distance between herself and her would-be captor to risk a short rest? Ahead rose the dim shape of a massive tree. The breeze of earlier days had shifted autumn leaves to tangle into grass grown thick beneath. Though doubtless damp, the leafy bower promised a soft comfort difficult to find on rocky ground. *Don't stop, don't risk discovery,* her mind warned but, acting for her weary body, her feet veered from the path. She wrapped the cloak tightly about herself and stretched out on nature's welcoming pillow, cradling her cheek on palm-joined hands. Breath sighed out and lashes drooped as she willingly relaxed into the inviting tranquillity of night.

Suddenly a viselike grip clamped over the lower half of her face, stifling her shocked gasp for air. Green eyes snapped open to find her two pursuers from the fair kneeling above, looming shadows blocking the moonlight.

Before she could gather her wits enough to resist, the gaunt one wrapped a strip of cloth about her mouth, replacing the other's palm.

With speed unexpected from a man of his broad build, the shorter man's freed hands moved to still her initial struggles. Holding her immobile, he sneered with satisfaction, "What's happened to your lovin' husband?"

Dragging deep breaths in through her nose, she felt each painful thud of her heart and silently cursed herself for twice the fool. Desperate to run from the dragon, she'd again failed to consider other threats.

"Had little success with men of his stand, eh?" taunted the gaunt one, his raspy voice a whisper, "and would sooner come back to us—"

Taine stiffened with disgust and fury as bony clawlike fingers slid in rough insult over her generous curves. It was a repeat of that other time, that terrifying time when one had held her immobile for the degrading pawing of the other. With the strength of desperation, she pulled one hand free, intent on shredding skin from the leering face above. Caught a breath short of its goal by the crushing force of a deceptively weak hold, she felt her arm twisted down and behind as in the same motion she was jerked up and against his chest in cruel punishment. Held feet dangling, she kicked but found the futile motion merely impelled her closer, a deed welcome to her captor. He sniggered; she went still. His foul breath was revolting, and only by effort of will did she meet his growing triumph with courage.

"Leastways you know what we wants with no fancy trimmin's to fool you away." His smile jeered and, had her mouth not been gagged, she would have spat in his face.

"That's none of it, Will." Greasy hair hanging in thin ropes about his neck, the bull-built man leaned around to scoff, "Her only jest heard barbarians like as her husband gots many wives."

The tall, wiry man merely grunted at this jibe but the speaker laughed loudly, the sound echoing against the valley's steep sides.

"Quiet," hissed the other, "be it her run on her own or we stole her away, the dragon'll not linger to reclaim what's his or be the fool to all." His companion's brain was as sluggish as his huge body normally was. 'Twas his strength that made him so useful an ally.

The warning effectively wiped laughter from the other's face, bringing a flash of cruel amusement to the wiry man, who mocked, "Afeared of his fire same as a brat caught in forbidden deeds."

"You claim to be elsewise?" the other squared beefy shoulders and snapped back, temper roused by the scornful words.

"'Struth," the gaunt one answered with a superior sneer. "Cower afore him I don't. S'only I've got wits enough to beware of his power."

Still crushed against a narrow chest, Taine little heard their quarrel for the truth in the words of the dragon's pride lent an ominous foreboding.

"What matter be it one or t'other—we're awastin' time best used in gettin' clear of his path." The stocky man's fear was such it overcame even his injured pride. He glanced apprehensively behind to the dark and looming hill they'd descended.

"'Struth." Irritated by the need to admit his cohort capable of logic, with a sour frown the tall man harshly commanded, "Waste no more then, Guy. Bind her wrists so we can get back where we should be."

Guy hastened to do as he was bid, twining a leather thong about the maid's wrists so tightly it cut into the soft skin. Taine bit her lip to restrain a moan, determined not to give them the satisfaction of her pain. She thought to seek divine deliverance and found a desperate humor in her choices. Must she pray for the earl to rescue her from these human toads or hope that they would quickly spirit her back to her nearly lifelong prison and away from the dragon's domain?

Suddenly forced to lie on her side in the damp, leaf-cushioned grass, Taine again kicked wildly and to more purpose. Her assailants' muffled groans and curses were proof of her success until the full weight of her heavier opponent descended with the assault of a hurled boulder, stilling her struggles. He bent to wind another length of thin leather about her ankles but paused when the other demanded, "Leastways take the ring, Guy."

Taine's fingers reflexively tightened into a fist to deny its easy taking. A heavy hand wrapped about her delicate wrist to hold it steady for the prying of thick, stubby fingers. Rapidly approaching horses' hooves sent a resounding echo across the deep valley and stilled the assault. Three faces lifted toward the horseman cresting the hill behind, a dark silhouette against the night sky's glow. A black cloak fanned out from broad shoulders to spread like wings over a moon-gilded stallion hurtling down the slope.

"God's blood, man," rasped the gaunt captor, urging his cohort on. "Get the ring and let's be gone."

Guy bent back to his task with urgent determination, nearly crushing Taine's hand in attempt to force her fingers open and release the prize. She grimaced with the pain but held tight.

"Free my wife or risk my blades." Strangely magnified against the rocky walls of the steep valley, the low words reverberated, carrying as clearly as the bells of a monastery, as clearly as had the assailant's loud and urgent demand for Taine's ring.

Fighting to keep the convoluted band despite cruel prying, Taine clenched her eyes shut. Yet she knew exactly when her opponent again glanced around. The hand gripping hers went slack. Looking quickly up, she too saw moonlight gleam on the wickedly curved Saracen blades crossed over a golden head that shone almost as brightly.

Air fanned her cheek from the speed with which her gaunt captor jumped to his feet and leaped onto his horse's back. The bull-built man stubbornly hunched over her, desperately trying to wrench the ring free. They'd agreed, were they to lose her again, they must first remove the proof of her heritage. Only thus could they hope to lessen their own punishment.

"Let it be, Guy, else ye'll be the next victim of the Dragon's fire!"

The hand on the prize stilled for a moment while the meaning of the words came clear. Once they had, he lumbered to his feet as fast as his size allowed and mounted his steed.

Taine, though made awkward and off-balance by her bound hands, also scrambled to her feet. She ran from her attackers—but also from the golden horse and his rider. The slope before her was steep, only a few hardy trees fighting for soil between encroaching boulders. The sight was daunting, a nearly impossible climb, but desperation lent an unthinking courage. She must try.

Halted at the deepest point of the valley, through narrowed eyes Jorion watched as the fleeing men raced toward the easiest path from the valley. His cynical one-sided smile appeared as he ended the play of silver sparks on the edge of his blades by sliding them into the two sheaths strapped X-fashion to his back. With his reputation, the mere threat of his foreign weapons defeated as many foes as the strength of his arms. His attention turned to the still-gagged maid stumbling toward the nearly vertical and intimidating hillside on her left, hampered by bound hands. A grim smile touched his mouth. Did she think she could manage in the wild without their use? Indeed, unbound, how long could she hope to survive alone? Even in more peaceful lands, 'twas dangerous for a strong man to travel without companions. But here, he shook his head, here opposing armies fought; in the hidden reaches of these hills, desperate bands of the dispossessed roamed wide to prey upon the unwary or unprotected.

Even as he urged his steed into an easy canter that would quickly swallow the distance between them, a spark of admiration for the woman's courage grew. Her flight into the night alone was a foolish deed, but no less than he would do if involuntarily taken. In truth, her action was no more foolish than his own. Unwilling to be shamed before his men by a fleeing bride, he, who knew the danger, had come alone.

Heart pounding, breath coming in short gasps, Taine struggled onward, aware of the approaching horse but loath to admit defeat. In her blind haste, she tripped over a half-hidden rock and, without hands to cushion the fall, would have taken a bruising tumble, had not strong arms scooped her up. A ragged groan whooshed into the muffling folds fastened about her mouth as she abruptly landed face-down over the golden horse's back. Uninjured but burning with the ignominy of her position and unable to scream her anger, she resorted to the only physical form of expression available. Kicking wildly, she expected the nervous steed to rise up and toss her free. She was disappointed. Anticipating this repeat of her earlier ploy, Jorion held him calm.

"Only laid thus, have I the access needed to free you from your bonds." Caught between irritation and amusement, he added, "But I cannot safely bend my dagger to the deed 'til you cease your useless tussling."

At the humor in his voice, Taine's temper flared brighter but she stilled.

Jorion's dagger sundered her bonds in one quick motion. As the tight thongs snapped open, the bruised and torn flesh beneath was revealed. Golden brows scowled. He could understand, even sympathize, with their decision to still the volatile maid's struggles but had only disgust for the needless cruelty of bonds tight enough to cut. He cast a quick glance toward the hill over which her attackers had fled. Although he had an unexpected urge to set Apollo racing after the culprits and demand from them a price of no less than equal pain, he must content himself with sending others to track them on the morrow. His first priority was returning his claimed bride to the safety of his home—not the small house the king had allotted for his use in Dunfermline, but to Castle Dragonsward, home of the earls of Radwyn for more than two hundred years.

Lifted and turned in strong arms that seemed not to feel the strain, Taine found herself again cradled like a child. This proof of the ease with which he could control her did nothing to cool her temper. With freed hands she peeled off the gag he'd left in place, presumably by choice, and gave him a fine demonstration of the remarkably colorful vocabulary she'd learned from her rotating guards.

Deep laughter rolled over her words and she found herself surprisingly thankful for the moonlight that drained away color, for she could feel her cheeks burning with bright embarrassment. Although she'd heard the curses again and again, never before had she spoken them aloud.

"You sound little like a lady," Jorion said, suppressing his laughter. He turned their steed and with the moon at his back directed him along the return path. Though he knew well how to hide his reactions, her language had startled him, but her very apparent embarrassment at the sound of the curses falling from her lips was amusing. It gave proof of how uncommon they were to her tongue.

Pulling as far back in his hold as he would allow, Taine lifted her face defiantly before snapping, "I never claimed to be one."

Shining head tilted to one side, Jorion studied her proud, moon-bathed face for a long, silent moment. Taine raised her chin even higher and bravely met his appraisal despite the heavy thumping of her heart. At length he stated, "Your face reveals your heritage as surely as my dark visage reveals my own."

Terror-struck, Taine froze. Did his words mean that he knew exactly who she was? Through alarm-widened eyes, she steadily watched the face above. The silvery orb at his back made his hair glow as if with some inner light but left his face obscured. When the path rounded the side of the hill and shielded them from the moon's revealing light, she looked away to stare into the gloom ahead as steadily as if hidden within lay a scene of spellbinding beauty.

They traveled some distance through the deep shadows on the hill's far side, Jorion's thoughts filled with questions of this unique damsel's past. He had seen her moment of panic and by it knew how determined she was to hide her identity. It roused his curiosity more and strengthened his determination to find the answer to the riddle of her. His lips curled with self-mockery. She couldn't know how unusual it was for him to take personal interest in a woman; she didn't know how well he'd guarded his emotions against such invasions for all these many years.

In a silence that throbbed with her fear, the dragon's failure to speak further on the subject convinced Taine of his ignorance in the matter. Focusing on the dim view of white fingers twisted into a homespun skirt, she consciously forced ease to tense muscles even while searching desperately for a dampening response. Her mind must wax creative under such adversity, she decided, when from the muddle of her thoughts came a pleasing answer. She defiantly warned, "There's many a bastard brat with noble mien. You shouldn't risk taking one to wife."

"No matter." The cynicism in Jorion's smile tinged his words. "There are many who view me as a mongrel of even lower pedigree."

Beneath the cold dispassion hardening his voice, Taine sensed an aching hurt but quickly denied the sympathy she felt. What injury could touch, much less pierce this proud and mighty warrior? She would not weaken to a man who was no less and no more than any other—save Bertwald. Nay, the small voice in her mind mocked, look again. Physically, at least, he is considerably more than any other. Taine's lips compressed in denial of her thoughts, yet it slowly crept into her conscious mind that where she had once been rigid with stubborn anger in the dragon's hold, she now lay relaxed. Mindful of the possible dangers in their conversation, she'd thoughtlessly sought warmth against a night tinged with autumn chill, welcomed the arms that drew her nearer against his heat.

Lying so close, she felt muscles ripple when he urged their steed to turn from shadows into a moonlit descent. The firm arm crossing in front brushed lightly, casually across her breasts and her breath caught. She looked up into the face surely too perfect to be real. Renewed awareness of his masculine beauty and the strength of his other arm holding her gently against his powerful chest gave life not to fear but to pleasure. A new kind of tension grew, even as she brooded over the ability of the body to play traitor to the mind. She rushed into speech to waylay its flow.

"What sorcery did you work to find where I'd gone, once I slipped free of you after we departed the fair?" The words, Taine realized, were disgustingly breathless. She looked down again.

"No sorcery was needed," he answered. "You left a clear path behind." The cynical one-sided smile reappeared on his lips but did not affect the calm tone of his reply.

Though frowning in question, Taine refused to look higher than the strong column of his throat. Jorion understood her refusal to meet his gaze. He'd felt it the moment the tension of fear had gone from her body and too had felt tension of another kind building. So, he thought, she was no less affected than he by this mock embrace in the seclusion of darkness. In the quiet of the last long moments the very texture of night had begun to ache with awareness as the slim but deliciously shaped maid relaxed against him—a temptation almost beyond bearing. Though moonlight stole color from most in its path, it drew out the flames in auburn hair, flames that warmed his blood, speeding it through his veins and sensitizing him to her soft curves 'til they seemed to brand his flesh. Reminding himself of his famed iron-control, through gritted teeth he answered the question in her drawn brows.

"I merely followed the path of my cloak."

Was it a fancy of her too-active imagination or had his breathing grown ragged? A tiny tremor passed over Taine and she bent her head to hide a blush he might see even through the gloom, yet feared he was so close he had felt her body tremble. She tried to concentrate on her self-disgust for not seeing this explanation sooner, more, for taking his cloak in the first instance. Instinctively knowing the danger, she valiantly sought to hold her eyes from his but lost the battle when gentle fingers lifted her chin. Her gaze was caught and held in one as deep as the night that surrounded them. She felt herself drawn into their darkness until she shared the hunger within. Her lashes fell in an attempt to break the potent contact, but it only seemed the velvet depths had swallowed her whole. Wild sensations throbbed within, stealing her breath, leaving not even enough for a sigh as his firm mouth brushed achingly across hers once, twice, and once again before settling to nip at her lips until they fell open, offering access for the shocking excitement of a deeper kiss. Her hand flew to his powerful chest with vague intent to push away, but instead was tempted by its fiery heat to linger and feel the mighty pounding of his heart—an echo of her own. The joined beating accelerated as her fingers spread and moved to test the feel of rock-hard muscles beneath. A tiny moan escaped Taine's tight throat. She was drowning in a black void of the dragon's making, stunned by golden streaks of pleasure.

Jorion, too, was stunned. Though clearly an untutored innocent, her passion was real. Surrendering to the desire of her naive wiles, he unknowingly erred, drove desire from her with unbelievable speed. He turned her more fully into iron-strong arms, pulled her firmly against the formidable wall of his chest, and crushed her lips beneath his.

Taine's mind focused on the tight embrace, the hard pressure of his mouth—a terrifying repeat of the vicious attack that had sent her fleeing from her castle-prison, from the two men who pursued her still. In the confusion of her thoughts, he and they became one, all willing to use their superior strength to force her to their will. She began to fight, pushing against him in earnest, striving to twist free. When it sank through the haze of Jorion's desire that she was struggling against him, he lifted his head and Taine verbally struck out at the one weakness she instinctively knew.

"You dark-skinned barbarian, leave me be!"

Further words died unborn on her lips as she watched the planes of his face freeze into a harsh mask that frightened her. Though his hands still gripped her firmly, they now held her as impersonally as if she were a sack of grist for the mill. Again, she felt a deep well of pain beneath his facade and angrily forced down an unruly desire to apologize for her words. After all, he'd have forced himself on her as surely as would the other two. In truth, his was the greater threat, for he had first bent her willingly to his intent.

As they embraced, their golden steed had carried them down the hill and into the night shadows that stretched long fingers toward Dunfermline. In heavy silence they traveled the short distance remaining.

Jorion's thoughts were as somber as the maid's. Although she'd earlier shown no disgust for his background, her insult had given him cause to wonder if she, too, was repelled by his Saracen blood. He flexed his shoulders irritably, an unconscious attempt to ease the tension of the whole long day. Although he seldom had trouble finding willing flesh to fill his bed, there were those women who had an aversion to his dark skin and foreign heritage. Few men of his class would scruple to take an unwilling woman of lower station without regard to her preferences, but in the days of his youth Jorion had been too often forced to submit to another's wishes to carelessly demand the same of others. Too, from youth on he'd learned to deny the pain of such rejections and was annoyed to feel more than a prick of discomfort at the prospect from this nameless maid, this female he'd rescued by giving what he'd offered no other.

Taine was surprised to find the young squire wakeful and waiting near the door. As Jorion dismounted and lifted her down, she stifled an unwelcome regret for having earned this cold and impersonal handling by concentrating on the weight of his squire's curious stare. Doubtless he wondered what strange chase she'd led his lord upon. Feet again on the ground, she turned toward the boy who shrank away. Clearly he stood in awe of her earlier temper. Though wishing to inspire such dread in his lord, she was embarrassed to have terrorized one so young and undeserving.

The unexpected charm of the smile his reaction brought to her lips left the boy gaping. Few ladies deigned to so gift a mere squire, and despite her garb and the morals he'd first questioned, he'd never doubted she was one. A shy grin lit his face as she passed to enter the still unlit house.

The figures near the fire were sleeping in nearly the same position as when she'd slipped away, apparently unaware of the movement of the lord and his "wife." All too conscious of the tall man behind, Taine climbed the stairs steadily, reassuring herself that this night's action presented no more than a minor setback. Tomorrow or the day beyond, Bertwald would help her win free of the golden coil.

The door to the chamber she'd fled lay to the left, but as she made to turn toward it a strong arm suddenly wrapped about her shoulders. Her heart kicked up an erratic beat. For what purpose did he restrain her from her allotted bed? Confusion raked over the coals of her temper, bringing it to flickering life as he urged her through the door of the room that lay opposite. She came to an abrupt halt one step within.

Mayhap having spent thirteen years of her life, save the weeks just past, in a dour castle was the reason she'd mistaken her first chamber for the lord's. Now she saw it was a paltry thing compared to the luxury of his. A well-stocked fire blazed. Before it stood a huge, heavily carved chair and table on which rested the remains of a generous meal—roast pheasant, fine wheaten bread, sharp yellow cheese, and a bowl of shiny red apples. Her eyes slid sideways over wide-plank flooring, well-swept and free of rushes, to the squares of thick Saracen carpets laid next to the bed. The bed. Apprehensive green eyes lifted to take in the magnificence of that imposing structure. High and wide, it was draped with heavy tapestries to hold the cold at bay and laid over by a bed fur of a kind she'd never seen before.

Hands clasped nervously together, she sidled away from the dragon and away from the bed, questions bubbling up in her mind like the frothing waters of a high mountain spring. Did this mean that, after their embrace on the horse, he meant to take her as wife in fact? Was that the price she must pay for her misdeed? Most important, where was the horror that prospect should call forth? She struggled to whip resentment and fear into a wall of protection, but her fortress was weakened by the undeniable truth that once she'd sought freedom from his embrace he quickly released her, though easily capable of forcing her to his will.

Light from the fire seemed to strike sparks in the auburn mass of her tumbled curls, and Jorion watched her shy away from him like one of his spirited Saracen fillies. A smile without humor curled his lips.

"Rest easy. Your fears are groundless. This night, at least, I am too exhausted by your foolery to seek more than the assurance that you cannot easily flee from me again." He lifted his arms and loosened the leather straps crossed over his chest to free the dual blades from his back. Jorion turned away to lean the weapons against the fireplace's stone wall, then worked to tug free of his heavy shirt of metal links, a difficult task even with the aid of a squire. That worthy lad had hoisted the mail onto his back but couldn't come to him in a chamber with a lady present. Despite this garment's weight, it was more easily donned than the plate armor worn in full battle and was most oft worn for daily defense.

Unable to tear her gaze away, Taine watched as her foe pulled off the homespun shirt worn beneath. The play of muscle under the golden skin of his broad back held green eyes in fascination, but offered little ease to her qualms.

Aware of the maid's growing dismay, Jorion's lips went tight with irritation. He glanced back and motioned toward the bed. "Sleep there."

She hesitated, looking doubtfully from bed to devastating

man, as fearful of her own newly awakened passion as of his.

"I give you my oath," he said, derision for her fears thickening his voice, "you are safe from my ardor—tonight."

The coldness of his eyes convinced her that his words were true. Indeed, his disinterested expression gave more cause to question her sanity in thinking him ever drawn to her. Surely those hot moments on Apollo's back had been a fantasy of her own making, born of terror—or desire? That treacherous possibility lent a sudden heat to once pale cheeks.

Seeing suddenly rosy cheeks and assuming them to be fostered by fear for the future joining he'd warned of, Jorion abruptly turned back to the fire, grimacing at tenseness in his muscles.

Hesitantly, Taine moved to climb up into the bed's soft comfort. As she pulled the luxurious coverlet over her fully clothed form and settled back into the bed's tender arms, her eyes drifted to the man staring into the flames and rubbing his neck where it joined broad shoulders. He looked to be as much in need of rest as she. A twinge of guilt pricked. Where would he sleep? She shifted uncomfortably and resolved to blank her mind of the man—to no purpose. He was too near and her awareness of his discomfort lingered on until, despite her unwilling sympathy, the exhaustion of the day's events won surrender to weariness.

The flames on the hearth had turned to little more than glowing coals before Jorion stirred from his long contemplation. After bending to prod them to life and ease their hungers with fresh wood, he walked to the edge of the high bed. Staring down at the slumbering maid he wondered for the puzzle she presented. Was he wrong to insist on the marriage she had claimed?

In the days of his youth in the desert, his mentor had talked of a green land kissed by cool mists. He had longed for it. When his grandfather called him to England, he'd been full of excited hopes—all dashed by the lack of welcome he'd found. The embittered man who'd lost a wife and three sons to be left with only a half-Saracen brat for heir to his earldom and proud family name had died within a year of that heir's arrival. In all the years since, Uncle Thomas, his guardian, had reminded him with persistent regularity of two pride-wounding facts: the inferiority of his heritage and that no wellborn woman would be willing to wed him and see her children tainted with the blood of godless infidels. Having suffered rejection in great measure, Jorion had never given any woman the opportunity to refuse him as husband—until this woman had claimed him mate. He'd agreed before others, but now she sought to reject him as he'd disallowed all others. He could not, would not see it happen.

Dark eyes studied the fiery woman, amazingly vulnerable in sleep. Though dressed in rough, much-patched homespun, her hair was the color of passion, a passion demonstrated as much by her mercurial mood changes and her temper, as by her fiery initial response to his embrace. Although he wholeheartedly accepted the Christian faith of the West, from the environment of his early years survived a strong belief in kismet, fate. Taine had made her marriage claim, and on first looking into eyes as green as the land he had longed for as a boy, he strongly feared he'd met his.

❧ Chapter 4 ❧

AN ANNOYING DISTURBANCE SUNDERED the peace of sleep's oblivion. Taine shrugged her shoulder to dislodge the soft touch and scooted farther down into luxurious warmth.

A hand hovered above the shoulder once again burrowed beneath heavy sable, while indecision puckered its owner's brows. What to do now was the question. Her lord had bidden her wake his wife, the existence of whom none here had known until the evening past—an odd thing that. But the lady seemed loath to rouse and she was unwilling to force wakefulness upon her.

The sensation of another presence, of being watched, stole into Taine's consciousness, bringing memories of the day and night preceding—memories of the dragon. Was he here even now? Surely not, she couldn't feel his presence and she was somehow certain she would. Nevertheless, green eyes cautiously opened a fraction to peer through the shield of thick lashes. The same friendly woman who'd led her to a chamber the night past now stood beside the bed, curiosity clear in hazel gaze. Taine cringed. What must the other think—finding her in the lord's bed. She quashed the cowardly inclination to pull the bedclothes over her head and hide. Instead she forced herself to sit up. Though still clutching the bed fur to her chin in nervous hands, she sought to meet the stranger with calm grace, a talent unlearned in a castle where no visitors came.

The waiting woman sternly repressed the amusement that threatened to twinkle in her eyes. She harbored no wish to offend this lady who looked like a bright-plumed bird prepared to flit away at any sudden movement. Since the earl had brought her to them, she'd been the foremost topic of conversation for all in his service. Having led the lady to bed in one chamber but sent now to waken her in the earl's, interesting questions arose in her mind. "Milady, I am Halyse. The earl bade me help you bathe." Tucking an errant lock the vivid shade of fresh carrots back into the questionable confines of a net crespine, Halyse nodded toward the large tub waiting before a blazing fire. Surreptitiously she peeked at the beauty whose dark hair was shot through with red, the deep red of ripe mulberries and quite unlike the bright orange hue of her own.

The earl? Perplexed, Taine tilted her head to study the speaker and sent a profusion of auburn curls over her shoulder and down the rich sable to her waist. One of the dragon's friends from the fair? A niggling dread began to build. Another powerful lord? She desperately sought some gleam of hope in the thought, for 'twould be a lesser threat to her freedom—but found it impossible to deny a truth so clear. The earl and the dragon were one! What had she done? To claim any man as husband had been a great folly, to claim a famous warrior more so, but to claim an English earl worst of all! On first sight she had known him a noble and should have realized before now his power was more than that of warrior or minor lord. Hope sank to her toes while her heart climbed to her throat, threatening to block all intake of air with its wild pounding.

The rapid succession of expressions crossing the lady's delicate features—uncertainty, sudden awareness and dismay—peaked Halyse's curiosity more. The evening past, after she'd settled the lady for the night and returned to the great hall, the earl had announced his marriage—a great shock. He'd gone past a score and ten showing no inclination for that tender bond. Now, like the conjurors who oft performed their mysterious arts at fairs or in a castle's great hall, he'd suddenly produced an unexpected bride. One who, with her hesitant smile clearly masking an apprehensive heart, was little like the haughty ladies of the court. Halyse's protective instincts were roused.

"'Tis hard to waken in a strange chamber, I ken, but the bath will cool, linger you too long abed." The smile accompanying the words was warm and eased Taine's anxiety. Soft rose lips curved in response. Surely this bright-haired woman posed no danger.

Halyse motioned toward the waiting tub and Taine's eyes followed. The sight of steam rising from hot water was inducement enough to draw her from the bed's comfort. Sliding from the covers, she discovered her feet bare, a fact which rendered a subtle discomfort of another kind. After she'd drifted to sleep, her shoes had been removed, and the thought of being touched unaware by the golden-haired lord brought a rosy heat to her cheeks, as if warmed by the dragon's fire. She stood and her toes sank into the never-before-experienced comfort of a thick Saracen carpet's deep pile. Her dour castle-prison had possessed no such refinements. Even distant childhood memories offered nothing to compare.

Halyse's bland expression hid her surprise at seeing the lady she was certain had undressed in another chamber the previous night, now rising fully clothed from the earl's bed. Mysterious deeds must have passed in the night.

With a quick, self-conscious glance at the waiting woman, Taine moved toward the tub. Not even her discomfort at the other's presence could hold her long from the promised bath. For weeks she'd had to content herself with a quick dip in an icy-cold stream or the doubtful good of a cloth soaked in the basin of tepid, brackish water provided by the inn. Resting her fingers on its water-warmed rim, she peered into the largest tub she had ever beheld. It surely must be able to hold two such as herself, even a man of the dragon's size, in uncramped ease. Made of tightly joined wooden planks and cloth-lined, it would doubtless lend a pleasant rest hitherto unknown. She walked slowly around its outer edge.

"The earl had it brought when the king settled here for the winter," Halyse informed her matter-of-factly, coming up behind. "Still, 'tis not what he uses in his great stone castle."

Taine turned quizzical eyes to the speaker. How came Halyse to know the dragon's bathing habits? An uneasy twinge pricked at Taine. Jealousy? Nay, couldn't be. Yet in her mind rose unbidden a vision of the bright-haired woman bending over the dragon's broad bare shoulders from behind. Taine was unsure whether the rosy heat that came to her cheeks was due to irritation at her ill-controlled thoughts or embarrassment at the vivid image of Halyse slowly drawing a cloth across the muscled ridges of an unclad torso. Whichever, Taine silently condemned her unwelcome fancies even as she wondered at her own temerity, calling to mind so vividly the sight of a powerful male chest.

Seeing the lady's frown and guessing a portion of its source, Halyse's amusement grew. She explained, "My husband, Will, says how the earl's got a nicer one—even larger and formed all of metal but soft with thick padding."

Embarrassed to find her thoughts so easily read, Taine's smile was weak and she looked immediately away to fumble with the fastenings of her simple surcote. To her memory, she'd never stood unclad before another living soul and found the prospect so daunting it made her unnaturally clumsy.

From a world in which the lady or daughters of each house lent aid in the bathing of all guests of rank, to Halyse such modesty as Taine's was unknown. Without hesitation, she stepped forward to lift the lady's sleeveless overgarment away. While Taine struggled free of her kirtle, each finger turned thumb by some wretched spirit, Halyse continued, pride in her voice: "Will is a knight and the earl's guard captain. Once the winter court settled I was summoned to see to the running of this house. Mayhap now you'll be wanting to take that duty to yourself?"

Taine froze, one foot poised over the waiting water. Inhibitions momentarily forgotten, her gaze flew to the other woman. Although Morag had supposedly taught her all that a wellborn woman was to know, she hadn't the least notion how to run a house. How could she, never having lived in a normal household. As a pampered princess in the Norwegian court, she'd been secreted away to become castle-prisoner on the bleak Scottish coast. She shook her head in denial, dropping her eyes to the water as she lowered her foot to its warmth. Nowise could she explain her past to this woman—or any other.

Determined to put unsettling matters aside, Taine stepped fully into the bath, enjoying the welcome heat of the liquid lapping about her thighs. This delight, she sighed, sinking blissfully into the watery realm, would fortify her to meet the challenges ahead. Comfortably seated on the low stool within, she accepted the small irregular ball of soap Halyse extended—another curiosity. Soft yellow and sweet-smelling, it little resembled those formed from meat fat, wood ash, and soda to which she was accustomed. She brought it hesitantly to her nose. Appreciation of its spring lilac fragrance curved tender lips in a gentle smile.

While Taine slowly lathered petal-soft skin, Halyse quietly spread towels to warm by the fire and laid a light morning repast on the table temporarily displaced by the tub. Laying out fresh garments, Halyse set forth to beguile the lady's leisure moments with several of her favorite legends, legends that would surely be of particular interest to Lady Taine.

"At the dreaming dawn of time, human life was a precarious thing, shrouded in mists and subject to the capricious will of unworldly masters," Halyse began, awe in her tone and eyes gone distant with the vision she told. "In those days a great mountain rose spewing forth lava and molten gold. As the precious substance cooled and fell to the earth a beast of fierce beauty was formed—" her voice whispering into silence, she paused, then roared, "a mighty dragon."

In the dreary boredom of Taine's prison, only Bertwald had offered comfort. With tales of happy yuletides and merry fairs or stories of the wee elfenfolk he'd learned as a child, he'd provided escape for her spirit. He'd even coaxed from one of her early rotating guards several of the tales sung by minstrels in fine castles, tales of mythical creatures and magical enchantments. For years she'd submerged, though never drowned, the disillusionments of her life in the sparkling waters of the tales and fables he'd repeated again and again. She was an audience willing to be captivated, and this woman's words were so vivid, her tone so reverent that Taine's hands stilled. She listened breathlessly as Halyse continued with other tales from the past, each speaking with respect and not a little fascination of the creature's awesome power.

"'Twas said," Halyse concluded, "that by his magnificence alone the Golden Dragon ensnared his prey, and beneath the golden links of enthrallment's net they willingly yielded to his consuming fire." Halyse slowly held her arms wide and raised her face to an unseen master above, a willing sacrifice.

Transfixed, Taine's hands too lifted but as Halyse's suddenly joined against her breast and she fell dramatically across the bed in mock death, Taine's dropped into water that had begun to cool. A large measure splashed into her face, startling her from the tales' trance.

Embarrassed by her foolish action, Taine quickly wiped the shining droplets from her face and began wringing excess water from the thick swath of her freshly washed hair, darkened but undimmed by the damp. "You are a fine taleweaver," she complimented Halyse, then asked the obvious, seeking with little success to sound no more than mildly interested. "They are stories of your lord, are they not?"

"The tales from whence his name came." Halyse agreed, still caught in the excitement of her own story and nearly convinced of their truth. "But far predate his coming." It seemed to her this lady with dark-flame hair was the perfect mate for their dragon's fire.

Though reluctant to leave the tub and again stand unclad before the other, Taine was even more determined to break the tales' thrall. She rose abruptly, sending a sparkling silver spray out from the tub. Her effort was rewarded by the soft towel Halyse held wide. With her mind still atuned to the world Halyse had created, the fire-warmed folds wrapped about her seemed like the embrace of her dragon lover. She felt trapped, wanting free of her evocative cloak but repelled by the prospect of donning either of the coarse gowns in her wardrobe.

Before she forced herself to the distasteful deed, Halyse eased the towel away and slipped a kirtle of fine linen over her head. Bemused, Taine's gaze followed as the peach-toned cloth skimmed downward, making a soft whispering sound. Designed for someone shorter, it failed by nearly a hand's breadth to reach the floor. Taine thrust her hands through dolman-cut sleeves, wide at the shoulder but tight at the wrist, and lifted her damp locks to fall forward. Halyse moved behind and worked the laces in the back, attempting to pull the edges together. It was soon clear that the gown had also been made for one less generously curved. The material strained across Taine's breasts while a gap remained in the back to reveal a wedge of satin skin.

Taine glared down at the too tight kirtle, even as the chamber's heavy oaken door creaked open. As she'd known she would, Taine sensed the dragon's presence. He held a talent for appearing in doorways at inopportune moments. Modesty forbade her turning away and displaying her bare back, but her arms flew up to cross over the unseemly bodice and silver-green eyes met dark ones accusingly.

Jorion's gaze swept over Taine, who stood before the hearth, outlined by dancing flames. His first glance took in her problem and left him torn between amusement for her predicament and irritation for the fact that she apparently blamed him for it.

"As you commanded," Halyse spoke to the earl even as she stepped in front of Taine and turned her back on him. "I went to Queen Marguerite to beg aid in obtaining suitable garments for your lady. From her own wardrobe she provided these and bade Lady Du Marchand attend your lady here to fill her needs." She dropped a sleeveless green velvet surcote over an auburn head. "'Tis a fine thing the queen and her ladies have arrived, for where goes the queen, goes Lady Du Marchand."

Taine was mired in a quandary as difficult to navigate as a peat bog. She wanted to pull the surcote down over the revealing kirtle but was unable to find discreet means for moving her arms from their shielding position to jerk it into place. Still, she heard Halyse's account and wondered what position of influence this unknown Lady Du Marchand possessed.

Seeing questioning green eyes above the cloth still bunched about Taine's throat, Halyse quietly offered an explanation. "Lady Du Marchand is one of the three ladies of the bedchamber who accompanied Marguerite from her brother's domain—King Philip of France, you ken?—to wed our king. Fresh from the French court and knowledge-able of fashions, she is responsible for the creation and care of the queen's wardrobe. Her taste and creativity are well-respected, and she is much in demand by the ladies of the court." Under gently tugging hands, the surcote slid freely down, and Halyse turned and spoke again to the earl. "She and her minions will soon arrive. Mayhap she can rework this sorry garb to a better fit." She stepped back to doubtfully view Taine's apparel.

Taine slid her arms into the surcote, an easy thing as the armholes stretched from shoulder to hip. The style was strange to her. Ten years and more in seclusion, with only a bitter old woman for feminine companionship, had left her sadly unaware of changing fashions. She lifted her arms, looking askance for the missing cloth that the other two seemed not to find lacking. Beneath the weight of black eyes, she suddenly became aware that this sideless garment fell far short of providing the cover she felt demanded by the revealing kirtle. Dropping her arms to form some barrier, she shied away from the tall man's strong presence.

Lack of sleep had already raked over the coals of Jorion's temper, and at Taine's action (further proof of her desire to reject the honor he'd offered no other), sparks of irritation glowed. To dampen its fire, as the door shut behind the retreating Halyse, he stepped beyond Taine to brace his hands on the heavy oak mantle. He pressed down until his fingertips turned white, a physical display of the restraint he forced on his emotions. A faint shadow of his cynical half-smile appeared as he acknowledged the nameless beauty's ability to break through the iron-control he was famed for possessing.

Taine turned to stare at the broad back before the fire, as solid and unmoving as Hadrian's wall. Silence stretched painfully. She grew nearly certain he'd forgotten her living. With a concerted effort, she stilled the urge to twist the material of the velvet surcote between her hands. 'Twas a nervous habit she'd named childish, sworn to end, and long struggled to defeat. In this man's presence it only grew worse. Instead, she rubbed her palms down the precious cloth and found distraction in its lush texture.

"I had forgot the feel of such stuffs," Taine murmured absently, unmindful of the motionless man who seemed too withdrawn to hear.

Instantly alert, Jorion spun about. "When last did you wear such finery?" His full attention centered on the maid. Here was the first weakening of her citadel's defense and he meant to take full advantage.

Taine's head snapped up, color draining away and leaving her cheeks an ivory relief against damp-darkened auburn hair. She had erred in speaking of even so minor a thing, for the dragon had quickly scented his prey. Nerve-frozen, she sought some harmless response among the chaotic thoughts whirling in her mind.

When no immediate answer was forthcoming, Jorion hastened to question further, "From whence came you that such was yours?"

Having found a dearth of believable deceptions, still Taine made no answer. The waiting man watched her closely, a golden brow raised in demanding query. Standing silent before him, one hand thoughtlessly wound green velvet about the other with fine disregard for both its value and her own vows to cease such childish deeds.

Jorion sensed her confusion and, a skilled tactician, recognized his advantage. Now was the time to strike, now before she'd time to restore her defenses. He stepped closer, towering above Taine and setting her heart to thumping painfully. "For what reason did two men pursue you at the fair—and later?"

At last here was a question easy to answer. Taine's chin rose, disdain curling rose lips. "For the same reason men so oft attack women, the same reason you assaulted me as we returned during the hours of early morn." She flung her arm out toward the hills over which she'd sought escape, but pulled it back to restore her shield of the surcote's lack and carefully folded one hand in the other at her waist as any well-raised woman would do.

His eyes went as hard and cold as obsidian. This response was a well-placed defensive blow, did she but know it. Jorion took pride in never offering himself up to be spurned. Yet by publicly accepting the marriage she'd claimed, he had already placed himself in danger of a humiliating rejection. Her words now were a serious affront. He hadn't attacked her, and was experienced enough to know that, at least for a time, the embrace had been as much a pleasure to her as to him. His broad chest expanded as he drew a deep breath and forced calm rationality to order his thinking. He could believe that such was the reason the two men had followed her at the fair, but it was not why they had lain in wait to assail her a second time. Accepting such as truth, a question remained: Did she know a deeper purpose lay behind?

Taine saw the dragon's hooded eyes focus on her ring, and forcefully stilled the near-overpowering impulse to thrust her hands behind her back.

For seemingly endless moments, Jorion studied the delicate band Taine's assailants had sought to gain. Although a pretty piece of twined silver and gold, it contained no precious jewel or family seal. What then had fostered their determination to take it from her? What lay behind a desire so strong that, despite a clear fear of him, her persistent pursuers had lingered to further their attempt? Perhaps simple greed. Perhaps more.

"Never in past have I seen a band of like design. How came you to possess such a ring?" Jorion's tone was gentle and intended to lull her obvious tension.

Taine looked at him suspiciously but shrugged. Explain the origin of her ring was the very last deed she would perform.

Her guard was up, Jorion acknowledged, and resources clearly regrouped. Gentle questioning would never wrest the truth from her. Familiar now with her hot temper, he sought to rouse it in hopes of loosening her tongue.

"Did you steal it, as you stole my cloak?" With startling

speed, he changed his strategy from gentleness to apparent disdain.

Jorion's goal was achieved. Taine's temper flashed. Without pausing to consider the wisdom of her words, she retorted, "My father gave it to me. 'Twas my mother's and my grandmother's before." The bold retort seemed to mock her determination of only moments past. She cursed her hasty anger and unthinking words even as she prayed them too few to reveal that which she would hide.

As Jorion's lips parted to press for further details, an imperative knock sounded on the door. With a low growl of disgust for the ill-timed arrival, he turned to call entry.

A woman of formidable dimensions sailed into the room. Taller and broader than most, Lady Du Marchand relished her ability to intimidate men, whether noble or serf. Finding the earl within, she frowned her disapproval. This friend of the king's had never shown similar qualms. The lady curtsied to the earl as propriety demanded and reminded herself she was friend to the queen. That close relationship with royalty reinforced a pride that often led her to boldness. Her chin went up so high it threatened to snap her neck from the back, yet still she could not look down her nose at the tall man. The queen had directed her and she'd come, but had believed the dragon would stay absent, leaving such womanly concerns to others. She preferred to lead in these matters, and he was a clear threat to her sovereignty.

Golden hair gleamed as Jorion inclined his head in acknowledgment of the woman's reluctant homage, but one corner of his mouth lifted in faint cynicism, even as he directed the serf who had led her to the chamber to remove the tub.

Once the earl's command was carried out, Lady Du Marchand leaned her not inconsiderable breadth through the open door and imperiously motioned her retinue to enter. Two young women came first and moved to her side. They were followed by a parade of male serfs carrying bolts of cloth and baskets of accessories. The men deposited their burdens and quickly filed out again, leaving behind a colorful array of wools and linens, precious silks, brocades and velvets. Cream, mulberry red, rose madder, deep green, moss green, marigold and buttercup yellow were spread so thickly upon the mattress, they hid the bed's sable coverlet. Two shades of blue were draped over a massive chair, and bolts of heavy velvets and rich brocades were haphazardly leaned against walls. Indeed, lengths of material covered every available surface, save the small table where Taine's untouched morning repast still waited.

Stunned by the profusion, Taine had little appetite for the fresh bread, fruit, and milk. Nonetheless, given the chance to partake, the opportunity to busy her fingers and mind with other than the overwhelming man and the crowd of strangers, she would have eaten and drunk even had the meal tasted of moldy rushes and vinegar-tainted wine.

Well able to ride courageously into fierce battle or stride unfazed through a court filled with powerful political foes, Jorion was uneasy amongst such unfamiliar activities as these. He comforted himself that he had but one thing to accomplish before making a strategic retreat. Slowly he examined each of the offered materials, while a nervous Taine and three silent women watched. In the abundance Jorion saw the measure of the aging king's affection for his bride of barely four years, happily an affection the plain but sweet young queen fully returned. Surely several carts must have been devoted to transporting the queen's wardrobe and its makings alone, providing even what she had not requested. Yet, it seemed to Jorion, the queen was less concerned for her own appearance than for the happiness of others, and thus had he sought her aid.

At length Jorion paused before a heavy velvet spread out on the bed. Gathering up rich folds the same deep green shade as a forest in the rain, he carefully rewound the bolt and tucked it under one strong arm. Moving to the rolls of cloth against the wall, he selected a misty green brocade shimmering with delicate flowers embroidered in silver thread and turned to the waiting women.

Knotting her fingers together, Taine apprehensively stared at her captor and his burden. She possessed little experience of such stuffs but knew they were doubtless of great value and, even though sent by the queen, the dragon would pay dearly for them. That he meant to meet the price and see her wear such wondrous material was more proof than she desired that he truly meant to wed her.

Lady Du Marchand's brows lowered over flat grey eyes. Although she preferred to think of the bold lord as a barbarian heathen, she was forced to admit his choice unerring.

"By the morrow's nooning hour, she must have a gown suitable for a court visit." Amused by the lady's haughty demeanor, still the earl would brook no denial of his demand.

While slate grey eyes met black in battle, Taine bit back a gasp. Had her hasty temper, the words prompted by his question on her ring, exposed to him her heritage? By taking her to the English king's winter court did he mean to claim a crown? Her hands clenched tightly together, each finger of one imprinting red brands on the creamy skin of the other.

"The style I leave to your choosing"—Jorion continued, offering a sop to the woman's wounded pride, but even that was qualified—"yours and hers, so long as the result is a gown she can wear proudly, fearing the insults of none." He couldn't imagine the fiery maid who had fought him each step—with but a few notable exceptions—easily allowing another to direct her choices. Yet her retiring manner since the moment of this overbearing woman's arrival left him fearful of that possibility. He failed to realize Taine's concern was more for him and their interrupted conversation than for Lady Du Marchand's nature. Determined to ensure that Taine's preferences were consulted in the selection of her clothing, he added, "For the rest, provide her with wardrobe fit for a countess—my countess. Do not stint on her behalf, I am well able to stand the cost and would see her garbed as the equal of any. But of most import, be aware that her decisions are law."

Accustomed to others bowing to her dictates on all details in these matters, Lady Du Marchand opened her mouth to protest, but Jorion unexpectedly dropped the chosen material into her arms. Although the weight was no great strain, such tasks as fetching and carrying she delegated to others. It set her off her usual stride, leaving her flustered and nodding her agreement to the wide back disappearing through the chamber door. Her two young assistants struggled valiantly to suppress grins called forth by the strange sight of their mistress so neatly outmaneuvered and scowling heavily.

Once the earl had departed, Lady Du Marchand dropped the bolts to the bed and squared heavy shoulders. She turned to the others, determination to regain her usual control clear in iron-grey eyes.

Buried in her own concerns, Taine barely noted the exchange. So preoccupied was she that she willingly bent to the lady's dictates. The earl's efforts to see her in control of her wardrobe's planning were, unbeknownst to him, a wasted exercise. As she had learned in donning the green surcote, in the matter of clothing styles, her upbringing had severe limitations.

Taine's morning repast had been replaced by a midday platter that suffered a like fate while the two assistants bustled about at Lady Du Marchand's direction. She stood at the foot of the bed and issued quick, brisk commands like the leader of some deadly assault. Taine was their apparent foe, for by the time they finished with her she felt utterly vanquished. With their measuring they'd twisted her this way and that, holding first one and then another cloth against cheek and hair to test the suitability of its hue. They had measured and prodded and poked while their bickering voices swirled about her head.

When at last Lady Du Marchand called a halt, Taine leaned against one of the draped bed's solid posts, wearied by the unaccustomed strain of building a wardrobe fit for a countess. All she wanted was to sit, or preferably stretch out on the wide bed's beckoning comfort. She'd had little enough sleep last night. Eyeing the staggering number of bolts that now lay in the mound of those chosen, she valiantly struggled to squelch both the self-betraying temptation to remain and enjoy such a bounty of lovely clothes and the niggling guilt that the dragon had wasted so much in their procuring. He was a wealthy man, she firmly reminded herself, an earl, friend to the English king, and unneedful of her concern. Once the imperious woman's servants had neatly rerolled and carried the wide array from the chamber, Taine straightened and forced a polite smile as she bade farewell to her nearly day-long companions.

Words of departure already spoken and goods and assistants gone, Lady Du Marchand lingered at the door. Her gaze drifted over the dragon's lady one last time. The rumor of a bride had spread swiftly through the court, lighting fires of curiosity that burned many a fine lady with jealousy as well. But she had found a liking for this maid who, unlike the women of the court, smiled without hauteur.

A widow of minor dower, Lady Du Marchand had been lady to the French princess from nearly the maid's birth. Full of determination to see that none took advantage of Marguerite's sweet and generous nature, she had willingly accompanied the bride across the channel to her aging bridegroom's side. At the court of the wily King Philip, Lady Du Marchand had long since learned to meet, match, even outdo those who thought to intimidate and easily transferred those talents to the English court. Accustomed to people seeking to prove their position by issuing imperious demands, she found the dragon's gracious bride a refreshing change. Here was a woman who demonstrated the same noble character as her young mistress.

An unexpected but friendly grin warmed Lady Du Marchand's stern face and surprised Taine into an answering smile that sent silver sparks to lighten green eyes. Spreading her peach skirt to better display the magic that deft hands had wrought, Taine thanked the lady for seeing to the alterations. Cloth had been so skillfully added to the hem and bodice of the once ill-fitting kirtle that the additions seemed part of the original. Lady Du Marchand was pleased by Taine's appreciation of her design and generously promised to see she had not only the one demanded on the morrow but several more completed within a very short time. Once the heavy plank door swung shut in the lady's wake, Taine was left in peaceful solitude for the first time in all the long day.

Frenzied activity ended, exhaustion overtook Taine. The autumn day's chilled fingers stretched out to touch her. She moved into the crackling fire's circle of warmth and sank into a wide, deep chair padded with a soft pelt. The midday meal still waited on the table. The stew had cooled to an unappetizing mess, but she reached for the slab of fine wheaten bread that lay beside. Lifted in one hand, the golden crust caught the edge of the crockery bowl and would have dumped its congealed contents had not her free hand forestalled the plunge. Flamelight glanced across her twined gold-and-silver band.

Nibbling absently on the bread's flaky crust, she brooded over her last conversation with Jorion and her foolish response to his question about her ring. Far better had she removed the delicate piece the first morn of her flight and tossed it into the smooth, deep waters of the tarn. 'Twas a deed best fulfilled even now, yet she had not the will. The convoluted circlet was all that remained of a life long past and, though few and time-hazed, those distant memories were warm.

Bread consumed, Taine turned sideways in the generous width of the chair and cuddled down, settling more comfortably. Creamy cheek resting in contrast against dark, luxurious fur, her thoughts wandered to the last, clearest, and most disturbing. She had loved her father, a huge man with blond hair and ice-blue eyes. He had given her the ring the night before she was to sail away to marry a prince and someday be queen. To a small girl the expected journey had seemed the romantic stuff of which traveling minstrels sang. Putting her mother's ring on a thumb it was far too big to fit, he had told her to not be affrighted when strangers came and carried her from the ship, no matter the circumstances. He'd said to remember that she *was* a queen—would always be. No marriage was needed to ensure that.

Queen—a dreadful title that meant only betrayal and loneliness. Taine's right hand covered the ring, hiding it from sight. Her father had sent her into it, had sent her to a cold and dreary castle to live alone and unloved. Her father and all the ambitious men who saw in her only the crown her hand could give. For that goal they would let her pay the price in misery. Unconsciously her hand tightened over the ring with crushing force, laying its imprint into her palm. She did *not* want the crown and nurtured a disdain for men, the selfish animals who thought of none save themselves and their aims. A vision rose of Morag, tall and gaunt with a sour disposition turned bitter with advancing years, warning her with vicious glee as she had again and again that her treatment at the hands of men was no different from that which every woman could expect—manipulation to attain personal goals. Her hand slowly relaxed as weariness led her past dark and looming threats into the peaceful realms of dreamless sleep.

❧ Chapter 5 ❧

BERTWALD STALKED ACROSS THE lower end of the Great Hall
to peer out the window, although little but shadows could be
seen through its hide covering. A short, impatient sound
issued from his throat. He turned and marched back to the
huge hearth, completing the round-trip path he'd trod no
less than ten-score times in the last few hours. His impatience boiled forth, and he slapped his palm against soot-
darkened stones. He must speak with the earl!

Of Taine, Bertwald had seen naught the whole of the day
past. Not until all else were at table for the evening meal had
she descended from the chamber above. Then, dressed as a
lady, at the high table she'd been seated beside their host,
while he'd been accorded an honorable place to the left of
one of the earl's knights at one lower. Not before Taine had
gone up to one chamber and the earl to another had the
knight at his side mentioned his lord's intention to take
Taine to the English king's court. A dreadful, frightening
prospect. Aye, he must see the earl and convince him of the
folly in the deed. Toward that end he'd risen early, hoping to
waylay the earl for a private conversation. With disgust he'd
found his ploy foiled. The earl had already departed for a

purpose unknown, leaving Bertwald in a stew of apprehension.

From her vantage point at the top of the stairs, Taine viewed the busy hall. Servants garbed in dun-brown homespun bustled about, preparing the midday meal. A woman stirred the steaming cauldron suspended above the fire from a strong metal hook, while another turned chickens roasting on the spits, and yet another divided bread for the tables, dark rye for those lower, fine wheaten for the high. Men fed whole logs to the huge hearth's hungry flames. Others assembled trestle tables in two long rows extending at right angles on either end of the one on the dais, and dragged heavy benches to their sides. The paths laid through floor rushes by benches were quickly erased by the milling feet of the earl's guard, who gathered in small groups to idly discuss again the battles of earlier months.

Not anxious to meet curious eyes, Taine stood utterly still as she searched for the gleam of a golden head that would tower above all others. Although both knights and most of his guard were there, he was not. Apparently it was his wont to go about alone, for had he not been unaccompanied when she met him at the fair?

She'd failed to find the dragon, but among the milling group below she spied Bertwald abusing a stone wall with the flats of both hands. Relief lifted her spirits. The past eventide her desire to speak privately with Bertwald had been forestalled by the dragon. They'd shared few words, yet he'd kept her by his side for the meal and beyond. Aware to the depths of her soul each time dark eyes turned to study her, she'd been able to consume but a few bites that had lodged uncomfortably in her throat. Sitting so near she could feel his heat, a nameless longing had risen and threatened her calm. She could nearly see the golden links of his enthrallment and feared the consuming fire. By the time she escaped, tension was a living thing whose shape, though unseen, was a dragon. She'd lain awake through the dark hours, fearing his intention of leading her into the lion's jaws, into King Edward's court. The dull grey mantle of a cloudy dawn lay heavy on the horizon before her eyes closed. She'd long overslept.

This opportunity to speak with Bertwald without the

dragon's presence was an unlooked-for gift. She must slip unobtrusively to his side and convince him to take her away before the dragon returned. Moving down the first few steps with exaggerated caution, she discovered her action as a foolish thing, for it drew more attention than she might else have done. A sea of faces turned to her. Unaccustomed and uncomfortable as the center of all eyes, she drew a deep fortifying breath, pinned a bright smile to her lips, and descended the remaining distance with proud grace.

Reaching her goal, she softly murmured, "Bertie, come walk with me for the time afore the meal is ready. It has been days since we talked."

Bertwald proffered his upheld arm and Taine placed her hand atop it. But as they started toward the iron-bound outer door, they discovered their progress shadowed by a tall knight walking close behind.

Taine's hand dropped from Bertwald's arm as she turned to the dark, barrel-chested man, a delicate brow lifted in question.

"Prithee pardon, milady," he answered the unspoken query in a voice so low and rough 'twas nearly a growl. "I am Will Fitz Herbert and am bade attend you, should you seek to leave this place. My lord believes a danger may threaten and would hold you safe."

Although his wife, Halyse, had talked of this lady's grace and sweetness of spirit, Will's eyes narrowed on the lovely face. He, as all of the dragon's men, thought much of his lord and was leery of possible insult to the proud man.

Taine tilted her head in gracious acknowledgment, but nibbled at her full lower lip while tightly linking her fingers. Seeking to raise her ire and thus bolster her courage to calmly face this impediment, she silently mocked the knight's words. Hah, the dragon feared less for her safety against earlier assailants than for the possibility of her escape before he could seek the reward of her heritage. The prospect was so daunting it raised more alarm than anger.

Bertwald saw Taine's troubled gestures and felt her tension build like a river in flood and in danger of cresting its banks. He reached out to place a calming hand on hers. "Ach, lassie, clouds hie the sun away and wouldna rain ruin such lovely clothes?"

Thankful for his comfort and aid, Taine's smile broke forth like sun through storm clouds, stunning the watching knight with its sweetness. Her noble carriage and regal nod had near convinced him of her threat to the earl's vulnerable pride. But for that smile and her nervous fidgeting she might be simply another court beauty, though of surpassing loveliness, anxious to prove her strength in that by claiming what none other had attained, yet having no care for the prize. This lady was as vulnerable as the man, and Will could see why Halyse had come back from her chamber as her defender.

"Best we stay within and visit here," Bertwald added, nodding toward a settle only large enough for two at one side of the door.

Taine nodded and moved to sit down. Bertwald lowered his broad form beside her. They talked of the weather and of the new clothes she wore and the wardrobe in preparation until Will rejoined the crowd busy with talk of their own. Certain of the relative privacy offered by many involved in other matters, Taine rushed into passionate speech before Bertwald had gathered his words. She poured out her error in talking to the dragon of her ring and of his plan to lead her into her foe's hands.

"He's seen my ring and he knows! Moreover, he means to lead me to my enemy, to King Edward."

Bertwald's bushy grey brows flew up in surprise. So, the dragon had shared his intent with the maid. To him it was proof that he didna yet understand the ring's significance or her heritage. He shook his head, sending wiry grey hair flying.

Taine thought his action a denial of her words and argued, "Has not the English monarch long been foe to the Scottish? Has this king not already sought to use me for his own purpose. Even if he refuses to support his favored vassal in a like cause, will he not make haste to shut me away and thus forestall a legitimate claim to the land he claims his own." Panic raised the pitch of her voice. "You've got to help me free of them all." She paused, pressing fingertips to soft lips as she glanced furtively around, seeking reassurance her words were unheard.

"I doona think the earl kens, lassie," Bertwald soothed.

"Many's the ring that passes from one generation tae another. Wait awhile yet."

"Wait?" Taine straightened abruptly and glared at her companion with eyes of green fire. "'Tis likely been too late we've waited already."

Bertwald lifted his hands, palms to Taine as if holding her haste at bay. "I mean tae speak with the earl when he returns. If after he still means tae take you there, I'll hie ye away."

Taine's brows lowered in mute disgust. Yet she knew when once Bertwald's mind was set, no means she possessed would change it. Moreover, winning free of their appointed guard would take planning.

The sudden opening of the door startled Taine. Heavy planks thrown wide, the dragon stood framed in the open portal. Black cloak, whipped by the breeze, molded an impressive form while the weak light of a cloudy sky glowed on golden hair. Taine's breath caught in her throat but whether from fear or some elemental tension she refused to question.

As Jorion reached to close the iron-barred door, he caught Taine staring at him through wide green eyes and paused for an endless moment to meet their tempting power. He, too, seemed to stop breathing as his gaze locked with hers. A small sound of amusement from the men within woke him from his momentary trance. Irritated at having been twice observed caught in this woman's thrall, he sent the door shut with unnecessary force.

Taine's cheeks warmed even as her gaze was freed from its bond with his. Gold sparks had burned in the dark of his eyes, holding her captive—further proof of the danger in him. A strong bronzed hand came into her downcast view, stilled the unconscious twisting of her fingers, and drew her up to walk at his side to the high table. Although cursing herself for the lack of courage she found, her glance never strayed from their path. Too aware of the graceful allure of the woman at his side and their curious audience, Jorion fixed his gaze upon the high backs of the chairs waiting behind the white cloth-covered tables ahead.

No words were exchanged at the high table but conversation at those lower was lively, the men quickly resuming their discussion of a particularly fierce battle and a disagreement flaring on the matter of which tactic had won the day.

Taine felt lost within the massive chair, identical to the one in which the earl comfortably sat. The warmth of his body reached out and enveloped her. Again she felt his golden net falling about her but strived to hold her attention on the rich appointments of the table. At the evening meal past she'd been amazed by its white cloth covering and the delicate stands topped with waxen candles that were placed at regular intervals down its length. Now, not even the intricate patterns of the silver goblets could hold her attention. Slender fingers gripped the one before her so tightly 'twas a fine thing it was formed of no less sturdy substance else the pretty vessel would doubtless have snapped in two. Through lowered lashes she peeked from the huge man at her side to her grey-haired friend. What hope had Bertwald of turning this man's famous iron will? Aye, she'd learned much of him from Halyse in the hours of yestereve, yet the things of which Halyse had boasted only increased her unease.

By the time the savory stew and roasted pheasant were consumed, Jorion was aware of the furtive glances passing between Bertwald and the maid at his side. In the cosy conversation he'd interrupted, had they laid some plan to flee? That possibility, nay, probability did not improve his temper. First his noble companions at the fair and now his own men had seen him caught in this woman's snare. The humiliation of a rejection at her hand would be greater than any gone before.

"Milord, I crave a private word."

In surprise, Jorion looked up from the apple he had absently chosen, thoughts caught in plans to forestall Taine's deed, and found Bertwald standing before him, determination in every line. Apple still in hand, he rose and motioned Bertwald before him to his bedchamber above.

Taine watched Bertwald's sturdy frame climbing the stairs. Although he preceded the dragon and was thus a step higher, his grizzled grey head failed to rise to a level with the golden one that followed.

The earl's departure signaled the clearing of tables. Rising to leave trenchers holding little more than stripped bones, the men of the guard regrouped about the nearly deserted hearth. Some worked together to hoist and tote benches to positions of ease near the fire's warmth, displacing the hounds that had earlier sought its heat.

Filled with anxiety, Taine little saw the hustle of the servants dismantling the tables and cleaning away the meal's remains. Bolted to the dais, the high table was a permanent fixture. Taine lingered there in a chair whose back rose well above the top of her auburn head, its dark fire little subdued by the net crespine loaned her by Halyse. Unaware of the frequent admiring glances of the earl's men, she stared blindly at the wine left untasted in her refilled goblet. She prayed God her angry defense had failed to expose her secret to the dragon. More, forlorn hope though it be, she prayed Bertwald would alter his intent.

The sound of the heavy door opening again, scraping across the plank flooring, finally broke Taine's absorption. The impressive form of Lady Du Marchand sailed into the hall, her usual line of lackeys following obediently. Taine allowed herself to be swept up the stairs on the lady's wave of assurance, but insistently led the way to the chamber where she'd slept the previous night, rather than the earl's, where they'd met before and where he now discussed her fate with Bertwald.

"But you darena take her there!" Bertwald pled with dwindling hope, shoving both hands through grey hair, rendering further damage to already wildly disordered strands. He'd thought the earl would protect Taine, hold her safe in his strength.

Weary of standing and listening to this man's repeated entreaties, Jorion settled into the chair on one side of a small table set with his chess pieces, and waved Bertwald to the other. With a sharp shake of his head, Bertwald refused the offer. Jorion's breath came out with a sound of disgust. How could the man expect him to change his plans without explanation for its need?

"Why?" he asked again with no real expectation of an answer to the question he'd asked time and time before.

Bertwald felt again the frustrating limits of the oath he'd given his lady. He could not speak of the prize she meant for the ambitious men who filled the court—covert supporters of Baliol; Robert Bruce; and, likely the greatest threat of all, King Edward. Not even to save her this danger could he sunder the bonds of his oath, but could only skirt about the edges. Faded blue eyes narrowed; he said, "'Tis a den of predators."

Eyes as deep and black as night studied Bertwald until, near to being swallowed in their depths, he sank into the chair he'd refused.

"Tell me the threat and I will see her safe," Jorion responded at last.

Bertwald rubbed his hand over his face in defeat. Short of betraying his royal lady, revealing what she most feared for this man to know, he could not forestall their court visit. He was not such a fool as to believe it possible the two of them could escape the earl and all his men between now and the hour of their departure. They must wait until the visit was done and beg Providence to provide a later means.

"Think you I can do other than go to my king? The nobles before whom I claimed Taine wife will have spoken of that deed to him." He paused until Bertwald's face lifted and faded blue eyes met his. "I am sworn to King Edward and though we winter now, we are here for purposes of war."

Bertwald now saw the necessity for the earl's court visit. He and his noble lady were caught between the devil and the sea. The earl must go, yet for Taine the danger was too great.

"I owe my liege service," Jorion continued, "and can do naught else but go to him and offer explanation. Before we may return to Radwyn lands and Castle Dragonsward for the wedding rite I swore to you, I must have his release from my obligations to him."

While the older man struggled to accept his words, Jorion silently acknowledged the debt he owed his king. Since the day they'd first met, Edward had taken a strong liking to the son of the man he'd left in Palestine. 'Twas the king who had knighted Jorion and stood him as friend, nearly a second father, until all others in his court had little choice but to accept the half-Saracen boy. Although, in truth, Jorion's lips curled in one-sided cynicism, the path had been eased by his inheritance of the vast earldom of Radwyn and the power that attended it. Aye, he owed King Edward this and much more.

Taine hesitated at the top of the stairs. Although outwardly composed, her anxious gaze frantically searched the crowded hall below for Bertwald. Lady Du Marchand had come and stayed—and stayed and stayed. Indeed, even now as the cloud-hazed sun hovered above a crimson-stained horizon, she stood but a step behind. Her lingering presence had frayed Taine's nerves and prevented her from seeking out the conspirator who'd promised to spirit her away should he fail to turn the dragon's will. He'd not come, there was no sign of him below, but there the dragon waited to take her where she dreaded to go. Again the back of his golden head, so high above the others, drew her eyes like a beacon light.

The attention of the two knights with whom Jorion spoke shifted to a point above and behind and he knew what had captured their interest. He turned and let his gaze slide slowly over the slender nymph he'd claimed wife. Lady Du Marchand had fully proven her talents. Light glanced across a dark green velvet kirtle like morning sunlight through the woodlands. The lovely surcote of silver brocade worn over was nearly sideless and allowed occasional tantalizing glimpses of curves lovingly embraced by satin cut close from neck to hip before flaring to dance in full folds about graceful feet. Threads of silver formed a delicate net crespine that added sparkle to the dark-fire curls it confined. A few escaped to rest charmingly against the cream silk of cheek and brow.

Under his long examination, Taine's chin tilted up and he smiled with satisfaction. Such a regal beauty was she that none could doubt her a lady born. Nay, a sardonic voice whispered in his thoughts, many women were there of the court whose envy would overflow with spite. The thought lowered golden brows in a frown that had Taine fearing he'd found her lacking. Jorion had rather there be no need to deliver her into their midst, wished he could yield to Bertwald's pleas, but was duty-sworn to his king. He could only stand as shield between her and the women's barbed words. More, he offered a silent vow to free her with haste from their company.

His smile flashed white against his bronzed skin, and the attraction of that sudden smile sent Taine's gaze to the floor. She cursed herself for falling coward to a smile. Nonetheless, she kept her eyes on the long line of deserted steps at her feet as she mentally recited an oft-repeated lesson of the past: men hold all the weapons of attack, women can but defend. Small comfort. This was a battle of a different sort and she had no weapons of defense save retreat and that he would not allow. Her palms nervously smoothed down the luxurious surcote, whose style she still felt was woefully inadequate, and sent up a fervent prayer to all the saints above for aid in meeting both the dragon's attack and the potential dangers in this fearful court visit.

There was no help for it, she must go. Pray God the English king would offer no immediate threat. *Moonling,* she berated herself in an effort to bolster her courage, *how could he be a threat to you?* He'd never seen the child to whom he'd once betrothed his heir. Even had he, 'twas little likely he'd recognize that small child in her. Feeling nearly compelled by the dark unwavering eyes below, she drew in a deep, fortifying breath and started down the steep stairway determined to at least complete the deed with grace.

The earl met her at the foot of the stairs and offered his arm to her. All too aware of a sea of interested eyes, Taine acknowledged the courtly gesture by placing her fingertips lightly on his forearm. Though born to a court, she had few clear memories of its nature and feared for her ability to meet the high standards of the English king's. As they passed through the watching members of the earl's house, she surreptitiously peeked at them. Their open admiration lent some hope that her appearance at least was not inadequate. Jorion led her to the outer door held for them by his page, whose wide eyes spoke much of his awe for this exquisite beauty in their midst. His wordless compliment lent a measure of bravery to Taine and earned the boy another gentle smile.

One fear allayed, Taine found another once she stepped past the open doorway and into the lingering half-light that follows even the sunset of a cloudy day. The great golden stallion stood restively at the foot of the shallow steps. At its side waited a small grey palfrey, prepared for a lady's ride. Her heart sank and she came to a sudden halt, shrinking from the need to confess her inability to ride.

For Taine, confined to the castle and its close surroundings for nearly all of her days, 'twas a talent never needed nor deemed less than dangerous for her to attain. Somehow the prospect of admitting even this one lack to a man so obviously talented was a bitter draught to contemplate. Moreover, he might well simply place her in a cart for delivery to the court, like a sack of grist to the mill. Refusing to allow such a crushing blow to the dignity she would need to face the king, her once intended father-in-law, she squared her shoulders and stepped forward.

Seeing the maid freeze a second time in terror before a steed, Jorion's suspicions were confirmed. She had never learned to ride and feared even Halyse's small dappled mare, which, for its gentleness, he'd chosen for her use. That she found the courage to go on, he applauded—and rewarded.

"She's as gentle as a lamb and will not rise up even should you jerk at her mane as you did Apollo's." His low voice was quiet and, although he teased, it held no derision for her lack.

Taine's eyes flew up to meet a mockery for once gentle in his one-sided smile. She nodded but paused again, having no idea how to find her way atop the placid palfrey. Strong hands slowly wrapped about her narrow waist, giving her time to recognize and accept his intent before lifting her, as though she were no more than a lily plucked from the stock. Even knowing what to expect, her heart thudded with alarm as her feet left the ground. Slender hands flew instinctively to the reassuring strength of broad shoulders. Though filled with alarm for her precarious position, for the need to travel ahorse, and with trepidation for the court visit to come, Taine acknowledged the strong current of attraction that this man's proximity sparked. Awareness of the power in the warm muscles separated from her fingers by only the rich cloth of his deep-blue tunic distracted her thoughts from the directions he calmly issued.

Holding Taine a fraction above the mount, Jorion instructed her how to sit the strange saddle, then waited a moment longer for her to arrange the magnificent gown and surcote for their best protection. Looking up at the woman he held as easily as if she were a child, his half-smile again flashed in momentary humor. Her magnificent apparel allowed a tempting view of lush curves that proved her no child. He settled her securely upon the grey mare's back and reluctantly drew his hands from her tiny waist.

Taine smiled her thanks for Jorion's uncritical aid, stunning him. Although, left in peace, her smiles were far more ready than his, this was the first whose full power was directed at him. Soft rose lips, top bowed, bottom full, curved with enchantment. 'Twas an enticement that set golden sparks alight in Jorion's eyes. A muscle clenched in his jaw as he deliberately turned away to mount Apollo. Ahorse, he took Taine's reins, speaking no ridicule for her lack to shame her before the two knights and the men from his guard who followed at a discreet distance.

Dunfermline had long ago been an important city where kings had built their fortresses. In one of those, plain and built of wood but with a hall of a size to accommodate the gathering of his court, Edward had settled for the winter. Daylight had completely fled the sky and the clouds that lingered hid the moon as Jorion dismounted. Turning, he lifted Taine down and led her up the well-trodden path to the rambling structure at the crest of a steep, nearly barren hill.

The double, iron-studded doors slowly opened at their approach and Taine went rigid with tension at the scene within. A blaze of myriad candles, placed on iron circles suspended by three-way chains from rafters formed of whole tree trunks, joined with the light of oil-fed lanterns resting at intervals down both sides of the crowded hall. They lent a nearly noontime brightness. Many men and not a few women arrayed in a wealth of colors, fabrics, furs, and jewels such as she had never seen filled the hall to overflowing. For one unused to such splendor it was a dizzying sight—magnificent and intimidating.

Jorion stepped into the room, forcing Taine to bring motion to alarm-frozen limbs. Only pride kept even a tremulous smile on her lips when a wave of hushed whispers began close by and crested in the farthest reaches of the room, directing nearly every eye to the new arrivals. Several small stirs in the hushed audience brought forth the dragon's companions from the fair.

"Though we held to our promise to leave you in peace," the heavy-set man fond of garish garb spoke, "there've been many wagers laid on when the newly wedded would return to our company." He leaned forward to loudly whisper, "You've disappointed me. I deemed it a certainty you'd have better and more pleasurable occupations for at least a fortnight more!"

Another stepped in front, laughing at the jest. "I, at least, am pleased to see you here—I won."

"We are here," Jorion responded, smiling wryly at their foolery, "but will not tarry long."

"What ho?" teased the winner, waggling his brows suggestively. "You come late and leave early?"

Jorion shrugged his apology. "We come only to seek the king's blessing and his leave to return to Castle Dragonsward."

"You mean to steal your lovely lady away from us?" The first man dropped his chin into the folds of several more to glare from beneath lowered brows and scold, "And again without the honor of an introduction?"

The easy bantering of the fair companions drew other curious nobles, who added their demands for an introduction.

"Lady Martaine, meet here the Earl of Swinford and Lord of Rudgel." He motioned first to the heavy one dressed in colors that clashed, and then to the winner of the wager whose probing eyes sought fodder for the gossip mill. They reminded her strongly of a childhood story of two strutting cocks, each so boldly seeking to outpace the other and win a tender hen that they failed to note when the object of their promenade flew off with a third who refused to compete. Sweet lips curved in a smile that charmed. As each lifted her hand to brush lips across its smooth back, Jorion continued with a second round of names and her hand was passed from one to the next.

Her cheeks warmed with a blush until Jorion mentioned a name she recognized, although she had no memory of the narrow face surmounted by thinning grey hair—Robert Bruce, son of the competitor and one of the great lords of Scotland, even though he'd ceded the title to his son of same name. The blood left her cheeks so swiftly it made her dizzy, but she met his speculative eyes with equal curiosity. Here was the leader of a great family who'd struggled to attain the Scottish throne once—would he again? His gaze fell to the convoluted band about her finger. Green eyes followed.

Robert Bruce realized of a sudden that his prolonged stare had drawn attention, and he forced a bland smile before commenting on the curious ring as if of only passing interest. "Such unique design have I never seen." Unique, he silently reiterated, doubtless the only one of its kind, but one he had seen before—on the thumb of a girl-child he'd secreted away from ship to a rocky shore. To see it now on the finger of a vital woman of jeweled eyes and dark-flame hair was a shock and more.

Fears allayed by his easy manner, Taine relaxed. She reassured herself that she'd imagined his unnatural interest. The tension in days past had made her too sensitive about this ring that few had seen and surely all had forgotten. The Bruces were seekers for the Scottish crown, but so were many others of lesser claim. 'Twas their enemies, the Baliols, who'd held her for long years and though the Bruces were the Baliols' enemies, they were not of a certainty hers.

To another's cajoling to leave his mystery wife in their company no less than a fortnight longer, Jorion flatly responded, "My uncle has yet to be informed of the wife I've claimed. 'Tis only right we go to apprise him of the deed." From the corner of his eye he saw the Bruce surreptitiously studying Taine's hand. A young voice interrupted his thoughts.

"Prithee pardon, milord," a page piped at his elbow. Jorion looked down into eyes wide with awe for the famous man he had been bade summon. "The king awaits you in his solar and I am sent to lead you there."

The Bruce's reaction to Taine's ring raised further questions in Jorion's mind, but he had no time to ponder them. The king waited.

Taine heard the page's words and felt her heart climb to

her throat. She swallowed hard. Her emotions seemed to jerk up and down as did the limbs of a marionette. Most anxious to leave behind the avid curiosity of those gathered about them, she willingly turned to follow the young page—and found an even more difficult trial ahead. Like the Red Sea at Moses' command, the crowd parted to bare a clear path to the king's door. Even the minstrels and jesters had ceased their arts to join the multitude of curious onlookers who stood on either side in fine imitation of the Red Sea's steep walls of threatening water. Their calculating stares seemed bent on examining each detail of her person for no kinder purpose than to determine the cost of her gown, the refinement of her manner, and if the fire of her hair were her own or born of a henna potion.

Jorion felt his lady's tension. Golden brows lowered over dark eyes shooting gilded sparks that threatened any who would offer insult. He proffered his arm in escort of Taine, wishing he could do more to ease her discomfort.

Bertwald would have recognized the determination in eyes turned silver-green. Taine laid her hand again atop Jorion's arm and surprised him with a flashing smile. She silently vowed to prove herself the equal of any. Never mind the heart pounding in her ears or the struggle demanded to hold her hands relaxed rather than tangled in the green velvet of her gown. She met the sea of watching eyes with a faint curve of soft rose lips and tilted chin.

Concerned with navigating the treacherous sea, she had no opportunity to ponder the dangers of the meeting to come. When the chamber door quietly closed at their backs, she went nearly limp with relief but pulled her defenses back to order on meeting a pair of piercing blue eyes examining her from beneath a thick mane of white hair. As Jorion knelt on one knee and lifted the other's hand in honor, Taine realized that the man she faced was King Edward. Though past middle years, he was nearly as large as the dragon and impressive. She sank into a deep curtsy.

"Your Grace." As Jorion spoke, he stood again and Taine rose, too, but her gaze did not. "I've brought Martaine, the bride I've claimed. We have come to ask your blessing on our union."

"Time and past that you do," the king returned in a soft, low voice that barely hinted at the booming power it held in times of anger.

Feeling the English monarch's slow appraisal, Taine reminded herself that this man was her greatuncle and held no higher title than did she herself, unwanted though it might be. 'Twas a fortifying thought that straightened her shoulders as she consciously calmed the thoughtless twisting of her hands. Eyes yet downcast, she couldn't know that their motion had drawn attention, but Jorion saw the king's gaze narrow on the twined-gold-and-silver band and was struck by the illogical feeling that his liege lord had seen it before.

The large, callused hands of a man who was warrior as well as king reached out to lift Taine's. "What delicate fingers are these," he smoothly commented, "to capture the elusive bachelor so well sought in my court."

Her eyes fixed no higher than the fingers he clasped, Taine blushed but wondered what he would think were she to explain that 'twas not the Golden Dragon but she who had been captured. A small smile peeked as one hand loosed hers and rose to gently lift her chin. Through effort of will, she unwaveringly looked into the broad face of the king while he studied her features. A strangely content smile of approval warmed his lips before he released her and turned to Jorion.

"Let us leave our ladies to their company for a time while we stroll in the garden. 'Tis a small one, but private." He motioned Taine toward a woman sitting quietly before the fire.

"Aye, come, Martaine. Sit with me here in warmth while they tramp through chill night air." The queen's smile held a welcome Taine had not seen in this structure. Reminding herself to guard her tongue, she went willingly to sink into the huge chair of dark carved wood. She refused to allow the knowledge that it was almost certainly the king's to intimidate her.

"Lady Du Marchand assured us we'd meet a gracious lady in you; and I, like all the others, have been anxious for that opportunity."

While the power of the queen's praise and openness mellowed Taine's mistrust and warmed her to the woman, still she recognized the danger in the other's curiosity. Though of nearly the same age, what common ground linked one raised in luxury to another raised in captivity? To her own surprise, as they chatted of gardens and rain and the difficulties of travel, she discovered her fears unfounded, for Edward's queen did not pry where she demurred.

On a moonless night only dim shapes could be seen in the garden, but two men walked unaware of the lack. Unchallenged ruler of all in his realm, Edward saw no need for covert questioning and plainly asked how Jorion had met Taine and from whence she came. Jorion responded freely, telling their story from meeting at the fair to her inability to ride to the court.

In the farthest corner of the barren autumn garden, Jorion halted and turned to boldly admit, "I have claimed for wife a woman I know little of save her pride of spirit and surpassing loveliness. Yet, my liege, I pray your leave to take her to Castle Dragonsward, where I would follow the custom of my ancestors and there wed her in the chapel."

Although he could see only the massive outline of the king, a dim shadow in the gloom, Jorion felt the weight of his long look and knew the moment of his slight nod. His attitude was odd, so long in consideration of a matter that should be no difficult choice. Odd, like his prolonged study of Taine, of her strange ring.

"You know her," Jorion flatly stated.

"I have never seen her before," came the king's quick response.

"But you know who she is," Jorion countered persistently.

Head tilted to one side, Edward paused and peered at Jorion through the night-gloom. "Mayhap" was his only answer, before he continued the slow walk.

Unable to demand answers from his king, Jorion paced beside Edward, frustrated by this seldom-endured feeling of powerlessness to order his world. The shifting of fallen leaves skittered by an intermittent breeze was the only sound to break the silence and no distraction for Jorion's questioning mind. What possible link might lay between English king and Scottish waif? He had full trust in Edward's word and if he said they had never met, then it was a solid fact—which only deepened the puzzle. Caught in a maze of the mind, Jorion failed to notice that they'd returned to the chamber door.

From atop the shallow stairs leading to the portal, Edward turned again to Jorion and placed his hand upon the younger man's broad shoulder.

"You are as a son to me, a more worthy son than my own blood heir. Marry her and fill her belly with your seed; thus you hold her safe."

Before Jorion could frame a query to the meaning of this strange pronouncement, Edward stepped into the room.

❧ Chapter 6 ❧

DAWNLIGHT, WEAKENED BY THICK autumn mists, sent but a dull glimmer through hide-covered windows. Floor rushes crackled beneath the shuffling feet of a drowsy house-serf, who carried a small spot of light across the silent great hall's dim expanse. With the taper in his hands he lit first one and then another of the candles in a tall metal stand, then moved down the wall to the next while the fires at either end of the hall leaped to renewed vigor beneath others' prodding feet. Under the growing light and sound, the men sleeping on benches or pallets began to stir. Stretching and rising to meet the new day, the rumble of their talk joined the clanging of pots and clattering of utensils as the servants began their preparation of the morning repast.

Clothed in black, as was his wont, Jorion stood unnoticed in the shadows at the top of the stairs and easily located the man he sought. Bertwald lingered on his pallet, only now sitting up to comb hands through sleep-disordered grey hair and down to massage stiff shoulders. Jorion descended and moved through the room, answering the morning greetings of his men but not pausing.

Filled with trepidation, Bertwald eyed the approaching

man whose steady dark eyes could surely pierce another's soul. When the earl halted, towering above him, Bertwald bolstered his courage and climbed quickly to his feet. The couple had not returned from the court 'til long after the house had settled for the night, thus he'd had opportunity to speak with neither. That he was so early sought out heightened his discomfort. Had the dangers of which he'd struggled to forewarn come to pass? Had his lady's secret been exposed? The earl motioned Bertwald to precede him outside and he hastened to obey, moving into a moisture-heavy mist that enveloped all who stepped within.

The heavy door snapped shut behind them and Jorion turned to his claimed-wife's protector. There were things to be done, arrangements to be made before they could depart for Radwyn lands, but he was uneasy at leaving the skittish damsel alone for a day, nay, for even a moment. His guard had earlier been commanded to prevent her and her companion from taking leave of his abode without full escort. Yet no warrior worth the name, and he assuredly was that, would underestimate his opponent. This wily man before him might well be capable of devising means to elude watchful eyes. Best, then, to have his cooperation. Already well acquainted with Bertwald's strength of honor in holding to an oath, he deemed his vow the most invincible guard he could place on Taine.

Fully expecting to hear some dread consequence of the past night's visit, Bertwald waited impatiently for the other to speak.

"Matters of import will keep me away this day. And, taking your warnings of danger to heart, I've come seeking aid in holding Taine safe."

These words, when they came, seemed to portend some nebulous threat. Bertwald nearly held his breath waiting for the earl to continue.

"I ask your oath to keep Taine secure within these walls." The black cloak swirled out as he motioned toward the house.

This request had little to do with Bertwald's expectations. He stared blankly at the speaker. Mind still on the more important subject of the past evening's dangers, met or evaded, he nodded his oath with little thought to the action and immediately asked, "But, milord, what of your court visit?" He had no business questioning the earl, but his anxiety was such that he would dare that and more.

Jorion knew and sympathized with Bertwald's concern for his lady and, although unwilling to describe the events of yestereve, answered without affront. "We went and returned in safety."

The response was an evasion but Bertwald was so relieved to learn none of the momentous disasters he'd feared had transpired that he failed to notice the lack. He dipped his rumpled grey head in thanks and earned a slight smile from the tall man before he turned away.

Satisfied that the strength of his men and, more importantly, Bertwald's oath would hold Taine safe, Jorion strode toward the stable, a roof and one wall, leaning against the house's far side and barely visible through drifting fog. Bertwald's questions brought clearly back to mind the king's enigmatic words of the night past. They had only further pricked his curiosity for the mysterious woman's past and his determination to seek answer to the multitude of questions it raised. He had dispatched men to trace her attackers shortly after bringing his claimed wife back from her attempted flight, but it would doubtless be some time before he had word from them. He was impatient and, once his travel arrangements were complete, planned to visit again the inn where he'd found Taine the evening of the fair. He had one or two queries for those within.

Bertwald watched as the tall figure moved through the grey fog and disappeared into the gloom of the stable before he turned to reenter the now bustling house. Attention immediately drawn to the high table, he saw thick lashes fall over deep green eyes in relief. His lovely lady had clearly spent some time anxiously awaiting him. Only now did he fully realize what to the dragon he had sworn. He gave her a weak smile and slid into a seat near the foot of a line of trestle tables below her. Throughout the meal that, for such a simple repast, seemed to drag on unnecessarily, he shifted guiltily beneath the weight of her hopeful, trusting gaze.

Taine nervously nibbled on the slice she'd cut from an apple still fresh and juicy from the tree, little appreciating its tangy flavor. For long hours the night past, despite their late return from the court, the soft down mattress had been unable to call her to sleep. The English queen, king, too, had been amazingly kind. But her presentation to them and, indeed, the whole court had driven hard to her the dragon's serious intent. Every day that he held her in his lair, escape grew more difficult. And the respect with which even the supercilious lords of the court had treated the dragon, once the four of them rejoined the crowd in the court's main hall, had increased her trepidation of him. With her own eyes she'd seen mighty men bend to the dragon's pride and power. A fleeing wife would lay him open to their ridicule, an unthinkable blow.

The core was all that remained of her apple, yet still men lingered at the lower tables. She began to toy with the small knife she'd used to cut slices of the crisp fruit, watching light gleam on its sharp edge. In the deepest hours of night, despair had grown that she'd never win her freedom and that punishment for an attempt would be harsh. He'd already claimed her wife, and a husband could do with his wife what he chose with none to say him nay. Only the comfort of Bertwald's remembered promise to see her free allowed sleep's call to conquer worriment.

Once green eyes closed, exhaustion had brought deep slumber, and she'd not awakened 'til the household's bustle rose to its daytime roar. She'd dressed as hastily as her stylish new clothes allowed, wishing she still possessed the disreputable brown homespun with dolman sleeves which grew tight only at the wrist. The multitude of buttons closing this pale grey kirtle's tight sleeves and the lacing fastening the back had forced her to wait for aid while impatience grew.

When finally she'd come down, neither Bertwald nor the dragon had been in sight. Her tension had grown. Finally, when all were at table, Bertwald had arrived and slipped onto a bench far away. Uncomfortable with her position as lone occupant of the high table, her dark green eyes returned again to the only person she could claim as friend. Bertwald must help her win free of the dragon—he'd promised.

Taine surreptitiously studied the men at tables below. They too fidgeted with mugs or knives, apparently finished with meal and anxious to be done. She wished they would stand and be about the duties that surely must await them. *Oh saints' tears!* A rosy glow burned on her cheeks as she realized the reason for their lingering. 'Twas one thing to learn a custom in theory and another to put it in practice. Even her limited education in noble life styles had taught that until the lord or, in his absence, his lady left the high table, those at lower must remain. Cheeks several shades brighter, she rose with such haste that her chair rocked violently, nearly falling back and down from the dais. She gripped the fine linen of her surcote so fiercely it would be a mass of wrinkles when freed. Within moments lower tables were deserted as at last the men were freed to take up their tasks. Still, they had seen the lovely lady flushed with embarrassment for her error, and their hearts warmed to her.

Taine tilted her chin to bolster her courage and set out through the confusion of the hall. Wending her way through the crowd, she kept her eyes on her goal, never allowing them to drift to the side for fear of finding ridicule on the faces of others. Thus, she failed to see their sympathy and support. Beside Bertwald at last, she rushed to speak, "Remember your promise of yestermorn." The words were soft and intended for no other. He'd said he would see her free of the dragon, should he fail to turn the man's intent. Though there had been no opportunity that day, surely in her captor's absence now he would.

Bristling brows lowered over faded blue eyes as Bertwald sent a quick glance about to be sure no other heard. "I dinna promise, lassie. Nay, I dinna do that." Green eyes widened at the denial and he hastened to add, "Only did I say I would hie you away if he wouldna heed my warnings. But I'd no opportunity and couldna do it." His face closed into a stubborn mask. He knew she would not allow the matter to rest so easily, yet he had given his word to see she remained when she had rather be gone. Moreover, he privately admitted to a further constraint than his oath to the earl. In truth, he believed her best interest would be served by the fate she would deny. Stalling for time, he led her to the same wooden settle they'd shared beside the door the day past.

Taine moved quickly to the wooden seat but, once resting upon the hard bench, she leaned away from its high back and turned immediately to Bertwald with her plea. "The dragon is away, now is the time to flee this place." The discomfiture of the scene at table only added to her determination for swift escape from the dragon and all his entourage.

In her rush to the hall, Taine had hastily and with little success tucked thick tresses into one of the net crespines Halyse had loaned. Bertwald reached out to tuck shining ringlets back into the delicate confines. The thick curls in the front refused to obey, bouncing forward once more to cheeks and forehead. They seemed to exemplify the fire of her spirit, undimmed despite dark trials. He wanted to see her free of the prison of her past but also of the prison of constant flight that threatened her future. To be forever pursued, forever in transit, was a nasty prospect she neither saw nor comprehended.

"The men you've eluded thus far canna return without you, else they pay a high price. They willna easily give up. And belike if they find you, they'll take care tae see I canna protect you again." He slowly shook his head, praying with little hope that the prospect would be enough to hold her back. But, even as he spoke, he knew she would choose to flee, if only to prove herself undaunted by her terror of the villains and their intent.

Her desperation was plain in tremulous lips and pleading green eyes. "They're no more a danger than he," she argued. "What they'd take by force, he would take by law, but what difference to me?" Even to herself she refused to admit her response to him was the difference.

"Aye, lassie, but doona you see? 'Tis a fine thing for us." Bertwald was pleased with this sudden inspiration and his smile was wide. "What better way for escape could there be than tae be escorted tae the heart of another country by one of its nobles?"

Delicate brows lowered over deep green eyes, but Taine could find no adequate argument against his sensible strategy. Bertwald would surely never understand her fear of the dragon's daily tightening hold.

* * *

A dense cloud cover hid the moon behind its impenetrable shield and the thick haze made travel difficult, hindering Jorion's return. The occupants of his house had long since settled for their night's rest when he noiselessly slipped from cool night air into the fire-warmed hall. Carefully, silently he leaned the Saracen blades and their scabbards against the wall just within the door. Sander, his squire, would see the blades honed and polished early on the morrow. Muffled in his black cloak, hood shielding golden hair from the seeking light of coals still glowing on both hearths, and nearly invisible, he moved up through the gloom of the stairs.

His day's search for some clue to Taine's identity had been fruitless. The people at the inn denied all knowledge of the maid, a fact not difficult to believe. They were the sort to make a point of knowing as little as possible of another. Nonetheless, 'twas disheartening. Between Bertwald's nebulous fears and Taine's persistent pursuers, he was well convinced of the truth in her danger. But, without knowledge of the threat, he was hard-pressed to protect her. As he quietly climbed the steps, hoping not to disturb the people already at rest, he comforted himself that, no matter what danger threatened, Taine was safe in his lodgings.

He found the error in his self-satisfaction the moment he gained the landing above. Though more felt than seen in the dark, he was immediately aware of others stealthily pushing open the door to Taine's chamber. Unarmed, save for the gold-hilted dagger at his waist, Jorion leaped forward. A thin blade briefly flashed through the dark and the next instant was buried in the man filling the open chamber doorway. His victim sagged into his grasp even as Jorion loudly called his men to arms.

The second man, trapped in Taine's chamber by the blocked doorway, whirled with broadsword at the ready. Hearth glow revealed a face fierce with desperation and a beard whose darkness was split by a violent streak of white, like lightning through a night sky. Jorion was impeded by the dead-weight of the man in his arms and the loss of the dagger still driven to the hilt and difficult to withdraw. The trespasser lunged, slashing randomly. Jorion jerked to one side, deflecting the blow's full force from heart to shoulder.

His foe pushed past Jorion's awkward position and leaped down the steps three at a time. Shoving aside sleepy, ill-prepared defenders, he flew out the great hall's door and disappeared into the night's dense fog.

Letting his victim slide like a limp rag to the floor, Jorion barked out orders for pursuit of the escaping man. A portion of his rudely awakened garrison raced immediately after him. The stamping feet and scuffling noises of others as they jerked on boots and snatched up weapons proved their haste to join the quest. Disheveled servants lit lanterns only recently doused and curiously watched the commotion.

A fighting man used to the minor wounds of battle, Jorion gave no thought to his wound as he absently pressed a hand to his shoulder. Blood oozed between his fingers as he turned to meet wide forest-green eyes. Taine huddled stiffly in the far corner of her bed, clutching the coverlet to her throat. Firelight burned on thick auburn curls cloaking fragile shoulders, their dark fire a strong contrast to pale cream skin.

Despite the desperate weariness left by two nearly sleepless nights, Taine's worriment over Bertwald's lack of support had kept her wakeful long after night's quiet had fallen on the dragon's lair. Though Bertwald's argument made sense, an irrational compulsion to escape consumed her. She had nearly decided to rise and flee again while the dragon was away, when a soft scraping at the door stilled breath in her throat.

The door had opened to the stealthy entry of a dark figure. Her mouth opened to scream for the aid of which she'd fooled herself she would have no need. The sound was stillborn by the sight of the dragon's larger shadow looming behind a second assailant still framed in the doorway. Relief had flooded through her, leaving her limp as tension drained suddenly from her muscles. As if from a distance she watched the scuffle. Though completed in a brief span of time, motion seemed to drag as flamelight glittered in a macabre dance down a long sharp broadsword that stilled only as it pierced the dragon's shoulder. She felt the blow as strongly as if it sundered her own flesh, and her hand flew to the same position on her own shoulder. 'Twas an unthinkable deed. Surely the dragon was invincible; the tales of him claimed it true. When Jorion's attention shifted to her, their eyes locked and held until gold sparks burned in the dark depths of his.

"Dinna I warn ye not to take her to court." A gruff voice broke the visual bond between Taine and Jorion. "Now they know the lass lives."

Jorion looked behind to find Bertwald glaring at him accusingly. With a cold half-smile he responded, "I asked you to tell me the danger, thus to protect her from its threat. 'Twas you who refused and left me unprepared for this attack."

Turning away, with the toe of one boot, Jorion rolled the body at his feet to lay face up. The man was a stranger to him, not one of the men who had pursued Taine at the fair and attacked her that night. The first two had been craven fools running from the first fight; these were professional soldiers. But whose?

"Is he known to you?" Jorion quietly questioned Bertwald, dark eyes compelling an honest answer.

Sleep-disordered grey hair stood in wild spikes on Bertwald's head and waved with the slow shake of his head as he denied all knowledge of the victim. It was not the knowledge of who they were that was so frightening, but rather the certainty of who they were not. They were not the known and expected foes, an indication that more had learned the secret and joined the chase.

"Search him," Jorion motioned toward the prone figure. Although certain the assailant and his master were too clever for so simple an error, Jorion would not make the mistake of failing to follow every possible source of information.

Bertwald bent to rifle through the dead man's clothing but found no clue to either his identity or purpose. Never one for easy trust of another's thoroughness, Jorion knelt at his victim's side and repeated the exercise to no better reward.

While the two men quietly murmured and searched for the assailant's identity, Taine's gaze was steady on one. He still wore his distinctive cloak but in the scuffle the hood had fallen back and firelight gleamed on golden hair, a stark contrast to his black-clad figure. Just looking at him made breath catch in her throat and tightened the muscles of her chest. Fear, she told herself. Disdain for him and all his kind, she further reiterated, refusing to admit how fascinating he was.

As Jorion stood again and grimaced fleetingly at the sting in his shoulder, Taine saw the brief expression before it was as quickly smoothed away. She rose, pulling the bedcover close and winding it tightly around and beneath her arms. Then, pulling the thick swathe of her hair free, she silently padded to his side.

"Take him to the stable," Jorion waved at the body and spoke as Taine halted just behind. Two strong house-serfs quickly answered Jorion's summons. "In the morning I'll . . ."

A soft touch interrupted Jorion mid-sentence. Expecting a servant and irritated by the intrusion, dark-gold brows scowled as he glanced down. His brows flew up and dark eyes widened on finding a sylphlike figure at his side. Flickering light from the hearth seemed to set fires in the abundant curls of hair so thick it appeared too heavy for one so slender, so ethereal—a fire-sprite born of flame. Surely the man who touched it would burn. Aye, Jorion could nearly feel her flames—flames of desire. If he was the dragon whose fire was feared by many, then she, of all women, could lie unscathed within.

Standing so close, Taine felt as if she'd stepped into his power. The tales must be true. She could nearly see the golden net spinning about him, drawing and holding the unwary who stepped too near. She could neither look away nor step free of his enthrallment.

Seeing the earl's sudden preoccupation, Bertwald grinned; but catching sight of the two serfs' wide-eyed interest in his lady, his amusement disappeared. They too stared closely at inadequately covered beauty. Although it was common practice for all to sleep nude in heavily curtained beds, it was unthinkable for the lady to rise and step forward less than fully clothed. The weighty coverlet, wrapped and tucked under Taine's arms, afforded no adequate covering. Unnoticed by the couple at the door, he urged the two serfs to turn their attention to the task at hand.

Forcing her gaze away, Taine's attention was caught by Jorion's strong hand still rubbing a wounded shoulder. Shame burned. She'd thoughtlessly wasted time gaping at him like a moonling while he stood in discomfort. "Come," she invited, lightly squeezing his arm, "let me tend your wound."

Jorion's eyes went to the hand gentle on him. This was the first touch she'd willingly given him, and it earned the small smile that, though rarely seen, had melted the heart of many a sophisticated woman.

The smile without cynicism mesmerized Taine until she noted the subject of his gaze was her hand and where it lay. Self-conscious, she let it drop like a stone-weighted parchment. Hampered by the thick folds of a coverlet designed for beauty and for holding the cold at bay, she turned to lead the way into her chamber. A few short steps demonstrated the inadequacies of her attire. It was no easy thing to walk with unwieldy material tightly wrapped and dragging behind. Moreover, it left her shoulders bare and its weight threatened to reveal more, slipping dangerously low. She was forced to fasten the fabric by holding her arms close to her sides, one hand tugging the front edge higher, the other jerking desperately at trailing folds.

Jorion followed willingly, closing the door behind him. He complied with Taine's command and sat where she indicated, on the side of the bed closest to the fire. Hiding a renewed smile behind a bland expression, he looked up at the maid struggling to pull her heavy wrap high enough to shield lush curves unexpected in one elsewhere so slender.

Self-conscious, Taine stared at the area on Jorion's broad shoulder where the wound must be. It was difficult to see. His hand no longer covered the broadsword's damage and no blood was visible against black velvet. Presented with this wounded man sitting where she directed and waiting expectantly, it came to Taine that her offer had been a foolish thing. She had no knowledge of healing arts, no notion of even the smallest deed to mend the flesh or ease the pain. Seeing a sparkle in the dragon's eyes, Taine suspected he found her predicament entertaining. Her fine brows knit with determination. She had offered and she would do the deed.

Watching the hesitant maid, Jorion's amusement grew. Yet she was so resolute—and lovely—he struggled hard to hide it for fear of raising her temper and ruining this excellent opportunity to have her near and willingly touching him.

"Doubtless, milady," he addressed her formally, his one-sided smile returning as he rose to his feet, "you'll need a clear field for your ministrations."

Standing, he was perilously close. The heavy coverlet tail, bunched behind Taine's feet, made stepping back nearly impossible. Her gaze slid slowly up and up the long length of him and stilled on the strong hands working on the clasp at his throat. Cloak unfastened, Jorion tossed it aside to the foot of the bed. Green eyes widened. Before she knew what he was about, he loosened his gold-buckled belt and stripped off the velvet tunic.

At the sudden close view of a man's bare chest, Taine gulped. Dark gold hair spread across a wide expanse of bronzed skin. Rose lips fell open. Drawn uncontrollably, her eyes followed the V's arrowing path downward until it reached a cloth impediment—and clenched shut.

Standing on the small trunk beside the bed, an ewer held what remained of the steaming water provided for Taine's evening ablutions. Jorion lifted the vessel to pour water grown tepid into a basin. He rinsed his hands, rubbing away dried blood, and wiped them on the bottom edge of his discarded tunic. Curious for the sound, Taine looked up as he turned toward pegs driven into the wall on either side of the bed. From them hung some of the new clothing Lady Du Marchand had delivered with Taine's stunning court gown the previous day.

The dragon had stepped far enough away that Taine felt safe in watching him. Another foolish deed. She discovered herself unable to pull her gaze from the play of muscles across the broad back as he rummaged through her garments. Firelight flickered over gilded skin and hair, catching her in the snare of his attraction. She could nearly believe him truly the Golden Dragon of unspeakable beauty.

At length Jorion found a camise of fine linen. First dampening it with fresh water from the ewer, he returned and held it out to Taine. She stared at it uncomprehendingly, as if it were some strange creature from the sea. Jorion shook his head slightly at the blank look and lifted one of her hands free of the coverlet to pull her behind him.

Desperately clutching the weighty wrap to her breast with the other hand, she stumbled after the tall man, apprehension for his intent growing as they approached the bed. He merely sat down to face her. Into the hand he'd held he deposited the wet camise. She stared dumbly at the cool cloth wadded in her palm.

"I assume you mean to cleanse my wound and see my night's rest eased." His voice held no mockery, but his eyes were alight with gentle laughter.

Feeling a fool for her witless response, Taine attacked the broad shoulder with unnecessary force. Jorion flinched initially but made no protesting sound, and embarrassment for her thoughtless action tinted soft cheeks a delicate rose. A few fresh droplets of blood appeared on the edge of the gash already closed. Bending near, with care she wiped them away and softly rubbed the cloth across his wide shoulder to remove brown stains. Fascinated by the firm texture of his bronze skin, so unlike her own creamy flesh, she continued her ministrations long after the task was complete. Absorbed in her actions, mindlessly wishing she could touch without the cloth barrier between her flesh and his, she failed to realize her covering had slipped perilously low in her slackened hold and revealed more of alluring curves than her modesty would knowingly allow.

Caught in the tantalizing view, Jorion little noted her lengthy attentions. Generous breasts rose from the constraints of the tightly wrapped coverlet, so near to freedom that the smallest tug would see them liberated. Pulse pounding, a nearly ungovernable compulsion grew to loose the barrier to his goal and see the bounty of pale ivory flesh draped only in the dark fire of luxurious curls. But doubtless such action would raise her anger—and her defenses. To forestall the ill-conceived compulsion, he forced his head up and eyes away from her unknowing enticement. The motion drew her gaze to his.

Lured by dark eyes, Taine tumbled into depths where golden fires burned. The gilded net of the dragon's attraction wrapped around her, pulled her toward him. In a gaze gone soft with desire's dense mists, Jorion read her fascination, and, unbidden, his arm lifted to draw her near. Drawn by the power of her own longing to an unknown but inevitable end, Taine barely felt the hand sliding beneath her thick hair to cup the back of her neck and bring her face to his. His mouth moved gently, enticingly across her smooth cheeks to nibble at the corners of beguiling lips and sear them with the tender heat of joining. He wanted to taste her in full measure, swallow her in his embrace. But, from a remote corner of his mind, memory warned that too fervent an embrace would drive her from him.

The melding of their mouths seemed to drain strength from Taine's limbs. She trembled but gave no protest when powerful arms gathered her slowly nearer, easing her down across the hard muscles of his thighs. All logical thought ceased, lost in the kindling sparks of the hungry flames only he could ignite. She failed to notice that the action had tugged her covering almost to the waist.

Gently drawing Taine close, Jorion felt the unexpected sweet-silk brush of full curves against his bare chest and a low groan rumbled from him. Only by effort of his famous control did he keep from crushing her against him. Instead, he gradually deepened the kiss until, under its slow torment, Taine let the wet cloth slip unnoticed from her grasp.

The devastating kiss and shocking feel of his powerful torso against her breasts drove the last vestige of restraint from Taine. Falling to an earlier temptation, she ran her fingers over broad shoulders, learning their strength by touch, and let them move to tangle in the cool weight of thick gold hair.

Jorion's large hands burrowed beneath an auburn cloud to nearly span her tiny waist and slide slowly up a satin back. Taine arched instinctively beneath the caress, shudders of wild excitement shaking her as she tightened her arms about his neck. She burrowed her face in his throat and crushed herself against him, wanting to be closer and closer still.

The feel of her soft flesh melded with the hard muscle of

his body, and awareness of her sweet trembling hunger were unexpected gifts. Jorion swallowed the anguish engendered by a control difficult to hold. Despite his urgent need to immediately merge their forms in passion, he exerted no pressure but held her for long aching moments feeling her pulse pound in rhythm with his own.

Filled with nameless wanting and unable to stay motionless beneath its demand, Taine leaned back and looked up at him. The slight distance between them allowed Jorion to slowly move his chest back and forth, dragging wiry curls across sensitive tips while staring into misty green.

Taine couldn't have looked away from the glowing depths of black eyes to save her soul from perdition. Jolts of lightning flashed from his vibrant body to hers. Jorion lowered his face and Taine's lashes fell. Expecting relief from the thrilling visual bond, she found instead that with the distraction removed sensations intensified. A soft whimper slipped from her tight throat and a small satisfied smile curled the lips which teasingly moved from her eyelids to cheeks to chin.

Slipping ever deeper into the dark void of desire, Taine surrendered to, nay, sought the dragon's fire. Luxurious curls shimmered as she tilted her head to lay tentative lips, untutored to seduction, against his. Her lack of skill was no impediment. Jorion responded immediately, nudging her lips, coaxing them open for the deep kiss he craved. It grew and burned until she felt herself melting against his hardness.

Breaking off the kiss to draw a deep, ragged breath, for long aching moments Jorion leaned back to survey the bounty he had claimed his. In times of elemental emotion he reverted to the language of his youth and now murmured his admiration in soft words unrecognizable to her.

The strange words were a dash of cold water on flames. Desire yet sizzled but receded enough for reason to weave through lingering smoke and bring Taine to a sudden awareness of her own nearly ungovernable response. It frightened her badly, this loss of self-command; more so to a man who, for his ability to steal her will, she now had even greater reason to fear. Horrified by her own actions, she went rigid in his arms.

So close and once joined in mutual passion, Jorion sensed Taine's rising panic. Again, she would reject him and this time he could not lie to himself that a harsh embrace was the reason. Fear darkened soft, sea-mist eyes as with great gentleness he grimly set her aside and rose to leave with no further word spoken.

Jorion crossed the corridor to slip into his own chamber and bed, but for hours lay sleepless. A familiar emotional ache far worse than his minor wound returned and grew to hitherto unknown anguish. Once again his mixed heritage had repelled another. But where he had turned the hard shield of cynicism to previous rejections, this one drove a barbed lance deep into his soul. He had claimed her as wife but feared she would never be able to bear sharing his bed, and he'd find no pleasure in forcing an unwilling woman.

Across the hall, Taine, too, was awake and confused. On three occasions Jorion had saved her from a threatening danger. But was he not a part of that very danger? By force of her own longing had he not stolen her will? Clouds had fled and dawn-light shed its softening glow on steep, nearly barren hills before either found rest.

❧ Chapter 7 ❧

In Taine's exhaustion, the morning clatter of a household making ready for departure failed to disturb her long-delayed rest. Even did she lay so deep beneath the restoring layers of sleep's oblivion that she was not roused by the hushed sounds of the woman moving stealthily about her chamber, carefully folding new clothes into huge open chests. With a sudden crash the heavy lid of one accidentally fell shut. Taine jerked upright, heart pounding in fear of yet another attack. Anxiety deepened the green eyes searching wildly for the perpetrator.

She found an equally startled Halyse clutching the indigo velvet of a soft wool kirtle to her bosom and glaring at the offending trunk that had slammed closed just as she bent to lay the kirtle inside. Unmindful of a possible audience, Halyse forcefully kicked the inanimate object. Regrettably, she'd paused to consider neither the flimsiness of her leather slipper nor the firmness of her victim. The pain was all hers. She dropped the kirtle to hop wildly, clutching her toe in an agony held silent for fear of disturbing the lady she'd not stopped to consider might have awakened at the sound.

Her mood already lightened at finding so innocuous an intruder, the orange-haired woman's antics tickled a ripple of laughter from Taine. Halyse dropped her injured foot, swung toward the sound, and glared at the woman still abed.

"I pray pardon," Taine apologized quickly. "It must pain you." Sorry to offend, she sought to explain her mirth. "I rose in fear of another assault and found you launching a vicious attack on a defenseless chest. My relief at not being its goal earned the laughter." Her demeanor was repentant, but silver gleams danced in her eyes as she grimaced her apology and sheepishly added, "Your one-footed dance was an odd sight and made holding my amusement too difficult a task."

Halyse's natural sense of justice defeated her indignation. She must have appeared the fool. Wide mouth curving into its usual broad grin, she shrugged. "I failed to heed Will's warning. He's told me oft enough to never underestimate the strength of a foe."

Taine returned the smile, relieved. She liked the friendly woman and had not wished to affront her. Other than a few dour castle-serfs and the stern Morag, Halyse was the first female she'd shared more than passing words with in many years.

First bending to retrieve the heap of indigo cloth, Halyse once more lifted the trunk's lid to place the kirtle within. Though unwilling for the conversation to end, Taine quietly watched as Halyse gathered other garments from wall pegs to neatly fold and add them to those already resting in chests. She refused to acknowledge what Halyse's methodical tasks portended.

"I chose for you garments suited to our travels," Halyse told Taine, "and left them on the peg there." She waved toward the far side of the bed.

Self-conscious of her nudity, Taine rose to quickly lift the thick mulberry kirtle free and pull it over her head. She silently applauded Halyse's choice. Although of rich cloth and fine style, this kirtle was meant for practical daily wear and had simple dolman sleeves. Thus, endless time need not be wasted fastening a multitude of buttons from elbow to wrist. Her satisfied smile faded. No sooner had she congratulated herself on the easy donning of sleeves than she realized the limitations of a design that fastened in the back. She was used to old fashioned gowns which gathered and tied at the throat. The back lacing of this garment was difficult to reach and still more difficult to maneuver. Hands bent behind in strange angles, she tackled the task but accomplished no more than aching arms and tangled laces.

Unaware of the lady's discomfort, Halyse folded the last garment and carefully closed the chest. Looking over her shoulder, she discovered Taine's stubborn struggle. Stepping near, she brushed Taine's hands away and straightened snarled laces before beginning to pull them closed.

When Taine winced at an overzealous tug, Halyse apologized, "My turn now to pray pardon. 'Tis the blame of my haste to be on the road to Castle Dragonsward. I long to hold my baby again and would force others to my will."

Taine's startled glance drew a wry smile from Halyse.

"Bryce is five winters and no longer a baby nor even a toddling. A fact he felt compelled to prove by exhibiting a new skill only a day before we were to begin our journey here. He'd learned to climb a tree—but not how to get safely to earth again."

Taine laughed softly. She had no trouble picturing a son of the impulsive Halyse risking such a foolhardy trick.

"Aye, he tumbled down and broke his leg." Though still adjusting Taine's back fastenings, Halyse shook her head with mock disgust, wiry hair catching and vividly reflecting the light from an unshuttered window. She continued, smile settling into wistful melancholy. "I was assured it would heal clean, but that the journey here would be too uncomfortable for him. I had promised to come administer the earl's home and felt the need to uphold my husband's honor by keeping to my oath. And so I did, even though the earl would have excused me. It tears my heart daily to be apart from that small part of me, thus I am most grateful to you for seeing to our quick return."

This sounded ominous and in growing dread Taine looked questioningly behind.

Halyse laughed. "'Tis your nuptials that give reason for our departure. Elsewise we'd spend all winter long in this godforsaken land. Even then, only I would return while the men remained to continue their warring through another season." With a final tug on the laces, she stepped away, smiling happily. "Now, pray God, 'twill be not more than a few days 'til again I hold my son."

Taine's hands had tightened on mulberry wool and at the final words threatened to rend it asunder. Despite the open trunks and folded clothes, even after Halyse started her talk of a return, she'd comforted herself that they were only in aid of the eventual fulfillment of the dragon's intent. The compression of sweet lips stole their sweetness. Although she'd been in his company the night past, he'd not warned her of an imminent departure!

In the hall below, a loud scraping heralded an arrival. Jorion turned toward the opening of the heavy door at the entrance. A square of daylight fell through the open portal, gleaming on bright hair and revealing Jorion's expression of hopeful anticipation. Golden brows lowered in a frown when a large figure blocked much of the light. Will, carrying a massive chest as if it were no weight at all, entered first. Jorion's broad shoulders tensed while the attention of he and all in the suddenly quiet hall centered on the empty doorway. At last a hunched figure slowly moved into its frame. Bent with age and leaning heavily on a gnarled, use-smoothed staff, an elderly man shuffled forward. Thick white brows jutted over eyes of failing vision, squinting in anxious search, and Jorion strode forward to place his hands gently on stooped shoulders, as he bent close to meet the other's gaze. Faded, nearly colorless eyes studied the younger man's bronzed face in silence. Then, slowly nodding, a benign smile laid a wreath of wrinkles about the visitor's mouth.

"Aye, ye've changed hardly at all." For a man of his years, his voice was surprisingly strong.

Jorion's rare true smile appeared. "Would that were so, Father." The term of address surprised their observers until they noted the visitor's garb—a monk's robe.

Taine had stepped to the top of the stairs in time to see the welcoming. Though filled with many, the hall was still, watching in silence. She lingered, too, unmoving as the old man responded, words carrying easily over unstirred air.

"A golden child, ye'll never be elsewise to me." Affection warmed the response.

Jorion's lips slid into their more common one-sided mockery. "No child now, I am the Golden Dragon."

"Ah, well," the priest nodded in acknowledgment of the allusion. "'Struth, you're beautiful enough to captivate a lady, but I hear 'tis your fierce skill at foreign arms that terrifies your foes." A teasing glint brightened faded eyes.

Embarrassed as few could make him, Jorion shrugged away the compliment, answering, "The years have surely not changed your teasing tongue."

"My speech and, of more import, my mind I yet have and so cannot bemoan slow feet nor weak eyes. I expect the good Lord only wanted to slow me so I could better learn appreciation of his gift of long life."

From his superior height, Jorion looked down to the one below, bent but undefeated by age. His tender expression shocked observers, Taine not least of all. As the two men spoke, she had slipped silently down and stood no more than three paces away. Who was this man who brought such warmth to the impassive dragon?

Jorion searched the older man's face and form, bitterly noting each wrinkle, each sign of age or pain. He remembered clearly the strong, loving man who, in a land of hot wind and sand, had devoted ten years to him. At the demand of Jorion's grandfather, this man had accompanied a twelve-year-old boy to England, only to be sent brusquely on his way with small reward for all he had given.

"Why would you not come to me before?" Jorion questioned. Once he'd attained his majority, he'd sought out his mentor and invited him to live in the comfort of his castle but had been refused.

"The Almighty still had work for me then." Thick, snow-white hair brushed narrow shoulders as he slowly shook his head. "But I have been his 'good and faithful servant,' have earned my reward, and can now rest where I will."

The talk of rest brought Jorion to an awareness of his position, still standing in the doorway barring the path of one ailing and nearly blind. The aging cleric would soon be incapable of caring for himself, and Jorion was determined to return the care he had been given as a child, a plan best begun now. Shaking his head slightly with irritation for his thoughtless delay, Jorion stepped to the weary man's side and reached out to help him toward a bench before the fire. As he straightened, he caught sight of Taine and smiled. Hesitantly standing near, slender fingers buried in a dark red kirtle and surcote that brought out the deep fire in curls escaping a respectable crespine to cling lovingly to cheek and nape. She looked the ethereal fire-sprite, skittish and ready to fade into the mists at any threatening deed.

The sweetness of Jorion's smile stunned Taine, even though she realized it was simply a reflection of his fondness for the aging cleric he had so solicitously aided. From where he stood beside his seated guest, Jorion motioned her forward into the fire's sphere of warmth. Moving to answer the bidding, Taine saw a flash of apprehension quickly cross a deeply bronzed face. She blinked and it was gone, yet she was in no doubt that the dragon feared her actions before his friend and wondered at it. What more could she do to pain him? He'd gone unbruised when she cursed him with foul names and even when she'd fled his protection.

"You are the maid that would wed my golden boy, hmm?" White hair fell forward as the elderly priest leaned closer, squinting at the slender blur in effort to study her more closely.

From the corner of her eye, Taine saw the "golden boy" stiffen and knew the source of his fear. She opened her lips to deny the claim and fulfill his dread but was defeated by the trust in the speaker's kindly smile of welcome. More, she felt the pain and shame that would come to the dragon from such denial before a friend and would not be its source.

"By Scottish law, Father, we are that already." Even as she spoke the words, she silently consoled herself that doubtless the dragon would still have held her to her marriage claim. Moreover, a wife belonged to her husband body and soul, his to discipline as he chose. She stilled the silent and mocking voice reminding her he'd not used his exceptional strength to punish her earlier rebellion.

Relief flooded through Jorion and tense muscles relaxed. She had sidestepped her one avenue of escape. Had she denied the marriage before his mentor, he would have felt honor bound to release her. His warm smile returned as he moved to Taine's side.

With the earl's powerful form close and towering above, Taine froze. Simultaneously overwhelmed and drawn to this source of alarm, the only statement clear in the muddle of her thoughts was that he must surely be the dragon of legend—using irresistible lures to capture and hold his prey. His strong hand engulfed her slender fingers as he turned with her to face the priest.

"'Struth, Father Aleric," Jorion addressed him formally, "this is Lady Martaine, to whom I would have you wed me in the chapel of Castle Dragonsward."

The white head nodded in benign satisfaction.

Releasing Taine, Jorion motioned her to sit at the new arrival's side. Her relief at being freed of his near embrace was so clear that even the failing eyes of the one man who had a clear view of her did not miss it.

As Taine gratefully slid onto the bench at the father's side, Jorion turned to their quietly watching audience.

"Cease your gaping and give haste to completing your tasks." Filled with more anticipation than he'd felt since the day he'd set out for England as a boy so many years ago and hoping the results would be to better end, Jorion's smile was wide as he added, "I wish to be under way before the day reaches middle age." All within were equally anxious to set forth and the hall itself seemed to spring into motion.

As a parade of men burdened with chests descended from the chambers above and marched out through the open door, Will scowled down at the heavy one still at his feet. He looked up at the watching earl. "You would have me hoist it out again?"

Jorion nodded, behind a solemn face suppressing his amusement for the taciturn man's disgust.

"Why then did I bring it in firstly?" The question was forced through tightly compressed lips.

"I confess I wondered for your reasoning," Jorion responded, wry smile breaking through.

"Aye, Will, chests will be the downfall of we both this day." Will turned to find his wife watching from the foot of the stairs. Halyse explained, "We came to battle, the chest above-stairs and I." Will's heavy black brows lowered, but Halyse shrugged. "The chest won."

Shaking his head at her deranged words, Will bent to shoulder the offensive burden, muttering darkly. "Gone witless, I shouldn't wonder, shackled to a daft woman and sworn to a lord who finds cheer at my misfortune." As he rose, the soft warmth in the gaze he gave Halyse belied his imprecations. Far from offended, Jorion laughed at his knight's complaint.

Taine was surprised. She'd thought the match between the outgoing Halyse and stern Will an odd one, but saw now the compliment of one to the other. The dragon's easy acceptance of his knight's bantering was her first indication of how the man she'd thought so fearsome had won and kept his men's loyalty.

"He's very special." Though limited vision could not clearly see the object of his words, his eyes easily followed the distinctive golden head. "It was clear the first time I saw him, and not alone because his bright coloring stood out so clearly among his dark brethren, nor even that he quickly grew to stand tall above them."

"You knew him in the deserts?" Taine asked, surprised, turning to the man beside her. The white head nodded, eyes still on the subject of their talk. "But surely you're English?" Again he nodded. "Then how came you there?"

Father Aleric smiled at her puzzlement. "As the fifth son of my father, a lowly knight, I had but two paths open to me. Having no taste for the fight, I chose the church." He paused.

That simple choice was no explanation of his time in the deserts and Taine waited patiently, quietly watching him despite the bustle of activity filling the hall. At last his face turned to her.

"Yet my choice I made for selfish reasons. I'd no true vocation or love for my Blessed Master and thought only of the learning I could attain. I went to Bologna, Paris, and Salamanca. In all the great centers of education I sought to learn more, rise higher than any had ever. In my arrogant search I traveled too far. Though warned, I ignored the caution of others and their tales of slavers."

"Slavers?" Taine straightened, green eyes wide.

"Aye." Again faded eyes twinkled. "'Twas a foolish deed that God turned to good for, in being humbled before Him, I attained the highest knowledge. I learned to trust and allow Him to lead the way. He took the misfortune I brought on myself and used it to His own purpose." His gaze went again to a golden head bent in close discussion with another. "God sent me to Jorion, and I've never rued the deed."

Taine's eyes followed the path of the priest's and she fell prey to the opportunity to study the unique man unobserved. Calmly directing the many tasks and toilers, he was all authority and devastating masculinity. Unwilling to admit interest in the dragon's past, Taine refused to ask questions but feared it was the power of her curiosity that willed Father Aleric to speak further.

"Sultan Bibars, Jorion's Saracen grandfather, promised the boy's dying father that Jorion would be raised a Christian. For that purpose, he purchased me."

Caution overwhelmed by desire to know more, Taine tore her eyes from Jorion and turned to ask, "If the dragon's grandfather was a Sultan, why did he not object to such upbringing?" Hard on the first question came another. "And why did he let the boy be taken away at the request of his English grandfather?"

Amused by the maid's unconscious naming of Jorion as the dragon and pleased by her interest in the husband he sensed she would deny, Father Aleric gently explained. "The men of those lands have several wives and many" —he paused, searching for an acceptable description— "companions, in proportion to their importance. The Sultan's children were numerous and his grandchildren a multitude. Jorion stood out among the multitude only because he was the son of a man the Sultan had admired. When the request came, I suspect the Sultan was relieved to see the boy go. It was clear he would never be accepted by—"

Absorbed in the cleric's words, waiting to hear who dared reject the dragon, Taine failed to notice Jorion's approach. When the priest stopped mid-sentence, she glanced up. Taine's breath caught at the unexpected meeting with black velvet eyes ringed by dark gold lashes. Refusing to be intimidated by their hold, she jumped up, rocking the bench with her haste. A foolish reaction for it only brought her closer to their power.

Jorion's wry, one-sided smile appeared and he lifted a brow in question for her motion as he handed her the new fur-lined cloak he'd provided.

The sudden appearance of the subject of recent talk had unnerved Taine and a blush stained her cheeks to the hue of a peach kissed rosy by the sun. She numbly accepted the heavy garment and cursed herself for the guilty reaction that would only lend amusement to the man she glared at without thought of the watching priest.

"For whatever foul deed by which I've offended you, I beg pardon," Jorion offered in mock apology, wry grin deepening the groove in one lean cheek. "We're set to depart, all in readiness and waiting on you."

Taine glanced about and found the hall empty. Her conversation with the priest had been so absorbing she'd failed to note everyone else leaving. Flinging the deep green cloak about her shoulders, she marched several paces toward the open door. A sudden question slowed her step. Would she be expected to travel ahorse? Her feet slowed, began to drag. She'd managed the ride to Edward's court only by Jorion's hold on the reins. To travel thus in company with his whole household would be a shaming thing—and surely not feasible for any distance? Nervously clutching a handful of soft green velvet, she glanced hesitantly behind. Jorion, although slowed by Father Aleric's lagging pace, was close to overtaking her.

"I've assured Father Aleric you would be willing to lend him your company in the cart." Jorion made his proposition sound a generous favor. "Our journey is a long one and—"

"Oh, yes. Indeed, yes." Taine rushed to assure the aging man, who looked close to rejecting her kind sacrifice. "It will give us the opportunity to continue our talk." She even gifted the dragon with a relieved smile, willing to forgive him his mockery for this thoughtful cover of her lack.

A niggling discomfort lowered Jorion's golden brows as he glanced from Taine to the priest. What common subject for conversation could they have but him? Father Aleric knew him intimately, but only from the days of his youth. All too familiar with the disgust his foreign heritage roused, Jorion did not want his claimed wife burdened with its details. Yet, the offer of companionship having been accepted, Jorion could do naught to see it forestalled. As they stepped from the hall, it was difficult to know if the darkening of his expression into a scowl was the result of the heatless brilliance of the autumn sun or irritation at some unfathomable deed.

Taine was cheered to find Bertwald waiting and in his hands the reins to the cart in which they had arrived at the earl's home. Unprepared, Taine gasped softly when, from behind, strong hands wrapped nearly full about her narrow waist and lifted her with ease into the cart. She steadied her breathing and calmed the erratic thumping of her heart as Jorion settled Father Aleric carefully beside her on the pile of bedcovers spread for their comfort. Once done, he quickly mounted his golden stallion and lifted his arm to signal a start.

The cart jerked into motion, taking its place amidst the entourage that started down the well-packed lane skirting the town. Though the direct route down narrow village lanes was a quicker departure for one or two mounted travelers, their collection of wagons, cart, and guard would find the longer outer road an easier path. The earl led the way, his knights at his side. Next came Lady Halyse, on the grey palfrey Taine had ridden to court. Bertwald's cart followed and more loaded wagons trailed after. On either side of the procession rode the men of the earl's guard. A festive air traveled with them, as all save one were anxious to reach their destination. Taine alone dreaded their goal.

Dunfermline left behind, the lighthearted talk of early travel settled into occasional murmured comments. As they passed over near barren hills and through colorful patches of bright-hued woods, the sun passed its zenith and began the downward fall. The only steady sounds were the monotonous squeaking of cart wheels and plodding of horse hooves that eventually lulled Father Aleric to sleep.

Watching the passing countryside, Taine began to see what she'd only heard rumors of before: areas scarred with the stark devastation burned by the English king across the land he meant to conquer. Where men rebelled against his control, he had sent fires of retribution, destroying home and harvest to leave neither sanctuary nor succor for his opponents. A small shudder shook Taine. Here, in blackened earth and destroyed villages, lay proof of the violent lengths to which men would go for the sake of power. Her gaze dropped from the sight of the charred remains of a small village to focus on hands twisted in mulberry velvet. The Golden Dragon was King Edward's man and had been a part of this destruction. Further proof of the absolute need to keep him unaware of her identity, to escape before he could lure her into willingly yielding to dragon-fire. Still, jeweled eyes were drawn again, as so oft in past hours, to fasten on the broad back ahead. He was unique, enthralling —inescapable?

She tore her gaze away and looked up to meet Bertwald's steady gaze. She wanted to immediately deny his knowing look, but held silent for fear of waking the priest from his one sure escape from suffering. Although he'd voiced no complaint, the cart's jarring discomfort must surely be near torture to arthritic bones. Glancing his way, she was surprised to find him awake and sitting quietly, deep grooves of unspoken pain marking the face he held in tight control. He smiled and in its serenity Taine saw that the same simple faith which had given him solace as captive in a strange land now gave him peace in facing physical disabilities.

Only to distract the uncomplaining man, Taine silently told herself, she leaned forward and urged him to speak more of the desert kingdom they'd talked of earlier. Again she was rewarded by the elderly priest's delighted smile, as he happily launched into stories of the child Jorion had been, from unsteady toddling to bold young warrior. Clear in every word lay his love for the boy, now man, whom he had raised.

Although Taine listened to proud tales of how Jorion had early exhibited his superior intellect and advanced skill at arms with an interest she would not have admitted, previously uttered words had left a question in her mind. When Father Aleric's stories slowed, Taine bent close and spoke in a soft undertone.

"Before we were called to depart, you said the Sultan let

him leave because he would never be accepted." Although flatly stated, it was clearly a question.

Father Aleric slowly nodded. He must admit to the trials of the dark-skinned, golden-blond, boy but the necessity brought an unhappy droop to his mouth. It was only just—if she would wed Jorion, she deserved to know the contempt that had built his armor of distrust.

"By his coloring alone he was separated from the other children of the harem. They rejected the child whose golden hair identified him as the Christian in their midst, a member of the religion whose adherents had been their blood enemies for generations." A tremor of anguish passed over Father Aleric's sharp features—anguish not for the physical discomfort which he bore so well, but for a pain of the soul. "I strived to be both friend and father, but he grew up lonely, longing to play freely with other children."

Taine, feeling somehow that the proud man would not relish her hearing of any weakness in him, glanced furtively again at the broad back ahead, where a dragon of golden threads seemed to take life. Sensing their time limited, she looked quickly back to the speaker, urging him to go on and complete the story.

"Once," the priest continued, "with the juice of grapes common to that land, he darkened his brows and lashes and slipped out to play with the children of the streets." Papery lips lifted in a sad smile. "It must have been a joy to discover such delights for the first time. But when the play grew rough, the cloth wrapped about his head was knocked away to reveal bright hair." He paused, obviously fighting an emotion that rose even after more than a score of years. "With foul names the other children taunted him and ran away."

Taine sat quietly, unwilling to force further painful memories, but the priest turned to meet her eyes. "I comforted him with stories of his father's cool, green land and the welcome he would surely find among the people there." Light from the setting sun glowed on white hair as he shook his head ruefully. "Yet, since that moment, I do not think that Jorion has ever given another opportunity to reject him."

Taine barely had time to register the knowledge that he

had given her that opportunity when a gruff voice interrupted.

"I hope the ride has not been too difficult, Father. There is a stream on the other side of this hill where we will spend the night." Jorion frowned up at the quickly darkening sky. "These short days will lengthen our journey." His expression softened as he looked down into Father Aleric's drawn face and added, "But it will mean traveling in easier stages more bearable for you." Dark eyes turned toward the path ahead but he remained by the cart's side. Only after they had crested the hill, and ridden through a stand of trees to the stream at its foot, did he urge his golden horse to the front and signal a halt.

Twilight's short glow had nearly faded into night by the time the fire's hungry flames gained strength enough to offer warmth and light. Halyse motioned Taine to join her on a pallet stretched out on one side of the heat, while Jorion helped the priest to a seat beside him on a fallen tree trunk on the circle of light's far side.

They shared simple fare: salt pork, dark rye bread and crisp apples washed down with ale for the men and berry wine for the women. Meal finished, the two women laid back, relishing the cessation of motion and stretching muscles cramped for long hours. In private undertones they jestingly argued which offered the more discomfort, horse hide or cart bed. Each held her own experience the more painful. At length their soft voices fell silent and they listened to the murmur of the stream, the gentle rustle of a breeze through leaves and the muted words of men gathered close about the fire.

As Halyse dozed, Taine turned her face toward the blaze to quietly watch the man whose blond hair and bronzed skin were gilded by leaping flames. In the perpetual mockery of his one-sided smile, she now detected the lonely boy rejected by those he'd sought in friendship. Her eyes drifted briefly to the man who had told her of his rejection but irresistibly returned to the center of her thoughts. A steady view of his firm lips brought feelings far from childish and she could not halt the memory of them burning against her own. Even now she could feel their welcome heat and the tender strength of his embrace. It felt as if an invisible cord were pulling her to him. No!

Rolling to her side, she stared into the black void. She would resist the dragon's lure to his consuming fire, for his goal was the same as for all men—the power she could give. A small voice reminded her that he'd claimed her wife with no notion of her heritage and all it promised. She quashed it. Surely he'd use her birthright to his own advantage were he to discover the secret, and that must never happen! One arm pushing back the heavy weight of the luxurious hair she'd released from its bonds, she pillowed her cheek on the other. Then, jerking the cover close to her chin, she determined to blank her mind of all concerns and drift into dreams—a goal neither easily nor quickly attained.

The touch of mist-green eyes had kept Jorion distracted from the soft conversation flowing about him. He had known the moment they turned to Aleric, then back to him, narrowed and darkened to forest green. When she flung her hair behind, it had seemed to reach toward the fire and trap all the fierce flames in its tangled curls. Lips compressed into a firm, straight line, Jorion looked down to the man at his side. Despite his love for Aleric, he cursed the man's joy in reminiscing, certain that all his talk of the years in the desert had crystallized Taine's disgust of his Saracen half.

He rose abruptly and, striving to keep harshness from his tone, pointed out to his men that, although the hour was early, they should seek their rest. They would rise before sunrise to obtain the longest day and travel as far as possible before another ended.

❧ Chapter 8 ❧

A MOMENTARY GRIMACE PASSED over Taine's weary face as the cart jolted over yet another unseen hole. Her whole body seemed to have become one large bruise. She shifted uncomfortably and cast a quick glance upward. Praise the saints who had offered one mercy at least. Although the skies had been filled with clouds for most of their journey, no rain had fallen to turn their path to mire and muck; and on this fifth day the sun had at last returned. Weak and nearly heatless, still it was a welcome.

The days of their journey had passed, much like the first with Taine riding in the cart's back with Father Aleric while Bertwald held the reins. The three of them had talked of many things, but never again had Father Aleric spoken on the desert years of Jorion's youth. Taine suspected he had been cautioned from the subject. Despite that lack, both she and Bertwald had come to know and respect the aging man, who never complained of his own suffering and always offered encouragement to others.

They had crossed rivers and streams, and wound through the dim caverns of dark forests where towering trees forbade natural light. Now they traveled over broad rolling meadows which, even this late in autumn and without man's farming talents, boasted lush green growth. Afternoon shadows had appeared and conversation had long ago drifted away. The soft thud of horses' hooves and constant rumble of turning wheels were nearly the only sounds. Discomfort strong, Taine again shifted cautiously on the pile of furs, seeking to ease the pressure on a tender portion of her anatomy. She still dreaded arrival in the dragon's domain, but even that would be preferable to continuing this subtle torture. Taine glanced at the priest whose lashes were lowered in worship as he quietly worked over his rosary. He was silently enduring the same discomfort and more, and she was ashamed of her unspoken complaint.

Feeling an intruder on the priest's private worship, Taine slid green eyes away from him to the company's lead and found their oft-sought goal. Though doubtless as fatigued as the rest of his party, broad and black-cloaked shoulders failed to share the weary droop of others. Fine brows drew into a tiny frown of perplexity. His treatment of her in days just past were a puzzlement. By all means, short of physical bonds, he'd forced her to this journey, but had not spoken nor yet turned the dark power of his gaze to her since its first beginning. All the while, she found her own eyes drawn to him repeatedly despite constant self-condemnation for the lack of control that allowed it. With renewed determination, she looked blindly down at cloth twisted between slender fingers.

It had been Halyse who attended to Taine's needs and tarried to talk while the men gathered about their lord for discussions not of past battles alone, but of those expected, nay, anticipated in future. More proof of the joy men found in seeking power at any price, she cautioned herself, and further reason to win free with all good speed. Still, the quiet voice of honesty whispered a mock question in her soul. Why then did she rue the lack of the dragon's attention? Even as the silent query raised a tall and mighty image in her mind, she felt his unexpected presence and looked up to find the golden horse slowed to the cart's plodding pace. Her hands tightened on soft wool, threatening to rend it asunder.

Jorion had seen the fatigue of several days' journey grow

on Taine's pale-cream face and, too, had felt the repeated touch of her sea-mist eyes. Yet her clear disgust for him the last night in Dunfermline and the first night of their journey had made him hesitant to approach her before his guardsmen. He had nothing but disdain for weak fools who could vent frustration and prove strength only by striking the women of their families. Nonetheless, were she to reject him openly before his men he would be constrained to wield the gauntleted fist and force her to his will or appear the weakened fool. He had sworn to wed her and so he would, but he was loath to use a physical strength that would likely either damage the pride and spirit that intrigued him most or build between them a barrier impossible to surmount. For this reason he had held his distance 'til now, as they fast approached his home.

He doffed his helmet, dropped it to the cart's seat beside a surprised Bertwald, and looked then to Taine. Pushing back the mail coif beneath, ruffling blond hair, he offered, "If you would appreciate a change in vantage point, I will swear to hold Apollo on tight rein and spare you any unseemly descent."

As he spoke, one corner of his mouth lifted in his usual cynical smile, but Taine saw the diffidence in imperceptibly raised brows. It brought to mind the golden-haired boy rejected by the children of the desert and earned him a gentle smile and nod of acceptance.

Even expecting the motion, Taine gasped as a strong arm swooped down and lifted her to 'Apollo's back. She landed abruptly, wincing at the abuse to her tender derrière, and glanced up to find dark eyes alarmingly close. This had surely been a decision of no merit for she'd not paused to consider the effect of such sudden proximity. One mail-clad arm was scant distance from her rib cage, one was warm against her back and his broad chest lightly brushed her shoulder. She was very nearly within his embrace and the feel of his big, hard body so close did strange things to her senses. As on the first occasion they'd shared such a ride, Taine went rigid.

Aware now of her lack of equestrian skills, Jorion ascribed her reaction to a simple anxiety for their mode of travel and began to speak in a quiet, soothing tone. "At Castle Dragonsward I have an extensive stable. Thus I was unwilling to choose a steed for you from among the limited choices available in Dunfermline."

Taine laced her fingers tightly together, consciously restraining them from clutching the horse's mane. Had he even considered the possibility of her traveling this distance unskilled but ahorse?

Jorion's one-sided smile came again as he noted entwined fingers, white with the pressure applied. "Once you've settled in your new home, I will take you to a secluded meadow beyond prying eyes and instruct you in the skill you lack."

Surprised by his offer and more by his plan to spare her shame before others, she glanced up and quickly back down, unable to risk meeting his attractions so near. As it was, the warm maleness of him wrapped about her, stealing her composure and beckoning her closer.

"In my stable there is a beautiful mare surely destined for you—" A touch so light she couldn't be certain of it brushed the riot of deep auburn curls which had escaped the net crespine's confines to lay a fiery halo about her face. "She's near the hue of your hair, and when you've learned to master a horse, she will be yours."

Even distracted by his gentle caress, Taine realized he'd promised to gift her with something he valued. Other than the ring her father had put on her hand so many years past, she could remember receiving no other gift and didn't know how to respond.

The steed carrying the self-involved couple had returned to the front of the entourage and moved a distance ahead. Wrapped in her thoughts, Taine unknowingly answered a summons earlier denied and relaxed against the solid, reassuring wall of the Jorion's chest.

Not so impervious to her sweet temptations as his carefully controlled face would indicate, he welcomed the soft warmth she yielded to him and smiled with self-mockery. Now, before the whole of his company, she became an all-enticing woman in his arms, now when he could not answer her unspoken invitation. Indeed, it seemed the rigors of their travels had banked the fire-sprite's flames for since he'd lifted her before him, she'd spoken no word. He deliberately turned his mind to matters certain to cool his ardor.

"Mayhap you would appreciate some"—he bit off the word "warning" before it was spoken, no need for such alarm on the discontent of one man—"knowledge of those you will meet in Castle Dragonsward?"

Taine wondered at the curious flatness of his voice. What had stolen the prideful note ever in his voice when speaking of his home? She risked a quick glance up and found his cold gaze trained on a lone tree at the summit of the long, gentle slope they were climbing. The leaves remaining on its soaring, spreading limbs displayed all the colors of autumn in a final glorious show before surrendering to winter's deadly call.

"Uncle Thomas," Jorion drew a deep breath and began, "became my guardian after my grandfather died, when I was fourteen winters. His mother was my grandfather's sister and he divided his time between his lands and mine until his were held forfeit to the crown." Jorion paused and his wry smile was nearly a sneer as he added, "He then moved permanently to mine."

Taine peeked up at him. Although his voice was carefully controlled, dislike of this arrangement was clear in eyes flat black with bitterness.

Jorion dwelled in bleak thoughts until the sudden skittering of a small creature in tall grass startled Apollo, and his full attention was demanded to soothe the nervous horse. Moving smoothly onward once more, he looked down at the maid nearly full in his embrace, lush curves pressed innocently against him. His blood warmed again while she seemed completely unaware of the temptations she offered. A curious thing that. The beautiful women of the court were fully aware of their allurements and wielded them as skillfully as a warrior his broadsword. Wary of needless rejections, he'd refused to enter their amorous lists and left his cousin to uphold the family honor on the field of love.

"You'll like Rhyming Richard," Jorion told her, certain of his statement's truth. "Uncle Thomas' son and my cousin."

Taine glanced up into the slow, sardonic smile lifting one corner of his mouth.

"Most women do," he added with a slight shrug. "Although his rhymes are lacking, his voice is sweet and he plays a fine tune."

By the affection in the description, Taine realized the dragon's cynicism was not for his cousin but for her expected response. Certain her experiences would hold her impervious to his cousin's charms, still her curiosity was pricked by the dragon's words.

"Richard is as unlike his father as day from night." Jorion had sought, with limited success, to hide his opinion of Uncle Thomas from earlier words, but this comment revealed more than he'd have allowed had he paused to consider and heightened Taine's interest.

"Then there's Elspeth." An unusual gentleness softened Jorion's face. "She's my ward and, as sweet as apple-honey, although Uncle Thomas ofttimes appears to think her his responsibility."

Taine blinked at this unexpected mention of another woman—one who brought warmth to his words. As she pondered his revelations, they crested a small hill and halted in the deep shadow beneath an autumn-bright and towering elm. Little noticing their location, Taine at last opened her lips to speak but was forestalled.

"Castle Dragonsward." The muscles of the broad chest she rested against flexed and his cloak rippled in the breeze with his sweeping motion toward his home.

From a wide green meadow the sharp angles of a rock-based hill rose with startling abruptness, lending a commanding position to the massive fortress on its summit. The late afternoon sun was sinking behind it, lending a gilded outline that seemed to prove it truly the Golden Dragon's lair.

"Isn't it beautiful!" Halyse, on her little grey mare, had stopped beside them. Her normally cheery spirit, undampened by days of travel, bubbled over with admiration.

Taine returned her infectious grin despite her own apprehensions. Behind the high shield of the inner bailey wall, she could see no more than the tops of whitewashed towers where pennants rippled and danced on the wind. To her it seemed a powerful and awesome place that inspired shivers of alarm. She tilted her chin to glance over a broad shoulder at the dragon's standard, the same black-and-gold image he wore on his cloak's back. When once again inside his mighty fortress, it would wave from the highest point to show him in residence, an act that signified to her the joining of two powerful restraints to her freedom. Bolstering her flagging courage with renewed determination to yield to no man, she swallowed hard and looked once again to the castle.

"I, too, saw it first time beneath this tree." Jorion's words were soft but filled with clear pride. "Aleric had explained to me that a sward is a wide expanse of grass, and I looked at the castle rising from the broad green meadow and knew I'd found my home."

Willfully, Taine submerged her apprehensions in the memory of Aleric's promise of a green land, the promise that had prompted a boy's longing for his father's home. By it, she understood the love for this place of the man grown from that boy.

"Aye, far above the sward." Will, drawn to a halt beside his wife, joined the conversation. "'Tis an appropriate base for our dragon."

Will and Halyse remained beside the golden horse on a circular approach to the castle's far side, where the hill made a more gentle ascent and the front gates allowed access. At the outer bailey wall that began at the base of the cliff they'd first faced, a bright sparkle against the rock face caught Taine's eye. High above, a waterfall sprouted unexpectedly from between the cliff's solid rock and the castle that stood on it. Her stunned expression brought a delighted laugh from Halyse and smiles from others, even Jorion.

"I didn't point it out before because 'tis such fun to discover for oneself." Halyse informed Taine. "A spring bubbles up in the courtyard. It doesn't seem right working so hard to come up there rather than down here, but then, that's the surprise of it all, isn't it? And we can be heartily glad it does, for it'd make a successful siege most difficult."

By concentrating on the unexpected loveliness of misty spray and tumbling water made silver and gold by the setting sun, Taine did not have to look at the overwhelming structure above. Soft green eyes stayed on the beautiful sight for as long as possible, which encouraged Halyse to talk on of the castle's amazing history. When the waterfall was lost to Taine's view, Halyse's bright chatter was a welcome distraction from her concern for what was yet to come.

Jorion welcomed Halyse's ploy. He liked Will's lady and admired her ability to maintain a positive disposition. Yet seeing the two redhaired women so close together, he couldn't fail to note the physical differences between them. Though Halyse's wiry curls were neatly coiled beneath a net crespine, their carroty hue was undimmed while Taine's rich hair burned with dark fire only where light was caught and held—in the coil of every curl. The sun appeared to double its brightness and gleam equally on vivid orange and deep wine red. Intent black eyes narrowed and by effort of will he stayed his hand from tangling in thick auburn satin.

Under the steady weight of his eyes, pale rose crept into Taine's cheeks and she looked determinedly away. They were now fully on the far side of the cliff and, nervously twisting her ring, she began to carefully catalog every detail of their surroundings. Harvested fields stretched out to woodlands so dense they must form a sizable forest. Any serious threat would surely come from that approach.

The castle's first line of defense was the outer bailey wall they had followed. Halfway up the long slope of the castle's approach, they came to a gate in its wide stone wall. It was flanked by guards who stood on the wall above and had carefully watched the advancing company. On seeing their lord's standard flying above and the gleam of his golden hair below, they had already unbarred the massive, metal-bound doors and begun the slow lifting of the heavy iron portcullis. The waiting group had only to listen to the chain's final groans before passing within.

As they moved toward the portals, Taine glanced fearfully up at the vicious teeth of the nearly invincible grillwork above. She shivered with thoughts of what agonies it would mean were the restraining chain loosed, allowing a sudden fall. Jorion saw her upward gaze and felt her immediate shudder. With no words of comfort to offer for a deed that could and, hopefully, would befall any foe seeking entry, he clasped her tighter and urged Apollo quickly beyond its threat.

Fool! A few days in the dragon's company and you fall to fear, Taine berated herself. Moreover, she'd allowed him to see her quail, and all when no true threat was offered. Pulling away from his broad chest and straightening her shoulders, Taine turned her attention to the sizable village of Radwyn. It clustered near the edge of the moat flowing around the castle's inner bailey wall. On the village's far side was a barely seen orchard planted in orderly rows. By concentrating on her surroundings, Taine sought to ignore the chill that came from the loss of the dragon's heat against her back. As they traveled the dusty lane through the village, the people stopped their chores and gathered at the edges. Their surprise turned to warm welcome for their lord, obviously a popular figure. Yet clearly they had not expected his return. Had he sent word of his coming to the castle inhabitants at least?

Taine had just begun to consider a whole new set of concerns when they halted near a small cottage on the village's edge nearest the castle. Nicely thatched and partly shaded by an old apple tree, it looked a cozy retreat. Even as she wondered for the reason of their stop, she wished it were her destination, rather than the intimidating structure towering ahead.

Jorion dismounted, leaving Taine suddenly sitting alone and terrified on the back of the powerful horse. Rigid with fright, not daring to move for fear of irritating the steed, from the corner of her eye she saw a golden head bent solicitously to a white one. The earl and Bertwald led Father Aleric between them into the cottage and Taine saw the purpose she'd questioned. Father Aleric had told them of his refusal to so far leave his vows of poverty as to live in a great castle. Thus it was reasonable he be provided with this humble abode. She was surprised, however, when Bertwald came out and walked to her side with the earl.

"He's nearly blind, lass, and canna be left alone." Green eyes clouded with suspicion of a meaning she prayed was not intended. "And I wouldna be comfortable where you go." Surely she would understand that he couldn't enter so imposing a castle as guest. He'd spoken to the earl and offered his company to Father Aleric. A fine plan, he'd thought, enabling him to remain close enough to come to her aid, if needed. "So, I mean to stay with him."

Taine's lashes clenched shut for a long moment to hide her pain, and when they lifted she looked not at Bertwald, but glared at the dragon who had left her ahorse to hear this plan. He'd known she'd be so frightened she hardly dared breathe, much less vehemently assert her disgust with this plan to steal away her only support.

Bertwald saw the maid's dislike of his decision and her unhappiness. Though he was certain she'd be safe within the great stone walls of the earl's castle, he realized she saw his action as a defection. He reached out and laid his hand over her tightly laced fingers, and she looked to him with bruised-clover eyes. "Ye musna fret for me." His voice was soft and reassuring, watery blue eyes pleading for understanding. "I'll still be here and the earl swears you can visit whenever you please." Bertwald looked to Jorion for his confirming nod before squeezing her hands and turning to stride into the cottage.

Taine watched his stolid, bowlegged frame disappear, feeling deserted, defeated. Black cloak flaring out like true dragon wings, the earl mounted behind her. All the tension that had drained away in their earlier travels returned, and the feel of him looming behind her strengthened her resolve. What matter that another man had deserted her, had accepted the soft life her trials laid in his path. Only further proof that she could count on naught but herself.

She hardly noticed the wide moat while they waited for the slow descent of a heavy plank drawbridge. Halyse's description of the laborious work involved in planning and building a moat fed by the spring's waters flowing downward around the fortification to fall from beneath the castle's back, was wasted on deaf ears.

Once across the lowered drawbridge, they passed through the tunnel opening in the thick stone wall guarded by a portcullis at each end, little noticed by Taine. In the courtyard the last gleams of a setting sun lit the orange hair of a small boy hurtling across the dusty, wheel-rutted ground. The bright mop caught Taine's eye and she smiled.

He could only be Halyse's much-missed son, a thought confirmed when the little body leaped into Halyse's wide-spread arms. Ecstatic welcome dissolved into happy tears before Will could urge the quietly sobbing woman and her precious bundle into privacy.

Closely watching the reunion, Taine failed to notice when the dragon dismounted and, as so oft in the past, was caught unaware by hands lifting her down. Startled by the suddenly renewed closeness, she pulled immediately away.

Jorion's wry smile reappeared when Taine quickly stepped back from him and turned resolutely toward his home, the place she had striven to avoid. She looked to it with the same hard-held bravery she'd shown at Edward's court. Although Jorion had no doubt but that she would find his castle impressive, he wondered for her response to those within.

Facing the castle entrance, Taine sought to force her full attention on standing prepared for whatever welcome awaited her inside. Yet having little experience in meeting strangers, she found it impossible to plan for the unknown and determined instead to distract herself by concentrating on inconsequential facts. Allowing Jorion to lead her up the long wooden stairway, she realized that under attack such steps could be burned to make entry into the main body of the castle more difficult to achieve.

When they entered the great hall, she gave it her full attention. That the room truly deserved the name was her first thought. Filled with a mass of humanity, each trying to be heard over the roar of another, it was the largest room she'd ever been in. Morag had told her that in the castles of powerful nobles there were separate chambers for family and guests and an additional guardroom for the men-at-arms. Thus none slept in the great hall save servants tending fires, and even then the food was prepared elsewhere than in its massive fireplace. It seemed that this was such a place. Two lines of round stone columns were necessary to hold the ceiling in place. She followed the line of the first up to a magnificent display of carving. From chains between every two columns hung metal circles within circles, each supporting a parade of candles that lit the room, while firebrands held by rings driven into stone walls brightened even the furtherest corners.

Taine glanced down in time to see a young girl, small and plump, hurtle herself into Jorion's arms. Green eyes widened to see him laugh, lift the ebony-haired lass above his head, and whirl around before lowering her for a quick hug.

"This is Elspeth, my ward," Jorion explained, still laughing. Taking the girl's shoulders between his palms, he turned her to face Taine. The girl grinned shyly at the newcomer but leaned possessively back against Jorion.

An odd ache filled Taine at sight of another's easy claim of the one she must refuse.

Jorion's eyes rose to a point beyond Taine and went hard. "And this"—he nodded to someone behind her—"is Uncle Thomas."

Taine turned to find a ruddy-faced older man towering above. Staring at the heavy figure, as tall as the dragon, she was struck with a feeling of familiarity. But how could that be? Before her escape, she'd met no men in the past decade and more, save her rotating prison guards.

"Welcome to Dragonsward." Beneath the apparent warmth of his greeting a coldness lay.

The wide smile seemed to rest uncomfortably on his stern face and in Taine's mind rose an irrational image of a fat, black, and poisonous spider. She had to force herself not to recoil from the hand stretched out to lift hers. As he brushed slightly damp lips over the fingers he held, his eyes never left hers, and she was unable to still a slight shiver of distaste. She had reason to like few men, but her sudden aversion to him was stronger than any she'd known before. Even her pursuers seemed little more than bumbling threats compared to this unknown peril.

The smiles exchanged by uncle and nephew went no further than a forced bending of lips, and their cold, guarded eyes revealed the uncertain nature of their relationship.

"It appears I'm not to be formally introduced." A light voice tinged with sarcasm broke the others' visual duel. "Thus I'm released to introduce myself."

A slender but well-proportioned man, little taller than

herself, stepped in front of Taine. With an elegant flourish he lifted her hand to lips outlined by a well-trimmed brown moustache and goatee. Still bent over her fingers, he peeked up and winked one twinkling blue eye. Such foolery in the midst of a tense moment surprised a bubble of laughter from Taine.

"I am Richard," he explained as he straightened, still holding her fingers. "His cousin." He inclined his head of thick, shiny brown hair toward Jorion. "And his son." He shrugged with a mournful pout. "An accident of birth— neither his choice nor mine."

Much of the hall had stopped and stood listening to the exchange. A growl of disapproval from the older man only brought an impish smile to Richard and an urge to unbounded laughter to Taine.

"Ah, my sire disapproves." Unrepentant, Richard grinned into the reddened face stiff with iron control. "That's good."

Taine darted a quick glance to the dragon, curious for his reaction to this wicked wit and caught a look of— admiration?

"'Tis only fair that she be warned." In mock-seriousness Richard turned to Taine and continued. "I am the family scapegrace who prefers games of love to games of war."

Taine looked at him, disbelief lightly puckering delicate brows. Was it possible for any man to disdain the struggle for power?

Richard saw her expression and shrugged again. "Have you ever tried to heft a broadsword?"

At such a strange suggestion, Taine's frown grew.

"I thought not. Try it sometime. It weighs near as much as I do! I'm deadly with a dagger, a blade just right for my size. But if I tried to swing one of those ghastly swords around, I'd fall flat on my ar—I'd fall in an ignominious heap. An unwilling sacrifice to the Gods of War."

Taine grinned at the picture he painted, and he squeezed her fingers once before loosing them. "My felicitations." Richard's merry blue eyes swept quickly over her with appreciation. Jorion had brought home a tasty morsel. "You've survived the meeting of our family group. Now, may we ask who you are and why you've come to our happy abode?"

Jorion stepped forward to place his hand on Taine's shoulder. He announced, "She is Martaine and my wife as soon as the arrangements are complete."

A gasp drew Taine's eyes to Elspeth's suddenly white face. From there they moved to Uncle Thomas who looked like thunder and on to Richard whose grin spread from ear to ear.

After long moments of stunned silence, Uncle Thomas drew himself up and called orders to a servant to lay the family's evening meal in the solar above.

Jorion's one-sided smile was full of derision for his uncle's command of the servants in a castle not his own, but he quietly turned to Elspeth. "Take Taine to a chamber to wash away the dust of our journey before the meal," he gently directed, "and wait to lead her to the solar where uncle dictates we eat."

Although softly sniffing, heart apparently wounded, Elspeth led Taine to the steep corner stairway that wound a narrow, circular path upward. When they reached the second level above, Elspeth started down the hall but paused when she realized Taine was still standing in the stairway gazing up. Trying to put a brave face on matters she did not understand, Elspeth went back.

"From here"—Elspeth pointed to the corridor branching off from the one she'd taken—"you can cross the curtain wall to the second tower where lies the chapel."

Taine looked confused by the sheer size of the castle, and Elspeth, empathizing with an emotion she herself was suffering from, was glad for this sign that the strange beauty was not some haughty lady of the court. She smiled. "Jorion and Uncle Thomas have wonderful apartments along the curtain wall above the great hall. You and I have chambers on this level. Richard's room and the solar are below. The guardroom, with chambers for Will and Halyse, are another level down." She paused dramatically. "The lowest level, below ground, is the dungeon."

Taine's brows rose, much to Elspeth's satisfaction, although she hastily added, "We use them for storage as none dare risk conflict with our dragon and the serfs are disciplined in other ways." Elspeth shrugged and went on to more interesting things. "At the very top of these stairs are the battlements where, on a fine day, you can nearly see the sea beyond the forest." Brown eyes went misty. She'd oft leaned over the parapet visualizing the unseen. "Not really, but sometimes I'm sure I can smell it."

This was not a pleasant prospect to Taine. The pounding, vicious sea had been near the only view from her lonely castle-prison.

Elspeth's fond description of the battlement's delights wandered into a new vein. "At night if the sky is clear, you can nearly touch the stars. Jorion—" Memory of the recent scene and the identity of her companion washed over Elspeth bringing a fresh wave of tears. Mortified, she whirled and dashed down the tower hallway.

Surprised, Taine still stood in the archway from stairs to corridor. Elspeth, from the door she'd flung open, announced in a watery tone her intention to soon return, then ran farther on to her own chamber.

Feeling guilty for a deed not of her choosing, Taine moved down the now empty corridor to peer through the open doorway. She was startled to find her chests not only within but one unpacked. Without pausing to consider the room's contents beyond a hasty realization of their rich appointments, she rushed to pour warm water from the pitcher to the basin. She was relieved that, for whatever reason, she'd been left in privacy to strip off travel-grimed clothes and hastily cleanse away as much of the dust and weariness of the trip as she could without the full bath she promised herself soon.

Being in a large company of strangers was even harder than Taine had expected, and not alone for the dissension flowing about them. What possible conversation could one long-held in remote confinement and still bound tight by secrets that must be kept?

Taine had trouble finding clothes that could be donned without aid, but by the time Elspeth returned, tear-shiny face scrubbed dry, she was ready and waiting.

Unable to meet the lady's eyes, Elspeth kept her own on the door latch she clutched, frustrating Taine's hope for some reassurance in her choice of garb. She glanced down once more, smoothing the green-velvet surcote over a simple saffron kirtle. She only hoped it was appropriate for the family meal. The younger girl led her down narrow steps to the open door of the family solar.

"How could you wound Elspeth this way?" Uncle Thomas' voice boomed out, berating Jorion. "How could you let her, let us all believe you meant to wed her, only to bring another to her home."

The two girls stood unnoticed in the shadowed doorway, fresh tears sprouting from Elspeth's overready supply as Uncle Thomas continued.

"You cannot marry one whose family we know naught of," he emphatically stated, smashing a meaty fist into waiting palm as he added, "I will not allow the marriage that would see Radwyn pass to the whelp of a Saracen brat and a nameless wench."

Jorion, who had been sitting, back to the door, stood slowly and faced his uncle. The blustering Thomas stepped away from the fury on his face.

"This castle is *mine.*" Voice cold as ice shards and just as dangerous, Jorion growled, *"I* am the Earl of Radwyn. In my absences for the support of my king I have let you assume control, too much control in my life and Elspeth's. For the care you once gave me I am willing that you abide in my home, but no longer will I allow you to hold the reins in your hand. Now I will take them and drive to the destination of my choice." He lifted his hands and slowly closed them into mighty fists. "The choice of wife is *mine* and none of yours." Fists thumped against a mighty chest. "Moreover, the choice of Elspeth's husband is mine. She is my ward, and I am no husband for her."

Face beet red, Uncle Thomas stomped past Jorion. More irate still for having given way before the force of Jorion's rage, he barely saw the girls he brushed by.

Once Uncle Thomas had gone, Jorion's fists unclenched. Yet cold anger still filled him when he turned to find himself observed by the two standing in the doorway. When he strode past them, Elspeth shrank back but Taine's chin lifted and she met his eyes directly. She would not allow herself to show fear of his temper—neither would she allow him to drive her to the destination of his choice! She'd had enough of men twisting her life to meet their own goals.

Taine led the shaky Elspeth into the solar and pressed her into the stool closest to the fire. Uncle Thomas' claim of an anticipated marriage and Elspeth's earlier warm welcome of Jorion explained her watery reaction to an unexpected bride and earned Taine's complete sympathy. She'd clearly been poorly used, a condition Taine understood too well.

No sooner had Elspeth regained control of her tears than Richard made his appearance. A quick glance told him who was within and who was not. It took little shrewdness to guess the gist of what had transpired. He advanced toward the two near the fire with a teasing smile that held more than a touch of bitterness.

"What will you do now that your 'perfect lord' is to wed another?" he asked, quirking one dark brow over mock-serious blue eyes.

Stung by his words, Elspeth gave him a stricken look, burst into fresh tears, and ran from his taunting presence.

Taine, herself too often the brunt for cruel words, turned on Richard with a flash of temper for his callous action, but stopped. For an unguarded moment his face held as much pain as Elspeth's.

"Is Jorion truly the perfect lord?" she asked instead.

"Near to," Richard responded with a characteristic shrug meant to lighten all serious matters. "He's the embodiment of all the courtly virtues: loyal, kind, and brave."

"Is that all?" Taine questioned sarcastically, unable to believe any man possessed such a host of virtues.

"No." Richard met her sarcasm with total seriousness. "Though he is all of those. More important, he is a warrior skilled enough to win most any tourney, has even distinguished himself in the king's wars." He leaned forward as if intending to impart a state secret. "The Scots frighten naughty children with tales of the Golden Dragon." He sat back and shrugged again. "But King Edward loves him." With a forlorn smile he added, "Jorion is all that my father and his grandfather admired in a man, all that I admire—if only the Saracen blood were not so evident."

"Of what matter is that?" Taine questioned sharply, not recognizing in her tone her own defense of the man. She was unable to believe these words of near hero-worship. Surely, she silently ridiculed, faced with a man of such perfection, none could find fault.

"No matter to me," Richard answered, "but to my father and his grandfather it was enough to ruin all else." A merry grin returned to hide his melancholy. "Most probably 'tis the reason we get on so well, despite our very different natures. We each accept the other without criticism for the truth of what we are."

Richard was never comfortable thinking long or seriously of his own shortcomings and wanted to turn from such introspective thoughts. He clapped his hands and asked, "Well, then, shall we dine on this feast of welcome provided for the returning lord?" With the wry query, he motioned toward the lone trestle table laid with a white cloth and splendid silver goblets.

"What of the others?" Taine was hesitant to begin alone.

"Be assured they will not join us again this night. 'Tis one of the little quirks you must become accustomed to—the many meals taken in bedchamber when both Jorion and my sire are in residence."

Taine was self-conscious, sitting with only Richard at the table, but he demonstrated his considerable charm by putting her at ease while the pages stepped forward to proffer each course on bended knee. Once the overabundant meal of leek broth, roast venison, and a salad of fresh herbs, vegetables, and flowers had been consumed, they moved to chairs before the fire. Richard fell to telling the bride of her intended husband's long-ago arrival at Dragonsward, with ten swift and graceful horses and the lack of any real welcome for him from a grandfather willing to accept even a half-Saracen rather than let the family name die out, but unable to love the dark-skinned boy.

"The killing blow fell when Jorion's grandfather asked him to demonstrate his skill at arms. He brought out two large, curved blades and, holding one in each hand, gave an amazing demonstration of skill and dexterity—further proof of his foreign ways. His grandfather was horrified and immediately set out to train Jorion to the broadsword and lance, a training my father continued after the old earl died."

Richard looked down at the maid whose attention was firmly caught by his words. "It's amusing that although he possesses and, in tilts and jousts, frequently demonstrates a superior skill with our native weapons, his serious fighting he does with the curved blades of his youth." Richard grinned at Taine and added with a laugh, "He says half the victory is in the fear engendered by the two spinning blades. His foes are not trained to meet such a threat and are easily overawed. His reputation precedes him, the strange weapons make him easily identified, and his mere presence intimidates the enemy.

"Wouldn't his grandfather be amazed to find his heir the most successful and feared warrior of his day because of the weapons he'd disdained?" His merry smile took on a bitter twist. "How unfortunate that neither Jorion's grandfather nor my sire were happy with their heirs. Jorion is all they desired but not clear-blooded, while my blood is pure but I have no skill to arms, no desire for power."

This second confession of a lack of desire for power, though hard to believe, tempted Taine to a liking for this carefree man far different from the romantic fascination Jorion had expected.

Beneath her suspicious eyes, Richard laughed self-contemptuously and retrieved a lute from the shadows of a far corner. Strumming it softly and winking at Taine again, he settled down to sing a delightful love song of his own devising. His voice was so clear and pure that it stole her tensions and soothed nerves jangled by the atmosphere since her arrival.

She gave her rare smile of enchanting sweetness and when the last note died away told him, "Now I understand why you are so popular with the ladies of the court."

Stunned by the magical smile, Richard looked at her in some confusion. Although he'd claimed to be popular with women, he'd not expected her to take him seriously.

"Your cousin told me it's true," she explained.

Richard shook his head and with a wry smile denied, "Nay, I merely console those he rejects for 'tis he they ever pursue. That he never accedes to their wiles only succeeds in making him more desirable in their eyes. Each woman believes she may be the one to gain the prize."

Through narrowed green eyes, Taine looked at the laughing man with obvious disbelief. She could only just believe one man capable of preferring music and laughter to war and power. This idea of any man, the dragon least of all, denying himself an offered pleasure was too implausible.

Seeing disdain curl soft lips, Richard misinterpreted its source and hastened to reassure. "Do not mistake, although he abstains from the court's rich feast, he's far from ready to take the monk's oath of celibacy. He has no aversion to ladies of less exalted station and there's ever a willing supply about."

❧ Chapter 9 ❧

TAINE SLEPT OVERLONG. THE sun had fully risen before the sound of a tiptoeing servant awakened her. Bedcover clasped across her breasts, she peeked through the bed's night-drawn draperies. With narrow back turned, a young girl bent to stir the banked fire to renewed heights. Drab brown hair fell in limp strands over her shoulder.

Rustling sounds from the bed drew timid eyes to the lady's fragile face, near overwhelmed by a wealth of auburn curls. Though enthralled by the figure in the bed, a gaze the same brown as her hair skittered away from eyes the deep green of a shadowed forest glade. Turning to the tray waiting on the small table before the hearth, the girl lifted a sample of offerings from the meal already done in the hall below. Leaning the emptied tray against the stone wall, she neatly arranged the frothy milk, wheaten bread still warm from the oven, honey, fresh apples, and raisins on the smooth planks.

Still holding the coverlet to her breasts, Taine leaned over the high bed's edge in a long reach to the floor and retrieved the kirtle she'd laid neatly at its side in fear of such need. Sliding back into the shadows behind still-closed drapes, she pulled the garment over her head. Covered with some modesty by the gown's shield in front but gaping open in back, she thrust one side of the heavy draperies open and dropped bare feet to the floor. Toes curling against the cold, she rose, wishing for the soft carpet that had lain beside her bed in Dunfermline. In the next instant she condemned her desire for such comforts when she would deny such seduction to new captivity. Lips compressed with self-disgust, she approached the meal she had thought herself unable to partake of. But, after forcing one bite, she finished the whole with shocking haste.

As the servant-girl removed the mug and crumbs, Taine thanked her and earned a hesitant smile from one unused to appreciation for the performance of a commanded deed. Taine returned the smile with a warmth that sent the girl from the chamber full of near worship for the kind lady. Once she had gone, Taine was left with time to ponder the difficulties of her position. It had been a shock to learn that she, an unwilling visitor in her own view, was unwelcome to at least two of the castle's inhabitants.

Reluctant to rejoin the quarrelsome family group, Taine chose to remain in the chamber lost in contemplation of her woes. She washed in fresh warm water from the ewer the girl had brought. Unable to close the back-fastenings of any gown, she donned the earlier kirtle and climbed back into the dim cave formed by the deep blue brocade shielding three sides of the bed. Sitting with chin resting atop updrawn knees, she stared unseeing at the flickering dance of orange and yellow fire. She failed to note either the intricate carvings on the mantel or the quality of the table and its two chairs. Unlike the first morning at the house in Dunfermline, the richness of this chamber's furnishings, doubtless superior, save its lack of Saracen carpet, could not waylay her concerns. The problem was clear but the answer befogged. How could she end this enforced stay in the dragon's lair? A lair, moreover, shared by the growing web of a fat, black spider. Threatening creatures whichever way she turned.

In this tower, an early portion of the castle whole, a long arrow-slit served as window. A shaft of sunlight slid down its length, fell across the floor, and climbed up the bed's high edge before the creaking of the heavy door broke

Taine's preoccupation. She leaned around the curtain's edge to find Halyse coming in and closing the door behind. The unchanged friendliness of the freckled face drew a pleased smile from Taine. After the cold misgiving of her thoughts, such uncomplicated warmth was welcome.

"I've come to aid your dressing for the midday meal," Halyse announced brightly. The young servant had earlier been sent to aid the lady in dressing, but had not found the nerve to explain her purpose.

Taine's heart sank even as her eyes rose to the long, narrow opening on the sky. The sun was nearly at its zenith, and tension knotted her fingers together. She dreaded the company of the group below, the spider most of all. Through the uncertain fog drifting across her memory, she had searched the dark, monotonous days in her castle-prison for some hint of his niche in her past—and found none. Yet even the thought of him sent a shiver of foreboding over her. For years she'd taken all meals at table with only the embittered Morag, a disagreeable task that would have turned even fine fare sour. Now, she almost missed the security of a known evil whose habits were expected and more easily dealt with than this vague-looming menace. *Fool!* she berated herself. *You've not struggled this far to cower before another.*

Reading the unwanted apprehension on Taine's expressive face, Halyse offered discreet encouragement. "Our numbers are reduced this morn."

Taine looked to Halyse with dubious hope in soft green eyes.

"The earl's uncle leads his men on a hunt."

Heartened by the news, still the odd wording caught Taine's attention. "His men?" she asked. Surely all here were the earl's.

"Aye, his." Halyse turned toward the packed chest in the far corner and tossed the explanation back over her shoulder. "There are some that came with him from his forfeited estates in Scotland."

Rummaging through the chest for suitable garments, Halyse failed to see the silvery flare of alarm in Taine's eyes at the mention of Scotland. The vague menace had begun to take form. Taine was standing, face cleared of any sign of her qualms, before Halyse turned, holding a neatly folded square of cloth. As Halyse shook the creases out, Taine let the unfastened kirtle she'd first donned drop to the floor.

"The earl's been out this morn as well, been visiting the village leaders—and not afore time." A kirtle the shade of sky before dawn slid down over Taine's slender form. Halyse stepped behind to pull the laces tight before continuing, "Long they've awaited his taking the reins of this demesne into his own hand."

At this description of his personal management, nearly a quote from the earl's argument the past night, Taine cast a quick, suspicious glance back at Halyse. The castle's gossip-vine must be healthy indeed. The faint flush brightening freckles confirmed her assumption. The embarrassed Halyse's unnecessarily sharp tug on the laces sent Taine's gaze down to discover the cloth laced so tightly it outlined generous curves with shameful precision. She opened her lips to request an easing of the constraints, but a surcote of deeper blue unexpectedly descended. Tugging it into place, Halyse rushed into a patter of meaningless talk that Taine found difficult to interrupt with a demand to loosen the under kirtle. And for what purpose? After studying the surcote closely, she decided the armholes were not so deep as to reveal the kirtle's improper tightness. Leastways, not if she kept her arms down, and that should be no difficult thing as she planned to return to this chamber as soon as the meal was done.

When Taine was fully dressed, Halyse summoned the timid girl who had awakened Taine and bade her brush the lady's auburn hair. First pressing Taine onto a stool before the fire to give the girl clear access, Halyse settled in the one opposite to chatter of Bryce and his mischievous ways. Taine had wanted to deny this luxury, feeling the earlier reaffirmed need to avoid comforts for fear of growing too used to and mayhap weakened by love for what she must flee. But not wanting to rebuff the shy girl so anxious to please, Taine submitted to her long, soothing strokes.

After the nearly tamed profusion of Taine's curls were confined beneath a crespine, save only the few escapees that lovingly framed her exquisite face, Taine followed Halyse to the stairs. I am a queen—a queen—a queen. With each

downward step Taine shamelessly used the disdained title
to bolster her pride and courage. Yet on reaching the foot of
the winding staircase, though she kept her fingers still, she
refused to look at the high table's occupants. She was
unwilling to risk the precarious bravery she'd need to cross
the hall's wide expanse against direct contact with the
dragon's power. It was an intimidating distance to the dais
where he likely waited. Horribly self-conscious in crossing
the open expanse to this first public meal in the intimidating
fortress, she felt as if every eye followed her progress.
Hoping to calm what was surely a foolish fancy, she peered
surreptitiously about lower tables—only to find it true! Her
heart thumped erratically, but she tilted her chin and
pinned her gaze to Halyse, carefully following her lead.

Each person in Jorion's household, whether guardsman
or castle-serf, had heard their lord had at last brought a
bride to them. Clearly this graceful woman was she. They
studied her unabashed, seeking proof she was worthy of
their dragon. Halyse and Will, even Sander talked warmly
of the lady, yet they too had heard Thomas' repeated
warning that no wellborn woman would accept their lord as
mate. Amongst his people, the famous warrior was well
regarded, and on his behalf they were wary of possible
rejection.

His black eyes half-shielded by lowered lids, his face
expressionless, Jorion, too, closely watched his claimed
wife's approach. With the dark flames of her abundant hair
restrained, the fragility of her slender beauty was fully
revealed. How could so delicate a form contain a spirit of
such fire and pride? He stood as she neared the high table.

Although Taine had kept her eyes firmly on Halyse's back,
she could feel the dragon's presence, his gaze. When Halyse
stopped at the edge of the dais, Taine was forced to look up
into the power of his eyes. He motioned her around to sit at
his right hand. As she moved to take the seat commanded, a
sparkle caught her attention. A tear slowly welled in a
brown eye and quickly followed the glistening path laid
down a flushed cheek by one earlier. Elspeth's red-rimmed
eyes told Taine that this seat of honor had once belonged to
her. Having long been the pawn in others' games, Taine

understood the ache in the tender sensitivities of the girl now sitting on the earl's left and felt guilty, though the choice was none of hers.

It was difficult for Taine to eat. Not only because she'd eaten so much and so recently, or because of the resentment of another at the table, but because once seated at the dragon's side the golden snare of his attraction settled about and drew her in, robbing her even of steady hands. She curled her fingers together and buried them in her lap to still the strange urge to touch him. Yet she remembered how firm bronze skin with warm muscle beneath felt against her hands and the sensations the memory roused were shocking. She looked up into dark eyes where golden fires sparked and knew he, too, was remembering the feel of skin against skin.

Jorion's jaw went tight and he forced his attention from the enticing maid, unwilling to show to all his captivity by one who had attempted to reject him. To Taine, who desperately wanted to be free of the dragon's thrall, the meal seemed never-ending; but when it was done and he rose, she felt as if a part of her were pulling away.

"Elspeth." Though to both women the low, gentle velvet of Jorion's voice seemed meant as caress, in truth it held no more than the warmth of affection.

Brown eyes fairly melted as Elspeth looked up at the man she'd worshipped for years, the man who, until last eve, she'd thought to wed.

"I go to inspect my orchards—come walk with me there?" There was little to be seen in the orchards of late November, but they offered the quiet, private place to talk that Jorion sought. He'd spent long hours the night past, considering the best way to handle this matter. Though it was hard to admit, Uncle Thomas had been just in naming him cruel for introducing a bride to Elspeth without warning and without explanation of her place in his life and affections. 'Twas a blunder he must try to right. He offered Elspeth his arm and warm smile.

Although Taine told herself she must, she couldn't force her attention away from the couple. Well aware of the rarity of a smile without cynicism, she was disconcerted to feel a sudden sharp stab. Jealousy? Looking sharply away, she quickly quashed the unwelcome and dangerous sign of any emotion for the dragon save disdain.

Smiling sweetly, Elspeth stood to lay her palm on Jorion's proffered arm, nearly certain that this whole charade would soon end. She prayed so, for it threatened to rend her small, safe world to shreds. She couldn't bear to consider any future save the one mapped out long ago.

Jorion's all-too-perceptive gaze had not missed the quickly hidden flash in green eyes. It gave him the encouragement to continue his quest for the secrets of her past and her heart. Surely once wed, once freed from the self-imposed bonds of his oath to Bertwald, he could breach the citadel's defenses and attain his fire-sprite. Then, with the heat of their passion, her restraints would fall into soon-dissolving cinders.

The orchard was laid with a merry carpet of bright fallen leaves that offered comfort for the stark, nearly barren branches above. Jorion plucked one of the few remaining from a limb and twisted it between his fingers as he sought gentle opening for a well-rehearsed speech.

"I am sorry my heated disagreement with my uncle caused you pain and would unsay it." He offered the words of penitence as cushion for those meant to follow, but before he could speak further the small girl launched herself against him. He cursed himself for a weak-wit. He'd ruined his carefully prepared speech by phrasing his opening so badly.

"I knew it wasn't so." A bright smile of relief curved cherry lips. "I knew you wouldn't desert me."

Jorion was accustomed to dealing with experienced women, even to dealing with Elspeth on a far different level, but of young innocents suffering from amorous hero-worship, he had no experience. While she snuggled against him tenaciously, he softly patted her shoulder. Uneasy with the awkward position he'd led himself into, he could only be thankful that none of the men who relied on him for quick decisions and wise actions could see him in this self-induced quandary.

Long silent moments drifted by until Elspeth's thrill of

relief calmed and it occurred to her that the light touch on her shoulder lacked the warmth she felt certain a lover would demonstrate. It was more the comforting gesture of a father or far older brother. Her arms slackened. Warily she looked up into dark eyes that offered solace and a hint of embarrassment, but no passion. She stepped away, gazing at him with growing dread.

Meeting those apprehensive brown orbs was, Jorion discovered, more difficult than facing an enemy's bared sword. He loved the girl—as little sister—and had no wish to bring her unhappiness.

"I meant to say that I did not mean to discuss our relationship with another before I'd talked with you. Still" —his voice gentled and he brushed the tip of her upturned nose with one long finger—"'tis true, I am no husband for you." Fresh tears began to rain silently down paled cheeks, but wanting to help her understand his reasoning, he continued: "You were terrified last night when uncle and I argued. I have a fierce temper. You must see how miserable you would be wed to a man whose anger so frightens you."

"I could learn," Elspeth began in a trembling voice but halted as Jorion shook his head, golden hair glinting in the sun.

"Nay," he refused with a rueful smile, "'tis only your tender heart that turns you to me."

Elspeth shook her head firmly in denial.

Two large hands settled on either side of her face to hold it still. "I am your guardian, Elspeth. Don't argue with me." He'd teased her often with this restriction, but it failed to win a smile this time. He sighed and added, "I know you—always ready to defend the defenseless, champion those ostracized by others."

She opened her lips to argue again. This time, instead of teasing her, he laid his thumb across the opening. "'Tis a trait near as much a part of your beauty as black curls and dimples. Don't deny it."

The compliment earned a watery smile.

"Near as oft as I, you've heard Uncle Thomas declare that no lady of good blood would wed me and bear my sons. For purpose of proving him wrong, and naught else, you've conceived a desire to be wife to me."

Jorion watched brows gather into a scowl above the gentle-souled maid's damp eyes. As with many like-natured people, Elspeth had a streak of stubbornness, and he could see that she silently refused to accept his words.

Unaware of the stricken expression in her deep green eyes, Taine had watched the golden-haired man escort an adoring maid from the hall with apparent solicitude. Others saw her dismay and found it reassuring, this concern for their dragon's attention to another.

"Milady," a laughing voice called. "Mi-la-dy."

Only after the second, more prolonged summons did Taine turn toward the sound, a rosy blush creeping into her cheeks. Although in the last fortnight she'd heard it oft enough, she still found it difficult to identify with the term. Even in the years of her imprisonment, she'd been addressed as "Your Highness"—to her a bitter mockery.

Unbeknownst to her, Richard had slipped into Jorion's vacant chair and was grinning wryly at a preoccupation so deep he must call repeatedly to earn her attention.

"The sun, though weak, is shining and this castle is dark. Come for a stroll with me?" Richard was curious by nature, and Taine presented an irresistible puzzle. He'd heard gossip of his father's loud denunciation of the "nameless wench," but her bearing spoke of gentle breeding.

Nibbling her full lower lip with indecision, Taine cast a quick glance between the outside door and the corner stairwell. Her plan to return immediately to her private chamber above was even more inviting now than before. Yet, though wary, she was as intrigued by this unexpected man—who claimed to possess no desire for power—as he was by her.

"I will show you the famous spring that bubbles up through our rock-based mound," he enticed.

She hesitated, peering at him from the corners of her eyes unable to halt the suspicion born of bitter experience. What purpose lay behind his friendliness?

Richard's white smile, teamed with roguishly sparkling eyes, had justly earned him a reputation as a ladycharmer. Taine had never seen the like before and she blinked against its full force.

"Even will I take you to see Jorion's desert-bred horses," he offered. He took her hand and rose to his feet, nearly forcing her to rise as well, though he did not step down from the dais.

Taine succumbed to his earnest plea. For the whole silent walk past reproving eyes in the still crowded hall, she wordlessly berated herself for so easily giving way.

The sun was indeed a poorly thing that offered no warmth. Before they had even descended the long wooden steps from castle door to courtyard, Taine wished she'd insisted on returning to the cosy, fire-warmed bedchamber —or at least demanded her cloak before departing. But the discomfort of chill air was forgotten as Richard wielded his practiced wiles. She followed his lead across the packed earth of the broad courtyard and found herself laughing at his slightly wicked observations of court and the people who inhabited it. They examined the abundant clear waters bubbling up inside a small stone structure. It was locked to protect the liquid resource, which when siege threatened was more precious than gold, from being poisoned or otherwise fouled. He pointed out the covered troughs through which the spring sped water to the castle, separate kitchen, and moat. He then led her toward the inner bailey gate.

Enjoying Richard's humor, Taine little noted the heavy iron grating of the two portcullises they passed under before crossing the drawbridge. She was more interested in the moat beneath, where steadily flowing waters moved over a gently downtilted track before forming the sharp, sparkling fall at the castle's back. Beyond lay the village, orchard on its far side. The distant pattern of dark branches against a pale sky like delicate lace brought to Taine pricking thoughts of the earl and his young ward.

Richard saw clouds begin to gather in her soft green eyes and lightly touched her arm. "The horse yard is over here." He motioned toward the opposite side of the village.

Taine welcomed the distraction and, experienced as Richard was, the captivating smile she rewarded him with nearly halted him mid-step.

In companionable silence they skirted the village and meandered down a path through harvested fields. Richard jestingly described a childish prank he'd played on his father, for which Jorion had willingly shouldered the blame, saying one mark more or less would mean little difference on the whole. Listening closely, Taine failed to notice when he trailed to a stop and idly leaned back against a strong stone wall.

"These desert horses of Jorion's are a special breed." Richard waved toward a cluster of sleek, beautifully proportioned animals on the far side of the grey rock barrier.

Surprised, Taine looked quickly where he indicated. She hadn't realized they'd reached their destination. Richard's gesture had startled the mighty stallion standing near. He leaped into motion, and others followed. They raced across the wide meadow toward the dark shadows of the forest at its far edge, then suddenly back again. Enthralled by the animals' swift grace, their hooves scarcely seeming to touch the earth, she rested her hands on the rough stones of the wall and leaned out to better view the magical sight.

Richard's attention was caught by a gleam on the hand resting close by. Glancing down he examined the band he'd little noted before. The women of the court were most times laden with rings of far greater value, but this had an elegant symmetry seldom found. With one finger he lightly traced its convoluted design.

Taine froze at the touch. Eyes widened with dismay dropped to the hand he lifted for a closer view of the interesting object.

"Delicate and unique, like you." He flashed her another of his famous smiles. "How did you come by such a lovely thing?" His casual question on an item surely of small import earned a defensive response little expected.

To Taine his words seemed a challenge much like the dragon's and she snapped, "It belonged to my mother and grandmother before—a gift upon a daughter's betrothal."

Startled by her curt answer, Richard's curiosity leaped higher. "I see," he quietly responded, watching her closely. "Then with your recent betrothal to Jorion, it must be newly given you."

Taine jerked her hand from beneath his and tightly twisted it into the folds of her periwinkle surcote, angry with herself for revealing this detail to yet another.

The haste with which Taine hid her hand was a useless effort. Richard had already noted the permanent crease on her finger that could only be created by a ring worn for long years. He studied the down-bent head whose hair even in cold sunlight glowed with dark flames. What matter the truth of the maid? Jorion had chosen her as his own and that was enough to earn his acceptance.

"Whatever my blunder, I am sorry and to whatever purpose lies behind your words, I yield." Richard softly reassured Taine, reaching out to untangle her fingers from ill-treated cloth. "Although many women are willing to offer their company," he smiled sardonically, "Jorion is near the only man who truly stands me as friend—and I him. As you will be his, I would be your friend too." Holding her hand upon his palm, he laid his other atop and closed his hands to warm the cold fingers between, quietly adding, "Jorion has had enough of rejection. I only beg you to spare him yours."

Taine looked up into the steady blue gaze of a man who offered friendship, with a price—a promise she could not give. Her earlier suspicion of a purpose behind his warmth seemed confirmed.

Richard saw the unspoken conflict in eyes deepening to the green of a storm-darkened forest and cursed himself. What weak, useless friendship would it be that depended on one's compliance to another's restraints. He prided himself on his ability to quickly judge the value of a person and was almost certain this mysterious maid was worthy of unqualified support.

"Whatever choices you make"—he gently squeezed the fingers in his hold—"I would be your friend."

Jorion's lips thinned to a tight line on seeing the two figures nearly entwined and absorbed in close conversation. He'd thought to distract Elspeth from her useless tears with this visit to his horse yard, but found more than he'd sought. It seemed Taine, like so many other highborn women, had fallen under Richard's spell. To see the others succumb to his practiced charm had been amusing, but Taine was a different matter altogether. Taine he'd already claimed for his own.

Over his companion's shoulder Richard saw the scowling

man approach and had difficulty restraining a grin. Ever invincible to feminine wiles, for the first time in his life the cynical, hard-shelled dragon was jealous. But even enjoyment of the rare sight could not long hold Richard's gaze from Elspeth. For all he felt no sorrow for the cause, the petite maid's downcast and red-rimmed eyes smote his heart.

Elspeth, too, had seen the couple so close that in sunlight they'd nearly cast a single shadow. An unexpected but sharp dagger seemed to pierce her unwary soul, instantly driving self-pity away. To ease the pain, she dropped her gaze to the tufts of wild grass at her feet. When Jorion stopped, she stopped, and only then allowed her eyes to travel up the blue-gowned woman.

Richard was shocked by the venom in the brown eyes glaring at Taine. Jealousy here too? For Jorion? Nay, her burning gaze had locked with concentrated spite on joined hands. A small spark of hope began to glow. Mayhap she begrudged Taine's time with him? His spirit soared with the possibilities in dreams he'd never dared aspire to fulfill. He'd long ago accepted the need to face reality with unbiased practicality—if one had no skill to arms, one found other talents to build around. In this instance, however, the prize was so precious he would risk all in pursuit, and the possibilities in Elspeth's jealousy were a matter he planned to test at the earliest opportunity. But now—

"Come, we must leave the newly betrothed in privacy." Richard released Taine's fingers and stepped forward to lightly lift Elspeth's hand, intending to lead her back to the castle.

Elspeth snatched her hand from Richard. His hurtful taunt of the previous evening was still fresh and not something she would easily forgive this man who dallied with her replacement. She whirled to rush away.

Richard's eyes widened with surprise, but he shrugged, feigning an unconcern he was far from feeling. With a merry wink at Taine he followed Elspeth's path.

Alone with the dragon, Taine again turned toward the horses whose beauty sudden tension left her too blind to see. He'd moved close to stand a mere handbreadth away and she'd never been more conscious of the sheer size of him. The golden links of the dragon's enthrallment crept around her, bringing awareness of the overwhelming man that danced on her nerves. For the first time since leaving her chamber, she remembered all at once the tightly laced underkirtle. Mindful of her intent to keep her arms close, she wrapped them about her midriff.

It did nothing to lighten Jorion's mood, this immediate turning away of his soon-to-be bride who, without quailing, had shared such close commune with Richard. Pushing aside the unwelcome comparison, he looked toward the animals feasting on the quickly browning grasses of autumn.

"There"—Jorion pointed toward a small roan filly—"there is the steed I promised you."

Remembering his earlier description of the horse as nearly matching her hair, Taine easily picked out the one he intended for her. Warm pleasure rose unbidden. To cover the fluster its coming evoked, she rushed into speech. "Richard told me these are the horses you brought from the deserts." She looked up and found narrowed black eyes examining her every inch. Breath caught and fingers twisted into the periwinkle cloth where they clenched beneath her arms on either side.

"Nay," Jorion denied, his sardonic smile appearing. "Here mostly are descendants of those few."

Taine's creamy cheeks warmed at her foolish lack of thought, and Jorion's deepened with approval of his firesprite's artless allure. He added, "I've come to appreciate the strength and stamina of the great destriers, yet the grace and speed of the desert breed draws me more."

Focusing her eyes with determination on the roan horse, she responded. "Aye, they are the most graceful creatures I have ever seen, beyond the soaring of a highlander bird." It came to her of a sudden that by twisting her kirtle she further tightened the cloth where she would rather slacken it and immediately loosed her hold to wrap hands palm flat around her waist.

Jorion saw Taine's arms tighten yet again about her slender frame and assumed her suffering from the cold. He doffed his gold-embroidered cloak and draped it about delicate shoulders even as he silently questioned the thoughtless haste that had sent her walking without her own.

Although thankful for the shield, the dragon's cloak increased Taine's discomfort. Suddenly enveloped in the garment still warmed by the heat of his body, she rushed even more determinedly onward, giving voice to the first thought that came to mind. "It must have been difficult to leave the home of your youth."

Jorion was surprised at her willingness to talk of his Saracen past. The subject made the women of his experience uncomfortable and was one he avoided whenever possible. "There was no difficulty in either the choice or the doing," he slowly responded, looking down into eyes the same misty green as the land his mentor had promised. "Father Aleric spoke of it so often and so vividly it seemed more my home than the place where I lived."

Taine could have bitten her tongue for the ill-considered words. Knowing of his childhood trials she should have seen how unlikely was a fondness for the desert home.

"Only would I have missed my horses," he continued, "and thus I brought them with me. They're my friends—near the only ones."

"Nay," Taine immediately disagreed, Richard's words fresh in mind. "Richard is your friend." To forestall her fingers from twining in the black velvet cloak as instinct demanded, she rested them on the cold, rough stones laid up to form the waist-high wall.

Jorion's eyes narrowed on Taine's earnest face. Had she some ulterior reasoning for her immediate defense? And how did she know who was friend and who was not? He merely nodded, leaning forward to rest his forearm on the wall next to her hands.

"There are others, too," Taine rashly continued, seeking to stave off the warm tingles of awareness his closeness brought. "Your companions at the fair and in the English court."

Jorion's smile had taken on its sardonic one-sided twist. "Just as my grandfather accepted me for the sake of continuing the family name, many others accept me for the sake of all that name means."

Taine's eyes flew up to meet the contempt in his.

"They accept and claim me friend for the strength of the dragon and the power I am, no matter the extent of their private disdain for my tainted blood."

Jorion's eyes shifted to stare bitterly at the dark edge of the forest while Taine watched, realizing anew that he had been as poorly used as she by the powers of their past and present. But to what path had they driven his nature? Had he learned to return like with like? Despite the questions, sympathy grew and although she struggled to push it aside as a weakness she must disallow, her spirit reached out.

Feeling her gaze, Jorion looked down and in eyes of soft sea foam found a gentle comfort and a simple understanding seldom seen.

Downcast, Elspeth huddled on a small three-legged stool drawn near the family solar's low-burning fire, brooding over her doomed dreams. What would become of her now that Jorion had claimed another? She heavily sighed her dejection. There was no mystery in the answer. As heiress she had no lack of applicants for her hand and one would be chosen. Most likely some fat and elderly lord who'd worn out a wife—or two—and had need of another. One young and strong with much to add to family coffers. Distaste quivered through her. She pressed her hands to her eyes as if by so doing she could block the vision of an obese and aging groom smiling lecherously at her. *Oh, pray God,* she silently pleaded, *let him be young and handsome like Jorion—or Richard.* No, she immediately denied the last thought, hands dropping to her lap. Richard was not and would never be a possible husband for her.

Having followed Elspeth's path, Richard stood in the doorway watching the anguish clear from his view of her slumped back. When her hands fell with seeming despair to her lap, he deemed it time to interrupt her flow of self-pity for the loss of Jorion as bridegroom.

"Have you forgiven me yet, sweet cousin?" he asked, his smile not reflected in eyes that steadily watched her abruptly stiffened back.

To suddenly have the object of her thoughts speak from behind made her self-conscious and defensive. "You are no cousin of mine," she snapped back, turning to face him with dimpled chin tilted defiantly.

Richard's smile vanished as he met her eyes with a long, unwavering gaze, only at length responding. "'Struth, there is no blood between us."

Elspeth's eyes fell away from his. What did he mean by that? Her mind raced but she rejected the most obvious interpretation as wishful thinking born of her recent lapse. Richard was popular with the ladies of the court, his reputation well known. He had his pick of their number and would find no use for one such as she, plump and shy, at least not beyond greed for her extensive dower lands. Though she knew her worth lay, as that of all women, in her dowry, she found a distaste for the thought of Richard seeing only gold and land in her. Nay, she thought, softly nibbling her lip, well she knew his lack of desire for the power of riches. Therefore, it seemed plain, he could have no use for her.

Seeing the gentle maid's confusion, Richard silently berated himself as an unfeeling oaf, forcing on her a clearly strange and doubtless unwelcome concept. He immediately sought to turn her thoughts to warmer patterns by questioning, "Remember the song-story game I taught you when first you came to live within these walls?" Laughing softly, he tweaked the small curl resting against her rosy cheek just as he had when the shy girl-child had first come to this awesome castle. He, as a stripling lad quickly proving a disappointment to his father, had taken delight in the undemanding company of that little maid.

The tug was an oft-repeated gesture from Elspeth's past, and she glanced up to meet a familiar teasing smile. He'd suddenly reverted to childhood friend. More than willing to accept the transformation, she was relieved to revert to their traditional relationship. There had been enough changes in the past two days. Happy with the reprieve, she nodded the answer to his query, her eyes dancing.

Richard moved to the edge of the wide fireplace where a lute hung by deep green ribbons tied around its graceful neck. He lifted it down and began to lightly strum a familiar tune. They had played the game often during her childhood, filling many an evening and rainy-day hour. Following the usual pattern, he began a story in rhyme, playing the tune again as she added the next verse and portion of the story, then he again, and so on and on. The stories thus told, sometimes sweet and sometimes sad, but most times silly, renewed their once-warm companionship.

Chapter 10

THE DAYS OF AUTUMN were growing short and darkness fell even before the evening meal was in readiness. Daylight had deserted the land, but a yellow glow was cast across the room by the light from firebrands along stone walls and candles held aloft on metal circles within circles. On the far end their light was met and joined by the massive fireplace's flickering blaze while at the lower tables waxen tapers burned, each a white star against an orange sky. Behind the high table the brilliance of a full moon shone from the rows of candles held by three iron pyramids.

Involuntarily, soft green eyes watched as white and orange reflections danced over Jorion's hair, apparently in time to the gentle rhythm of timbrels and pipes that had begun now the meal was near concluded. Earlier, at the horse-yard wall, their visual communion had been broken by the nudge of a horse recognizing his master and coming close. As they walked back to the castle, they'd talked quietly of Will and Halyse, their mischievous son's antics, of Mercia—the girl who daily came to brush Taine's hair— and of other simple matters. In the growing harmony, Taine

148

had begun to dream of the life she might have led had she truly no past to drag behind like heavy leaden chains.

In deference to the music, the dull roar of voices began to fade. This meal was a banquet specially planned in honor of the earl's return—one that more than his family could share—and Taine had not been prepared for so large a gathering or for the din that filled a hall of a size to easily hold two and more of the one in her castle-prison. At right angles on either side of the dais, two long lines of trestle tables stretched down the room's full length. And even now, when filled with feasters replete with the plentiful meal past, the hall teemed with people.

Young pages, anxious to please, had attentively served at table. Following each course they brought small bowls of scented water for rinsing of the fingers used to eat; and, for drying, they held out clean cloths folded over upraised arms. Taine silently watched and saw the truth of the dragon's claim of nobles seeking his friendship, despite private disdain for the dragon's blood. By sending their young sons to foster under Radwyn, first learning noble ways as page and then training for knighthood as squire, they sought strong ties with the powerful lord. Taine's attention was caught by words that fair dripped with scorn.

"What use is there in wasting time with serfs and villagers?"

Taine looked to the speaker of sniping words. Sir Thomas' sneer was only nominally covered by lips twisted into the parody of smile.

"It met my purpose," Jorion coldly replied, meeting the older man's gaze steadily.

"Hah, you think that such actions are proper means to manage such extensive lands?" Uncle Thomas' false smile had gone and his eyes gleamed with derision for so foolish a deed.

"Aye, proper indeed and glad I am for the doing." Jorion's face was completely motionless but for the muscle pulsing against his jaw. "With my own eyes I've learned the truth of recent management with more haste and clarity than ever I would from the reports of others."

Sir Thomas' dark brows lowered into a threatening scowl,

while the normal high color of his face brightened several shades. "What charge are you laying at my door?"

"The people have been taxed beyond their endurance. They're near to starving with winter coming on." Jorion's voice was so calm and flat that those who knew him best would take heed.

Richard saw the brewing storm his father was too angry to perceive, but could only stand back from the fray, for neither man would accept pacifying words from him.

"How did you think you earned the money to go warring with your king?" Uncle Thomas snapped back at Jorion.

"My coffers are already full to overflowing. I have less need for gold than for healthy serfs to till the soil and keep my demesne strong."

"Healthy serfs?" Ridicule heaped bitter gall on the words. "What value that? So a few die, there's ever more to take their places. Thinning them out only means fewer to consume the harvest's bounty."

Mesmerized by the conflict between the two men, but never in doubt as to where her sympathies lay, Taine watched the fury lighting golden fires in Jorion's dark eyes and held her breath waiting for his response.

"I was born where people are bought and sold, where the value of one like Aleric is measured in coins. Early I learned that a man's worth cannot be measured in coins or by the amount of produce it takes to keep him alive." Jorion's mouth clamped into a firm line as if biting back further words.

Taine was impressed with the dragon's control and amazed by this man more concerned with the people of his lands than with enriching himself, but had little time to ponder its meaning in the midst of the heating argument.

"So, you will strip me of my role as manager of Radwyn?" Uncle Thomas demanded, countenance achieving a vivid ruby hue.

"Did I not tell you so last eve?" Jorion's answer was prompt and harsh.

"I had hoped, on further reflection, you would remember the debt you owe me for the years I gave in care of you." The words were as stiff as the back of the man who spoke them.

Jorion's one-sided smile was all of bitterness as he responded, "Uncle, when have you ever let me forget the debt of gratitude I owe you for the great favor of your care? Whereas another who gave more has asked naught of me and accepted only a humble abode on my lands." Jorion paused, regaining control over his escalating ire. "Have you not lived in my home these many years, since in your support of a deposed Scottish king you threw your own heritage away?"

"Threw it away? Threw it away?" Furious, Uncle Thomas jumped to his feet. "It was not thrown away but stolen by that greedy king you follow."

"Nay." Jorion firmly shook his head, eyes never leaving the older man's. "You had but to submit to him and it would still be yours."

"Aye, and submit to him will I never!" The crack of fist against palm resounded in the amazingly quiet hall, where every ear was trained on the heated dispute.

The black gaze never wavered. "The loss of your lands is your own folly, and I will no longer give you control of mine. Be content that I yet allow you to remain in my castle."

Uncle Thomas whirled and stomped from the hall. Once his ascending footsteps could no longer be heard on the stairs and the sound of a chamber door slammed shut above had ceased reverberating, Richard spoke sotto voce: "Methinks he still believes John Baliol will regain the Scottish throne—a measure of the fool he is."

From the moment Jorion spoke of his uncle's support of a Scottish king, 'til the confirmation of Richard's words concerning the Baliol, Taine heard nothing through her heart's loud pounding. The shock of finding the spider a supporter of her foe had parted the mists of youthful memory with a stunning lightning bolt of recognition. Happily the argument had held the attention of all in the hall or the terror on her face would have been revealed. From the arms of a dead man on a rocky, storm-darkened shore, she, as a young child, had been lifted and spirited away to a dismal castle-prison—by the dragon's uncle. Unwittingly she had stepped into the spider's web.

Consumed with alarm, Taine soon found an excuse to withdraw to her chamber, where she paced uselessly until long after the castle settled into sleep. Her only hope was to back out of the spider's web before he sighted his prey, before he learned who she was. Clearly, she reassured herself, he had not the knowledge now. Proof of that lay in his derision of Jorion for taking to wife one whose family they knew nothing of. Moreover, he'd described her a nameless wench. Yet certainty that he was unaware of her identity offered only temporary comfort. Were he to discover her secret, doubtless he would see her delivered back to her prison—or furtively see an end to the threat to Baliol goals that was she.

Weary, aching with growing tension, Taine undressed and climbed up into the high bed, leaving one side of the draperies slightly open to admit warmth from the hearth. Praying for sleep's oblivion, still she lay staring up at ever changing patterns of flickering firelight on the bed's canopy. Nerves as jagged as the edge of an unhoned dagger, strong apprehensions for the future and memories from the past tangled in her mind. When the slumber of exhaustion at last overtook her, terrifying dreams replayed endlessly in her mind; but, even as she began to scream her fears, a golden dragon whose kiss was fire appeared. Drawn inexorably to the flame, she struggled against an overpowering hold. Her eyes snapped open to find a dark face framed by hair of molten gold. Dream-hazed, she was uncertain whether this dragon was born of myth or flesh and blood. Fearing either, her struggles wildly increased.

After the attempt to capture Taine their last night in Dunfermline, Jorion had lost confidence in the safety of any abode, even this great stone castle in the heart of Radwyn lands. Thus, although it was believed he occupied his own chambers, he slept each night in one adjoining Taine's. Now, wakened suddenly by desperate cries and fearing another attempt at abduction, he had rushed into Taine's chamber. He swept one edge of the bed's draperies completely aside to find the delicate maid full caught in the grip of fearsome night-terrors. Dropping immediately to her side, he'd tried to waken her with a gentle shaking that only seemed to increase her fears. He had then attempted to still her struggles by lifting her close against his hard chest. When a delicate chin lifted, sending thick curls of flame over his arm, and eyes flaring with green fire met his, he knew her awake and fighting not dreams, but him. Powerful arms loosened their grip.

Heart pounding erratically, Taine leaned as far from him as his slackened hold allowed.

Through the gloom of the bed heavily draped against autumn chill, Jorion looked into eyes near as dark as his own. "Share the source of your fear," he quietly invited, "and I will try to ease it for you."

The low-burning fire, blocked from Taine's view by the dragon's broad form, glowed on golden hair, but she could not discern the face laid in shadow. She had awakened from a dream assault to find herself in this man's arms, from the pull of the dragon's lure only to find herself caught in the temptation of his soft words and gentle arms. Thus was confirmed her belief that truly he was a man to fear above all others, a man who could entice her into giving what she had sworn would she never.

"You," Taine cried, pushing away. "You are the source of my night-terrors." Staring up into the dragon's face, so quickly she could not be sure it was true, she saw a fleeting shadow cross his features before they blanked into his usual impassive mask.

At her retort, Jorion's arms dropped immediately from her tender curves, as if sundered by one of his double-edged swords. This afternoon he'd been a fool to read more than pity in soft green eyes. Crushed to find her disgust for him so deep it induced night-terrors, Jorion turned and left without speaking.

Taine felt his pain in the rejection pierce her own heart, but it was too late to call back the words—he was gone. Lying back and pulling the heavy coverlet over her suddenly chilled body, she sought with limited success to reassure herself of the rightness of her action, justify her claim. What matter in rejection now or later? She could not stay, must be gone before the dragon knew his prize or the spider sighted his prey. She rolled over, burying her face in a soft pillow to muffle her shameful sobs.

"Aye, we found them." The speaker, short, dark, and filled with his own self-importance, nearly sneered the words. "An' never have I seen such inept men. Their masters must be desperate for aid as to find such incompetent fools, 'tis certain, they've drained the dregs of the wine barrel."

Staring into the busy courtyard with hard eyes, Jorion had waited for news the other delayed. Gifted rather with another's useless observations, for all its truth, he turned the power of his gaze to the two men at his back. They had been sent to track Taine's pursuers from the fair and had only now returned.

The man behind the speaker, though nearly a head taller and barrel-chested, fell back beneath the command in his lord's eyes and hastened to tell what the other had held back for greater effect. "We followed them to the castle of Duncan McLewell."

Jorion's eyes hardened to the power of sharp black knives, but he nodded his understanding. Distracted, he waved the two men away and stood alone pondering the news of McLewell's involvement. The Scottish noble had submitted to King Edward and retained his lands, but none doubted that his loyalty lay with Baliol and he had never been called to join Edward's battles. Aye, he was a staunch Baliol supporter. The question was how did one delicate maid figure into Baliol intrigues?

"Held back for your coming, the morning repast awaits."

The words broke Jorion's preoccupation and he turned to find Will behind him in the half-light of the stable's morn.

Taine had awakened from a heavy, troubled sleep that had crept over her unbid, foiling her crazy plan born of desperation. She had decided to rise in the wee hours and flee before others were about and had closed her eyes only to work out each detail. In the next instant, it seemed, she'd opened them to discover Mercia slipping into her chamber and the castle already astir with the many demands of a new day. At that hour and from a castle filled with curious people it would be impossible to slip away unseen.

She was waiting at the high table when the dragon appeared and shied away as he took his seat at her side. Yet, netted again in his tantalizing aura she looked up straight into intense black eyes. The impact trembled through her.

She couldn't pull her gaze from his and her heart thumped wildly. She wanted to reach up to touch him but consciously curled her fingers into her palms, preventing a fall to forbidden temptation. Jorion's jaw went rigid. But, more aware of their surroundings and audience, he forced his attention toward the waiting page and the tray he held. The encounter had lasted no more than a few moments, but to Taine it seemed time had stopped and stolen her breath. Drawing in a deep, ragged gasp, she bent her head and kept her traitorous eyes grimly on the plate they shared.

As the meal progressed he steadily ate all that was offered, while she refused most and did no more than pick at what she took. In the dour castle of her imprisonment, frugal meals had offered few choices—oat cakes and goat milk a part of near every one. But here in Castle Dragonsward even the morning repast consisted of a wide variety of dishes, so many they were long in the serving.

Jorion felt Taine's tension and misread its source. Her rejection of the night past was too fresh. Curious as she clearly was, had she such distaste for him that she could not bear to so much as sit by his side and share with him a meal? Bravely deciding to play upon her curiosity, willing or no, he took his cue from Richard's practiced skills and turned to Taine with a stunning smile as he lifted a portion of fresh wheaten bread to her.

She had once thought Richard's charming smile attractive, but now found it a poor imitation of the one that graced Jorion's face, absent of cynicism and filled with warm invitation. Her mouth fell open only to be nudged by the flaky crust he laid against her lips. She accepted the bite, but its fine taste was lost on one caught in enthrallment. Elspeth's frown called her to a realization of her silly expression. She bent her head to diligently study twined fingers, as if without such visual restraint they might fall to temptation and touch the strong hand still holding the golden bread toward her. A short shake of her head sent light glancing over the cloud of auburn curls only partially restrained by a crespine. Richard had not come down to the morning meal and so Taine could not turn to him for distraction.

"I havna seen Bertwald since we arrived." Tension thickened Taine's brogue as to forestall further such temptations she rushed into speech. "I go tae visit him this day."

"Hold till I have been to the stables where a mare of mine sickened last eve," Jorion quietly suggested, "and I will accompany you, for neither have I visited with Aleric during that time."

'Twas precisely what Taine did not want and silently rebuked herself for sharing the plan. "Oh, nay, 'tis unnecessary," she hastily refused. "I can find my way alone and, in truth, would appreciate private time with him." She spoke without pausing to consider the wisdom of her words and could only hope they would not tell him the intent of her deed.

Though Jorion nodded acceptance of her wishes, beneath his apparent complacency, he caught the unnatural haste of her refusal. It struck a note of suspicion in his soul, and he decided to follow her path, unseen.

Anxious to be gone on her errand, the meal seemed never-ending to Taine. Only to allay the dragon's doubts did she force a few bites down.

Jorion was not fooled but continued his meal as if unaware of her growing strain. Fearing she would snap like a bow drawn too tight if he lingered longer, as soon as seemed natural, he rose to depart. A conscientious guard captain, Will also stood.

"Nay, Will," Jorion quickly waved him back into his seat, "I go only to my stables to check on the ailing Moondream."

Will nodded, straight dark hair falling over one eye. He knew of the mare's plight, and the earl's love of the animal made his concern aright and the task a natural one. Never one to question his lord, he did not wonder at the earl's rejection of his company.

"After all have done," Jorion directed, "set up the quintain for the squires to practice their tilting. Now we've come back to peace, 'tis time for their training to continue." An excited hum immediately began from where the squires took their meals at the bottom of one long line of lower tables. Brushing back his hair, Will grinned while Jorion's one-sided smile appeared, its teasing mockery holding no bite.

Taine watched as the golden-haired lord, all masculine grace and power, strode toward the outward door, unaware of the attention her rapt gaze drew from those still within. Pulling her eyes from the iron-bound planks closing behind him, she found herself the object of Elspeth's resentful glare, a small blow, only mildly disquieting compared to the steady, narrow scrutiny of the watching man who seemed more than ever an evil spider waiting to trap the unwary. She must escape before he recognized her as his prey. Desperate to elude his threat, she stood and made excuse to leave the table.

A light drizzle had begun to fall like dew from the wrong direction. Hastily descending wooden stairs to the damp courtyard, free for once of dust kicked up by every breeze or passing step and foreshadowing the mire of winter, she moved purposefully toward the day-opened portcullis and then across the lowered drawbridge. This was the first time she'd had opportunity to walk without guard or guide from the castle since meeting the dragon. By his own words she knew his intention to visit an ailing horse and, enjoying the feeling of freedom, she looked neither left nor right as she made her way to the small cottage Bertwald shared with Father Aleric.

She knocked twice at the wide oaken door and waited, nerves stretched taut. No answer was forthcoming. She lifted her fist to rap again but paused a breath from her goal when Bertwald spoke from behind.

"Ah, lassie, you come tae visit wi' me?"

Taine whirled and nearly threw herself into Bertwald's arms, her heart responding to the affection in his tone and forgetful of the harsh thoughts she'd earlier harbored for his choice to desert her and live with another beyond the castle's inner bailey wall. Her friend he was and she could ask near anything of him.

"Bertie, you've got to help me. I've fallen into my enemy's hands, did he but know it and I fear he soon will."

Bushy grey brows gave Bertwald's craggy face a fierce expression and when, as now, he scowled, 'twas a fearsome sight indeed. He wasted no breath in answer but flung open the cottage door and shoved her unceremoniously inside.

For such talk privacy was imperative. As Father Aleric had gone to morning mass in the earl's chapel and not yet returned, the cottage would fill the need.

"I dinna ken your meaning." Bertwald spoke only after he'd sent the door shut with a snap. "Speak it plain."

Safe with Bertwald in private, the enormity of the danger revealed at the past evening's meal swept over Taine. She trembled and stepped near to him. "You've got to hie me away, Bertie." Her fingers curled into the loose cloth of his tunic with a death grip. "You've got to, else I'll be trapped for all my life."

Bertwald felt as if he'd been set adrift at the edge of some accelerating whirlpool. She'd not complied with his demand to speak plainly. What reasoning lay behind her plea? He floundered, searching for some firm mooring to bring sense to her words. Had the earl done some alarming deed to make her ponder a marriage with him as a lifetime trap? Sparse grey strands whipped about Bertwald's face as he shook his head in confusion, opening his lips to demand a clear explanation for her panic.

Caught in the passion of her entreaties, both failed to note the opening door. True to his intent, Jorion had followed Taine's path and heard her desperate appeal for freedom from a lifelong trap. The clear rejection added to the one in dark hours was a fierce, near-killing blow to tender vulnerabilities opened to her as to no other. After the strength of her night-terrors, her disgust of him was so strong that she would rather seek the dangers of roads in a strange land than share a soft life with him. He nearly groaned with the pain of that truth. The thought of those dangers, and the perils her secret past clearly offered, filled him with a fear that proved she unknowingly had caught him firmly in her snare. He was fated to see her protected, even though she would deny him reward for the deed.

"There is nowhere you can go that I cannot find you." Jorion's words were as bitter-cold as the first snowstorm of winter. He hoped to frighten them into remaining, for although, in truth, he would find them even should they flee, he might be too late.

At the icy words, both Bertwald and Taine whirled toward their speaker, a broad shadow against heavy grey skies.

Taine was startled but not surprised to find the dragon again demonstrating his habit of filling doorways when least-expected and little-welcomed. He stepped forward into the light of a small peat fire. His bronzed face, stiffly controlled, could not hide from her the dragon's injured pride. If she ran now, 'twould be a terrible attack on his abused self-esteem and an insult that could not go unpunished. Strangely, she found the notion of suffering his punishment less a deterrent than the desire to protect him from another hurtful injury to his self-respect. 'Twas a frightening discovery, this caring for a man.

❧ *Chapter* 11 ❧

HEAVY CLOUDS AGAIN LAID an oppressive mantle over Castle Dragonsward. What brave light survived the battle through their thick barrier was severely weakened by the fight and offered little more than the colorless light of pre-dawn hours. Into the massive walls, halfway between the level of Taine's bedchamber and the solar level below, had been cut a small room, barely large enough for two to stand within. Taine stared out from its small window into the day's perpetual twilight, a depressing reflection of her mood.

She'd had few nights of good sleep since falling to the dragon's snare, and this morn had longed to linger abed with privacy to continue the same search for means to escape that had prevented much-needed sleep the night just gone. But Halyse, in her cheery manner, had replaced the shy servant, Mercia, and come to awaken her, a deed not appreciated. The brightness of Halyse's spirits made it clear she was happily home. Though pleased for the woman, now friend, such bubbling spirits were difficult for Taine to meet so early after a night of despair. The request she'd come to deliver was even less welcome. The request—hah, command more like—for her to meet him in the solar came from the dragon.

The solar was but a few paces further. She really must go. Still, Taine lingered at the window cut through thick stone. Impressive always, on this grey day the view without, a vast panorama of field and woodland, was dismal. Even the few autumn-toned leaves remaining on ever more barren branches, whether on the fruit trees in neat orchard rows or the thick-grown trees of the forest beyond winter-barren fields, seemed stripped of color.

Reluctant but fearing to worsen the dragon's mood by her late arrival, at last Taine forced herself to leave the small embrasure and move to the solar's door. Hand on its iron latch, she hesitated. The roar of a loud voice carried through the solid oak barrier. Her brows puckered. She'd come to meet the dragon, but nowise could its source be he. In past she'd heard him in rage and his voice deepened to a rumble but was deadly calm.

The door slowly swung open under her hand. She saw Elspeth clasping a small black cat protectively to her bosom and cringing away from the room's other occupant. In the moments before the door opened wider, Taine wildly wondered who would offer threat to so timid a girl? Her protective instincts rose for Elspeth, who as heiress was prey of men as surely as she.

"I'll not have such an evil omen in my home." The threatening words were so loudly spoken they seemed certain to rattle even the castle's thick stone walls.

Taine tensed even before Uncle Thomas' broad form came into view. His face the brilliant crimson of an English poppy, he reached out and snatched the hapless kitten from Elspeth's arms.

Taking a deep, ragged breath, Taine stepped across the room with determination. "I wouldna credited it possible for a strong man to fear so small and defenseless a creature." Her words were calm but burned with sarcasm. In response to rough treatment, the "defenseless" kitten hissed with pointed teeth bared and flashed amazingly sharp claws. Undeterred by such minor blocks, Taine stretched her hands toward the animal.

Caught in their own battle, none within the solar were aware of the tall blond man who'd entered the chamber through the door Taine had left ajar. Will had slowed his arrival with urgent questions but he'd been only a few paces behind Taine when she opened the portal.

Back to Jorion, Thomas' eyes dropped to approaching hands. Stunned, he allowed the kitty's removal without argument. His eyes were fastened on the entwined gold-and-silver band he'd last seen on a small girl's hand.

Fool! Unthinkable, incredibly witless fool! Taine's silent self-castigation filled her thoughts to the exclusion of all else. Why, in the name of all the saints, had she not rid herself of the ring when first she'd won her freedom. Failing that, then after the dragon noted it. Aye, once sighted by the dragon she'd thought its sudden disappearance would raise too many questions. Thus, she'd kept it. Now she wished she'd risked the dragon's curiosity rather than the spider's certainty. For, as surely as the sun follows the moon, the spider had sighted his prey.

Jorion had heard his uncle's words and Taine's response but was unaware of the undercurrents swirling about them as he spoke in her support.

"Have you forgot so quickly, uncle? 'Tis my castle and the animal is welcome here. If for that you find my home uncomfortable, mayhap you should seek lodging elsewhere." Eyes dark as night met the other man's renewed but impotent fury.

Having relinquished the subject of their words, Thomas' hands clenched into fists with no possible goal. He whirled and stalked away. *'Tis only a matter of time now 'til the deed be accomplished,* he told himself. Having waited these many years, he could wait the little time longer to get his own back. He'd not hoarded Radwyn's resources all this time to see the fief grow wealthy nor to support Edward's wars against his own. No, never that. The door slammed behind him.

Once the loud crash reverberated into silence, Taine looked back to the younger girl whose cheeks were pale and eyes were wide with alarm for the scene she'd been party to. Seeing a fear momentarily greater than her own, Taine thrust her desperation into temporary abeyance and soothed the other.

"The kitty is yours and safe to you now." Taine held the bundle of silky black fur toward Elspeth. Having settled against the soft comfort of Taine's breasts only to again be dangled precariously in offering to another, the subject of all the fuss again bared her teeth.

Elspeth fairly jumped back, hands held palm up to ward off the gift. When the kitty rested calmly once again in Taine's arms, Elspeth let her arms fall. "I—I—" she stammered. "You are her savior. Clearly she prefers you." By her willingness to aid the little cat, Taine had taken a great leap up in Elspeth's estimation. Elspeth herself, as much as she might wish it untrue, shared some portion of the superstitions that turned even the overwhelming Sir Thomas to coward.

Jorion tweaked a shiny ebony lock of Elspeth's hair. "'Tis as I said, you will ever go about defending even those unacceptable creatures you yourself fear."

Elspeth's cheeks suddenly burned near as bright as Thomas' and her eyes dropped to examine the pattern she meticulously traced with one leather-clad toe.

"Take heart," Taine softly consoled the shamed girl. "I have no fear of an animal so small and will care for it." Then, fearing she'd further insulted where she wished to heal, she added, "There are things I fear"—green eyes sliding sideways to peer at the overwhelming man at her side. Even over the anxiety for Sir Thomas' discovery, she felt the power of him. In truth, she feared him, not for his physical strength but for the strength of his attraction.

Elspeth's gentle brown eyes rose to Taine's warm smile. Another defense was broken. Nowise could this lady be the ogress she'd wanted to believe the day past. Elspeth nodded her gratitude and shyly returned the smile.

Assuming Taine, too, in reality wished to be free of the creature both had protected, Jorion moved to relieve her of the purring burden.

Taine saw only the dragon reaching toward her, a dreaded yet anticipated deed. One that had recently offered a nearly irresistible temptation to forget the dangers of her past and yield to his fire. She reflexively stepped back, reminding herself that so powerful a lord would doubtless use her to attain more by forcing her to a life she refused.

Gold sparks flashed in Jorion's eyes, the sign of the dragon's fire, and Elspeth's fear strengthened fourfold. Alarmed by the prospect of further harsh words the girl rushed toward the door. Her skirts whispered across the rush-strewn floor and as she departed carefully shut the door without sound.

Once the door was closed and she was alone in the corridor, Elspeth stumbled to a halt. She dreaded the possibility of meeting curious eyes in the great hall below or sympathetic platitudes from the servant undoubtedly waiting in her chamber above. Brown eyes settled with longing on the same window embrasure Taine had earlier sought— the only hope for peaceful solitude in all this great castle, but too near the busy solar. She glanced hopefully up the stairway and was pleased to find it deserted. There was a similar nook one level higher. Thankful for the inspiration, she climbed the stairs and slipped into the small niche to tentatively sit on the cushioned ledge below the window. The seat was amazingly soft. Caught in weighty thoughts, she wiggled into a comfortable position, curled up and leaned against one wall, like the little black cat come seeking sun-warmed comfort despite the grey day.

Timid, far too timid, she berated herself. Jorion was right and she wrong. She knew Jorion well, trusted him more than any other, yet without fail his dark temper and aura of dangerous strength only temporarily at rest made her uneasy and more. A steady rain began to fall, casting a grey veil over the rolling view and blurring the softer tones of meadow into the forest's deep hues. The mists seemed to spill into her thoughts, and she questioned what she never had before. Had she convinced herself that she loved Jorion for the same reasons she had defended the kitty? Was Jorion right of this too? Was her love of him love for brother, much as she felt for Richard? No! Sitting up sharply, she emphatically rejected the thought. She didn't think of Richard as a brother, she had never fooled herself of that. She rubbed hands over her face, unwittingly seeking to erase her futile confession of a doomed love.

To Richard it was clear the winsome maid was deeply troubled, and he felt her discomfort as fully as if it were his own. So caught was she in her distress that she'd not heard him ascending the stairs nor felt his prolonged gaze. Her pain doubled in his heart with the belief that her sorrow was for the loss of another. He had loved Elspeth since she was a child, an emotion which had matured as she did, although he'd always known her destined to a greater man than he, who had only the paltry lands of his mother's dower. Had his father not stubbornly allowed the hereditary lands to be held forfeit, there'd have been hope for his suit—a fact adding a piquant acid to the relationship between him and his sire, although the elder man never understood and probably little cared for the cause.

"Are you reflecting on who your new betrothed will be, now that Jorion is to wed another?" Hopeless love left an edge of bitterness on the words.

Suddenly come upon by the subject of her thoughts, Elspeth wrapped her arms about herself to stave off a cold she'd not noticed before and stared determinedly down at the folds of her cherry-red skirt.

"Sir Osbert, mayhap?" Richard suggested. "Or James of Swiefert?"

A strong tremor passed through Elspeth. Both possible bridegrooms fully met all the characteristics of her worst fears. Old, fat, and lecherous.

"Or me?" Richard suggested after a long pause. Elspeth's eyes were firmly trained on innocent cloth and didn't see the seriousness in steady blue eyes or note the lack of teasing in his voice. Her heart had leapt with the words but now thudded painfully. 'Twas a cruel jest. How could he tease by offering what she had only admitted was her heart's desire as he spoke it. Pride triumphed over childish tears.

"I'd sooner bed a serf!" she snapped back, chin tilted defiantly as she met shocked blue eyes. She stood recklessly and rushed past Richard.

As she disappeared from sight, Richard's shoulders sagged in defeat. After Jorion had announced his intention to wed another, he'd entertained a dim hope. But expecting a sweet, innocent heiress to find him suitable was a jest. Oh, indeed, he was very popular at court for his entertaining ways and skilled gallantries, but a young girl had every right to dream of a strong, valiant warrior for her lord, and he was not that. Richard sank down on the seat still warmed with Elspeth's heat.

Eyes blinded by scalding tears, Elspeth did not see the man she brushed past on the winding stairway.

Once Elspeth had departed the solar, Jorion had thought to speak frankly with Taine as he had intended when summoning her to meet him there. But Halyse had arrived and at Taine's invitation had stayed to talk of fashions and kitties and trivial matters that wore dangerously on his nerves. At length he had slipped up the stairs, intending to walk the battlements despite the steady rain. The rising storm matched his mood. Starting the final curve to the top of the castle wall, Richard and Elspeth's voices carried to him. Not wishing to interrupt what seemed a private disagreement, he had paused and heard what he, too, thought a crude jest on Richard's part. He silently applauded the gentle maid's surprising response and her unexpected display of temper.

ᴥ *Chapter* 12 ᴥ

"A TOAST TO THE coming nuptials!" Sir Thomas' voice rang out above the great hall's mealtime din. "A match I whole-heartedly support." The jovial mien of the man standing with goblet raised sent a hush over those seated at the two long lines of lower tables. Light from the nearest brightly burning wall-braced firebrand spread his broad shadow across the dais, casting Taine into an ill-boding shade. The castle's healthy gossip trail had given all within reason to doubt the truth of Sir Thomas' claim. Quiet dissolved into a rush of whispers like the breeze that gathers momentum to forewarn a storm.

From the shield of lowered lashes Taine examined her foe while tables rocked and feet shuffled as all within the great hall rose to meet his toast. Beneath the table's white cloth cover her fingers tangled into a soft woolen surcote. She was far too leery of the schemes of men to be less than deeply discomfited by so startling a shift in attitude.

After taking a long, long drink of the amber liquid, Thomas settled down into his tall-backed chair. The smirk on his ruddy face proclaimed him well satisfied with his deed and the speculation it roused. He enjoyed inciting unease, setting people out of kilter and the feeling of power it gave. One reward not denied him by his enemies.

Through vast experience, Jorion blanked his face of expression. Although certain that, after much spirited discussion and wild conjectures, most observers would come to believe Uncle Thomas' words merely a conciliatory gesture, to Jorion the sincerity of his approval was clear, a fact raising further questions. Cold eyes studied without seeing the heavily engraved goblet in his hand. What earthly purpose lay behind this action by a man who did nothing for another that did not aid himself? Knowing, from the men he'd set to follow Taine's pursuers, of the link between them and Baliol, he wordlessly questioned the connection between his uncle's sudden content with his marriage and the accomplishment of Baliol goals.

Thomas felt Taine's surreptitious gaze and his smile deepened. Stunned earlier by the recognition of his nephew's betrothed, he'd spent the day pondering the problems and possibilities it posed. Though the marriage brought an end to one plan, it offered a different and finer opportunity. The deed could now be more easily accomplished—by another's hand and no blame laid to his door. He was far beyond feeling guilt for his intent. Deprived of his hereditary lands by the greedy English king, he convinced himself that the Baliol cause had become all that gave meaning to his life. The end to Baliol's only legitimate threat would be a fine thing. If it also aided his personal goals, 'twas just, for even a portion of Radwyn's wealth would go far in support of the Scottish rebellion. Heavy hands rubbed together with delight.

Taine's fingers dug hard into her thighs as she watched Thomas' hands express his satisfaction, the satisfaction of a fat spider who sits confident of the power of his web and sadistically enjoys the squirming of his trapped prey. She shuddered. What wickedness had he spun to give him such joy?

Jorion felt the maid's tremor and looked down to where torchlight shone upon a bent auburn head. He would have spoken to soothe her troubled spirit had the man seated at her other side not forestalled his attempt.

The strength of his gaze added to Taine's tension. She was

caught between the spider's growing web and the equally dangerous dragon's golden net. The former seemed to coil about her feet and the latter to twine its seductive strands through her thoughts and emotions.

"So, now we are all satisfied with the coming event—nearly all." Richard's words were low and plainly meant only to prick the maid on Jorion's left.

If Taine had been less upset by her own growing dangers, she'd have been irritated by the obvious jibe at Elspeth's disappointments. As it was, she welcomed any distraction to lessen her fear of Sir Thomas' plotting and, nearly as important, divert her awareness of the dark-eyed man at her other side. She turned to Richard with a smile of blinding sweetness.

Again its potency caught Richard unexpectedly, but he recovered with haste enough to note the disapproving expressions of both Jorion and Elspeth. He was pleased. This was the perfect opportunity to test his theory that he could make Elspeth jealous. Following the afternoon's devastating confrontation, he held a need for some ray of hope to prove the maid not so indifferent as she'd claimed. He turned his practiced charm on the inexperienced Taine.

The almost complete seclusion of the decade past had left Taine with no experience of such maneuvers as Richard displayed. She was soon laughing at his jests and blushing with his compliments. This hoped-for diversion from other concerns was more successful than Taine expected. Glancing sideways and meeting a frigid stare, she suddenly realized that not her attention alone had been diverted. The toast and its mystery was forgotten by the high table's occupants. Mary's Pity it be, she was now the object of at least a portion of their censure. She wanted to end the source of disapproval but was at a loss to know the means. How did one compel a man to cease blush-inducing compliments or halt gentle smiles and teasing words?

Richard flirted and Taine blushed, while Jorion's eyes hardened to cold agates and Elspeth looked dangerously near to fresh tears. Of all on the dais, only Thomas sat seemingly impervious to the new tensions while beneath his facade of mild interest he registered the possibilities revealed by Elspeth's jealousy and Richard's satisfaction.

He'd thought himself forced to yield a portion of his original plan (a great pity that for its revenues, too, would be welcome to the cause), but mayhap he'd not lose any part. At last his offspring could be of some value.

When a page knelt between him and Taine to offer a platter of apple slices and sharp cheese, Richard paused in his close attentions to the maid. Taine peeked up at the huge, glowering man at her other side. Sensitive to the rejections of Jorion's past, she saw the harsh lines on either side of his firm mouth and bitterness in eyes of black ice. Guilt for his pain at her actions rose. Nay, she nearly shook her head in silent rejection. This hard man had survived and triumphed for all these many years without her sympathy. The thought lacked certainty and gave little comfort. Moreover, she reminded herself with more conviction, he'd not likely feel as much for her trials. Indeed, were he to learn of them he would doubtless turn them to his own advancement.

The sound of a lone piper's spritely music interrupted Taine's thoughts. A second piper joined the tune whose rhythm was soon accentuated by timbrels, and Taine smiled despite her anxieties. The players, arrayed in gay colors, strolled into the open area between the lines of lower tables and faced the dais as their first tune came to an end. They bowed low to the castle's lord and the ladies on either side before striking up another. The melody was apparently well-known to the hall's occupants, for more than one laughing voice called out urging Richard to fetch his lute and add words to the song. Delighted by the opportunity to change attention to others, Taine turned to the prospective singer and added her pleas. Moreover, merry music and joyful laughter had for long years been no more than a part of Bertwald's fantasy-inspiring tales. Here was another chance to experience that wondrous custom of entertainment.

As Richard rose to fetch his lute, his father excused himself from the company with vague words of a matter nearly forgot. Jorion was too preoccupied by green eyes that danced with silver lights for another to find his uncle's departure curious. Aching for similar reasons, Elspeth kept her gaze down. Others in the crowded hall were caught in anticipation and gave no notice to the leaving of one whose presence was seldom a cheering addition.

Pleased with the ease of his leavetaking, Thomas climbed the narrow stairway whose gloom was lit at regular intervals by resin-soaked torches braced in iron rings. On reaching the second level, he turned into a wide hall that connected old to new. Here in the addition begun by the old earl and completed under Jorion's command were the chambers he, on moving permanently to the castle years past, had claimed his own.

Though Thomas normally found pleasure in the luxury of his surroundings, tonight he marched past the huge fireplace that kept the chamber warm even in depths of winter and cast no glance at the long window of nearly priceless glass which looked down on the protected courtyard. He seated himself behind an ornately carved table to pull a parchment sheet and sharpened quill from a small box on one corner. He bent laboriously over the cream-colored square and wrote a few well-chosen words. A light knock sounded at the door. Thomas' eyes flew quickly over the writing one more time before he folded the sheet with little care spared for the dryness of the ink. The door opened to his call as he closed the missive with the seal of his forfeited Scottish lands.

Davie, one of the men who had come with his lord into exile, took the parchment handed him. Sliding it into a hidden pocket in the lining of his heavy cloak, the newcomer spoke one word, a question. "McLewell?"

Thomas nodded with slow deliberation. The other turned immediately to depart.

The hall below rang with laughter and Taine clapped with delight at Richard's song of foolish deeds. When that tune was done he rose from his position in the midst of the musicians before the dais and approached Taine. Reaching across the high table, he lifted her hand and gazed up at her with exaggerated soulfulness as he sang of an exceedingly beautiful faerie princess. Jorion's face looked as hard as the great stones of his castle and a golden goblet fell to danger in his crushing grip.

Not formed of such stern stuff as he, Elspeth jumped to her feet, offering a mumbled desire for an early rest. Yet, as if beyond her control, brown eyes settled on Taine for a brief moment. Though wanting to blame the beautiful newcomer, Elspeth found she couldn't, for how could any woman fail to fall beneath Richard's charm? Tears broke their restraints and flooded down pale cheeks.

Watching Elspeth flee the hall, shoulders shaking with her sobs, Taine's guilt came back full force and would not be denied. She'd been ill-used by men too oft not to feel the younger girl's pain. The misleading appearances she'd unintentionally been party to left her frustrated. She would never knowingly aid a man in hurting a woman but saw now that she had—repeatedly. By both Jorion and Richard, she'd been used thus, and to the younger girl it must appear that she had come to her home, stolen her betrothed, and was seeking even to take Richard's attentions for her own. Aye, she'd been used by them and it left Taine more resentful of all of their kind.

Beneath his merry mask, Richard's face was white but he finished the song without noticeable pause. Of late, Elspeth had run from him often enough and with this action he'd meant only to prove her interest, not to pain her.

Once Richard had done, Taine pulled her hand back and hid it beneath the table's cover to tangle fingers into the folds of her skirt. She refused to flee and reveal her disquiet to all. Neither would she lift her eyes above the now barren platter she had shared with Jorion. Richard returned to sit at her side as the musicians half heartedly played on.

When important visitors came, the high table could be extended to accommodate more, but for family meals the chairs were placed closely together, flat tall backs rising high above their occupants' heads. Richard's small frame left a handbreadth between him and Taine, while Jorion's broad shoulders left none. The dragon shifted and brushed against Taine, drawing her attention. Beneath the thick shield of lowered lashes, her eyes settled on the strong hand still clasped tightly about the sturdy vessel half-filled with amber liquid. As she watched, his fingers eased and began to brush slowly over the engraved pattern. Taine nearly felt their touch on her skin. She cursed herself for thinking of the moments she spent in his arms when she had such recent proof of the perfidy of men, but could not halt the images that flashed through her mind—she, burning beneath his kiss, swallowed in the depths of dark eyes, singed by his touch, overcome by golden sparks of pleasure.

When at length the music dwindled away, Taine stood and quietly begged leave to seek her rest. Without waiting for words of formal acceptance, she descended from the dais, forest-green eyes melded to her feet's path.

Jorion watched the departing woman with an expressionless gaze, but his hold on the goblet, relaxed only under effort of will, once more clamped tight, gripping it in a fist of iron strength. He had claimed her his and his she would be! Straightening, he tossed back the remainder of his wine and rose to leave without words of excuse.

Determined that they not be excluded from castle life, Jorion had insisted Bertwald and Father Aleric join the castle's evening meal. Although holding firm in their refusal to sit on the dais, they had bowed to his command in accepting places of honor at the top of the line of lower tables on Jorion's right. Throughout the meal Bertwald had watched the growing discord, and Father Aleric, although he could not clearly see the scene nor hear words there spoken, had sensed the building tension. When first Elspeth, then Taine, and next Jorion left the hall, Bertwald told the priest of their going. Yet, although his bristling brows lowered in a fierce frown, Bertwald spoke no word when, following long moments of contemplation, Richard jumped to his feet and hurriedly took the others' path—offering no excuse in pretext of normality.

Jorion climbed the stairs in measured deliberation and with each step recalled another of Richard's compliments, another of Taine's smiles, another laugh shared between them. His temper heated until gold sparks nearly hid the black velvet of his eyes. Moving quietly down the corridor, he opened the door of Taine's bedchamber with equal restraint.

Taine's back was turned to the opening door and, expecting Halyse, who was later than usual in coming, she did not look behind. She had already removed her surcote and loosened abundant curls whose weight she now lifted, revealing a tender nape. "I've looked forward to your coming." Her words were softly spoken. She was still uncomfortable in disrobing before another, but knew herself incapable of unlacing the gown alone. Although she had fallen into the luxury of having Mercia brush her hair each morn, she resisted evening aid in undressing, thus Halyse made a practice of coming each night. The cheerful woman often lingered to visit and was near the only truly friendly face in this castle now that Richard had proven himself unworthy. Feeling in need of a friend, Taine had been anxiously awaiting her arrival. "This kirtle was drawn far too tight, I fear. Loose these ties I cannot reach and set me free of its constraints." Auburn cloud held high with one hand, the slender fingers of the other searched for the ties beyond their touch.

Golden brows snapped together. Surcote already removed and luxurious fire of her hair gathered up, the snug-fitting kirtle gave a clear view of her slender back, tiny waist and gently rounded derrière. She had expected another to come, one so familiar she need not turn to welcome him. Had this happened before? With so little time preceding, it seemed unlikely, yet Jorion was beyond cool reason and had heard of the seductive powers Richard could wield. The mere thought broke the final threads of his restraint. Eyes on the tempting maid, he shoved the door closed.

"If you are so anxious for a man's caresses, then you will have mine! My wife you will be and no other will you have!"

Leaf-green skirt billowing out, Taine's arms dropped and she whirled to find Jorion striding toward her, eyes blazing and face harder than granite. He caught her shoulders and pulled her against the unyielding wall of his chest.

Even as she opened her lips to explain or protest, she knew not which, his mouth came down with bruising force and swallowed the sound. Her body trembled but she stood steady beneath the harsh embrace until the iron band loosened, grew unexpectedly gentle. His hands slid caressingly down her back, urging her closer as his mouth softened to cherish her with short, tender kisses. She weakened to their seduction, irrationally wanted to reach up, tangle her fingers in golden strands and hold his lips against hers. His tongue lightly probed between her lips and steam seemed to rise. A whimper of longing escaped from deep in her throat.

Breathing hard and fast, Jorion drew a breath away and found wounded green eyes filled with unwilling passion and uncertainty. Beneath his intense gaze, Taine's heart went wild, agitated by the chaotic combination of fear for, in the first moment, the very real re-enactment of her nightmare attack and, in the second, for the strength of his temptations. In panic she tore free.

Richard hesitated in the dimly lit hallway before Taine's iron-bound and forbidding chamber door, unsure of his earlier certainty until the sound of a deep growl from within confirmed his suspicions. He straightened and squared his shoulders, preparing to charge into the chamber and face a far superior foe—a task he'd never thought himself capable of performing. His actions had brought this response from the dragon. Fool that he was, in his anxiety to prove Elspeth not indifferent to him he'd failed to consider either the pain he might render to Elspeth or the price Taine could be called to pay for his deed. He owed Taine this. But, before he was able to match action to intent, the door burst open. Richard fell back as Taine raced past him, curls flowing behind in a dark-fire stream.

❧ *Chapter* 13 ❧

EMOTIONS IN A CHAOTIC tangle, Taine flew down the stairs, hearing neither the steady click of heavily booted feet descending in pursuit nor Richard calling her name. For the same reason, anguish-filled eyes failed to see the shocked faces of those in the hall as she, clad only in tightly laced kirtle, dashed through before fleeing out into the night. Not until chill air swept over her, as she stood outside the closed entrance, did she realize what foolish thing she'd done. *You witling,* she rebuked herself. There was only folly in running poorly dressed and without thought to a destination. Aye, she'd run before, near always without thought to her journey's end, but never without some form of planning aforehand.

Wrapping arms about herself in poor protection against damp cold, she desperately searched for a haven, somewhere in the unwelcoming gloom of a cloudy autumn night. She shivered, but cheered herself with the minor blessing that at least the steady drizzle had ceased. Guards stood about the walls, no light burning near to impede the view below, but torches blazed around the drawbridge's mechanism to prevent an unseen foe from gaining control. Torches also lit the castle's stairs; and, unwilling to stand revealed in their glimmer, Taine hurried down steep wooden steps to huddle in the dark on one side. Away from torch glare, a small previously unnoticed gleam caught her eye. Anxious to find a private retreat where she could seek order in her confusion and plan escape, she cautiously moved through shadows toward the promising gleam. It led her to the special stable Jorion had constructed for his Saracen steeds.

Her hand was cold but the metal latch colder as the door opened wide enough to slip through. A long, broad aisle stretched before her, stalls on either side. At its end a soft glow beckoned. Without thought to a possible stableman and ignoring the neighing of horses disturbed in their rest, she hurriedly approached the light. The aisle opened into a small room, clearly the metalsmith's shop, deserted but warmed by the strong heat of a banked fire. Protected in an earth pit surrounded by stones reddened like coals, it was left burning through the night so on the morn little time would be lost in restoring its intensity. Taine registered only that the room offered a welcome warmth.

From the unused stall around the corner, Taine gathered up armfuls of fresh straw, carried them back to the shop, and stacked them in one corner, safely back from the fire's dangerous flames. Task complete, she settled into the pile's prickly comfort. With nothing more to waylay black thoughts, they rolled over her like heavy storm clouds threatening a rain of tears. Not since she was a child had Taine let tears conquer her control but tonight, like the night before, weakened by lack of sleep and wildly vacillating emotions, they rose in a hot tide and burned down cold-reddened cheeks. She'd been frightened by the initial force of the dragon's embrace, but had yielded to his tender fire as she ever seemed to do. And, worse, despite a struggle to deny it, she longed to yield to his demand for a lifetime at his side. She sobbed the harder for the self-betrayal in the admission.

From the top of the castle's entry steps, Richard searched for some sign of Taine. He'd nearly caught up with her in the inner stairwell but, on seeing the attention she drew running through the hall, had thought better of dashing after her and adding more grist to the gossip mill. Consequently, he had wasted precious time idly taking a circuitous route, pausing to jest with one, question another and had apparently lost his opportunity to apologize. Mentally searching for her probable path, he thought of the one place, outside the castle-proper, offering both warmth and privacy. Jumping down the steps two at a time, he hurried across the courtyard with little regard for deep ruts slimed by two days of rain.

Taine's sobs filled her own ears and she did not know another present until a hand lightly touched her shoulder. She instinctively flinched away.

"My actions were unpardonable but I beg you to forgive me." Richard's hand still hovered over Taine's shoulder. To see the proud lady's pain doubled his guilt, and he cursed his thoughtless action taken without consideration of others' responses.

Richard touched Taine once more but she burrowed deeper into the loose straw, not in condemnation of him but for her own humiliation in an emotional display to which she'd taken pride in never succumbing.

Stabbed by this apparent rejection, still Richard reached down and determinedly lifted Taine to lay against his chest. He patted her back as he repeated his remorse for his heedless behavior over and over like a church litany. "I swear to perform any penance for my unthinking deed, any penance you name. On my honor I swear it, I swear it."

The harder Taine willed her tears to cease, the faster they fell. Richard was nearly hoarse by the time she had mastered them enough to speak. "You have naught to beg pardon for," she assured him in a wobbly voice—and meant it. He had done only what the nature of all men commanded, and her disgust was more for the whole than the one. Indeed, the condemning voice of honesty silently rebuked her, disgust was more appropriately directed to herself for so easily falling in with his ploy. She pulled away and scrubbed dampness from her cheeks, shamed at revealing her lack of control to another.

"No," Richard denied firmly, not willing to absolve

himself. "I, who have known him so long, should have been wiser than to tempt the dragon's fire."

Ragged emotions left Taine ill-equipped to soothe another's fears. Moreover, she could not allow the one clear notion in the tangled skein of her thoughts to be denied. "You are *not* to blame. At least not beyond the fact that 'tis the character of all men to force a woman to their intent."

Surprised at her vehemence, Richard's brows flew up and he started to deny her generalization, but in Taine's emotional state her temper was near.

"You had a goal," she flared, bitterness flavoring the words, "and thought only of what your actions would earn for you."

Richard, having no real argument against this statement, looked stricken but did not deny it.

Green eyes clouded with sour memories. Taine shook her head, catching firelight in dark curls, as she spoke her thoughts aloud. "There's not a grain of difference between you and all the men of my past. Neither those who seek to bend me to their will for the sake of a crown they would force me to wear in order to share its power—no matter the cost I am called to pay for their ambition—nor those who imprisoned me to protect their own goals by preventing another from claiming that prize through me."

No great fighter, Richard prided himself on his acute mind. He had been raised by a father deeply involved in conflicts for the Scottish crown and was well-acquainted with its intrigues. Presented here with a woman who, by her voice, was clearly Scottish, he began to see through the mysterious mists surrounding her. Although never taken into confidence in the plotting of Baliol schemes, he had heard gossip of the only Scottish woman with the power to give a man claim to a crown, of a living queen. Blue eyes narrowed to study her ring. "Is your mother yet living?"

Taine saw where his eyes rested, and her heart plummeted with the devastating force of a catapulted stone even as she answered: "My ladymother died soon after giving me life."

Richard only nodded slowly, but Taine knew he had guessed the truth and rushed into an impassioned speech. "Already have I been forced down a path I would deny—for a crown I do not want! I beg you not to force me back to a life I cannot bear." Silent tears slid down flushed cheeks, leaving silver tracks soon traveled by others.

Pulling her back into comforting arms, Richard reassured Taine. "Your secret is safe with me." He had caused enough damage and was determined to do no more. The gentle rain of her tears grew into a deluge that drenched the shoulder of his favorite sapphire tunic before, drained by violent emotions, she slipped into exhausted slumbers. Richard resigned himself to spending an uncomfortable night and waking her early to slip them both back into the castle unseen.

After Taine ran from his harsh embrace grown tender, Jorion sank onto the edge of her bed and let his head drop forward. Firelight gilded blond hair while he rubbed his neck to ease tense muscles. He'd claimed a bride who ever turned from him—a rejection he'd sworn no woman would have opportunity to render—but could not let another take the one he'd named bride. Still, he was upset with himself for the mistreatment he'd never meant to give any woman, Taine least of all. He sat in disgust for his actions and hers, until a noise at the door drew his guarded attention.

"Oh!" Halyse halted one step into the room, round hazel eyes taking in the sight of her lord seated on Lady Taine's empty bed. "I am sorry—I—" she mumbled.

"Come you often into this chamber unannounced?" he demanded, irritated by the unexpected visit that caught him with guard down.

"Aye—that is—I come every night to aid your lady in disrobing. 'Tis a difficult thing, you ken? Back lacing and buttons aplenty." Amused by her own stammering words, Halyse shook bright curls carefully restrained, threatening to see the wiry mass freed.

Jorion's lips compressed but he nodded his understanding. It explained all too much—whose company, in truth, Taine had anxiously awaited and who she had directed to hurry in unlacing her kirtle. He'd been a fool. It was not an experience he enjoyed and Halyse's merry smile did little to lighten his humor.

"I was overlong in coming tonight," Halyse added. "Bryce ate too many apples and suffers from an aching belly. I could not leave till he slept." Narrow shoulders lifted in a casual shrug but hazel eyes probed curiously into the chamber's every corner, clearly seeking some sign of Taine. "If I'm not needed"—she paused and looked into a steady black stare—"then I will go back to my naughty, ailing child." Jorion nodded his acceptance of her plan.

Not wanting to follow too close on Halyse's path and raise her curiosity more, Jorion waited until she'd time to return to the rooms she shared with her family. Sitting yet on the side of Taine's bed, Jorion sensed another presence and turned toward the shadows of a far corner. Unblinking gold eyes gleamed. For a long moment he returned the steady gaze of the small black cat, invisible in a dim corner save for the strange eyes whose stare felt like an accusation. Rising, he bowed to the animal with a mocking smile. "'Struth," he said, "I've made a muddle of it all."

Quietly closing the door to Taine's chamber behind him, he climbed to his own in search of his cloak. He had decided to find her and make amends for his mistakes.

A time after Taine had climbed above, two men close on her path, with all others in the great hall, Bertwald had seen the improperly clad lass rush wildly through. The look of fear on her face he'd seen before. By it he was fairly certain what had transpired between her and her jealous husband. While others' attention turned to speculation, he visually followed Richard's deceptive route in pursuit of her. He rose to his feet. Now was the time to speak with the earl. One secret he must share.

A cloud of thick white hair bobbed as Father Aleric turned his head toward the gruff man whose movement he more felt than saw. Bertwald had appointed himself guardian and shared his eyes, talking freely of the high table's occupants and their actions. Thus, when Bertwald had suddenly sunk into a heavy silence, it was more telling than words. Long accustomed to learning through his other senses, the priest heard the gasp and noted the thick hush that preceded the opening and closing of the outer door.

The rush of words that followed in a hall unrestrained by a lord's presence told him all Bertwald had not. Feeling Bertwald's gaze upon him, Father Aleric lowered his face. Lifting his tankard he took a long sip, keeping his gaze averted. Clearly Bertwald wished not to speak of his lady's strange actions, and he would not seek a confidence unwillingly given.

Presented with the top of a white head, relief swept over Bertwald—and appreciation for the priest's tact. The hall was still humming with speculation. Men had risen from lower tables and were gathered in small self-involved groups shielding Bertwald's path. Unnoticed, he turned into the stairwell and began to climb. By the time he reached the first level, he realized the futility of his action. In a castle this size he'd have difficulty finding the earl's chamber without aid. As if in answer to his silent plea, a young castle-serf turned into the stairway from the first level archway.

"Where is the earl's chamber?" His question was short and curt. The girl looked at him through narrowed eyes, suspicion for his motives clear. "I—I bring a message from Father Aleric, who is too infirm to climb these stairs himself." The girl's furrowed brow smoothed miraculously at mention of the earl's gentle mentor. Guilt smote Bertwald at the lie and shameless use of the other's name. He controlled the urge to curl his lips with self-amusement at the amazing influence close contact with a priest could bring to bear on a previously less than pious man. As he followed the girl's soft direction up one level and down a wide hall, he wordlessly promised to confess his small sin to Father Aleric and, without complaint, do whatever penance was commanded.

There was no answer to his knock on the earl's chamber door. Refusing to question the rightness of the girl's directions, Bertwald sank down next to the door to wait. The earl would return whether sooner or later.

Jorion, preoccupied with self-disgust for his lack of control over his own emotions—he'd never experienced jealousy before—and his misjudgment of the maid, didn't see the figure hunched beside his door. Like a strange jinn from the mythical tales of his desert youth, it leaped up with a whoosh that sent torchlight flickering to weave mad shadows on the wall. In an instant Jorion crouched, drawn dagger a threat in his hand.

Bertwald flattened himself against the wall, arms crossed defensively in front. "Ach, you're overfond of threatening me with that wicked thing."

Jorion stood tall but kept his dagger before him as with lifted golden brows he demanded explanation for the visit.

"'Tis a puzzle." Bertwald's short crack of laughter did not move Jorion. "Firstly you bare that nasty blade to compel me to speak of milady; now you do the same when I come to fulfill a wee part of your demand."

With a brief silver flash and soft whispering sound the dagger slid into the sheath at Jorion's waist. He reached out to thrust his chamber door open. Torchlight glowed on golden hair as he nodded Bertwald inside.

Bertwald hesitated for a long moment. Watery blue eyes considered the hard bronze planes of Jorion's face, the black wall of his eyes, the overwhelming height and breadth of him. The man looked so unyielding that Bertwald questioned the wisdom of his decision.

Jorion watched the indecision in Bertwald's expression but betrayed no response. His training to patience came not from his warrior skills alone but from Aleric's example in trusting to a higher command.

Nay, Bertwald decided, shaking his head and moving through the door, if the man would stand husband to the maid he had a right to know, leastways of one part of her story. The part she'd never felt he'd need an oath to hold secret—and he'd sworn none.

The chamber was nearly twice the size of most. The massive, draped bed was dimly seen in the shadows of the far half. Before the fire stood two high-back chairs and on the sizable table between resided a flagon of ale and several tankards. Here the earl met privately with the important men of his domain. Bertwald strode with assumed confidence to one of the chairs and sat down without awaiting the earl's pleasure.

Jorion smiled at the other's unknowing error in etiquette and poured out two measures of deep brown liquid before taking his chair across from Bertwald. "You wished to speak, and I am listening."

Bertwald shifted uncomfortably beneath the steady dark gaze. "I saw you—er, I saw Taine leave the hall. From her agitation I know her discomfort."

Dark gold brows snapped together. Did the man take his father role to such lengths he would dare reprove him for his treatment of a girl who would be, nay, was his wife?

Bertwald saw the other's growing ire and cursed his own unwieldy words even as he rushed to clear their murky meaning. "I come to tell you of a deed that made the girl react as she did." The words were plain-spoken with no tactful cushion. Far better that than to have the dragon misunderstand again. "She was alone with only a near-deaf old woman for companion when two of her gaolers drank far too much of this—" Bertwald lifted his tankard in an unsteady hand. Bitter ale slopped over. "With its fools' fire in their bellies they were struck with the pleasure to be had in taking the virginity of their lovely lady"—the words trailed away while Bertwald watched black eyes flare with golden flames. The hard jaw jerked erratically like stone moving under the force of an earth tremor.

"They dinna succeed." Bertwald hurried to reassure. "I come and with me cudgel gave the sotted oafs a sounder sleep than the ale woulda—and a fiercer headache I ken." His lips twisted in a satisfied smile.

Jorion's cold half-smile dawned as he consciously relaxed clenched fists and knotted jaw. They'd failed and been chastised for their attempt. Nonetheless, he wished he'd been the one privileged to render the blows.

"We been running since that night," Bertwald added. "Do you ken my reason for speaking of it now?"

Preoccupied with his disgust for her assailants, Jorion stared at Bertwald blankly.

"I kept them from fulfilling the deed, but they attacked and frightened her badly. She canna bear to be handled roughly—mayhap not handled at all." Bertwald's shoulders slowly lifted and he shook his head. "I feared in your anger you might'a roused her terror and deserved to know its source."

Jorion appreciated Bertwald's reasoning, but cursed himself. He had known from the first that, for whatever reason, too strong an embrace repelled her. Nonetheless, he'd allowed his unreasoning jealousy to overcome good sense. This night's actions would only strengthen her fear of him and his passion.

Even as these thoughts whirled through his mind, another matter weighed heavily. Bertwald had revealed one certain fact. Taine had been prisoner—but why? In their world it was not uncommon for a woman to be held in seclusion by a father, guardian, or husband—husband!

Cold eyes turned their full power on Bertwald. "If I lead her to the church door, will we be placing ourselves outside the hands of God?"

Momentarily flustered by this lightning change of direction, Bertwald frowned. Church door? 'Twas where marriages vows were exchanged. Ah, bushy brows rose in comprehension, the earl asked if his bride were already wed. "No," he emphatically responded, "no."

Relieved of one fear, Jorion's mind leaped to another question. Aware of the link between Taine's pursuers and the Baliols, Jorion asked, "Are her attackers still seeking her return?"

Bertwald mentally struggled to keep pace with the earl. "Mayhap," he answered, then added, "Most like they are."

"Tell me then who they are," Jorion commanded softly. "Tell me who she is."

Bertwald, suddenly aware of just how much he had unwittingly disclosed, clamped his lips together tightly and shook his head.

"We seek the same goal, protection of our lady." Jorion argued logically, but Bertwald sat unmoving. "Yet you limit my abilities through your stubbornness," he quietly warned.

Bertwald closed his eyes to shut out a compelling gaze. The dragon spoke true and he believed Taine would be best served by giving him her secret to protect, but an unshakable oath prevented him from giving what the earl demanded.

Jorion continued his logical arguments like a barrage of arrows until at last Bertwald responded. "If you give your oath to King Edward, would you not die to hold it?"

"Are you telling me," Jorion responded, irritation breaking through his calm control, "that you feel your promise to the maid to be as strong as an oath to your sovereign?" His words were a measure of his frustration, for in his own habit an oath to a serf or an oath to a king were of equal import.

"Aye," Bertwald answered with a grim smile and strangely intense gaze, "'tis exactly my meaning!"

Seeing the futility in further arguments, Jorion shrugged and stood to offer his arm to Bertwald in recognition of his strength of honor. Bertwald rose and, for a long moment, clasped his forearm to the one proffered before making his escape.

Sitting down again, Jorion's thoughts whirled with the implications of the revelations he'd heard. Her attack explained how the brave maid's passion could so quickly change to fear. Knowing the pain it meant for Taine, he was slightly shamed by the relief he felt in learning her rejection of him might be from a source other than disgust with his heritage. Although Bertwald had feared her incapable of sensual fires, Jorion knew it was untrue. But her attack might well have left her fearful of her own desires and thus be the reason she denied their call. He must, Jorion promised himself, approach her only with great gentleness and tempt her beyond fear—if he had not already driven her to another's arms.

Taine he would forgive for her actions at table, but Richard was experienced enough to know better. For his love of Richard he would warn this once of the punishment to come of another such exhibition. The heavy chair scraped across the plank floor as he shoved it back to stand. Snatching his black cloak from a peg by the door, Jorion purposefully strode from the room and down the corridor to Richard's chamber. He rapped loudly on its heavy door. There was no answer. He thrust the door ajar and stepped into the empty room. Bertwald's earlier words, little noted when spoken, sounded clear in Jorion's mind. He frowned. Bertwald had said he'd seen Taine's agitation as she ran from the hall. Something Jorion knew but had not questioned. Had she run from him again? His chin lifted and fists clenched. Did Richard mean to aid her escape and claim her for himself? Nay, Jorion wrapped his ire under tight constraints. This path to unreasoning anger had earlier led him to misjudgment. More like Richard had followed the maid to offer consolation. The mocking voice of cynicism questioned: And more? The door shook with the force by which it was slammed behind his quickly departing figure. He would at least put an end to his unpleasant conjectures.

Although most of his men had descended to the guard-room one level below the great hall to seek their rest, a hardy few huddled about a table drawn close to the fire. So involved were they with the dice game in progress and their wagers upon it that they gave no attention to their lord as he moved across the room and out the massive double doors. The clouds of day left the night a murky void but Jorion wasted no time hesitating at the top of the entrance stairs. Intending to be atop his great steed and upon Taine's path, he immediately strode to the stable where his fleet Saracen horses were housed.

Sensitive to his mettlesome steeds, Jorion slowed at the stable door and slipped quietly inside. At the far end of the aisle between dim and quiet stalls, an unusually bright glow burned. Jorion paused, getting his bearings. With deliberate stealth he moved toward the light until his silhouette filled the open doorway—a sight as threatening as the black eyes glaring beneath scowling golden brows.

Richard dozed lightly against a soft cushion of straw while Taine, with an ease she'd never shared with him, curled peacefully against Richard's chest. Her flushed cheek nestled in the curve of his shoulder and dark-fire hair flowed across his shoulder and arm. Jorion's open palm slapped with a sharp crack against the small tree trunk that formed one side of the doorway. Taine jerked up, fear flashing silver in green eyes. Richard, for all his vaunted dearth of military skill, in less than a moment had dagger drawn and held threateningly. Jorion might have smiled at this demonstration of a skill Richard claimed only in jest, had Taine's eyes not deepened with apprehension once she recognized the man she faced. Her expression reminded Jorion forcefully of his oath to restrain his jealousy until he'd proven his desire no thing to fear. The goal was made more difficult for facing a man rumpled by the sweet burden once slumbering in his arms. In silent command Jorion curtly jerked his head toward the door.

Taine, feeling Richard coil in readiness to reject the

demand, quickly squeezed the arm still holding the knife in defense. When questioning blue eyes turned to hers, she smiled slightly and nodded toward the door.

Scrambling to his feet, Richard cast one last look between Jorion and Taine as he brushed away the straw clinging to his clothes and spiking his hair. To Richard's surprise, although Jorion was implacable, he spoke not a word of dispute. Taine clearly wanted Richard to go without further confrontation, and he was willing to accede to her wishes. He'd not last long in a battle of strength with Jorion and a battle of words, of logic would be more successful in the cool light of day after calm reason was restored. Still feeling guilty for desertion, Richard departed, comforting himself that his goal was to see the two together.

Despite the earlier harsh embrace, when Jorion held his hand out to her, Taine laid hers in his without hesitation. He pulled her up easily and then released her hand to unfasten his cloak and swirl it about her shoulders. It nearly fell to the ground, but he bent and suddenly lifted her in his strong arms. He carried her from the stable and through the black night toward the castle where lights blazed like bright stars in an empty sky. Emotionally exhausted, caught in the snarled confusion of her own thoughts and justifying the action with the certainty that no struggle would set her free, Taine nestled quietly into strong arms, savoring their forbidden warmth and power.

❧ *Chapter* 14 ❧

AFTER THE PAST DAY'S dreary cloud cover, a welcome sun atoned for its lack of warmth by bathing the earth in clear, bright light. It lifted Taine's spirits and gave hope where there was little. Standing unnoticed at the foot of the castle's entrance stairs, she pulled the hood of a brown homespun cloak lower. Its thick wool cast her face further into shadow as she gazed around the bustling courtyard. The usual throng of villagers and tradesmen milled about, urchins dashing through their midst. Although harvest was past, its fruits were still arriving to be stored in the cool recesses of the castle's lowest level. The neighing of workhorses and groaning of carts became a clamoring din when joined with children's shrieks, parents' futile admonishments, and sober business talk.

Determined to speak privately with Bertwald, Taine congratulated herself on escaping the castle undetected. The dragon would think her still resting after their late-night return to the castle. She'd taken care to establish that misbelief by sending word of such intent to the morning table and waiting patiently behind closed bed draperies until the chapel's bells rang tierce. Well, perhaps not patiently, but she had waited and surely at this hour the dragon was too involved in his own business to notice her action.

Still, for fear he would again interrupt her visit with Bertwald, she'd taken care to ensure her departure unseen. Claiming she meant merely to play a trick on Bertwald, Taine had begged Halyse to lend her workaday cloak. Ever one for a jest or mischievous trick, Halyse had at the first suggested herself as company for the deed. Taine had struggled to find some excuse to go alone and had been greatly relieved when the other remembered her promise to Bryce of a visit to the horse yard and time watching squires training with lance and sword. As to the cloak, Halyse had shrugged, what matter that when on their arrival the earl had publicly agreed Taine was free to visit Bertwald whenever she liked.

Taine set off winding around carts and through the busy crowd. Suddenly, two paces in front of her, a burly serf lost his hold on a basket and a measure of apples spilled over the edge. He snarled a clipped but colorful curse as they bounced on the rutted ground and rolled in all directions. Startled laughter burst from Taine as she sidestepped two red freedom-seekers. The thought reminded her of the task ahead. She quickened her pace through a group of playing children. Attention full on her goal, she failed to see the tall man on the far side of a heavily loaded cart.

Distinctive laughter, clear and light as a tune from silver pipes, had caught Jorion's attention immediately. He turned in time to see a brown-cloaked figure moving toward the inner bailey gate with unmistakable grace. His lady bride had gone to some pains to depart unnoticed. He turned to his companion with a smile that did not warm his eyes.

"I trust you, Will, to go and learn the right of the matter." Jorion laid his hand on the other man's shoulder. "My uncle will have it that only his way will solve the dilemma, but I cannot trust his word."

Will was a man who, like the dragon, seldom revealed emotion. Still, squared shoulders and lifted chin demonstrated his pleasure in his lord's trust of him, and he met black eyes directly as he nodded his acceptance of the charge.

"Go then"—with the final words Jorion's smile turned true and teasing—"but return with all good haste, else Halyse will turn her wicked tongue on me." He lingered no longer although, nearly certain of his bride's path, he followed at a distance.

Once beyond the lowered drawbridge and on the packed dirt of the village lane, Taine's breath came easier. She met few along the way, and as she walked through the shade of a towering elm, her heart lightened with the success of her ploy. Her good fortune held. Green eyes smiled at the sight of Bertwald putting his strong back and brawny arms to good use chopping wood on the far side of the cozy cottage he shared with Father Aleric. In rhythm with the ring of metal against wood, she quietly approached. She halted a few paces behind the laboring man to lean against the daub-and-wattle wall and waited for him to turn.

Across the open ground below his castle Jorion walked with no shield for his unmistakable figure. With false security the prey he stalked had not glanced behind. After Taine had passed beyond the lone tree along the path, he moved beneath its shelter to watch as she approached the cottage he'd felt certain was her goal. He'd earlier warned them of his response to any attempt at stealthy departure and would not interrupt their visit this time. Moreover, he'd come to trust Bertwald's good sense and had hope of his support in holding the maid safe on Radwyn lands.

Tiring under the strength of his labors, Bertwald stopped to mop a sweaty brow with his tunic's sleeve-end. A wry smile split his rugged face. He'd gone soft with the easy life of past weeks in the earl's company. In confirmation, one finger rubbed the fresh calluses on a palm grown nearly smooth. With inactivity came a feeling of being watched, and he slowly looked behind to find a slight brown-draped figure stepping toward him. Wary of any who need hide in voluminous cloth, he whirled and fists braced on hips. The visitor's hood dropped back, allowing sunlight to flame on carefully confined hair.

Bertwald leveled a steady, disapproving gaze at Taine as

he spoke. "Lassie, am I to ken the dragon has forbidden you come to me?"

Several bright curls sprang loose from their net restraints as Taine shook her head. Although affection was clear in his soft tone, she saw a lack of welcome in Bertwald's eyes and the deepening of grooves around his mouth. Her heart sank. Where had her supportive friend gone?

"Why then did you don a strange cloak to hie away to me?" Bushy brows rose with the curt query.

Bertwald knew the maid's fear of the earl, and it doubtless had increased by rough handling the night past, but he'd also lingered in the castle great hall until the golden-haired lord carried her back into the castle with tender care. It now seemed clear she'd come to complain of the dragon's treatment of her and, for that, to demand he free her of the dragon's bonds. Irritation pricked at her denial of the way of their world. He loved his lady and would not willingly see her come to harm; but no longer doubted that the earl meant to offer her all good care. He would wed her and she, as all women, must accept and submit to her lord.

"I wanted to speak with you alone, Bertie." Taine stepped quickly forward, hands raised in supplication. "When last I came as myself, he followed and prevented me from speaking what I needed to say."

Not proof against the plea in soft green eyes, Bertwald moved to take Taine's outstretched hands into his own. "Aye, he did that." His face gentled. Could be he'd misjudged the maid. "Speak then for here you have but to cast your eyes about to see none are close enough to hear your words." He waved one newly callused hand about. On one side 'twas clear to the next cottage and to the orchards on the other.

Taine squeezed her lashes shut tightly for a moment in relief for the return of her familiar friend. Then, looking directly into faded blue, nearly whispered words rushed out as if anxious to be said afore they could be again forestalled. She told of the child lifted from a dead man's arms on a stormy beach by Sir Thomas, of his recent recognition of her, and of the dragon's needle-witted cousin who'd put one fact with another to come to the right sum. She ended with a plea.

"Surely you see why 'tis a desperate need for me to fly free of this place and people who know my name."

Bertwald turned to pace a short distance away and stare unseeing into the line of forest on the horizon. Despite her gaolers' attack, the lovely woman was far too naive to see the many others who would force her to their will in more than the matter of a crown. He wouldna always be able to protect her. She must have a stronger, younger man; and, after their previous night's talk, Bertwald was even more convinced the earl was that man. After all, having neither gold nor property, she couldna make a life for herself and must marry someday. Indeed, without such enticements, 'twould be difficult to find an acceptable husband. Although few men of her class would hesitate to force a lone and alluring woman to their bed—there would be no thought to marriage.

"The earl spoke truly, lass." Bertwald turned to face her again, braced for her distress at his response. "Wherever we would run, with his vast garrison he would find us. And a fine thing that, for without his aid life in this land would be a difficult thing. The countryside is unfamiliar to us and clear foreigners we be and ever suspect for others' misdeeds."

Green eyes widened to hold crystal tears captive within. She could not explain to Bertwald her elemental fear of the man into whose care he would give her—the man who would not fit the mold she had cast for all men of power and who could so easily draw her to him with enthrallment's golden net. From the early days of her confinement she'd depended on Bertwald for sympathy and affection. She could see his unquestioning support slipping away, opening a chasm in her soul. Clenching her hands tightly together, she compressed soft lips into a thin line to contain a cry of anguish.

Bertwald knew she heard his words as defection and saw her brave facade. He shared her pain but comforted himself that he spoke for her own sake. "I grow old, lassie, and canna protect you always. Tell the dragon your secrets," he quietly counseled. "Wed with him, give yourself into his care, and thank the good Lord for providing so mighty a protector."

Taine silently studied Bertwald with burning eyes. He was lost to her, a friend no more. One shining droplet broke free and ran down an unnaturally pale cheek. Having early learned to freeze tears into ice for her soul, she wordlessly condemned the escapee. Not until the dragon's arrival in her world had they begun to thaw as if his fire were melting the frozen chambers of her heart. Nay, that she could not allow. She would fill the void Bertwald left with ice-block memories of his defection, his willingness to give her over to another man's goals for the sake of his own comfort. She forced stiff lips into the parody of a smile.

"You leave me little choice but to do as you say." Her throat was tight with repressed sorrow that strained her voice. She must seem to bend his way for she no longer trusted his loyalty. Were he to know her intent to flee alone, he might well betray her to her foe.

Bertwald's heart ached. He wanted to step forward and wrap her in his arms, promise her any reward. But he believed the dragon better suited to the deed and would see her in that powerful man's embrace. For now, he would do nothing to break her proud facade, humble her by emotions revealed.

"I only remind you of your oath already made," Taine continued, still certain his honor would hold him to it. "I will speak to the dragon but in my own way and my own time."

Bertwald nodded his agreement and Taine turned away. She pulled the brown hood up, again casting her face in shadow. As if a spring thaw had come in earnest, tears broke free and flooded all restraints in a silent torrent. Rather than returning to the crowded courtyard and busy castle, Taine moved toward the quiet of a deserted orchard stripped of fruit. Nearly barren branches reached dark fingers to clear skies, while the ground was layered with the false fire of bright leaves. Well into the trees, the brown figure dropped gracefully upon the soft comfort of earth's bright cushion.

Of a sudden she'd grown nearly as weepy as Elspeth, Taine scolded herself. She was shamed by the tears of past days. Since her escape, new sensations, new emotions had assailed her at every turn. Seemed she'd been safer within the tight confines of her castle-prison. That craven notion mocked her victory over long confinement and immediately halted the flow of tears. She'd gain nothing by cowering safe within prison walls. In truth, those new emotions and sensations, she reminded herself, were small price for such joys of freedom as sweet music, tasty foods, laughter—strong embraces and exciting kisses. She sat up abruptly. The final two traitorous thoughts she would deny, would flee from in earnest even if it must be alone. Aye, alone and at night while others slept.

She rose to dust away clinging leaves, bright patches against deep brown. Such a plan had failed once but surely would not a second time. It had only been a matter of luck, she reassured herself, that the dragon had discovered her gone the earlier time. Even he couldn't be so fortunate twice. Carefully planning every detail of her departure, she barely noticed the few who passed her on the lane approaching the drawbridge. The dark-clad figure leaning against a broad elm trunk, lingering scattered leaves shielding gold hair from the sun's revealing rays, she saw not at all.

Jorion watched as Taine passed by, immersed in heavy thoughts. Bertwald's assurance that 'twas her fear of a man's embrace and, therefore, not his heritage that repelled her was a hope Jorion held as comfort. Surely only his embrace, begun harshly and too quickly turned to wild passion, had frightened her—badly. It took no great wit to guess how strengthened now was her determination to win free. He cursed himself for the damage he'd done to the tentative bond between them. He'd talked with the maid of things no other was willing to hear and had found a comfort in sea-mist eyes he'd never seen in another's. The graceful figure passed beneath the iron teeth of the first portcullis and began the journey over the drawbridge toward the second. He pushed broad shoulders away from the rough trunk, reaffirming his decision. He must guard her closely, entrust the duty to no other. And remember all the while his oath to Bertwald, which decreed that until they were wed he could not prove his desire a less than frightening thing. Thank the saints, the time to the day of their vows grew short.

* * *

The silence of another cloud-shrouded night had fallen over Castle Dragonsward. The eerie feeling of a thing done before swept over Taine as she fastened her forest-green cloak at the throat and pulled its hood lower to conceal the pale oval of her face. She bolstered her courage with the thought that to this escape she went better prepared. The fine linen of her deep blue kirtle lay across the table. Atop it Taine had piled the supplies she deemed useful for her journey. She'd surreptitiously taken fruit from the evening table. From Halyse who'd come to aid her disrobing, she'd begged a small round of cheese (for treats against hunger pangs in the night) and several sizable hunks of meat (supposedly for the wee kitty).

As Taine folded and tied the corners of blue cloth, the intended recipient uncoiled from her perch at the edge of the bed. Stretching sinuously first, she leaped gracefully to the floor and padded forward to rub repeatedly against her mistress' legs. Taine bent to lift the little animal and smooth her cheek over its silky black fur. A raspy tongue lapped at her face and the smile it earned was tinged with regret. Who would care for the defenseless creature once she had gone? Impulsively she tucked the purring ball into the wide pocket of her cloak. The kitty apparently found it to her liking for she curled up inside, only ears and golden eyes peering above the edge. Tying a final knot in the blue kirtle, Taine lifted it in one hand and reached out to carefully ease the door open.

The cat in her left pocket hissed, startling Taine. She looked down at her defender's bared teeth and then up at the broad form filling the open doorway. Her bundle thudded softly to the floor. Only a small gasp of surprise came from Taine's tight throat, but she took an involuntary step back and then another as the tall man moved into the chamber, firelight glowing on bright hair. Truly, the man held some unworldly sense that put him in her doorway at the worst possible moments! A less courageous woman might cross herself to ward off his power, but Taine knew enough of the wounded boy beneath cynical man to assure her that whatever put him always in her path, 'twas not for his being devil-cursed.

Jorion had felt Taine's desperation at the evening meal

and saw her stealthily slide fruit into a pouch beneath her surcote. Holding to his oath to watch his bride closely, he'd lain wakeful in the chamber adjoining hers and had known the moment someone began to stir in her chamber and moved to block the path. Without turning the dark power of his gaze from her, he lightly kicked the bundle further into the room and pushed the door quietly shut behind him.

Held captive by fathomless eyes, Taine heard the ominous sound of the softly closing door. Certain of his fury, she braced herself for an attack. Thick lashes fell and clenched shut when his hand reached toward her. She waited for a blow or a rough grip to jerk her close but felt only the light brush of fingers against her throat loosening ties. A nearly imperceptible touch brushed her hood aside and slipped the cloak from her shoulders. Surprised by this response to her transgression, she peered at him suspiciously. Two strong hands lifted toward her throat. Her eyes shut again. She was certain he meant to strangle her. Senses heightened by apprehension, she felt the curiously light brush of thumbs tilting her chin. Then came the gentle pressure of firm mouth against her own. An unexpected pleasure trembled through her, even as his hands spread into the rich tangle of unbound curls.

Warmed by the heat of her skin, firebright curls twined about Jorion's fingers like a living caress and rose-petal lips opened on her small wild gasp. Striving for control, he silently commanded himself to damp down the flames that set his blood to steaming and not panic her with his fierce ardor. Eyes blacker than midnight, he drew back, preventing himself from plundering her mouth. Instead, applying no pressure to hold her within his grasp, he rubbed short tantalizing kisses to the corners of her mouth, cheeks, eyelids, and in the sensitive hollows beneath her ears.

Caught all unawares and with none of Jorion's experience in desire and its restraint, Taine swayed. Strong arms offered but did not force support. She settled into their tender cradle, his clean masculine scent and the feel of his big, hard body overwhelmed her with dangerous sensations and drove away all rational thought. Still, innate inhibitions built of a lifetime kept her from reaching out to caress the bronze skin of his firm jaw or stroke across the well-remembered muscled strength of his chest. But, too weak to prevent the action, too far under his enchantment to care, she melted against him, wax to candle flame.

Lush curves full against him, a temptation near beyond bearing, Jorion went rigid and laid his cheek atop auburn silk as he forced himself to remember his oath not to claim her before the marriage rites. Nonetheless, he rationalized, she must learn how gentle loving could be, must learn his embrace was not of force but sweet pleasure. They'd shared passion's fire before, yet always she drew back. This time, to them both, he meant to prove that the combined flames of dragon and fire-sprite could consume such inflammable reticence.

Wrapped close in his arms, Taine felt him go suddenly still like an iron statue, albeit one fresh from the forger's fire and red-hot. She looked up into eyes where glittering gold sparks swirled in dark depths. Mesmerized, she tumbled headlong into blazing hungers and felt her knees go weak. His arms contracted gently and he lifted her, turning toward the bed. Deep into desire's fiery well, Taine didn't realize her feet no longer touched the floor. The tilting and movement seemed only an extension of the whirlpool of hunger she was drowning in.

Jorion laid her across the soft mattress in the draped bed's warm cavern and followed her down, mentally arguing with the small voice of cool reason. For a moment, only a moment, no more. Then he would leave her alone and unclaimed till vows had been said.

Feeling the warmth and strength of his body so near, Taine instinctively moved closer. His mouth touched hers, pressed her soft, yielding lips apart, and eased his tongue inside to taste her like a bee after nectar.

Taine's heart went wild, loving the intimacy, the feel, the taste. Drowning in blazing sensations, she shifted restlessly. Mindlessly she wrapped her arms about his neck and spread her fingers into his thick gold strands. Spinning ever faster, her world began and ended with the man in her arms. His hands swept down the long arch of her back, pulling her deeper into his embrace, bringing her hips against his. Still Taine wanted a closer contact, wanted something unknown, something more. She arched against him, nails digging into the firm flesh of his neck. A rough groan tore out of his tight throat and a shudder ran the length of him. Knowing he must stop now or surrender his honor, forswear his oath, Jorion pulled abruptly away.

From beneath passion-heavy lids, Taine looked into eyes blazing gold. Mind fogged with smoke of her dragon's fire, Taine did not quickly comprehend his action. Desperately wanting to continue, to build the flames to new heights, she lifted her arms in yearning invitation. Only through effort of years of restraint was Jorion able to pull from enticing arms and look down at the hunger in deep-green eyes and at soft, trembling lips that silently pleaded for his, without falling again to her pleasure and his own.

"You can never escape me, nor I you," his deep velvet voice warned. "We are fated to be one." His gaze held hers as he added, "Surely you feel the cord that binds us?"

Taine's arms fell but the power in gold-flecked eyes seemed to force her nearly imperceptible nod. His smile was strained and tilted with self-mockery. He rose and after a long, steady look departed.

Feel the cord that bound them, the golden net that drew her ever nearer? Aye, she did that, always had no matter how she would deny it. But in the quiet of the room she could no longer deny its forbidden name: love. What a day of defection this had been. First Bertwald had deserted her and now she had been forced to admit her own self-betrayal. Not once but twice. Once for allowing the birth, nurturing, and maturing of an emotion which in her experience meant only pain. And then again for surrendering to the pleasures he so easily roused. She had sworn she would never yield to a man's desires, never give herself to further a man's goals and what but that could come from the union? Surely, given the opportunity her heritage offered, like all men—even Bertwald—would he not use her to his own ends?

❧ Chapter 15 ❧

In but a few short days the growing weight of winter cold had crushed the bright shades of autumn into the dull straw of dying grass and deep brown of barren tree limbs. Near the only green here in the midst of the orchard lay in shadowed eyes of the maid glancing upward to clouds gathered overhead, a heavy grey cover pressing the earth with ominous discontent. To shield herself from the nipping air, Taine pulled the hood of her fur-lined cloak closer to cold-blushed cheeks. The weather seemed only to echo the foreboding that oppressed her with a growing sense of impending danger.

Without serious need, few would venture beyond the castle's walls when storm clouds gathered above, but she had welcomed Richard's invitation to walk as they had many times in the past few days.

Since her attempted escape, a sennight, seven tense days and seven lonely nights, had passed in strained monotony. In the labyrinth of Taine's entangled thoughts they nearly blended together. With the spider watching closely from the shadows, she was trapped within the dragon's domain but found herself less frightened of captivity than of her weakening resolve to win free.

All too aware of the tempting dangers in the dragon's company, she refused to meet his eyes for fear of tumbling again into their depths. Yet within his presence she could feel the golden net twining ever more tightly about her. Unsought, inescapable love strengthened each cord. When he was near, her gaze inevitably followed him. She surreptitiously soaked in every detail—the way firelight glinted on blond hair and burnished bronze skin, the strength of arms lifting small Bryce for a ride on broad shoulders, the velvet voice that offered encouragement to a new and somewhat clumsy page or low laughter rippling at the jest of another.

Studying Jorion from beneath lowered lashes, she'd been struck again by the paradox in bright hair and dark eyes. Was he in truth the merciless warrior feared by naughty Scottish children or the gentle lord who would care for the hungry serfs of his land as well as he cared for his prized steeds? Was Bertwald in the right when he named Jorion her only sure defense? But if defense against confinement, what difference between one and another? Between her first castle-prison and the dragon's? She shifted uneasily as a silent voice in her thoughts mocked the question. If this was a prison, then 'twas exceedingly soft. Moreover, her gaolers were unlike as lions and lambs, mighty dragons and skulking dungeon rats. With love admitted she could not compare the two. Nay, she argued back as so many times since the day they'd met, such love was merely the path to self-betrayal, for would he not use her as others had sought to do? That argument so oft-repeated had lost its heat. At least for the time before he learned her true identity, a soft enticing voice called, she could live a life of love and joy as it might have been but for the curse of her birthright. Nay, the mental dispute continued. If, to gain his full protection as Bertwald urged, she admitted her heritage, would he not see her as merely the key to a crown? Mayhap, mayhap not. Nay, responded her cautious side. And so it went in her thoughts—round and round to no purpose. Others might fear the fire of the dragon's temper, but she feared the lure of the dragon's passion, for it tempted her to give what she had sworn would she never.

Seeking distraction, she spent her days talking with Halyse, playing with Bryce, even visiting with the castle-serfs and guardsmen. But most often she walked with Richard through the outer bailey's orchards and fields. She'd caught only glimpses of the tactful guards, who followed her every step and knew she would be restrained from walking far alone. Though Richard appeared genuinely sorry for his unthinking use of her, repeated again and again his promise to perform any penance she named, she would trust not him nor any man. Still, she welcomed his companionship on the long walks doubtless otherwise forbidden her. Without trust, she offered him little conversation beyond the state of the weather, the delights of past meals, and talk of castle inhabitants. Usually, as now, they walked in quiet companionship.

A short distance from Richard's side, Taine leaned against the gnarled trunk of an old apple tree and stared up at the lone leaf still stubbornly attached to a branch above her head. Tenacious but doomed to failure—like her? Nay, Taine refuted the dismal thought. She would find some way free. Driven by fear of her own weakening resolve, she had searched long but found no means of escape—a depressing reality. She looked toward the great fortress above, white-washed towers bright against threatening grey skies.

"Was your castle much the same as Jorion's?" Richard asked curiously, stepping near as he wrapped his stylish scarlet cloak close about his slender form.

The same as Castle Dragonsward? Taine glanced at him sharply but on meeting steady blue eyes looked as quickly away. In her mind rose the image of her cold and gloomy castle-prison. It and Castle Dragonsward were no more alike than sweet peaches and bitter tansy. Aye, they both stood on fearsome cliffs but whereas the first clung to a jagged precipice above mighty waves that crashed and battered a rocky shore, from between the back wall of the latter and its high stone pedestal liquid silver sparkled down, ending in a shining spray of diamond droplets. Compared to the hostile Morag, dour servants, and rough gaolers of her prison, Taine realized how welcoming was Castle Dragonsward. Despite the mists of danger swirling around and through its mighty walls, within were friends as well—Halyse and Will and Bryce and Mercia and Sander, even Richard and Elspeth. In the depth of summer her former prison was cold but, even with winter fast approaching, Castle Dragonsward seemed warm, a place of beauty where people laughed and music was heard. Not seen for several days, Taine's sweet smile reappeared although she answered simply, "Nay, nothing like."

"Tell me of it," Richard persisted, curiosity increased by the combination of warm smile and cold words.

"A dreary place with nothing of beauty within." Her answer was curt. She had no wish to think more on the dismal past nor see more bright comparisons to further tempt her to remain where she stood, full within the spider's web.

"You were there." Richard argued her claim of no beauty.

Taine shook her head in denial of the compliment.

Undaunted, Richard advanced a weaker example, the only one he could think of, having no knowledge of her past years save the truth of her heritage. "And your ring."

Taine looked at the dainty circlet of twined metals, sorrow in her eyes. "I see no beauty, only a symbol of the treachery in all men."

Having heard her speak of her prejudice before, Richard did not flinch as he lifted her hand to gaze at the band. It was too delicate and charming to mean aught of such ill, just as the maid was assuredly too tender and sweet to carry such bitterness. "'Tis lovely," he said softly, eyes on her as he spoke.

Rose lips firmed into a bitter line and sea-mist eyes never left the fingers he held. "Aye, lovely. My father said 'twas known as the 'cherish ring,' one my mother should have given to me the day of my betrothal. As she was gone, he gave it to me in her stead the night before I was to sail away and become child bride to a prince." Taine paused, feeling again a pain she'd thought long since stifled by disdain. Pain that welled out in aching words she'd meant never to speak. "My father said he loved me—even as he sent me to spend my days in dreary confinement. He *lied.*"

Richard saw her anguish and desperately sought to turn

its course with meaningless talk. "You are Margaret?" Taine tilted her head and nodded, looking at him from the corner of eyes filled with suspicion.

"Your mother and grandmother were Margarets too?"

Again Taine nodded. Why did he ask of her forebears? Was he checking the validity of her claim in preparation to earn some reward by use of her?

"A curious fact," Richard lightly commented, hoping to draw her into talk of this oddity and others. He collected small tidbits like some birds collect useless bits of cloth and straw to build strong nests. Seeing Taine's pain turn to misdoubts for his intent, he recognized the failure of his strategy. Shrugging away the talk of so idle a fact, Richard changed his course full about. Some said that speaking of trials and wounds would lessen their pain, much as lancing proud flesh oft brought relief. He boldly asked, "Tell me about your years of confinement and the method of your release. Tell me how you came to Jorion's side."

Suddenly turned stone, Taine's heart sank to her toes, for here was the embodiment of her fear. She only wondered what form his reward would take and from whose hand it came. Not from Baliol, who knew the whole and would learn her whereabouts from Sir Thomas. Then from whom? From Jorion? And why question now? Although he had already learned her most threatening secret, she would not share more.

Richard saw the hopeless resignation on her face and knew his blunder. "I have but raised your fears, not lessened them as I'd meant." He shook his head with self-disgust. "I only wanted to show myself a friend to whom you can speak plainly and safely of your past with no worry I will disclose your words to another." Her delicate brows were drawn and green eyes narrowed. She was plainly full of suspicion, and Richard saw he would have to prove his sincerity with more than words. "I see I have not yet proven myself worthy of your confidence and can only beg you again to charge me any penance to prove my good faith. But, until I've shown myself equal to your trust, we will speak of other matters."

He went on to talk of his mother and happy memories of his youth, which brought further stories of Jorion, the friendship that grew between the reserved, wary boy and the extrovert so unalike. Too, he spoke with respect of Jorion's honor in caring not only for the elderly priest whom he loved but for the uncle who disdained him and fought the king whom Jorion followed.

Although the winds strengthened and whipped cloaks about chilled forms, some capricious sprite of nature held the threatening storm at bay. The grey sky had deepened almost to night and the evening meal was near begun by the time they returned to the warmth and light of the imposing castle.

Huge platters laden with pheasants stuffed with a savory concoction were reduced to a bare skeleton with no aid from Taine, who only laid aside a few tender strips for her kitty's repast. An unpracticed page knelt carefully at her side to offer the meal's final course, a selection of fruit and cheese. Biting his lip in anxiety, he studiously balanced the precarious tray. She lacked for appetite but couldn't bear to see his careful effort go useless and thus accepted a deep yellow wedge. As the youngster turned fractionally toward his lord, she wondered at what point a bashful boy grew hard and learned to scheme and turn all to his own advantage. From the corner of her eyes she glanced sideways to watch Jorion lift a shiny apple to firm lips. Hearing the snap as he bit into its crisp flesh, she found herself unable to sustain such all-encompassing disdain when she knew his strength was built in self-defense. The quiet voice of justice whispered that he had done much for her and asked no payment but that she stay and fulfill what she had claimed.

Jorion felt himself watched but knew if he turned to meet that gaze, it would drop away. During the long walks Taine shared with Richard, Jorion had paced his castle and snapped at his guardsmen, 'til they began to mutter amongst themselves of their lord's metamorphosis into a true and snarling dragon of irritable flames. Nonetheless, in Taine's presence he kept his temper tightly reined. She'd turned from him since the night he'd prevented her flight and he'd cursed his oath to Bertwald a thousand times. Only for its sake had he torn himself away even as she surrendered, lifting beckoning arms to him. And still now, days later, he dared not touch her again for fear he could not restrain their fierce blaze. Burned on one hand with fires of jealousy and on the other with flames of desire difficult to leash, 'twas a wonder he'd not scorched the castle with his displeasure. He liked to see her temper flare in opposition to his own ('twas something no other woman had braved) but trod softly, wary of frightening her and losing what ground he'd gained.

Although he knew the result, Jorion looked swiftly down into her wide eyes and watched in fascination while sea-mist darkened to forest-green.

Caught by his unexpected glance, Taine discovered anew the power of even so brief a contact with the depths in the dragon's eyes, burned by suddenly flaring sparks of gold. She tore her gaze from his with a tiny gasp and looked quickly down, startled to see chunks falling free of the wedge she'd unconsciously twisted between her fingers. Before her eyes small irregular balls bounced and rolled across the table's pristine cloth—and she knew that he saw too. Horrified, she dropped what remained and tucked her hands under the table's white cover to curl fingers into her peach-toned surcote while hunching beneath a steady black gaze.

Had Taine glanced up, she would have caught a glimpse of Jorion's odd expression. Sitting at Taine's far side, Richard saw the quickly masked look and his brows flew up. Never before had he seen such gentle longing on a man's face, the dragon's least of all. He'd known Jorion jealous but had thought possessiveness its source and was stunned by the idea of the proud lord laying himself vulnerable to love's sharp pangs.

For Taine's embarrassment, Jorion wanted to offer the comfort of shared amusement but knew she would likely misunderstand and feel herself ridiculed. He bit back gentle raillery and instead sought to divert attention.

"You must come to the tiltyard, Richard," Jorion said seriously but his eyes smiled. "You could provide a fine example for our young knights in training."

"'Struth, I am a fine example of all that must not be done." Richard shook his head in mock disgust. He had seen Taine's nervous reaction and quickly picked up on Jorion's diversion.

"If you prefer," Jorion answered, "but I thought you perhaps more suited to a demonstration of how to send a sharp dagger dead to point."

"Why me when they have the famous, or is it infamous, Golden Dragon?" Richard asked, one dark brow arched as he stroked his short, pointed beard.

"I am neither famous nor infamous for my dagger skill," Jorion responded immediately, one-sided smile appearing.

"Mayhap not," Richard replied, "but were we to come to a battle with daggers alone, I would not leave the victor." He grinned suddenly. "And a fine thing it be that, as I lack in martial skill, I have the cunning and caution of the fox and would never tempt the dragon's fire."

Peering around the earl's broad form, Elspeth watched the two men diligently easing the other woman's discomfort. Strangely her irritation was only for the one. Jorion would be Taine's mate and it was just he should soothe his bride's unease, but surely Richard's efforts were an overdone thing—particularly for so minor a thing. Brown eyes burned on the offender, as they had for much of the week. She, too, had watched as Richard escorted Taine on lengthy walks. Although never beyond sight of the castle walls nor beyond convention, they'd walked in privacy.

Having already forgiven Taine for falling under Richard's irresistible charms, though it was far from conducive to friendship between the two women, the full power of Elspeth's jealousy fell on Richard. With neither temperament nor nerve to relieve her jealousy with such fiery displays as the earl loosed upon his men, Elspeth could only glare at the dark-haired man when his back was turned. Even their childhood friendship seemed at an end. She couldn't bear to have him treat her as a child, while he lavished his attention on another. Thus she took care to stay clear of his company.

In his chair at the end of the table, Sir Thomas leaned back. From beneath half-lowered lids he observed the others, studied their words and reactions. He saw the closeness between Richard and Taine and the younger maid's disgust that it was so. Again in this would Richard, that most unworthy of sons, frustrate his father's goals. From behind the impervious mask of his ruddy face, he schemed. It was clear he must take matters into his own hands, put the concept before Jorion himself.

"My lord." A voice from below startled the self-involved gathering at the high table, and nearly of one accord they turned to the speaker. Suddenly the focus of so many eyes, Halyse fell back a step, yet their expectant expressions demanded she continue and speak her business. "I crave pardon," she dipped politely to Jorion, "but I have found little opportunity to speak with you in the day." In truth she'd had ample opportunity but, knowing from Will the ease with which the dragon's fire was roused of recent times, she'd chosen to speak with him only in the company of his lady, where his restraint was strong.

"Have you news for me?" Jorion prompted gently, feeling remorse for the leery expression on Halyse's open face. He prided himself on dealing justly with others but knew in past days they'd learned to move about him with care. Another fault to lay at the door of his inability to immediately claim the maid his and end the "friendship" that raised his ire.

"I've come only to assure you that, with the dawn of your wedding two days hence, all will be in readiness."

Halyse's words jerked Taine from her contemplation of Jorion's strong hand idly twirling the dregs in a silver chalice. In all the hours they'd spent together over past days, her friend had never mentioned the wedding nor the arrangements in which she must have been fully involved. Hard on the passing of the first thought rose a stunning realization of the shortness of time. In the haze of recent days, she'd been so caught in the conflict of her soul that she'd not comprehended the inexorable passage of time to a destination she must escape. While Jorion asked after the completion of wedding details, she desperately cast about for a last-moment plan to forestall the rite they discussed.

No sooner had Halyse rejoined Will at the top of a lower table than Thomas called up a pleasant face and turned to Jorion with a benign smile that held all the sincerity of a winged serpent. "I also have matters to discuss with you," Thomas informed his nephew. "A matter that calls for privacy."

Taine froze, breath trapped in her throat. With the

marriage unexpectedly close, did Sir Thomas mean to disclose her heritage? Until the possibility of imminent exposure, she had not realized how well-cherished was the dream of living as wife to Jorion without threat of her past, for a little time at least. Both the possibility of exposure and the power of her dream strengthened her resolve to find escape before the morn of their wedding rite—so fearfully near!

White light from a pyramid of candles behind glowed on shining hair as Jorion nodded his assent. Remembering his determination to hold irritation in check, he rose to his feet without question and led his uncle to the corner stairwell. As they climbed the circling steps and passed through the deep shadows between widely spaced firebrands, he had the sensation of a cold blade approaching his unprotected back. Though he derided the impression as a flight of fantasy, he glanced sharply behind to find his uncle puffing in his wake. Softened by age and a life of ease, Thomas' normally pink cheeks were deep crimson and his breath labored. Plainly, Jorion thought, rejecting his momentary unease, his uncle was in no shape to offer a threat, even were that his desire.

On gaining his chamber, Jorion led his uncle to the chairs arranged about the table. Struggling to catch his breath, Thomas sank into the nearest and was thankful for the time Jorion spent in pouring a measure of wine into goblets kept ever waiting. The task spared him the time to regain control of his breath and speak evenly.

"As you are not to wed Elspeth," he said at last, "I've come to propose an alternative." Elspeth was Jorion's ward and as such he must approve any marriage agreement. A thing that stung Thomas. He was convinced 'twas he who had played the role while Jorion was so oft absent on his king's violent missions.

Settling in the chair opposite his uncle, Jorion's face was impassive, his eyes shielded by half-closed lids. What plot had his conniving uncle now devised?

"I know you bear her an affection if only that of brother for sister, as you claim. Thus surely you will wish to see her happy in her marriage." That Jorion had not immediately called halt to his subject encouraged Thomas. He leaned forward and continued with overdone affability. "She's a shy and oversensitive child who has known no man of noble birth save me and you—and my son."

"Richard?" One golden brow lifted in question. 'Twas clear Thomas suggested that worthy for her mate, but the idea of a match between the timid girl and the wicked-tongued lady-charmer seemed a farfetched notion. Richard had been her childhood friend but of recent days even that tie had been sundered.

Despite the other's discouraging exclamation, Thomas added, "Although the lands he inherited from his mother are not so great as those she is heiress to, surely the great fondness Elspeth bears for him will be compensation."

Considering the conversation Jorion had overheard between Elspeth and Richard, the claimed fondness seemed an unlikely thing. However, already burdened with far more serious concerns, Jorion was loath to add another source of contention to the many already lying between him and his uncle.

"'Tis a serious matter and one I cannot give answer to without thoughtful consideration. With my own wedding so near, I have little time and can only say I'll give you my decision after I've had time to think on it." He rose, forcing Thomas to stand as well.

Although irritated by the younger man's dismissal and call for more time, Thomas dared not ruin the warm camaraderie he'd affected. He offered his arm in hearty salute and as agreement to the other's promise.

❧ Chapter 16 ❧

EBONY RINGLETS FELL FORWARD against fire-flushed cheeks as Elspeth bent closer to flamelight. The solar boasted only a small window, and the poor light of a heavily overcast morn was not sufficient for the close needlework in her hands. On a three-legged stool she sat before a blaze that filled the lack. Threads of bright hues worked in close stitches would become a lovely tapestried chair cover. With a sharp exclamation, she dropped the intricate design and jerked her hand away to keep a crimson drop from staining painstaking work.

Fingertip in mouth to ease the sting, she glared at the offending needle still thrust into cloth. Her skill had deserted her and she knew the cause. She'd begun this piece while Richard accompanied Taine on the first of the past two weeks' many walks. During all those that followed, she'd had more than adequate time to see it complete—if only her jealousy had not grown apace and turned nimble fingers to thumbs. The tears provoked by the loss of Jorion for mate had been but the pouting response of a youngster forced to leave childhood dreams behind. A truth made

211

plain by the fact that the distress of Jorion's loss was nothing compared to the pain in watching Richard bend all his practiced charms on the lovely and mysterious lady in their midst.

"Something gone amiss?" asked Richard from the door he'd silently opened in time to hear her cry of pain.

Elspeth's hand dropped away as she hastily turned toward the subject of her irritation. More than once her thoughts had summoned him. A lock of glossy brown hair fell boyishly over his forehead and he brushed it aside as he came forward. "Methinks the needle is cursed," she babbled her answer, tension growing with his each step nearer, "controlled by some small demon who takes delight in my discomfort." Richard grinned, and beneath his smile's charming power Elspeth's gaze fell to study her injury as if it were a wound of great concern.

Richard knew Elspeth's disgust with his attentions to Taine. He'd not meant to use the younger girl ill, but felt he must make amends to Taine to prove himself her friend. Not wishing to turn Elspeth away with his actions, still he could not suppress the pleased warmth her jealousy inspired. Such reaction proved she bore him some degree of interest. Whether less or more should be no worry for he knew well how to play upon it. Yet this time, when the result was of such import, he felt an unaccustomed lack of confidence in his amorous talents.

Kneeling at Elspeth's side, Richard lifted the injured hand in a gentle grasp. "Aye," he solemnly agreed, lightly touching the tiny red dot. "'Tis a serious wound, for which there is but one effective cure."

Elspeth's breath stopped when he bent his head to kiss the needleprick. Clasping her fingers still, he straightened to meet her eyes on a level. Blue met brown as he slowly brushed his mouth across their soft tips, then turned her hand over to press it against a vulnerable palm. Sensitive flesh felt the touch of firm lips, the silky brush of moustache and beard. Caught for the first time in a haze of sensation, she found no will to break the visual bond drawing her closer and closer. His mouth lightly touched soft lips and her lashes dropped. With a sigh she melted nearer.

Richard was not immune to the invitation of a delight

he'd never seriously thought to taste. Gentle arms swallowed the softly rounded maid, folded her against him, while his warm mouth moved on hers with a slow, lazy pressure that coaxed hers to open for him. One kiss melted into the next, a slow exploration which deepened hunger.

Unaccustomed to partners innocent of loveplay, Richard bumbled the most important encounter of his life. "Your kiss," he murmured, nipping at a passion-swollen lower lip, "is the sweetest of all those I have tasted."

For Elspeth, his words turned sweet kisses sour. She knew his popularity at court, had heard teasing talk of his rakish reputation. His comment seemed confirmation of a momentarily denied fact—fall to his practiced charms and become merely another in his long line of conquests. Plainly he'd turned to one as plump and inexperienced as she, only from the boredom of being held long from the court and its wide selection of willing ladies. Oversensitive in the first instance, this culmination of tensions of the past several weeks lodged an unwelcome knot in her tight throat. She pulled free and, under effort of will, held scalding tears at bay until she reached the solar door. Throwing it open, she rushed toward her chamber, moisture-filled eyes unable to see the woman she brushed past.

Richard, still on his knees with hands braced against thighs, stared after the fleeing woman and wondered what he'd done to deserve such response. With shoulders hunched, his head drooped forward disconsolately.

In the dimly lit corridor outside the solar door, Taine watched the wet-cheeked girl disappear before turning to move into the chamber. Her questioning frown deepened on seeing the richly garbed Richard in so unusual a position. How had timid Elspeth brought so experienced a man to his knees?

A movement brought Richard's attention to the puzzled newcomer standing hesitantly one pace within the room. He quickly jumped to his feet, smoothing anguish from his expression, but Taine had already seen the pain. Green eyes studied the slender man for a long moment, noted the mask of welcome he'd forced over unhappy features and realized they shared the same complaint. Even merry Richard suffered the pangs of unreturned love. She tilted her head, sending thick clouds of hair the color of deep berry wine cascading forward over her shoulder. An oddly pleasing possibility came to mind. After she was gone, would Jorion suffer any part of such torment—beyond wounded pride? She wished he might share her love, but the difficulties of his past had built heavy armor about him and she doubted him vulnerable to such gentle emotion.

Moonling, she silently berated herself, running nervous hands over the soft wool of her leaf-green surcote. No time now to waste pondering such useless dreams. The night past, Halyse's talk of the imminent wedding had shocked her from days of lethargy. With but a few hours to forestall the vows she both feared and dangerously longed for, she'd spent the night frantically devising first one wild, improbable plot for escape and then another. In the end she was forced to acknowledge what she already knew: she could not safely flee at night, nor during the day—by herself. Bertwald would not aid her cause, but Richard claimed himself willing to perform any penance to atone for the dragon's fire he'd turned upon her. She could not flee the castle alone, but no one would halt Richard, even if she, as so oft in past days, was in his company.

Taine tossed back over her shoulder the tresses she'd wasted no time to decorously bind. Only well-bred ladies wore fine nets or rich cloth. The common woman allowed her hair to fall loose or braided it simply. As she wished to hide her noble background, she'd chosen the former, never realizing her delicate features and graceful carriage were a revelation in themselves. With a brave smile pinned to her lips, she approached Richard. She must reveal a further secret to him and pray it would gain his support. Although Richard might well have some spark of love for his sire, she was certain he bore little respect for his father's blind devotion to a cause lost long ago.

"I've come to collect on your offer to make amends." She hesitated, twining fingers into soft wool and watching closely for his response to her words.

Richard was surprised. His remorse was true and his words were sincere. He had even hoped she would name some duty so he could prove himself a worthy friend, yet he'd not truly expected her to name a price. Beneath his warm and steady smile, he was uncomfortably aware that he'd laid himself open to this mysterious woman's unknown demands. She was a gracious lady, he reassured himself, and could surely ask no more than what others demanded: a new length of costly material, a trinket fetched from some distant place, or a song written for her alone.

"Whatever penance you name," Richard gallantly acceded, sweeping an exaggerated bow, "I'll perform without question. But first sit here at the fire. The day is bitter cold and its warmth welcome." He waved her toward the recently deserted three-legged stool and bent to retrieve the forgotten tapestry at its foot.

Legs weak with tension, Taine willingly complied. His decision on the matter would be the breaking or making of her plan and could still be denied. The stool was short for one of her height and her knees rose high. She tucked her legs sideways and arranged the soft green of her kirtle carefully, then ruined the graceful effect by twisting her fingers nervously into the cloth. Too caught in far weightier matters, Taine had long since given up on her intention to teach her hands gracious calm.

While Richard studied the skillfully stitched cloth in his hands, Taine took a deep breath and dove headlong into the secret she had come to share. "I was taken from a boat carrying me toward alliance with the English prince." She pleated the soft wool of her surcote, carefully matching each fold in width. "'Twas your father who delivered the wee bairn I was to a remote and chilling fortress meant to hold me the length of my days." She looked up to find a frown gathering above blue eyes.

Richard turned from sea-mist eyes to stare into low-burning flames. He was not surprised to learn of his father's part in preventing Scotland's rightful sovereign from taking its crown to the hated English. As a child he'd heard whispers of such a deed. When grown he'd come to consider those stories merely products of gossip born in inventive minds, and his certainty of his father's involvement merely the work of a child's overactive imagination. He kicked a smoldering log and sparks rose like gleams of truth from the inert dark of the past. On learning Taine's identity, he'd not paused to consider the danger his father could be and even now sought logic to gainsay it. He shook his head. No, it couldn't be.

"From the day he delivered you there to the day you arrived here"—his sharp glance returned to Taine—"had you seen my father or he you?"

"Nay," Taine answered immediately. She saw his reasoning and would have explained the nature of the threat, but Richard spoke again as if unconsciously anxious to hold back her words.

He little esteemed his father but would hide from the possibility of one close in blood harming so sweet a maid. In instinctive denial he reasoned, "If you were a child when last he saw you, he cannot be certain who you are and thus is no danger to you."

Taine recognized his hurt and sorrowed for it, but she could not give up now or her plan was lost. She lifted her hand. Flamelight glowed on the curiously twined band. "As you once said, my ring is unique and one I have worn since my father put it on my finger. Unique, but one your father has seen before and by which he knows who I am."

Richard kicked the logs again, sending another storm of sparks upward. It was a truth he'd known in his heart from the first she'd spoken. And another example of how little he found to love in the man who had given him life.

"Don't you see?" Taine jumped up and clasped Richard's forearm anxiously. "Each moment I remain in his sight, the danger grows. He was willing to steal me away once and would surely not balk at the need a second time." Eyes now deep-green wells of pleading, she squeezed the flesh in her hands. "You must help me flee before he sees me again confined." She could speak of her fear of captivity, but would not burden him with the possibility of his father seeing the threat of her existence ended with violent finality.

"Not I but another," Richard shook his head, sending an unruly brown lock again to lay against his forehead. "Jorion is your best defense against any foe. Tell him your plight."

Thick lashes dropped over cloudy green eyes, Taine let her hands fall and stepped back feeling defeat creep upon her. How could Richard understand her dread of the dragon's learning her secret?

"Aye," he renewed the argument she'd immediately refused. Jorion was more than able to hold his wife safe. "Surely you have seen how my father backs away from the dragon's fire." Misunderstanding the reason for her denial, he added, "As you are not on terms of ease with Jorion, I would speak to him for you, tell him your story. Once he knows, he will stand between you and all others."

"Nay!" She shook her head wildly, auburn hair whipping about slender shoulders with her adamant refusal. "He would be the first to see me forced where I would not go. 'Tis *my* story to tell to whom I choose, and none of yours."

Surprised at her vehemence, Richard stepped forward but Taine fell back another pace. The thought of Richard revealing her identity to Jorion sent a sharp lance of pure terror through her. With such information, doubtless Jorion too would seek to bend her will for his own ends—and his powers were far more effective than others, his fire too alluring. Until he knew her secret she could dream, if only in memories, that he had seen in her a woman he could love, rather than the promise of a crown.

"Promise you will not speak of my past!" Desperate thoughts whirled in her mind. A simple promise was not binding enough, nor even a simple oath. "Swear on the Holy Cross that you will not!" Surely Richard feared the punishment for profanity of the Cross. Yes, the Cross, it must be on the Cross.

To calm her anxiety, Richard easily bowed to her will. "By the Holy Cross I swear my oath to speak never of your heritage." He spoke so quick and confidently that she did not hear the care with which he chose his words. A small idea nibbled at the edge of his thoughts.

Having his oath, Taine's stiff-held shoulders dropped in relief only to tense again with determination. He'd not heard her plan but it was lost, and she must find another. With a light frown of concentration, she turned to the door, intent on finding some way to depart, even if it must be down over the castle wall. She'd no skill at descending a rope and had rejected the plan the past night, but in her desperation mulled the improbable idea over again. The first step was to find a rope of sufficient length and strength, one inconspicuous enough for her to furtively carry away.

Watching Taine's chin lift with renewed determination,

Richard knew she would go even without another's aid. Could the fragile woman not see that to a lone female the dangers of the road were far greater than mere captivity? He opened his mouth to caution her but saw in the stiffness of her slender back that she would no more listen to that warning than to the counsel he'd given. His conscience pricked. He could not let her go alone into danger, and he had repeatedly offered to perform any penance.

"Hold, Taine." His voice was unintentionally sharp.

Taine turned, distrust darkening her eyes. Did he mean to wield some unexpected weapon and keep her from her intent?

"Tell me the plan," he continued softly. "I gave you my promise and I hold to my words." His father, having set out at dawn on a day's hunt, would likely not return until after nightfall. Thus, he would not be aware of Taine's flight until at least one day had passed.

Although suspicion slowed her steps, she returned to face him. "If I seek to pass through the lower bailey gate, I will be stopped." She halted a pace before him and looked into blue eyes that met hers steadily. "If you seek exit, none will question you—even if I am at your side."

"You mean to *walk* free?"

"Why not?" Taine was defensive. "The steeds here are the dragon's and precious to him. I will not take one." Her chin tilted and silver glints of determination flashed in her eyes. This was a fact Richard could not deny and one which did not force her to admit her lack of riding ability.

Glossy brown head tilted to one side, Richard quietly studied her. Slowly stroking from moustache to goatee tip, he sought some satisfactory rebuttal of her plan.

"To ride in a cart pulled by donkey or on a farm horse would raise questions for which we would have no explanation." Taine furthered her argument with words dropped into a lengthening silence like pebbles into a smooth pond.

Though no warrior trained to strategy, Richard knew himself outmaneuvered on every front and shrugged his acceptance. He must accompany her on the absurd attempt if only to protect her until Jorion arrived, as he no doubt would and burning with fury for their flight. Smiling in self-mockery for his oft-denied willingness to risk the dragon's fire, he asked only, "Do we go without provisions to ease the trip?"

Taine shook her head lightly, seeing very well his belief that it was a foolish deed not to be taken seriously. A strange thing that, for he knew she'd already escaped from one well-guarded fortress. No matter, once he had aided her through the confining gates, she would bid him return while she traveled on alone.

"Bread, meat, and my cloak are all I need." She met his gaze bravely, daring him to point out her ridiculously limited resources and for that refuse his aid.

Richard's brows rose but he said only, "Well enough." He'd learned the stubborn maid's nature well enough to know she would no doubt deny any attempt from him to show how seriously she lacked. From the escape of her first imprisonment, she must surely know as well as he the bare minimum for any attempt included weapons and some small cache of coins. Weapons. That, as with going afoot, was another ticklish point. Even with a soon-following Jorion, it was necessary to stand prepared for the dangers of the road.

Taine laced her fingers tightly together as she steadily watched the elegant man who plainly pondered some important matter. Silently she waited for him to speak.

"Were I to carry a sword, suspicion would immediately be roused, for"—he smiled in self-mockery—"unskilled as I am, I never do. But this," he said, pulling a heavily jeweled dagger from the stylish scabbard at his trim waist, "though no match for the dragon, I wield with great efficiency."

Taine nodded her acceptance. It was not a matter of great import as he would not be long with her. They agreed to meet, as was their wont, in the courtyard after the noontide meal. She would secrete her meager hoard away beneath her flowing cloak, and he would dress in dark hues and carry the dagger he was seldom without.

As the two in the solar plotted escape, in the courtyard the golden-haired lord listened to the plea of a distraught serf. Standing on rutted ground cold with winter death and twisting a rough woolen cap, the man in rough brown homespun petitioned his lord for mercy.

Sir Thomas had claimed the produce of his field, leaving naught but gleanings to keep his family alive. With the barren days of winter fast approaching, already that meager supply was gone.

Jorion was irritated by this example of the cruel management his uncle had wreaked on his land. It was confirmation of the rightness in his decision to take the position from him. He looked at the gaunt man, saw his misery, saw the fear in trembling hands, and knew only desperate need would bring to him a man so clearly frightened.

"They's caught me oldest poaching rabbits." The voice was hoarse with emotion. "Stephen's a good lad. 'Tis just that the babe is so small and grown weak with hunger. Me laddie loves the frail child and only done it to keep him alive." Dull eyes pleaded for understanding.

Jorion silently cursed the uncle who'd demanded his people's all and driven a lad to forbidden lengths for survival.

"He done it and they's said they gonna take his hands to keep him from doin' it again. He's so afeared that he ran to the woods." The agitated serf paused, Adam's apple bobbing as he swallowed hard before continuing. "Yestermorn Sir Thomas come to our hut and said the lad got to give hisself over by the time the chapel bells ring nones, else he'll send men to torch the thatch on our home and see me next oldest boy pay the price for his brother." The petitioner fell back before a fierce scowl, assuming his lord's anger directed to him for the rash plea.

Jorion's fury blazed. Here was proof that his uncle yet sought to control at least a part of his domain. And not he alone. For this threat's completion he must have aid—the men he'd brought from Scotland and still loyal to him. His fire was fanned by the knowledge that his home contained men he fed and housed, but who followed another's bidding.

The despair on the serf's face brought Jorion back to the problem at hand. He forced his features to relax. "Sir Thomas," he coldly stated, "has no power to command punishment on my lands."

As other lords, Jorion believed poaching a serious matter for which, to prevent its easy undertaking, serious punishment must be meted out. However, unlike others, he believed it was the lord's duty to see his people provided with at least the minimum foodstuffs to see them through cold and barren months. In that manner he'd long meant to prevent the desperation often cause to the deed. No fool, he also realized well-fed serfs were loyal and had strong backs to till his soil. He blamed himself for this lad's plight, for he'd allowed distractions to keep him from earlier filling his people's lack.

Jorion saw the humble man's gaze lift fearfully, and black eyes followed their path to find the sun fast approaching its zenith. "Where is your home?" he demanded.

A gleam of hope burned in hollow eyes as the man told the earl its location.

Jorion's lips clamped into a firm line. Time was short. The distance was such that only a hard ride would see them there before the named midafternoon hour arrived.

"Go then for your lands while I summon my knights. We'll mount our steeds and soon overtake you." The serf, he knew, would have little skill at riding, and as they must move swiftly they could not risk the slow pace required to carry him pillion. "Have no fear," he reassured. "We will prevent the carrying out of this wrong, and when you arrive it will be a danger past." His smile flashed white against bronze skin before he turned to stride quickly toward the stable, calling loudly for Will and two more knights.

At the meal meant to be her last in the dragon's lair, Taine was relieved to learn Jorion had gone. Though an unruly part of her longed for one last glimpse of the fascinating lord, the rational part lauded the ease his leaving lent her plan. When he was near, as if he bore some unnatural instinct, he seemed always to know what she planned before she began.

Meal complete, like most days the week past, Richard awaited Taine's coming at the foot of the castle's entrance stairs. He smiled jauntily and lifted his hand to aid her in descending the last two steps. The promised storm had broken in the night, pouring rain over the waiting land and sliming the courtyard. Taine looked down to watch her path across its muddy, hazardous surface and hide her eyes. She irrationally feared one of the dragon's guard might share his lord's uncanny ability and see her intent within green depths.

At the inner edge of the drawbridge Taine turned to savor one last look at the mighty castle raising its proud face against a glowering sky, pennants piercing the mists. Aye, as Will had said the first time she saw it, an appropriate home for a powerful dragon. She understood Jorion's pride in his home, remembered her first glimpse of it, a jewel laid atop rich green cloth. In fleeing her castle-prison she'd felt no regret but could not suppress such traitorous pangs now. If only she had no crown to be won, she would happily remain in these walls, surrender to the temptation of the dragon's fire. Then would she devote the rest of her days to piercing his armor and driving love's sweet blade into his heart.

Richard stood quietly at her side, seeing on her face a longing she would deny. It eased the path he'd chosen. He would fulfill her penance, see her free of the castle; but, too, he would lay a path easy to follow and stay by her side to protect her until Jorion had come to bring her back and claim her his. Then one deed more he would do to ease her dangers, although another she would deny.

Taine shook her head as if to free herself from the clinging tendrils of love and desire that bound her to this place. Again she kept her eyes on the path and moved wordless at Richard's side, breathing easily only after they'd passed unchallenged under the fierce iron teeth of the portcullis in the outer bailey wall.

Richard started down the path through rolling meadows but Taine, pausing at the crossroad some distance beyond the yawning jaw of the final gate, called him to a stop. He halted and turned with one brow raised in question of the woman cloaked in forest green.

"I travel that direction." Her words were soft but firm as she nodded down the path opposite the one he had chosen. She had concentrated all her energies on the simple process of winning free and had not thought so far as her journey's goal. As before, she had no notion of the way to anywhere or specific destination in mind. To ask of towns or cities might well have raised doubts for her purpose and had therefore been too risky a deed. However, it seemed clear to her that the meadow's long, flat expanse offered ease to any pursuer and chose instead the distant shelter of close-grown trees. Though few leaves remained, in their dark clothes she and Richard would blend among the multitude of stark trunks and branches, fade into the shadowy woodland.

Richard was not overpleased with her choice but kept his unhappiness to himself. It was necessary to travel some distance over meadow to reach the forest's edge. He dawdled along the way. First, to remove a pebble in his shoe, he sat on the thick brown blades that remained of dying meadow. He comically rolled about far more than necessary for so simple a task—and pressed a revealing hollow into its depth. Then, claiming a foot made sore by the stone, he limped—slowly. Next, saying it was easier on his injury, he left the path and moved through the deep grass at its side—laying two deep valleys in its brown length like furrows through a wheat field.

Impatient with Richard's leisurely pace, Taine failed to notice the trail he left. It was no short walk to the shielding trees; and at length she halted to turn toward him.

"I want to be well into the wood before nightfall," she said in exasperation. "I know you are in pain and would not deepen it with my haste, thus now is the time to bid farewell."

This was not in Richard's plan nor had he foreseen her intent to send him back and travel alone. "Nay," he responded firmly. "I'll not leave you before your destination is achieved."

Taine shook her head so firmly the hood fell back, revealing dark-flame hair that glowed even on a sun-hidden day and emphasized her stubborn nature. "You cannot, for I myself don't know where that lies. Moreover, Jorion would roast you with his fire."

"And you think 'twill be less if I return now after stealing his bride away only hours before the marriage rite and leaving her alone in the wild?" His disgust was clear.

Taine was stunned. In her blind determination to win free, she'd not considered the price Richard would pay. Legs gone suddenly weak, she sank with little grace into the pillow of dead grass at the path's edge. How many times had she cursed men for their willingness to use her without care for the price she'd pay? Now she herself was guilty of the deed she'd damned. She lowered her face into cupped hands, filled with remorse; the same remorse Richard had professed in hurting her. What a fool she'd been to brand Richard the same as the cruel men of her past for one thoughtless deed. Had she misjudged Jorion as falsely? Was the man who had saved her from threatening danger, time and time again, like all others? Nay, even his appearance demonstrated that unique he was. Her throat tightened and eyes burned. No matter his willingness to aid a nameless woman, she scolded her softening determination, likely the powerful lord would not hesitate to use a queen to his advantage. Even such cold censure could not halt her doubts for the rightness of her choice. Yet, it was too late now to question her wisdom, too late to accept the delights he offered. Scrubbing tears from her eyes, she pulled her tattered composure together. One thing was certain. She could not send Richard back to face the dragon's anger, a fire doubtless stoked by their deed. Richard must come with her.

Richard was startled by her reaction to his words and helplessly watched her sorrow for the retribution he'd named. When she turned a brave face to him, he held out his hand. "Please believe, whatever I do, I do for your happiness."

Filled with her own regret, Taine accepted the cryptic words as a final plea for her trust. Nodding, she gave him a watery smile before pulling up the hood to hide her distinctive hair and allowing him to help her up. She turned bravely toward the dark line on the near horizon.

In the distant edge of the forest, where dead leaves scuttled across cold ground and a ragged child peered fearfully around the edge of missing door, Jorion stepped onto an upended firewood round. Backed by his knights, he faced the men sent by Sir Thomas to perform a grisly act on an innocent child. Eyes hard and unyielding as granite, he bent his gaze slowly on first one and then the next.

With flaming torches they'd come, laughing boisterously, to pound on the small hut's flimsy door. Beneath the dragon's booted foot, the door had been smashed from its hinges, catching the leader full in the face and knocking him to the ground. The others had fallen back from the gaping doorway in terror of the black-clad man whose golden hair gleamed as brightly in torchlight as the two curved blades crossed against his wide chest. He'd stepped forth and was followed by three knights well-known for their fierceness in battle. Dropping weapons and dousing torches in the trough near the door, his uncle's men submitted to Jorion with no swordblow given.

"You are here at Sir Thomas' command, but he is not lord of this land," Jorion began in a voice as cold as death. "His lands are forfeit, your fealty to him ended. I have known of your wrongful loyalties but, for my uncle's sake and believing he'd not use you against me, I've allowed it to continue. My patience is at an end. Choose you to remain on my fiefdom, here and now swear fealty to me and no other. Choose you the lost Baliol cause and my uncle, and be gone before the sun rises on another morn."

In front of a serf's small, dingy hut where a child weak with hunger cried and a mother sobbed her relief, first one and then another defeated man stepped forward. Kneeling before the dragon with the acrid smoke of doused resin torches swirling around them, each swore a binding oath to him. Deed complete, they rode back to the castle carrying his decree to the remainder of his uncle's supporters, offering them the choice to be gone by the morrow or come to the wedding feast and pledge to him their fealty.

After they had departed, although his three knights were already ahorse, Jorion stood beside his golden stallion, readjusting the position of his saddle. He heard the approach of the serf who had sought his aid and returned as oaths were given. Jorion turned. Tears of gratitude flowing freely, the gaunt man sank to his knees and kissed the strong hand which offered protection. Jorion nodded acceptance of the man's honor and motioned him to rise.

"Where is your Stephen," Jorion asked, "the lad whose action brought this calamity on you?"

Although his lord smiled, renewed alarm haunted the serf's eyes.

"Nay," Jorion rebuked his anxiety. "I do not seek him for punishment; but, as I will provide you and all my people with rations sufficient to hold hunger at bay, I wish to be certain he understands that a similar action will not receive such mercy."

The serf's eyes widened at the promise. Mayhap the earl lied, but the promise was more than any other lord had given. "Don't know where he be, milord, but swear I when he returns to tell him your words and I promise he'll not break your law another time."

Jorion's brows furrowed. "You don't know where he is?"

The serf's stringy hair whipped around his shoulders with his negative answer.

"But he hides in the forest?" Jorion patiently drew information from the apprehensive man.

A vigorous nod was his response.

"He can survive in the forest only by poaching more of my beasts, thus I will find him and return him here so you may ensure he does not." The man cowered at the truth in such comment, but Jorion's cynical smile appeared. "Do not fear, I'll not hold him accountable until he has returned and heard your chastisement to honesty."

Apollo stood steady as Jorion swung his not inconsiderable weight onto the broad back. Jorion had much rather spend the fast-approaching night before his wedding in his castle and with his bride, but accepted the need to first fulfill his duties as lord. He led the way deeper into the woods, a chill breeze ruffling his black cloak till the embroidered dragon seemed to take life and move.

On a cloudy December day twilight was short. The snapping of a branch beneath Taine's foot, the eerie call of an owl, the sound of some small animal skittering to its haven, all wore on her nerves. She was thankful for Richard's company now, when even the bare trees' queerly tangled shapes seemed a threat. As they moved silently forward a strange glow appeared in the dark forest in front of them. Taine froze and Richard went still at her side. What mischief lay ahead? Some faerie dance? 'Twas said that one who listened long to their music would lose his soul. Taine's heart thumped erratically and, though Richard put his arm comfortingly about her back, she felt his pounding just as hard.

It was well-known that faerie melodies were so sweet they stole the will, and the youthful, tuneless voice that floated to them proved no such dangers awaited. Near laughing with relief, yet cautious nonetheless, they approached the small bonfire on quiet feet. One on each side, they peeked around the wide shield of a broad oak trunk. A boy of perhaps ten winters hunched over the flames, peering fearfully into the dark beyond and singing loudly as if by such bravado he earned strength.

Taine stepped first into the circle of light. Hood fallen back, her thick curls caught the reflection of leaping flames and seemed to burn. To the lad, the woman with hair of fire and flowing cape made of night shadows seemed a creature of unearthly beauty.

"Be you the faerie queen?" he asked with fearful awe.

After her own recent fancies and fears, his question brought a sweet grin to Taine.

Richard, joining her in the ring of light, answered before she could respond. "A queen, yes. But not of the faerie realm." He heard Taine gasp and turned the subject. "But what, young sir, are you doing so far from home on a winter's night?"

The boy's lower lip jutted out and he cast them a sullen look. "What matter to you?"

"None." Richard shrugged. "We'll ask you no questions if you ask us the same."

The boy nodded but with the natural curiosity of a child looked to be sorry for the promise. He motioned to a fallen log he'd dragged to one side of the fire.

Before straddling the rough seat, Richard helped Taine settle on a cushion of fallen leaves in front of it. Toes toward the fire's welcome heat, she leaned back against the log's coarse bark and pulled a bag from beneath cloak. From its depths she drew a loaf of rye bread, a round of cheese, and a large hunk of roast venison.

The boy's eyes went round with longing and he unconsciously bit his lower lip.

Taine's warm smile reappeared. "Have you eaten?"

The boy shook his head, gaze never leaving the tender roasted meat.

Taine's amusement deepened and she tore a sizable

chunk from the slab to give him. He fairly snatched it from the outstretched hand and took a huge bite, eating ravenously until he noticed the eyes bent on him.

"Pray pardon, milady." He dipped his head toward her, momentarily obscuring his bright cheeks. "I ken I shoulda thanked ye firstly—me ma woulda smacked me wrist right sharp."

"You must have had a fearsome hunger to forget her teaching," Taine excused and, forgetting their pledge to ask no questions, said, "How long has it been since last you ate?"

"Don't know. Some days past. They kinda run together out here."

While Taine questioned the boy, who managed still to stuff his mouth, Richard's gaze fell on the rough blade of honed iron lying next to the boy.

"Why have you not trapped food for yourself?" Richard questioned, motioning to the knife. "You've the means."

The boy froze. Meat fell to his lap when his hands flew to cover his face. Taine exchanged a surprised glance with Richard.

"They'll cut off me hands—says they'll do it anyways." His face crumpled but he clenched his eyes shut to contain their moisture. "I jest done it for little Davie." His voice was clogged with suppressed tears. "Ma sed he'd die once the last of the oats was gone. Sed he needed a strong meat broth to ease his belly what got so unnatural big. So, I caught a rabbit, and the forest warder caught me."

The boy collapsed in tears, and Taine reached out to pull him into her arms. "I guess you'll have to join with us," she murmured, patting his back consolingly. "We're running, too, and what's difficult for one is easy for three."

At length the boy regained his control and sat up looking at the woman as if she were truly a faerie come to grant him respite. "I'm Stephen," he announced, straightening his shoulders with pride.

"A pleasure, Master Stephen," Richard answered, standing to offer a mock bow. "I am Sir Richard and this is Queen Taine."

The boy grinned merrily at the titles he could not know were true. "A queen," he grinned, "and a knight? A knight is what I would be if I could choose. A great, fierce knight like the Golden Dragon." He made a mock slashing, jabbing motion with an invisible sword.

Richard saw the quickly hidden flash of anguish in darkened green eyes and sought to turn the boy's attention. "You were singing when we arrived, but do you know this little rhyme?" Richard sang a catchy tune of his own making and taught the boy its words. They sang it over and over till Taine fell asleep and the boy's flagging efforts were interrupted more and more often by yawns. When the youngster curled into a childish ball close to his new heroine's warmth, Richard threw another log on the fire and stretched out beside them. What, he wondered, could possibly be delaying Jorion. He'd left a trail a babe could follow.

A sleep of exhaustion kept the three from hearing the approach of another group. In the lead, Jorion moved silently through trees, towering somber outlines against the fireglow ahead. A short distance from his goal, with the stealth of a trained warrior, he urged Apollo forward, ducking beneath a low-hanging branch. He straightened slowly. Expecting to find only a frightened child, he was stunned to see a blaze of dark-fire hair on one side of the boy and a slight man stretched out on the other.

A cold rage washed over him. Here, in front of his knights, only hours before their vows, lay his bride beside another. Never mind that a youthful poacher lay between and their array revealed nothing of passion. Together they'd run from him after he'd forced patience on his desire and restrained his temper from her—no easy task. Halting nearly beside the prone man, he dismounted with fluid grace.

"Get up, cousin." Jorion kicked none too gently at Richard's legs.

Coming abruptly awake, Richard leaped to his feet. "Well, at last." He grinned at Jorion. "Your tracking skills must have grown as rusty as an ancient and seldom-used chain—I laid down a path a halfwit could follow."

"Stop babbling," Jorion impatiently demanded, ignoring Richard's foolish words as he peered about the glade for their steeds.

"We walked," Richard stated matter-of-factly and drew a

black gaze. "She insisted," he shrugged, "and it seemed the slowest method and most easily overtaken."

Jorion scowled at him, too angry to examine his meaning. "Get up behind Sir James."

No sense in arguing now, when Jorion plainly preferred their confrontation to be a private one. Richard nodded and accepted the arm Sir James offered. He mounted in back of the aging knight with his fierce need to prove himself equal to any younger man.

Through the heavy weight of deep sleep, Taine heard voices and frowned. She forced heavy lids to lift. Firelight gilded hair and outlined the broad form of the man she'd longed for in her dreams, the man beyond her reach. She sighed even as the heavy anger in his voice slowly sank through the pleasant feelings which lingered from warm sleep fantasies. Suddenly realizing he'd caught her again, she returned to reality with a harsh jolt. She sat up abruptly, silver-green eyes wide and gleaming, to discover the boy awake and huddling in fear against her side. When the furious dragon turned to them, Taine wrapped her arm about Stephen as a shield and bravely defied the angry earl.

Jorion plucked the child from her grasp and nearly tossed him to Will, who sat astride a huge grey horse. "Take him to his parents and see he understands my position." Will nodded and wheeled the steed about. Stephen looked around the broad shoulder and gazed at his new friends until the dark swallowed them up.

Strong arms lifted Taine without regard to her wishes, but put her gently across Apollo's back and mounted behind. Now accustomed to this form of travel, she found that, with experience, the thrill of his closeness had not lessened but grown more potent. Even before they'd left the wood behind, she'd melted against his broad chest, laid her head trustingly against his neck. Had she not longed for another chance to accept his offer and live the life her heritage had stolen from her—at least until he learned its secret? Pray God that time was distant.

There were no words spoken on the return trip. Jorion was convinced that Taine had proved her preference for gallant Richard's gentle company. But why then did she snuggle so willingly against him? Nay, he must not question so sweet a gift. He let his bronzed cheek lie atop her luxurious curls and stared into the moonless night. Willfully he blocked his thoughts of questions that would distract him from the feel of her enticing form yielding all to him.

In their separate thoughts each wished the ride would never end. When they arrived at the castle, Jorion dismounted and lifted her gently into the cradle of his arms. Turning with his sweet bundle curled willingly in his arms, he turned to see Richard lightly jumping down from the back of Sir James' steed.

"Follow me," he curtly directed, reality returning with memory of the deed he had stumbled onto. He turned and carried Taine through the great hall and up to the deserted family solar, with Richard close behind. In the dim hall outside, he thought better of his plan. Richard would bear his anger, not Taine, not when on the eve of their marriage she yielded so warmly. He lowered Taine slowly to her feet. Green eyes met black for endless moments before he gently took her shoulders, turned her toward the stairs to her chamber, and nudged her forward.

He watched the graceful sway of her hips as she moved slowly where he directed. Fragile hopes were in danger and shook beneath the knowledge that she had run from him again, and with Richard. He turned to the younger man with golden sparks in his eyes.

Standing in the arch to the stairwell, Taine watched Jorion glare at Richard as he moved threateningly nearer to him. She feared the price Richard would be called to pay, but feared more that he might be forced to reveal the secret she wanted to keep now more than ever before. If the dragon were to learn the truth, then all of her bright new dreams would be lost. She'd never know if he could want her beyond a crown.

"Richard," she called.

Both men turned toward her, Richard with a questioning expression and Jorion with threateningly lowered brows and pain-darkened eyes. Again, she called to another.

"Remember your oath." Her command was short but effective.

Richard nodded and she turned to climb the steps. The dragon wondered what mysterious confidences they shared.

When she was out of sight, he turned on Richard again. "What lies between you?" he demanded.

"'Tis not what you believe." Richard shook his head, warily backing away from his furious and much stronger cousin.

"What then?" asked Jorion, face a cold mask.

"You heard. I've given my oath and cannot say, but 'tis not love of me."

Jorion shook his head in disbelief and disgust for a second man who shared oath-shielded secrets with his bride.

In exasperation Richard threw up his hands and asked, "Think you how much farther we could have gone had I not delayed the progress. Did you not see the trail I left behind?"

"I came from Bershill village to find the boy and stumbled on you as well."

"Then, indeed, we were all lucky. You'd not have found my trail till the wedding hour had come and gone." He shook his head at the near disaster.

"You laid a trail, but took her still. You make no sense," Jorion said, his voice still deep with temper.

"Makes little sense to me either, but 'twas the best I could devise to protect you both." Richard returned and grinned. "I would not willingly tempt the dragon's fire."

Jorion was in no mood for either riddles or jests. "Then tread lightly," he coldly warned, "lest it consume you."

❧ *Chapter* 17 ❧

"GOOD MORROW!"

As the bed's heavy blue draperies were swept aside, Taine jerked the covers over her head. How could Halyse be so eternally cheerful first thing in the morn?

"No slothful lingering abed, sweet bride," Halyse said, addressing the lump over which barely visible fingertips clutched a cream-toned coverlet. Although pressed down tight, from beneath its warm comfort a bright mass of auburn ringlets escaped to spread across the abandoned pillow in wild disarray. Using the enticing tone of a mother bribing a recalcitrant child, Halyse added, "This is your wedding day." Clearly things were not aright between the dragon and his bride, yet Halyse's optimistic spirit was certain that so special an event must overshadow all petty discords.

One corner lifted and Taine peeked out. Slothful? Hardly that. Save the first few days, had she not always joined the majority of the castle's inhabitants for the mass that preceded the morning meal—sitting with others wellborn on the hard benches ringing the chapel, while servants sat on the floor in the middle? Between the looped-back draperies, Halyse stood with hands on hips, looking like a well-pleased kitty triumphantly dropping its captured prey at the feet of its master. Taine had denied this day since first the dragon had said it would be, yet had come to long for its forbidden delights. Fear and hope warred. She was torn by worry over the question of the rightness in this irrevocable deed.

"Rise, soon-to-be-countess." Halyse stepped back and made an exaggerated sweeping motion toward the tub standing before the fire. "Your bath awaits." Aware of Taine's preference for solitary bathing, she spoke again, "While you soak, I'll fetch your morning repast."

Taine saw her friend's thoughtful ploy and appreciated her consideration. She sat up, tucking the coverlet modestly beneath her arms, and smiled with the sweet warmth of a midday sun.

Halyse was pleased by Taine's response. She had worried at the lady's strange actions—turning away from the earl, walking long with another, and showing no interest in the ceremony drawing nigh. "When the time arrives," Halyse added, as she turned away to drape a large towel for warming by the fire, "I'll help you dress for the ceremony."

It was a fine thing that Halyse's back was turned. Had she seen the apprehension her last words brought to Taine's eyes, her puzzlement would have returned.

After Halyse slipped away, closing the door softly behind, Taine berated herself for the craven beginning she'd given the day. Now was the time for courage and risk taking. From fear, unquailing, she'd attempted several daring escapes. How much more appropriate bravery for love. She threw back the coverlet, firmly rose to her feet, and moved to the steaming tub. Trailing her fingers into the waiting bath, she watched them sink without resistance into the watery realm. Would her life meld as easily with Jorion's? Only the night past she'd decided to take the offered opportunity to live life without the constraints of her past and pray Jorion would come to love her without motive of a crown.

Sweeping her hair up, she stepped over the tub's edge and sank into welcoming waters. So long as Jorion did not learn the secret she must keep, she could live in dreams. She leaned back against the padded side and loosed her curls to tumble over the edge in a cloud that brushed the floor. While she luxuriated in gentle warmth her mind drifted through fantasies of future days spent in peaceful comfort and nights in fiery delights.

The water began to cool and roused Taine to a deed left undone. Her hands were buried in soapy foam when Halyse returned. Beneath a lather-crown, delicate brows rose with surprise at the variety on the heavily laden platter the other carried.

"Cook prepared these special delicacies for the dragon's bride alone." Halyse flashed a teasing grin as she slid it gently onto the small fireside table. "She says 'twill lend you stamina to keep pace with him."

Cheeks already flushed with bath heat deepened to dusky rose. Taine ducked her head below the tub's edge for more reason than the rinsing of sudsy curls.

"Sit by the fire and let its heat aid in the drying of your hair." Halyse spoke when Taine lifted her head and began to wring excess water from wet-darkened hair. "Later I'll send Mercia to brush it for you. But wait"—Halyse wagged an admonishing finger—"until I return to dress you for the wedding rites. A bride should not be seen before the time is at hand." Never lacking for words, Halyse chattered on as she turned to lift a simple dove-grey kirtle from a bedside chest. "Visitors for Sir Thomas arrived only this morn." Closing the chest's lid again, she spread the garment carefully over the top, ready for Taine to don in the interim. "He says 'tis a lucky thing they've come in time for the celebrations, limited though they be with the court so far removed." Halyse turned and disgust for Sir Thomas laid a scowl above hazel eyes. "Ill-timed is what I call it."

"Guests?" Taine asked sharply, hands stilling amidst moisture-heavy curls coiled on her head. The spider and his visitors were a threat to her fragile dreams.

"Aye, Duncan McLewell and his knight, Elwyn Morton. Don't know why they've come. McLewell is a Scottish lord but has sworn fealty to King Edward, so's you'd think Sir Thomas would have little use for him." Halyse shrugged away her disapproval of the man's strange ways and moved on to matters more important. "I left Bryce in the bakehouse and had best deliver those there of his company, afore they're tempted to buy his good behavior with too many sweets, and I"—Halyse thumped her chest with mock-disgust—"end with an ailing child."

Taine laughed. It did seem a likely thing. The red-haired boy was as full of good-natured deviltry as his mother must once have been. "Pray waste no time on my behalf—haste away and perform your errand of mercy."

The two women shared a smile of amusement before Halyse turned to the door, calling back one last assurance. "I'll be back later to aid your wedding preparations."

Alone, Taine rose. Water ran down her willowy form in shining rivulets like streams in full flood. She stepped from the bath onto the rush-strewn floor, curling her toes against its minor pricks and wrapped herself in the fire-warmed towel, welcome after cool bathwater. The names of the spider's visitors were unfamiliar and mayhap had naught to do with her. A small voice of reason silently mocked that weak hope as she wrapped the towel more tightly about a body unnaturally chilled. Glancing toward the long arrow slit, a deep sigh escaped her. Plainly, some purpose lay behind the spider's constant stares and sudden approval of a marriage first disdained. Green eyes clenched shut, closing off the sight of the rain-bleak clouds without, as she closed her mind to the ominous specters rearing in her thoughts. Even did she wish it, she could no more halt this wedding than she could still the North Sea's tide. No profit now in letting unexpected and, to her, unwelcome guests mar her dreams. Likely they would be fleeting enough without allowing external forces to early shatter her illusions. She would savor every moment of the doubtless fleeting time, store up warm memories like a miser his gold. Then, were she again returned to her dreary castle-prison, more than insubstantial fantasies would brighten her days.

Brows of dark gold half-lowered over deep black eyes. The man they surreptitiously examined was tall, nearly as tall as himself and well-formed. Duncan McLewell had a pleasant face and a friendly smile. An honorable man, since taking oath to King Edward under threat of forfeiting his lands, McLewell had never failed to fulfill all the king's commands. Yet Jorion knew his heart lay with the deposed John Baliol. Jorion had sworn fealty to Edward and served him, too, from respect. Still he had wondered what, under similar circumstances, he might have done to preserve Radwyn to himself. McLewell's loyalties had led him to support an opposing cause, and they'd earlier met as foes on the field of battle. But until Jorion learned that Taine's bumbling pursuers had fled to McLewell's castle, the man had been one of the few Jorion admired. In a different time, they might have been friends.

Jorion carefully cleared his frown away as he stepped from the shadows to greet the man at his uncle's side. "Welcome."

McLewell moved forward to accept Jorion's extended arm in a firm clasp. "Thank you for the hospitality offered to two who came at another's invitation."

"My uncle is well-used to treating this castle as his own." The words were acid-tinged and accompanied by a cynical smile, but Jorion sincerely added, "And I am pleased to have guests bear witness to my wedding vows and share in our celebration." Jorion's black gaze steadily met Duncan's equally unwavering pale-blue one.

"I am sorry," Duncan said, dark head dipping, "for the poor timing of our coming." He turned to motion his companion forward.

As Jorion welcomed the other visitor, a slight young man with pinched face and winging brows, he wondered whether Duncan deemed his timing poor for being too early or too late.

"Nonsense, nonsense," Thomas stepped forward, pleasure glowing pink on his face. "The timing is perfect, perfect."

Jorion's eyes narrowed on hands again rubbing in satisfaction. His uncle clearly had some plan afoot, and Jorion wondered if Thomas knew yet that his former supporters had been commanded to swear an oath of loyalty to the dragon alone.

Taine willed her hands to refrain from tangling into the rich brocade of the same gown she'd worn to King Edward's court. Her morning had slipped all too quickly into a haze of soft dreams while, before the fire's drying heat, the young serf Mercia rhythmically pulled a horsehair brush through her long hair. On first arriving at Castle Dragonsward, Taine had denied the very soothing experience of a deed she could perform for herself. But 'twas a deed she'd learned to enjoy after Halyse insisted she submit to the gentle ministrations. Yet today it had not calmed her spirit so completely that she could face the imminent ceremony with ease.

Fingers tightly laced together for confidence, Taine again looked down over the beautiful deep-green kirtle and sea-mist surcote which sparkled with silver embroidery. The apparel was perfect and gave her the courage to step through the chamber door held open by Halyse. Lifting the long velvet train and draping it over the crook of her arm, Taine slowly descended the narrow, winding stairway.

As a captive queen expected never to wed, she'd learned little of wedding customs but knew a bride and groom commonly met at the church door to exchange vows. How could that be when a marriage ceremony took place in a castle's chapel? She hesitated beneath the arching doorway to the great hall, deserted but for Jorion's squire. Hovering beyond the edge of childhood, Sander was angular, all rapidly lengthening bones yet to be padded with adequate flesh. Her fine brows lifted in question.

Sander, shifting awkwardly from one foot to another, swallowed hard. Green-garbed, she looked like the woodland faerie queen with eyes gleaming like sunlight on dew-damp clover. A chaplet of shiny holly leaves and bright berries crowned the luxurious flow of her dark wine-red curls. "I been told to lead you to the chapel, milady." He spoke in awe and his young voice cracked on the final word, bringing a bright flush to his cheeks.

He was clearly uncomfortable with his assigned role, and in reassurance Taine gave him the stunning smile he remembered, the one that had earlier earned his undying admiration. She nodded her willingness to follow, but still he hesitated.

"Don't the holly leaves prick?" Unthinking, he questioned with the curiosity of a childhood not completely left behind. He nearly believed her able to command that nature reverse its laws for her.

Taine stepped closer and whispered conspiratorially, "Nay, look you close, you can see where they"—she tilted her head back to Halyse and Mercia waiting behind—"broke away the pricking tips." His serious grey eyes narrowed in close examination of glossy leaves. "All the flowers are winter-dead," Taine explained, "and Halyse says this is as near to the brides' traditional flower crown as they could manage."

A shy smile peeped, bashful for this attention given him by the dragon's bride. "You're the most beautiful lady I ever seen," Sander stammered.

"Why, thank you, gentle sir." Taine's smile widened and she dipped in a mock curtsy.

Embarrassed, Sander shuffled and hurried to add, "I'd best get you to the dragon, else he'll have my hide."

She followed him down the great hall's long length to the stairway in its far corner. He led the way up the narrow, spiraling steps of the castle's second tower. One level above lay the chapel. As they climbed, Taine reminded herself of the courage she'd vowed to maintain for the sake of the love she sought.

Jorion stood impatiently at the chapel door. With control ingrained by long years of experience, he watched the empty corridor, unmoving, with no hint of emotion on his face. He'd had little sleep the previous night, lying awake even after their late return, wondering if he'd erred in forcing Taine to hold to the claim she'd made. Could she bear to share her future with him or, despite her apparent acceptance of his heritage, would her disgust of it ever turn her from him? She had run from him, time after time. Would she again?

He waited, deaf to the whispers of the large group in the chapel at his back. Questions without answer churned in his thoughts. Did she merely flee the mysterious forces threatening her? If so, why would she not share her fears with him? Surely he had proven himself both willing and capable of defending her, whatever they be. No longer could he believe she turned from him for fear of an intimate embrace. In the dark chamber after her attempted midnight flight he'd proved the lie of that. The memory of the unfulfilled need that had overcome her inhibitions gave him hope. Surely the fire of their mutual desire would forge a bond between them, meld their separate lives into one. A harsh doubt mocked his assurance. First they must reach the point of the joining. His strong chin lifted as if prepared for the attack of some unseen foe. When she met him here at the door and he pledged his vows, would she reject him, shame him before his people? The thought was more terrifying than a thousand drawn blades and his face hardened to a stone mask as Sander appeared. She was his fate, he fiercely reminded himself. Surely fate meant her to be his.

When the lad stepped aside and a vision of grace glided forward, Jorion's breath, unconsciously held, whooshed out as if the unseen foe had landed a well-struck blow. The gleam of myriad candles placed to light her way down the hall shimmered against silver stitches on pale green and glowed in sea-mist eyes. But it was the warmth of the smile on tender lips that stole his breath away.

When Sander stepped from her path, Taine's eyes widened but never wavered from their goal, the dream she would struggle to make real. The corridor was edged with yew boughs rather than the flower garlands common to a wedding. Taine was unaware that the deep green of her kirtle's velvet skirts brushed against them as she moved steadily toward the waiting man who summoned and held her full attention. Cream velvet, gold embroidered at neck and sleeve, had replaced the dragon's unfailing black garb and intensified the gilded shine of his hair and bronzed skin. A man, in truth, formed of molten, living gold. Powerful, he was the epitome of masculine beauty and a prize she would claim hers before all. Nay, Taine reminded herself with lingering smile, for the memory of a hasty claim of unsuspected consequences, that had she already done. Now she would swear herself his.

Not until she reached Jorion's side did she notice the benignly smiling priest beyond his wide shoulder. Staring up and nearly falling into midnight-deep eyes, Taine listened while Jorion spoke his vows firmly, as if daring her to reject them. Unknown to him, they were the first scene of the future she'd chosen and would no longer run from but seek with brave arms opened wide. With Father Aleric's gentle coaching, she returned his words in a voice soft but unhesitating. After the last word fell from her lips, Jorion's tense shoulders relaxed, and he gave her a blindingly sweet smile seldom seen before.

Pleased, Father Aleric nodded, thick white hair waving with the motion. The lovely maid had plainly stolen past Jorion's defensive shield. The golden boy would not live his life alone and unloved in self-imposed restitution for a heritage not of his choosing.

Having given Taine no betrothal ring, Jorion slipped onto her finger a dainty band cunningly worked to fit its large, sparkling emerald into the twined ring already there, as if meant to be the other half of a whole. Feeling its cool addition, Taine wondered for its perfect fit and offered a quick prayer that their lives would fit together as smoothly and grow comfortable as speedily as this band would warm in contact with her skin.

Filled with happiness and relief for the completion of a decision made with difficulty, Taine hardly heard the traditional words Jorion spoke until he ended with, "—and pledge thee half of my estate in guarantee of your livelihood should I be called to judgment afore you." Horrified, she froze. She wanted no part of his estate, no more of any inheritance to make difficult the way.

Attention resting on the bride and groom, the quick look of irritation that crossed Thomas' face went nearly unseen. One-half had Jorion named to his bride, when one-third was most common. One-half then to the cause, when one-third would have been deemed a windfall of wealth. Ah, well, he smoothed his face. The whole laid a path to the return of the prosperity he'd lost, and he would not begrudge Baliol even half. Suddenly uncomfortable, he glanced to the side and found McLewell's eyes on him. He squirmed, though sweet Mary knew why, when they both shared the same aim.

Jorion bent forward and brushed his lips across Taine's to seal their vows with the marriage kiss. Its warmth drove her momentary discomfort away, and she smiled shyly when he drew back. He offered his forearm and she placed her fingertips atop its muscled hardness to be led into the chapel for the wedding mass.

Those waiting within murmured approval of the beauty

now their lady. Her friendliness and lack of hauteur had already won their liking and were she to continue to treat their dragon with the welcome she showed now, their affection would be assured. Father Aleric stepped behind the intricately embellished altar. However, neither its grace nor the awe-inspiring grandeur of the splendidly carved and painted chancel could hold interested eyes from their lord and his bride.

Unwilling to show her unease in standing before a large company, Taine looked up to the long window that faced the guarded courtyard below and soared unobstructed to what in the twin tower was a higher level. By Jorion's order it had recently been fitted in the new manner with colored glass in the pattern of Christ the Good Shepherd. Unable to understand the Latin words of the mass, Taine only heard their soothing rhythm. The discomfort of many eyes on her back faded before the awareness of the man so close she felt wrapped in his strength. Peeking up from the corners of her eyes, she could see the individual gold strands of his thick hair, the bronze cheek so near. She wanted to touch its hardness—here in the chapel before so many! It proved he was powerful in more than physical strength. He'd subdued her once strong determination to never willingly submit to a man. Indeed, now she had pledged him her life. Renewed uncertainty crept upon her bright content, a fog of doubt rolling in from an ocean of past disappointments. Her fingers twisted together and green fire flashed from the heart of the new band on her finger.

Jorion felt Taine's tension growing. Though she'd ever proved one for unexpected actions, after the previous night's attempted flight and despite her yielding on the return journey, he'd been stunned by her warmth and willingly spoken vows. Yet, he reaffirmed his decision the night past, nowise would he question the unexpected gift nor wonder for the length of her welcome cooperation. He laid one large hand over hers, engulfing twined fingers.

Forest-deep eyes flew up and breath halted in Taine's throat on meeting the tender golden blaze in black depths. For the second time in the space of an hour, he gave her his rare smile without cynicism. It caught her in the net of his enthrallment, drew her closer to its power. Only the priest's cleared throat brought them to an awareness of the ended mass. Taine's face flamed as she knelt at Jorion's side to accept communion and receive the priest's blessing on their union. Standing again, they turned toward the company that waited with smiling eyes and warm grins. Jorion laughed and proffered Taine his arm. Cheeks still nearly matching the holly berries of her chaplet, Taine walked with him through the cheerful company that parted to open a clear path for the newly wedded couple.

Watching his friends, Richard beamed at the happiness in Jorion's low laughter. Happiness was an emotion rare to the man. Richard had been near as surprised as his cousin when Taine came willingly, nay, gladly to bind her future to the dragon. Nonetheless, he congratulated himself on being father to the deed. For, to his mind, it was his action of the previous day that had seen her returned and made the rites possible. It lent confidence in the wisdom of the further measure he intended to take. Well-pleased, he joined the joyous company following the bridal couple down the stairs.

Taine's eyes widened when they stepped into the vast great hall. Clearly not all the castle's servants had attended the ceremony for, in the space of time since last she'd passed through this doorway, tables had been prepared and laden with a sumptuous meal. Venison, whole pit-roasted boar, and pheasants with golden-brown skin refeathered lay beside loaves of still-warm bread, steaming pasty pies, mounds of autumn-harvested fruits and vegetables aplenty.

Looking down, Jorion saw her amazement and he smiled. He laid one finger beneath her lowered chin and lifted it to close her mouth. "Come," he invited, "our wedding feast awaits." He waved toward tables near groaning under their weighty offerings.

As she walked with him to the dais, she wondered how the cook could have thought she'd need the hearty breakfast previously provided when this abundance awaited? With the thought came memory of the cook's suggestive innuendo and renewed color tinted creamy cheeks. To hide her sudden embarrassment, Taine said, "Surely, this is too much for even the whole of your household to consume."

"Aye, thus more than my household will partake." Jorion gently replied as he helped her to take her chair and settle the extravagant gown carefully out of danger's path. "All the people of my demesne have been summoned to join in celebration of their lord's joy." And a joy this day was, one he'd never experienced before. Even as he'd determined to force her into fulfilling the claim she'd made, he'd never expected the tender maid's open and willing compliance.

Although she had sat at meal with Jorion all these many days, this one was different. In the first instance, to make room for the two visitors on the dais, the chairs were set nearer together. Now Taine thought she understood the reasoning behind the overgenerous breakfast. The dragon's closeness stole her appetite. But this time when the gentle net of his attraction coiled about, beckoning her, she didn't turn from him. Rather, she let herself melt into golden eyes, a bond which could not be broken, not even by the merry entertainment of jugglers, tumblers, and jesters. During the whole lengthy meal, she merely touched the chalice to her lips for each fulsome toast and nibbled only on the tender delicacies her dragon lifted to her mouth. They could each have been straw for all she tasted of them. Caught between apprehension and anticipation of what was to come, she emptied her mind of all save the present.

When the fruit and cheeses of the final course lay on silver platters on the high table, a group of men approached the dais. Taine felt the dragon rise to his feet. Surprised, she looked quickly between him and the group.

"We have come as you bid," stated the short, muscular man in their lead, "ready to swear homage to you alone."

Taine gasped silently. She recognized these men as some of the spider's Scottish supporters and quickly glanced down the high table. Thomas' face, though impassive, was beet-red. Clearly he neither expected nor appreciated this event. Taine's eyes turned again to her new husband, tall and strong, as he stepped down from the dais to the open space before the high table. He extended his hand as the first knelt to swear his oath of fealty and bend his balding pate to brush lips across the dragon's hand in homage. He was followed by another and another, until all of Sir Thomas' former supporters had pledged their loyalty to the earl. Taine's heart lifted. It seemed a propitious sign, this taking away of the spider's support. By this, doubtless her safety was further ensured.

The first notes of a piper's tune were joined by a lute. When a trimbel set up a supporting rhythm, Jorion realized the time was near when he must lead Taine in a dance to begin the festivities meant to last the whole night through—without the guests of honor. His lips slid into a smile so sensuous the green eyes below flared with silver lights. He shook his head and came back to the problem at hand. Although he'd refused to join the amorous lists, he'd been too often at court not to have learned the courtly graces it demanded—double-edged small talk, silly games, and intricate dances. But in a past during which she'd not learned to ride, had she learned to dance?

Careful to phrase the question without insult of any lack, he asked, "Have you learned the steps to many dances?"

She had realized her peril when the music began and had twisted a piece of soft wheaten bread between her fingers until it was little more than a doughy lump. "I have danced seldom," she answered honestly, "and know the name of none." No purpose to claim more than she knew, when she would doubtless be called to prove her words. Only one time when the strains of a boisterous village gathering had drifted to her remote prison had she begged Bertwald to teach her to dance. He had tried, although as he was stiff and awkward it had all been to little purpose.

"Tell me the pattern you know," Jorion quietly directed, leaning near so their words were private, "and I will seek to match it."

Taine recognized his thoughtful attempt to save her from shame, and misty-green eyes met his as she quickly complied. He nodded and rose to lead her to the space bared before the dais. With long train draped elegantly over one arm, she faced him. He lifted her left hand in his right and began the simple steps. Inexperienced though she was, her natural grace covered any lack and together they moved in harmony of motion. While the music drifted its magic and she followed the dragon's path through the entrancing tune, Taine gloried in the never-before-experienced pleasure of submerging herself in a rippling stream of liquid notes.

The huge man and the delicate maid held the approving eyes of the assembled company. When the music had ended, Taine's shy smile of relief for a frightening thing successfully done and Jorion's clear pride of an exceptionally graceful partner brought another toast lifted to the bridal pair.

Jorion led Taine back to their seats on the dais as the once-open space filled with people anxious to begin the next dance. Taking her seat, Taine looked up at the man leaning close to help her arrange the lush velvet folds of her gown. The light of the three candle pyramids behind them gleamed on bright hair, and his dark face warmed again with a gentle smile. She fell deeper into enthrallment's net, feeling the banked fire of nameless hunger still simmering between them.

Jorion smiled with pleasure for the success of the easy rhythms of a dance surely meant to portend the intimate one fast approaching. His smile disappeared, however, as Duncan McLewell rose from his seat at the dais far left and stepped behind them.

"Milady." He bent and spoke to Taine.

Too involved with Jorion to note another drawing near, she turned politely to the visitor.

"I have seldom seen such loveliness of motion," McLewell praised, light-blue eyes smiling.

Taine graciously nodded, sweet smile peeking. His compliment was all the more appreciated for the anxiety with which she'd undertaken the deed.

Jorion closely watched Taine's reaction. Her clear crystal-green eyes and warm response revealed neither fear nor recognition of McLewell. Plainly she had not been held directly in his control. Questions for the reasoning behind her captivity again beat in his mind, but with the other man still speaking he had no time to dwell on them.

"I am Duncan McLewell, Lord of Arunswell." He politely introduced himself, as the dragon had chosen not to. Brushing his lips across the slender fingers he'd lifted, azure eyes narrowed momentarily on the flash of an emerald and the intricate band entwined about it. "I beg you honor me with the next dance." He motioned toward the swirling colors weaving in complex patterns below the dais.

The polite invitation shook Taine from her haze of warm

content. If forced to dance again and with a stranger unaware of her inexperience, likely she would shame herself by revealing her lack of skill. She shrank back from the prospect.

It was common practice for a bride to dance with all guests of rank, yet Jorion felt Taine recoil and knew her reason. "As husband, I claim the right to refuse your request." He would save her embarrassment happily as he preferred to hold such joys to himself for a while longer. Moreover, it was the perfect opportunity to warn his foe. "She is now mine," Jorion laid his strong arm about Taine's shoulders, "and what is mine I keep." Although the words were softly spoken, they held the tone of a threat.

Light blue met black in a moment of perfect understanding before McLewell smiled and bowed in assent. "Be she mine, I would feel the same."

Jorion's expression did not change, but his clenched jaw tilted and his face appeared carved of solid ice. He saw beneath the smooth compliment to a claim of prior ownership. His arm unconsciously tightened.

Drawn against Jorion's strength, Taine nearly snuggled into his encircling warmth. She didn't understand the threat in the response which held her safe from possible shame in a simple request, but felt protected, safer than ever in her life. The tiny, inescapable voice of caution, ever skeptical of men and their schemes, whispered: Safe from others, but safe from him? The same strength that wrapped her in safety, if turned against her, would be a terrifying thing. She looked up into the handsome face of the man she loved and willfully closed her mind to the warning.

Glancing down, Jorion met a green gaze gone soft with tentative trust. He smiled and renewed his determination to defend her against foes known and unknown.

Richard watched the table's byplay and knew his moment had come. Their visitors clearly knew Taine's true identity, as did he and his father. To protect her, Jorion must not be the only major player in this pageant still unaware. Richard had sworn an oath on the Holy Cross never to plainly speak of her past, but there were ways and there were ways. He rose to his feet and clapped his hands loudly together until the music faded away.

Over disgruntled muttering he announced, "I've written a new song, the tale of a mythical ring, and have dedicated it as gift to our dragon and his bride." Murmurs faded into anticipation. The people of Castle Dragonsward were proud of their lordly minstrel and ever anxious to hear first a new song that would be sung in high places.

Stepping from the dais, Richard fetched his lute from the corner where he'd left it in readiness. Moving into the space below the high table, which dancers had quickly cleared for him, he strummed a few chords and in a voice famous for its sweetness began:

"From three royal women all called the same,
 Through three generations from mother to daughter it came:
  A marriage of silver to gold,
  A betrothal ring,
  A cherished thing . . ."

In the verses that followed he wove a tale of the ring's mystical powers, of love lost and found. Each ended with a repeat of the lyrics of the first. When done, a thundering roar of cheers swallowed Taine's small moan. Her fingers twined viciously into the green velvet of the skirt beneath the table's white cover. How could Richard, the man who claimed to be her friend and the one she'd nearly come to trust again, do what he knew was a betrayal of the spirit if not the detail of an oath he'd sworn. From such words doubtless others, the dragon first of all, would discover her identity as easily as had Richard himself. Horrified eyes studied Richard, accusation for his faithless action clear in their green depths. His song was the first blow to the foundation of her bright dreams, one that weakened the structure and was near certain to topple the whole.

Richard felt Taine's wound but his absolute certainty of the rightness in his deed made him impervious, or nearly so. To quell his discomfort, he looked from Taine to Elspeth and caught solemn brown eyes studying him. One bright blue eye winked.

Unprepared for the sudden glance and even less prepared for the flirtatious action, Elspeth blushed and looked down, an action which did not hide a pleased smile. Now wed, surely Jorion would keep his bride too busy to notice Richard. With her rival safely removed, was there hope for her? She thrust aside doubts for her plump shape and inexperience, letting herself contemplate how wonderful the future could be.

As Richard sang, Jorion saw the sudden stillness of his uncle and the visitors, followed by glances full of meaning. Contemplating the curious words of Richard's gift, he didn't see Taine's glare at the songsmith. However, he felt her growing tension and wrongly assumed its source merely the length of a strain-filled day and apprehension of the hours to come. Sunlight had been swallowed by the depths of night, and the men at tables below had grown loud and boisterous, each coarse toast to the bridal pair bringing a hail of even cruder jests. He turned to Halyse.

She'd been awaiting his command and rose, motioning Elspeth to join her. The task ahead was one seldom attended by unwed maidens, but as they were the only gentleborn women in the dragon's mighty castle it was fitting she aid the bedding of the bride.

Seeing Halyse moving about the outside of the tables to approach her from the back, Taine's heart kicked up an erratic beat. She didn't know what to expect of the bedding rites that had been the subject of so many crude jests, and the unknown was difficult to face. But, she reminded herself, she'd sworn to hold her courage for love. Her dreams would likely be short-lived, and if Jorion were to learn who she was all was lost. More reason to waste no time in fear.

Halyse stepped to the dais behind her. "'Tis time for us to depart," she told Taine softly, sympathizing with eyes full of apprehension despite bravely squared shoulders. "Don't worry, the bedding is quickly past and what follows is worth the men's foolery." One hazel eye winked merrily, hopeful of diverting the new countess.

Taine stood, thankful for the long velvet kirtle that hid shaking knees. She thought she'd understood Halyse's talk of "men's foolery," for the toasts had been crude in the extreme. But as she followed Halyse's path to the winding stairway, she found the earlier words were mild compared to the lewd comments half-soaked men called after the one meant to be maid no longer. Her cheeks were as vivid as Halyse's hair by the time she reached the first step.

Jorion's sizable chamber was the bridal bower, and when Halyse threw open the door Taine followed her inside, leaving Elspeth, brown eyes lit with curiosity, to enter behind. While Taine hesitated a step within, Halyse moved forward to sweep aside the richly patterned tapestry of crimson and gold that draped the dragon's bed and neatly folded back the thick coverlet. In a stack against one wall lay several large cushions of red and cream silk. Halyse lifted and arranged them against the bed's back.

Apprehension born of inexperience grew. Taine looked away from the intimidating bed and focused on the black cloak hanging on a peg near where she stood. The gold-embroidered dragon's head appeared among the folds, flames shooting from its mouth. Taine swallowed hard. It was not a sight to calm the nerves of one who entered the dragon's domain knowing herself an offering to his consuming fire. *'Tis only a cloak, a cloak and a mythical tale,* Taine silently rebuked her increased tension but found no comfort in unconvincing words. She'd spent her whole life fearing a man's claim of her and was now struck by an unexpected anxiety for her ability to please.

Halyse touched her arm and Taine started. "You must shed this glorious gown."

Taine nodded and consciously released the delicate brocade surcote from twisting fingers.

As Halyse lifted the outer garment, a soft green blur flashing with silver rose past Taine's eyes and tangled in the thick mane left free for the wedding. Halyse knew Taine found it difficult to stand nude before others and, as soon as the lush velvet kirtle lay in a pool about her feet, hurried her into the bed. But when Taine slid down and pulled the covers to her chin, Halyse shook her head.

"Elspeth"—Halyse turned to direct the girl standing mutely nearby—"in the small box on the table you will find dried rosemary, lavender, and tansy. Strew them lightly about that the room may be freshly scented."

As Elspeth turned to do as she was bid, Halyse motioned Taine to sit up. Taine's cheeks went hot, but she complied and held steady when Halyse reached behind her neck and pulled a wealth of curls forward. Taine's horsehair brush lay ready on the small chest next to the bed and Halyse quickly applied it, leaving her hair a glowing cover for lush curves.

She stepped back to survey her handiwork and smiled. "My hair looks like carrots, but yours is flame. As I've long believed, you are the perfect mate for our dragon." Taine met hazel eyes and only prayed it might be so.

Below, Jorion lingered long. Great quantities of wine and bitter ale had been consumed. The majority of his companions were too sotted to exhibit sensible behavior, and he chose not to arrive with his bride unprepared, perhaps unclad and revealed to leering eyes. All too aware of the need, for his innocent and nervous bride's sake, of a clear mind and steady control, he had abstained from drink save in answer to toasts.

At length he rose to his feet, while in his wake others, all men of good blood, weaved and stumbled up the stairs. Only Uncle Thomas and his guests had maintained their clear wits and steady gait. Jorion spared a thought to wonder what secrets were guarded by sober tongues. He paused at the bridal chamber's closed door. An unsteady Richard, laughing at a particularly ribald jest, laid a hand on Jorion's solid shoulder. Leaning heavily, he reached past to throw open the block in their path.

The vision of loveliness waiting within stunned the boisterous group into silence. Against a pile of large, silken cushions from the desert kingdom of Jorion's youth, Taine reclined, bedcover drawn only to her waist. Flamelight seemed to live and burn brighter in the thick mass of dark-fire curls brushed forward in a tempting cover for the sweet cream of lush curves. In an effort to still the near overpowering urge to rush leering men from the room and immediately claim his delicious maid, Jorion tore his gaze from generous breasts, bare but for the teasing cloak of auburn silk.

As so oft before, Taine stared at the broad form blocking the door, power and masculine grace in every line. She saw golden sparks leap in dark eyes as he studied her barely shielded curves and hardly dared breathe for fear of disarranging the curls by a breath too deeply drawn. She knew little of the customs of wedding rites but did realize that this night would see the completion of the pleasure initiated more than once. Jorion had earlier proved she'd no reason to fear from him the harsh attack of her gaolers. In her knowledge of what was to come she found no fear, only a nervous anticipation.

Dried spring flowers, crushed and strewn about the room, wafted their tantalizing scent to the men in the doorway. Looking up, Jorion met soft green eyes full of welcome but saw also the nervous nibbling of her full lower lip, a sweet pleasure there too. Although his pulse had begun a heavy accelerated beat, again he pulled himself back from temptation, reminding himself of her innocence, her past fears, and the need to move with gentle slowness. Caught in each other, neither heard the coarse jests of wine-soaked men.

By effort of will Taine held her fingers relaxed on the cover drawn up to her waist, failing to realize her nervous tension had found a new outlet in nibbled lip until his intense gaze settled there. It felt as if he had touched her lips and they fell open on a silent gasp.

When soft rose lips parted in wordless invitation, wildfire flashed through Jorion's veins and he stepped into the room and stripped off his tunic with one swift, smooth motion. He wanted free of the others' prying eyes and restraining presence but, by tradition, they would not leave until he joined Taine unclad in the bed.

Suddenly presented with the close sight of Jorion's bare and powerful torso, green eyes widened. In treating his inconsequential wound in Dunfermline, she'd been too close to observe the whole. Now gentle candlelight flickered from many tapers clustered on a silver platter near the door, and blazing firelight glowed on both bronze skin and the dark gold hair arrowing down from broad chest to disappear beneath the belt at his waist. As strong hands loosed the buckle, Taine drew a deep breath that nearly freed soft mounds of their insubstantial auburn shield. Feeling the silky mass slide precariously, Taine's gaze fell. She carefully exhaled, determined to steady her breath and train her eyes only on the soft cover into which her fingers curled tightly.

Attention never wavering from his waiting bride, Jorion saw her predicament and frowned. He no more wanted to see her bared to the others' view than did she. He pulled his belt free with a crack and two thuds quickly followed as his shoes fell to the floor. As he stood only a pace within the chamber, only Richard and Will had found room to fully enter behind him. Without a word he motioned Elspeth and Halyse from their positions on either side of the bed. Detouring to first extinguish every candle's flame, they obeyed his silent order. As they passed, he turned to watch them move through the crowd of men. The cold command in black eyes was demand enough to back the men up, but did not quiet their ribald jests for his haste to be alone.

"Methinks he's overeager." Will laughed.

"Oh, nay," Richard responded, brows raised and staring at the bulge in the cloth covering Jorion's lower torso. He turned, wavering dangerously, to meet Will's mirthful grin. "Methinks the time for departure is—ripe."

Richard laughed so hard at his own words that Jorion had to catch the swaying man's shoulders to keep him from falling back. Jorion lightly shoved Richard through the door, and Will followed, to pick Richard up after he stumbled and fell. Jorion quickly shut the door and lowered the bar. For some moments others pounded on the closed portal in tipsy disgust for the untimely end to their play but at length the last disgruntled man moved away to rejoin the merrymaking below that would continue till dawn.

When the sound from without faded into a distant roar, Jorion turned to again face the bed. Unsure of what was expected of her, Taine had not moved and still stared at her fingers gripping the coverlet with a deathlock.

Seeing the action as a sign of her fear, Jorion cautioned himself to damp down the fire in his blood and move slowly. She was a banked flame he could either ignite or douse with the cold water of ill-considered action.

When the mattress tilted beneath Jorion's weight, Taine peeked sideways to find him sitting beside her on the edge of the bed—surely the image of superb masculinity.

Jorion reached out and gently lifted her chin, fingers spreading over her jaw to turn her face toward him. Thick lashes shielded her gaze just as dark-fire curls hid her bounty. Nay, the latter was untrue. Knowing the action a dangerous threat to his restraint and despite his intent, Jorion's gaze dipped down to find a rosy tip peeking through auburn silk. His hand involuntarily tightened on the fragile curve of her jaw.

Beneath the painless pressure, Taine looked at the man and saw the direction of his attention. She watched his lips part on a harshly indrawn breath, firm lips whose kisses were fire.

When Jorion forced himself to look up he found rapt sea-mist eyes on his mouth. Clearly she longed for a pleasure earlier sampled, one that had left a hunger for more. "No matter your fear," he murmured in satisfaction, "you want my mouth near as much as I want yours." Jorion leaned closer to study its sweet perfection and breath caught in Taine's throat.

Without thought she lifted her mouth in mute offering. Jorion answered the unspoken entreaty, brushing his lips back and forth across hers. A tormentingly inadequate caress. With a small, wild cry Taine twined her hands into cool gilt hair and stilled the teasing motion. Jorion's blood steamed at her offer of innocent passion but maintained his tight control, giving no more than she knew how to claim.

"Jorion," Taine moaned the need stirred to life by the dragon's command, fires of wanting smoldered and grew.

It was the first time she had called him by name and in her soft brogue it was an aching plea. Rather than comply, he pulled a breath away and looked down into eyes gone deep-green. "I would not frighten you with the strength of my desire. If you want more of me, for a time you must lead the way." He did not want her to wake on the morrow and say he had forced her to what she would have denied.

Taine had come to the bridal chamber with no question for the end, or her wish, for however short a time, to share the dragon's fire and did not hesitate to rise up on her knees. Her fingertips tingled at the remembered delight of a journey through gold-tipped curls. With renewed admiration and curious hands she stroked the hard, wide expanse of his strongly muscled chest. Jorion went rigid beneath the inflaming touch and fought to maintain his restraint. In some corner of a mind fogged with drifting smoke rising from passion's glowing coals, she saw his effort at control and grew determined to entice him beyond his intent, draw him down to join her in the flames. She twined her arms about his neck and let her soft curves melt against the heated contours of his massive torso. A strong shudder swept over Jorion when her small tongue tasted his lips, as in times past he had tasted hers.

His iron restraint broke under the temptation of her freely offered response and lush breasts separated from him only by fire-burning curls. With a harsh groan he crushed her teasing form against the power of his. Lowering her to the bed, his hunger for the elusive temptress almost tangible, he followed her down and stretched out at her side, taking control of the kiss and their path.

Before the dragon enveloped her in his heat, Taine felt a moment of triumph at having shattered the strong bonds of his control, her first taste of a power that could equal his. 'Twas her last intelligible thought as her senses overpowered rational thought. Even as he deepened the kiss, his hands spread slow searing paths from hips up her sides to beneath arms wrapped about him and then down. He repeated the motion again and again. Moving fractionally closer together, his palms brushed imperceptibly against the sides of her breasts. His repeated light touches were a fire of torment and a strong tremor shook her. He broke the bond of their lips.

Looking down at the enticing woman in his bed, Jorion watched her arch in response to the pleasure of his touch, watched her dragging in a deep breath as his palms returned to move more firmly against aching flesh. Dark-fire hair, flowing over the white sheet and burning with hearthlight, was a perfect foil for the warm-cream and deep-rose flesh. No matter a possible disgust for his heritage, this need at least she could not deny.

Lost in a haze of smoldering hunger, a small sob of protest escaped Taine's tight throat as the scorching touch slid back down to her waist. It was a burning torment but welcome, and when the upward path began anew, she shivered, every sense focused on the flame that paused to hover a whisper above tender curves. Unable to prevent the action, she reached up to clasp his hands about needful flesh. He lightly pressed her satin softness and she gasped, eyes tightly closed.

"Look at me." Only in response to Jorion's demand could

she lift heavy lids to stare up into his face, taut but for the sensual curve of his normally firm lips, and met the gold sparks leaping in black. "I wanted to watch while I touched you, see you shudder and cry out with need of me." Breath coming hard and fast, he renewed the warm, sensuous motion of his hands, and she writhed beneath its fire, again clenching her eyes shut. "No," he commanded in a low voice of husky velvet. "Watch me while I taste a pleasure no other has sampled." Taine did watch, helplessly, as he lowered his golden head to nuzzle soft white mounds and slowly, endlessly brush burning lips across tender crowns, touching, cherishing. Through the smoke of heated need he'd ignited, at last she saw his warm mouth pause and open over one. He drew it into a hungry cavern and a moan welled up from her depths as she trembled beneath flashes of wildfire even as she tangled her fingers in his cool golden hair and pressed his exploring mouth closer.

He rolled back, seeking some measure of control to lengthen their play, heighten her pleasure. He intended to at least see his fire-sprite so consumed by their joined flame that she'd have no care for the unavoidable pain. Taine followed his retreating form, determined to repay the torment in kind. Slender fingers burrowed into gold-tipped curls grown in a wedge across his prone chest, pleasured in the feel of every steely muscle beneath. He went rigid under her touch but did not deny the caressing hands stroking over the hard planes of his body in sweet torment, until soft lips bent to follow their path, settling with gentle seduction on a flat masculine nipple. A harsh groan was torn from his throat, and he turned to pull her full into his embrace.

Crushed against Jorion's hard length, breast to chest, hip to hip, thigh to thigh, Taine smoothed her hands over the strong muscles beneath the satin skin of his back. Clinging to him, she felt the heavy beat of his heart and twisted against him. Another deep growl came from the dragon's throat and his hands slid down her slender back to cup the perfect curve of her derrière and pull her tighter. She pressed even closer as he began to rhythmically rock her against him and felt the shudder that went through him when she writhed in helpless response.

Taine softly cried out her loss when Jorion pulled away.

Heavy lashes lifted and through desire-glazed eyes she saw flamelight burn in golden hair and polish firm bronze skin as Jorion quickly stripped off the last impediment to their joining. The golden dragon was hers. A slight smile curved throbbing lips. With feverish need she ached for Jorion to take her deeper into the flame and lifted her arms in willing surrender to the dragon's consuming fire.

Beyond rational thinking, Jorion yielded to her naive enticements. She clearly yearned for the final step in their erotic dance and he moved to settle above her. Resting on his forearms, he arched his back and stared down into eyes a green so deep they were nearly as dark as his own while he slowly joined his body to hers.

Lost in gold sparks which in that moment exploded and nearly obscured the black of his eyes, Taine barely felt the moment of pain, quickly overcome by hungry flames stoked to golden fires in his eyes. She shared the ever-building heat in their depths as he rocked her deeper into searing flames. Afraid she could not bear a greater intensity, still she clung desperately to the source, tinder to feed a hotter blaze. At last her cry of sweet anguish twined with his deep groan as the growing pyre burst into a conflagration of pleasure.

After endless moments at the unfathomable pinnacle of the hottest blue flame, Jorion rolled to his side and drew the trembling Taine close into the shelter of his arms. With gentle caresses and nonsensical words he eased them both through the wafting smoke of their descent and into the realms of contented sleep.

But for Jorion the whole of the night did not pass in peace. In the shadows of night he found unwelcome answer to the puzzle of his wife. It had long played at the edges of his mind, but he'd denied the unpalatable notion by simple assertion that so unbelievable a thing could not be true. Yet why else would supporters of Baliol be so determined to hold a young girl in seclusion?

Aye, only by subconscious denial of unwelcome facts had he failed to see the truth before. Too many clear hints had there been. Hints such as Bertwald's assertion that an oath to Taine was the same as an oath to a sovereign, and her pursuers' determination to take the ring by which Edward had known her. The refrain of Richard's song danced through his thoughts, mocking his attempt to refuse so clear a truth, for despite the flimsy assertion 'twas of a mythical ring, the lyrics plainly spoke of Taine's. Had she not told him herself that it had been her mother's and grandmother's before: "Three royal women all called the same . . ."? When added to her initial hesitation in giving her name (the long pause after she began with "Mar—"), the truth was undeniable.

Jorion had been with Edward at Westminster when came the news that dashed the king's hopes for a united English/Scottish crown. His heir's betrothed had died in the crossing from Norway. Small Margaret, daughter of Margaret, Queen of Norway, and granddaughter of Margaret, Queen of Scotland. There'd been questions for the truth of a death so advantageous for proud Scottish lords, but even Edward had been convinced of its truth when the child's father, King Eric, grieved heavily. 'Twas Margaret, the Maid of Norway and rightful Queen of Scotland, who now cuddled so sweetly against a form battle-tough from hard-fought conflicts to subdue her land to another's rule.

Over many years it had been driven into his thoughts that his mixed heritage made him an unsuitable mate for any wellborn woman. In defense of expected rejection he'd borne a cold and cynical shield keeping him impervious to the ladies of the court. Yet he'd let one delicate, nameless maid slip beyond his fierce pride to drive the sharp blade of love deep into his heart, only to find she was the most highly placed of them all. Given her naiveté in many matters, he doubted she understood that the play just past could result in a child. And if the ladies of the court could not bear to see their children tainted by the blood of the infidels, how much worse would it be for a queen?

❧ Chapter 18 ❧

WARM AND CONTENT, TAINE snuggled closer against a solid pillow. The sound of approaching footsteps was an unpleasant interruption to the gentle haze of happiness cushioning her semiwakeful state. Slowly thick lashes rose to find firm, bronzed skin a breath away. Memory flowed back and she smiled.

Muffled laughter roused Jorion from the heavy doze he'd slipped into only after predawn light first peeked through cracks in shutters drawn over sizable glass windows. Golden brows lowered, he turned his face toward the door and missed Taine's contented expression. He'd poor timing with his rest—awake all night but sleeping now and left unprepared as the door creaked open and prying eyes peered in.

In the forefront, with glossy brown head and one shoulder thrust through the barely opened door, Richard laughed. "Still abed," he loudly whispered to the small group behind, "and though the fire's gone to ashes we may be sure they've kept warm."

With no experience of wedding customs, no loving mother to instruct, Taine was shocked by this early morning arrival of curious people. She looked desperately about for

259

something to clutch over her bareness. Covers, dropped to her waist and half-fallen from the bed, were no aid in preserving her modesty. Her embarrassment was eased when Jorion lifted up on his side, shielding her tantalizing form with the wide expanse of bronzed back he presented to the door, now thrown open to admit the inquisitive party.

Dark-wine curls in a lovely, disheveled riot, Taine raised up only enough to peer over the edge of Jorion's broad shoulder. On meeting Richard's blue eyes, heavily veined by overindulgence but sparkling, and McLewell's sky-soft gaze, she buried her face in the warm crook of Jorion's neck.

Aware of Taine's lack of practical knowledge of many matters, it was clear to Jorion she had no notion of this traditional rite or its purpose. He lowered his lips to her ear and quietly explained, "They've come for the sheet." Jorion pressed the lush bounty of her slender form close against himself with one arm and reached over her shoulder to retrieve the heavy bedcover. While Taine wondered at the meaning of his statement, he quickly wound the soft coverlet about her, tightly covering her silken body from chin to bare toes. Once done, he rose, unashamed of his own nudity, and lifted her like a swaddled babe in his arms.

Halyse stepped from her position, linked to Will's side by his strong arm wrapped about her. She efficiently whipped the sheet from the bed and held it up for the inspection of all.

"Well and truly claimed," Richard called out, grinning wide and letting his gaze dwell appreciatively on the bundle trustingly curled against the new husband. The fiery abundance of Taine's hair flowed down over the strong arm holding her near to swirl about the bare flesh of Jorion's hip. Richard was still pleased with his handiwork and had nearly convinced himself he was solely responsible for their being together.

Rose-tinted cheek lay against the firm muscles of Jorion's broad chest; and while struggling to understand the meaning of this ordeal, Taine barely heard the pointed jests aimed at their joy of the night past. The assembled company looked, in the main, as if they'd barely forced themselves from their beds, a fact attested to by ruffled hair, heavy lids, and surely more than one pounding pate born of the past night's excesses. For what purpose? Quickly passing over the group, puzzled green eyes focused on the dark stain on a pristine white sheet—her virgin blood. Her cheeks burned and she turned to bury her face once more in the warmth of Jorion's shoulder.

"Nay, sweet wife," Jorion whispered again into her ear. "There is no shame here. 'Tis only proof you were pure and are now truly mine." The pride in the last words was unmistakable. Chin lifting, obsidian eyes sought Sir Thomas and McLewell to state his claim near as loudly as words: *Even be she queen, she is mine.* Here was the proof and he was glad they had seen it.

To Richard the meaning in Jorion's visual claim was clear, and by it he knew the dragon had found the purpose behind his small song. Despite a fiercely aching head, Richard's spirit soared and he gaily broke the wordless communication. "Our mission we have accomplished. Let us then be away to see what morning repast awaits us." The nearly unanimous groans of his companions deepened his grin. They had yet to recover from the previous night's enjoyment, but his appetite was renewed by the satisfaction in knowing that by his action Jorion was prepared and Taine thus more easily protected.

Deed complete, the small group stumbled out. As the feast had continued long past the hour of the bridal pair's bedding, most intended to seek again their rest. Once the door closed behind the last, Jorion carefully lowered his fire-sprite to the bed and stood for long, silent moments looking down. As he'd once thought, she'd lain unscorched in his fire and joined her flame to his in a blaze of incredible intensity. Dark eyes clenched shut and large hands tightened into fists of frustration. Aye, he had claimed her, but could he keep her? In the hours of night he'd decided he could no longer use force to hold a queen. Nor would he use the burning bonds of desire to bind her to him, no matter that by their passionate play he had proved he could tempt her beyond reason.

Seeing his expression of pain, Taine struggled free of the tightly wound coverlet. In solace she lightly stroked over the heavily muscled thigh close to and lingered to savor an enjoyable path of discovery through gold-tipped curls grown thick over bronzed flesh.

Jorion's eyes opened, and he fell into a gaze forest-deep where silver lightning bolts of rekindling desire flashed. Through the thick disarray of auburn curls, one silken arm lifted to caress perilously close to where, were it to venture, his control would be lost. Jorion stepped back. She might be willing to anonymously share in passionate play, but could she, as queen, bear to lower herself to love one such as he? Passion without love was a thing easily attained, but from her it would come to taste like bitter wine.

Taine frowned. One night in his arms was no assurance of experience, but she had learned enough to know the clear evidence of his desire when it was unshielded a short distance from her eyes. She was more than willing to surrender again to his fiery delights, but why then did he withdraw from her? Looking up, Taine discovered Jorion smiling at her—a smile once more full of cynicism.

He shook his head as if to clear a lingering fog. Lifting from the chest near the bed the black garb so common to him, he began to dress. Wanted she free, he would release her. The choice was hers. He'd been alone all his life and would be again rather than hold her unwillingly, force himself on one who would reject him. Bright head popping through dark folds, his eyes fell to temptation, returning to the yielding woman's barely hidden curves, soft and all of enticement. Had he tasted sweet heaven only to find it could never be his? He went rigid with control to hold himself from her. He would not take her again and increase the chance that she would bear his child until she was aware that the secret of her heritage was known to him.

Taine nibbled on the tender rose of her full lower lip. For her the hours past had been a delight beyond knowing, but in her inexperience had she in some way failed to return the pleasure?

Seeing doubts clear in crystal-green eyes, Jorion watched a tremulous smile curve the sweet mouth still slightly swollen from their ardent play. Yes, he must tell her he knew her secret—but not now. Having taught her that desire was a pleasure not to be dreaded, he could not leave her fearing herself inadequate. The bed tilted as his superior weight settled beside her. As a precaution against loss of restraint, he lifted the bedcover to just below her chin, placing a barrier between him and her lush curves. He leaned halfway across her, strong forearms braced atop the coverlet on either side of her slender form and imprisoned her arms beneath its tight-held constraint.

Startled, Taine looked up into a smile that, though stiff with desire, held no hint of mockery. Scorched by the golden flames in his eyes, her own lashes fell beneath the gentle touch of his lips.

He moved the teasing caress over cheeks to the corners of her lips and whispered, "You are the richest delicacy, the hottest fire I will ever know." His mouth brushed hers, cherishing it with light touches.

Hungry fires blazed anew in Taine and she lifted hers to seek his. He answered the unspoken plea, deepening the burning contact. The kiss grew long and deep and wild, but when she moaned and struggled against the obstacle between her and her desire, he pulled away.

Silently thanking her for calling him back the moment before his control evaporated into the steam of mutual passion, Jorion strode from the chamber. Only through the strong effort of will, which seemed ever a necessary trait about her, did he deny the nearly ungovernable compulsion to look behind at the sweet temptation he could not refuse again.

Taine stared after him in confusion. Was this part of some further bridal custom unknown to her? She laid back against disarranged cushions and let her eyes go dreamy with warm memories of the past night. With unconvincing fervor, she reassured herself that loving Jorion was not such a dangerous thing. So long as he didn't know who she was, he couldn't use her feelings for him as the first step to a crown. The concept brought to mind Richard's betraying song, an annoyance that disturbed her contentment. She drove away apprehensions with the comfort that surely if Jorion had discovered her past in its words, he'd have added that proud claim to the others made this morn.

Taine dozed again and her dreams were heated memories, and she awakened wishing Jorion would return to rekindle the flame. Though heavy clouds filled the sky and shutters were drawn against the weak light, she could see the day was well advanced. The coverlet's warmth was reluctantly tossed aside. Although most of her wardrobe still rested in the bedchamber she'd used till now, one chest had been installed in a corner of the vast chamber.

While she'd slept, someone had stoked the fire, and red and yellow blades tangled in a combat that sent out welcome heat. Still, when she arose her toes curled against the cold floor and led her to make a crazy zigzag path across the chamber so she could walk on thick Saracen carpets as oft as possible. A happy smile warmed her face as she reached the chest and drew out a kirtle not worn before, one saved for some special occasion. The soft blue-green of seafoam, its hem and the edge of long sleeves fitting tightly at the wrists were embroidered in a deep-green pattern of thick foliage. Most important, the kirtle laced up the front and she could don it unaided. Atop it she wore the deep-green, nearly sideless surcote.

Only as Taine turned to search for her horsehair brush did she spy the light repast awaiting her attention on a small chest near one side of the bed. Although Halyse and Mercia had left her in peace this special morn, someone had slipped in to leave a thoughtful meal, probably the one who had attended the fire. She smiled. Except for the spider, life in Castle Dragonsward was a joy unexpected. And with Jorion's demand for the direct allegiance of all men in his domain, the power of the spider's web had surely found boundaries. She was not hungry, but managed a few bites to demonstrate appreciation for the deed.

Wanting to look her best for the man she willingly admitted to love, to herself at least, Taine brushed her thick locks until they glowed with fire. Weaving ribbons of silver-green into their wealth she formed thick plaits and bound them into a heavy coil at the nape of her elegant neck.

She was ready, but where should she go? To the great hall? Nay, she would not willingly submit to the curious eyes of the many before it was needful. To the solar then. Jorion would doubtless come to her there when his tasks were complete. The prospect was pleasing. She smiled and, anxious to see him once more, hastily departed the bed-chamber where she'd found happiness.

Taine was vaguely disappointed to find only Elspeth within the family solar. The young maid was sitting on the floor before the fire, tentatively stroking the black kitty's fur and earning its loud purr. Wanting to lessen the strain between them, Taine advanced.

"Good morrow. I see you've found the key to Omen's heart." Firelight made silvery ribbons glow amongst dark-fire hair as Taine nodded toward the small animal lying in contentment beneath caressing hands.

"Omen." Elspeth laughed, eyes sparkling with under-standing of the allusion. "You named her what uncle called her."

"It seemed the proper thing to do." Taine grinned back and dropped down onto a small stool beside the other. They sat quietly for some moments, only Elspeth's occasional murmurs to the cat interrupting the companionable silence. At length Taine caught curious glances from soft brown eyes and wondered what query she hesitated to ask. Warmed by a never-before-experienced contentment with her life, Taine wanted to share her happiness and forge the first links of friendship with the shy girl.

"I would answer as truthfully as I may any question you put to me," Taine offered at last, certain the girl could know nothing of the one secret she would must ever hide.

Still Elspeth hesitated, clearly uncomfortable. Her question was personal in the extreme.

Taine assumed Elspeth had some query for the relation-ship between herself and Richard and found it difficult to form the words. "Any question. You need have no fear of offending me."

Elspeth tamped down her embarrassment and began, "Did you—That is—" She hesitated then rushed on before her nerve crumbled away. "Is the joining of husband and wife as horrid as old Agretta says or as exciting as Buxom Peg claims?" Elspeth knew that Agretta, the midwife and a bitter old widow, was unlikely to speak true. Besides, after her moments in Richard's arms, she was inclined to the scullery maid's view. Yet, with the innocent's lack of tact, she sought firsthand knowledge from one of her own station.

Stunned, wild rose stained Taine's cheeks. Never having heard such gossip before, no one had talked of these matters to her. Oh, yes, she'd known the mechanics of mating, but until Jorion came into her life, she had been as naive to passion as the younger girl. She'd promised to answer and it seemed only just that someone speak truth to the girl.

"I do not know how it will be for you. For me—I have been subjected to an attack meant to end the same and found only disgust and pain; but with the dragon it was fire and pleasure and joy."

Elspeth had asked but not truly expected so honest an answer and smiled her appreciation. Thereupon their talk moved into less personal subjects and both, having had few opportunities to speak plainly with another woman of like rank, save Halyse, welcomed the chance. By the time Halyse came to call Elspeth to a task undone, a tentative bond of friendship had been formed.

With a warm smile for Taine, Elspeth left while Halyse lingered to watch Taine lift the small bundle of black to her lap and gently pet it. Head covered with unmanageable carroty hair tilted to one side, she questioned, "How will you like having babies of your own?"

Startled, Taine looked up. Having spent very little time with children of any age, the idea was new.

"You'd best make up your mind to enjoy it," Halyse teased, "for you may be breeding even now." She broadly winked and withdrew.

Back to the door, Taine resumed her stroking of black satin fur. Of a certainty, Halyse's words could be so. The possibility of a child was a pleasant thought and she was smiling warmly at the vision of cuddling a small child with golden hair and bronzed skin, when a voice called softly from behind.

"So here you are, Margaret."

"Aye," Taine answered, turning with welcome on her lips for the father to her dream.

Standing in the doorway, Jorion was not smiling. He'd

felt the need to test his theory and, with little hope, had questioned the truth of his conclusion.

The meaning behind his words swept the color from Taine, blood receding so quickly she wavered, light-headed. He knew her identity, and her bright dreams shattered like glass against stone. Now she had lost all possibility of earning his love and knowing it not born of desire for a crown. No doubt he would turn her background to his own advantage, just as so many others had sought to do. Why else would he trick her into admitting her heritage? Her face closed into a cold mask, and green eyes glowed with disgust as she rose and walked past him to leave the chamber, careful to allow contact at no point.

Her action brought an unhidden anguish to Jorion's handsome features, and he slumped against the door frame. His worst fears had been confirmed. By naming her queen, he had driven the warm welcome from her. She'd gone from him, unwilling to so much as touch him in the passing. What he had gained was lost—the fire-sprite doused to bitter ashes. He would have to release her—but not before he'd made certain of her safety.

Once beyond the solar door, Taine ran to her old chamber, silent tears running down her pale cheeks. Throwing herself on her cold, virginal bed, she buried her face in the pillow to muffle unstoppable sobs. When at last the clouds of anguish were drained dry and she gulped only dry sobs, she named herself fool for yielding so easily to the dragon's fire. Such was only proof of a subtle chain to bind her to his will and ambitions.

Days passed on dragging feet like sinners to judgment. Wondering for the reason behind so sudden a rift, the people of Castle Dragonsward silently watched. All knew Taine slept in her old chamber—alone. She seldom left that solitude and, it was whispered, when she did she looked to be carved of ice—quite a feat for someone with hair of fire. Jorion's golden hair was the lightning crown for a face of thunder. He no longer raged at others or showed even a cynical smile as he walked about, speaking only when unavoidable. Sir Thomas appeared to enjoy the others' misery immensely and laughed often, a sound lending not joy but discomfort to listeners. His attitude was bearable only because the entertaining of his visitors, hawking and hunting, brought him seldom near.

In the central room of his small cottage, where afternoon shadows had gathered and darkened into early evening, Father Aleric looked across at the man grown from golden boy. He had summoned Jorion to a private talk that clearly the other would as lief deny.

Father Aleric, squinting to see Jorion's response, began in a voice soft with love, "You are dear to me."

Jorion nodded but, for the first time in their long relationship, let an impassive wall drop between them. Near certain of the reason for this summons, still he waited patiently, determined to allow no one, not even this man who held firm place in his heart, to meddle in the matter.

"My eyes are weak but could not fail to see the breach widening between you and your countess. Nor can I calmly watch you suffer with a pain that by action might be healed, and I urge you to seek the path of reconciliation."

Jorion's voice was ice as with words clear and distinct he replied, "She has denied me, and never will I force myself on any woman."

An intelligent man, Father Aleric understood much that was not said and divined the wheat of truth from the chaff of gossip. He had heard rumors of a bride seeking freedom before the wedding day. Such action had not kept Jorion from claiming her. What was unclear was the difference in denial between then and now.

Jorion had not wanted to offend his mentor but could not bear to discuss the matter with another. Instead he briskly stood. "The evening meal will soon be in readiness."

The priest struggled to rise as well but fell back, discomfort flashing across his face. Concerned, Jorion leaned down to help the elderly man, so frail beside his strength. He was torn by his mentor's confusion at his refusal to speak further of the inexplicable attitudes of bride and groom and did not want him to feel its source a lack of caring. "These days are short and already the sun has been driven into hiding." Jorion's gruff voice imperfectly covered distress for his inability to perform what the priest suggested and soothe his worriment. "I will aid your climb to the castle."

Father Aleric laid age-gnarled fingers on the strong arm offered him but stood motionless, gazing into dark eyes. "'Tis all right." He smiled gently. "I would see you happy; yet, though you deny my words I do not doubt your affection for me."

Taine was already at table for another uncomfortable evening meal, when Jorion led the faltering priest to his usual place next to Bertwald. On coming to the great hall she'd been surprised to find Bertwald already there, as it was his habit to help the aging cleric to the castle. Now she realized that he had come early to leave Jorion in privacy with his friend. Such consideration only served to make· Taine feel more alone. Even surrounded by Halyse, Will, Richard, Elspeth, Sander, and Mercia, more friends than she had ever hoped to have, loneliness engulfed her. Without the love of the strong man now taking his seat at her side, she was alone.

As every night since their estrangement, his warmth reached out to enfold her, as his arms would not. Lifting his goblet, he brushed her side and she responded to the inconsequential contact. Keeping her eyes on the slab of day-old bread on the platter she shared with him, she watched as a bronzed hand ladled over it a portion of savory stew from the pot held by a kneeling page. That hand had caressed her. She almost felt the remembered touch, the searing brush of fingers on bare skin. Unintended though its flames might be, the dragon's fire burned, and she dared not look up into a face always cold, could not bear to be subject of the icy stare she'd seen him turn on others. Beneath the table's white cloth cover, her fingers twisted into the soft wool of her skirt. Still staring at the platter, she saw him choose bites from their fare. She had no appetite, and he no longer plied her with delicacies. The thought drove a pang into her heart.

Clearly a crown was his only use for her, she proudly reminded herself, reviving her flagging defiance. Since he had secured it by claiming her and had displayed the proof to all, he'd turned from her, never again looking her way. While she, despite her best intent and strong will, could not hold herself from peeking at him whenever he was near, could not stem the tide of pleasure in his company nor the wellspring of love.

Jorion felt her gaze on him, but could not look her way, for surely she would read the truth of his love in his eyes and pity him for it. Pity—a humiliating response from the one whose citadel he'd thought to breach but who instead had slipped through his shield and pierced his heart. He forced bites that tasted of dust; he must keep up his strength if he was to be of aid in any battle to hold Taine safe. She did not eat and it worried him. He lifted a piece of fresh wheaten bread and stared at it as if he suspected some vermin might rest within. Shackled to him by wedding vows, had she lost her will to live? Had he stolen all joy from her by his proud demand of a tie she'd sought to deny? Feeling his throat close with self-disgust, he put the bread down untasted, hand closing into a fist.

Taine saw his action, felt the flexing of his arm, and wanted to reach out to him. To subdue the unmanageable but forbidden impulse, Taine turned her attention to the tables below the dais and found Halyse's eyes firmly upon her. Forcing a wan smile, Taine's gaze dropped again to the half-filled platter. Halyse could not understand the sudden rift between Taine and the dragon. Though Halyse had not broached the subject directly, she'd renewed her praises of the dragon's many fine qualities. She'd even taken pains to tell Taine how Jorion had ordered Will to deliver Stephen, her young forest friend, to his family's bosom unharmed. Moreover, after Jorion had pardoned Stephen for his unlawful deed and spared his younger brother, he had provided sufficient food to see the lad's family through winter. And not for Stephen's family alone but, too, for all the serfs of his lands.

"You missed a glorious sunset—purple and rose," Richard said softly, near whispering in Taine's ear. "I wish you had walked with me to see it." He wanted to be both friend to and creator of peace between the couple, who did not speak or even look upon one another.

Taine did not answer Richard. Caught between two men, she only gave a smile so brief it did not warm the deep-green eyes, which quickly dropped to stare again at the platter. From the first morn of the freeze between her and Jorion,

Richard had tried to draw her out but she refused his call. Empathizing with her new friend, she clearly saw the true subject of Elspeth's tender emotions and, as she ached with unfulfilled love herself, she would not be party to another's pain. Elspeth no longer blamed her for Richard's deed, but still grew more and more upset with him for his continued attentions to another.

While most eyes were on the estranged couple, Thomas watched his son and the heiress. He had seen Elspeth turn against the man so constantly attending the beautiful woman claimed by Jorion and cursed his son. If the plan were to be saved, he would have to push the point before the bumbling of its central parties destroyed all hope. A further consideration urged haste. It was certain only Jorion, a doting guardian, would consider an alliance between an heiress and Richard, thus the marriage must be an accomplished fact before his first plan was concluded—the two visitors were growing impatient.

"Jorion," Sir Thomas called and waited until black eyes turned to him. "Have you thought more on the proposition I made you?"

A heavy frown brought golden brows together.

"Time has passed since your vows were spoken." The dragon's expression was neither a welcome sign nor encouragement to continue, but the proposal must be addressed without delay else the plan would be lost. "I've waited as you requested but now ask again. Will you agree to a marriage between my son and your ward?"

Elspeth gasped, brown eyes wide with shock. Richard's frown was fierce and his hands slapped palm down, shaking the table. Of his father's plan, Richard had known nothing, and he was furious at his sire's meddling in a matter so important. Seeing Richard's anger, Elspeth misinterpreted its source. Pride rose, as did her chin.

The negative reactions of both parties to the proposed marriage seemed unmistakable to Jorion. "'Tis not to be, uncle," Jorion responded, irritated with the older man for forcing the issue. "I have it from a very reliable source that Elspeth 'would as soon bed a serf.'"

Sir Thomas, face bright with suffused color, merely nodded his head before casting a killing glance at his son and rising to depart even before the last course was served. His guests sat so quietly at meals that the others barely noted their presence—a useful talent—but being summarily refused before them hardened his intent.

Taine, aware of the unspoken feelings of both Richard and Elspeth, watched as the tangled strands of their relationship became inextricably snarled. Each pretended a pleasure in Jorion's denial of the future they most desired. Barely able to survive the disaster of her own relationship with Jorion, she could not bear to see another's destroyed, certainly not for so foolish a misunderstanding. If Elspeth and Richard would speak clearly to one another, so much could be avoided. Under the weight of unhappiness pressing the high table down, she wanted nothing more than to follow Sir Thomas' example and flee to the cool darkness of her chamber.

From the top of one long line of lower tables, Aleric and Bertwald watched the proud distance between Jorion and Taine with disgust for their foolish behavior. Although Bertwald held to his oath to Taine, they'd shared lengthy conversations on the respective natures of their onetime charges. A mutual concern for the couple's future formed a bond between the men, and they had discussed measures to see it happily fulfilled.

"You spoke to the man?" Bertwald questioned so softly no other would hear.

"Aye, I tried to speak reason," the priest answered, vexation showing through, "but Jorion is a stubborn ass."

Bertwald's eyes widened in momentary surprise at the priest's choice of words. "Stubborn, hah," he returned after a short pause, words nearly a hiss. "He can't be a scratch to the lass. She'd stand strong against the devil hisself."

A wry smile lifted papery lips. "I hope so. Indeed, I pray it be so."

"Ho!" Bertwald shook his head in wry response. Caught again. 'Twas only to be expected of a priest.

"Stubborn she may be," Aleric continued, "but as she is the only path left us, I will speak with her."

Taine had forced herself to endure the final stage of the meal, watching as Jorion took one bite of a sweet pear and shredded his cheese. After the battered remains on the platter they'd shared had been removed, she rose and made quiet excuse to leave. Stepping down from the dais to walk toward the corner stairwell, she was surprised to find Father Aleric behind her.

"Milady, I beg a word with you."

Surprised, Taine nodded and led the way to the now empty solar. Assuming he wanted to speak with her of the trouble between her and the dragon, a subject she had rather avoid but knew no kind way to refuse, she sat on the small three-legged stool near the fire, tucking her legs to one side.

The priest settled with difficulty into the chair beside the chessboard and wasted no time. "Are you repelled by Jorion's heritage?"

Whatever she had expected him to ask, this was not it. She looked at him carefully, as if suspecting his advancing years had suddenly misarranged his wits. They'd talked so long of Jorion's past on the trip to Radwyn that surely he could have no doubts on the matter.

Father Aleric smiled gently at her obvious disgust for the question and continued. "Whenever one turns from him, he will think it the cause."

Clearly, Taine realized, the priest believed Jorion saw her actions as rejection for his Saracen blood. She had turned from him suddenly. Was it possible Jorion thought her action a rejection for something beyond his choice? Nay, she scolded herself—with wavering fervor. What matter in such misunderstanding, if he would still seek to use her heritage for his own gain? But would he? He'd made no move yet and it had been nearly a sennight.

Aleric was still speaking. "A group of desert boys, despising Jorion for his Christian ways, assaulted him. He complained to none of the unfairness in one attacked by many, but worked twice as hard to build his strength and mastered the Saracen arts of defense until he stood strong, invincible to physical attack."

Ever interested in stories of the dragon, Taine listened silently, heart aching for the boy who surely lived on in the soul of the man.

"We then came to the longed-for home of his father; but, as you know, he discovered himself no more accepted here. He built about himself a protective armor against which belittling barbs and veiled rejections fell away, making him impervious to emotional torment as well."

Taine had seen the power of Jorion's armor turn away jealous barbs at Edward's court, had heard the pain of his past—in large part from Father Aleric himself. For what reason, then, did Father Aleric now speak of it again?

"Jorion has opened his armor to you." Father Aleric answered the unspoken question clear in cloudy eyes. "You, and nearly you alone, can pass beyond its shield to the man within. Turn you away now, and likely he will lock himself inside and withdraw still farther from disappointing humankind, until the gentle side of his nature turns as bitter as bottled wine that, allowed to go unopened beyond its prime, turns to vinegar."

❧ Chapter 19 ❧

A BLOODCURDLING ROAR JERKED Taine from the troubled sleep she'd been long in attaining. Caught bending over her, two dark shapes, indistinguishable against the dwindling firelight behind, stumbled back from the bed. Heart pounding erratically, she struggled to sit up, clutching the bedcover across her bare breasts with innate modesty. Shoving disheveled auburn silk out of her eyes, she looked to the open chamber door. In its frame stood the dragon, a figure of power. Dark garb blended with night shadows but bright hair shone its beacon-light, glowing with the same reflected hearth flame dancing on the finely honed blades crossed over his chest's broad expanse.

Jorion saw Taine's movement from the corner of his eyes, but his penetrating gaze did not shift from the taller of the men found uninvited within his wife's bedchamber.

Light-blue eyes, nearly colorless in the half-light, met dangerous, unflinching black ones. The arrow-slits that served as windows in this tower built long ago were not of a size through which a man could escape, and a threat loomed in the only path to freedom. McLewell had almost expected this foil to their plan. He'd faced the dragon in conflict before and did not underestimate the man, his foe once again. With a small smile and a slight nod of acknowledgment for the dragon's victory, he let his sword's point drop.

The younger man sidled toward the bed but Jorion pinned him with dark eyes that glittered in menace. Morton still held a small dagger that might well be turned against Taine to hold her before him as hostage and shield. Jorion jerked his head, summoning the maid whose attention lay heavy upon him.

Without a moment's hesitation, Taine snatched the thick coverlet free and wound it about her slender form as she went to this man who had again appeared unexpectedly in her doorway to offer protection. As she moved, Morton flipped his blade until he held its tip in perfect balance for deadly flight.

"My blade protects my heart," Jorion calmly stated, "and failing that blow one dagger cannot render enough damage to protect you from me."

Morton nervously bit at his thin lower lip. The dragon spoke true—he could not fell so mighty a warrior with a small dagger. 'Twas said the dragon with his dual blades could fight and defeat a full company of men. Their only defense was the lady clearly dear to him. Morton's glance went to Taine, swiftly calculating the possibilities.

"Harm you my wife while I yet live, and I will see you in hell," Jorion warned, words softly spoken but more menacing for that.

Morton's face went white, but he hesitated. She was the only effective blow they could wreak upon their foe.

"In the desert where I was raised"—Jorion's voice was deadly as black ice—"they practice many refined tortures unknown in this land."

The weapon clattered uselessly on the rush-strewn floor.

Amazing, the power of even unused foreign weapons and ominous threats of deeds unknown, thought Taine. Looking up, she found a slight, one-sided smile of mockery on Jorion's harsh mouth and knew him to be amused by nearly the same thought. The sound of approaching footsteps and muffled voices seeped into the chamber's unnatural quiet. Others had been roused and drawn by the dragon's battle cry.

"For what purpose did you rend the night with your shouts?" Sir Thomas demanded from behind Jorion. His normally well groomed hair stood in spikes, and his eyes were still puffy with rudely interrupted sleep. In irritation he sniped, "Some heathenish practice you've not taught us before?"

Jorion turned slightly to give the disgruntled man full view of the room. McLewell calmly stood, sword point-down, while Morton hovered nervously at his back. "Your guests have chosen to repay my hospitality," Jorion coldly informed his uncle, "by attempting the abduction of my bride."

Sir Thomas' brows rose in very real shock. Although he'd hoped for some action on their part, he'd expected nothing so overt nor that it would come this night. "You are fools," he nearly snarled at the two trapped men, voice thick with feigned disgust, while beneath his sputtering condemnation, satisfaction bloomed. They'd fallen into his snare, as he'd known they surely would, given time to contemplate the possibilities. Only a few subtle hints had been needed to ease the way.

McLewell did not respond but stared at Sir Thomas with such cynical disgust that the man nearly faltered. Despite the cold gaze, Sir Thomas drew himself up to further his charade and continued. "Don't you see that the marriage removes the need for such dangerous measures?"

Face unreadable, Jorion watched his uncle closely. He knew the older man too well to be easily convinced he was pleased by the marriage or content that, by alliance with one of unacceptable heritage, the one claim to the Scottish crown superior to Baliol's was removed. 'Twas unlikely any would support a monarch who might pass the crown to an heir of mixed blood.

"You are the fool, old man," Morton hissed from behind the protection of McLewell's back. "A widowed queen is as capable of sharing a crown as one still a maid."

Stunned as by a sudden frigid water drenching, unhindered by the cold of metal blades, Taine backed closer against the dragon's warmth. This talk of a widowed queen brought to light an unforeseen threat. Her heritage placed Jorion as much, nay more, in danger than she herself. As

Morton said, once her identity was known, any man coveting the crown had only to end Jorion's life and claim her as his own. Moreover, Jorion was a danger to Baliol plans, for so powerful a lord could well begin a struggle for the crown with greater and more lasting success than John Baliol had demonstrated. Heavy masses of bright curls tumbled over her bare shoulder as she tilted her head back to look up into black eyes, fear and horror darkening her own. By accepting a claim she'd initiated and protecting her from others' schemes, he'd stepped into a danger for which he'd yet to seek reward.

Pleased by her obvious concern for him, Jorion smiled down into her pale face before turning away. From the crowd at his back he beckoned several men of his guard and bade them deliver the foiled abductors to a dark cell in the castle's underground level. Then motioning Sander forward, Jorion handed the wide-eyed boy his curved swords with directions to see to their care.

As Jorion withdrew his heat and support, Taine wavered. She'd brought on him a terrible danger—and for what gain? He'd known her secret for a sennight and more, yet had made no move to claim her crown. Nor had he even contacted his friend King Edward with the news. The conflict between her bitter assumptions and the truth of his actions left her filled with uncertainty. Was she as guilty of foolish deeds as Elspeth and Richard, who fell to difficulty for not speaking frankly? Was it possible Bertwald and Father Aleric had seen the facts more clearly than she? Even with the truth of her past, was Jorion the man to trust? Did Jorion turn from her solely for a misbelief that her response to his calling her by name was rejection for a bloodline beyond his choosing?

After the two prisoners were taken from their midst and with no further gossip-fodder in the offing, the others drifted away, murmuring in excited undertones of the strange event and even stranger talk of a queen.

When the curious crowd had departed, silence returned. Jorion lifted McLewell's abandoned sword from the floor at the foot of the bed, then moved nearer its head to retrieve the small dagger deflected by words.

"Thank you for your protection of me, Jorion." Taine

spoke the words gently to the broad expanse of a black-covered back.

Jorion went rigid, arching as if the words were a sharp thrust into unwary muscles. After his grandfather had spurned a young boy anxious to please so many years past, he had learned not to hope for another's acceptance—at least not beyond those whose livelihood depended upon him and who were forced to the deed. But her soft gratitude sent a gleam through the bleak reaches of his soul. He steeled himself against a weakening that could end only in anguish, and his face showed no emotion when he turned to nod his acceptance before starting toward the door.

Watching the man she loved leave her again as if he could not bear to linger in her company, Taine took her courage into her hands. She had far rather know he meant to fulfill her worst fears than constantly cower, unsure of what the coming days would bring.

"I would know," she asked straight out, "what you intend for the crown of Scotland." Their only chance for a marriage true lay in the plain speaking she'd wordlessly encouraged Elspeth and Richard to attempt.

For long, silent moments, Jorion stared into hopeful green eyes. To hold his wife, would he have to break with Edward and start the doubtless bloody battles for the Scottish throne? He had little stomach for such an endeavor. Yet she had the right to wear the crown be it her desire; and, as her husband, he must support her cause.

Watching her closely, he answered her question with two of his own. "What path would you have me seek? What do you wish me to do—reclaim for you the power and wealth the crown holds?" A cynicism born of experience with women far different from Taine shaded his words.

Green eyes widened to deep forest pools. It had never occurred to her that any man would ask her desires in the matter. Still, she was quick to emphatically make her preference known. "Nay, I have no wish for the crown and would gladly forswear its unwelcome weight."

Though shocked by her vehement rejection of a prize others would kill for, relief flooded through Jorion and his tightly held face relaxed into admiration.

Taine was surprised. Jorion appeared to want the crown

no more than she, although he had clearly been willing to support whichever choice she made.

Beyond the first relief that he need not take a path unwelcome to him, suspicion grew in this man who could trust few. Either she was truly a woman like no other, or some deeper reason lay behind her wish to give up a possession so coveted. The women he knew would eagerly perform incredible tasks for such rewards. Had Taine some secret life waiting elsewhere? A life that offered more? A love that overshadowed even such treasures? The possibilities shot bolts of pure pain to his soul. He'd sworn to release her if she wished, and the ice with which he froze his emotions against so dear a loss coated the question he next asked, "What path then do you seek for your future?"

"To live peacefully here in Castle Dragonsward," she answered truthfully, swallowing pride for this chance at her heart's desire.

Jorion shook his head as if clearing cobwebs of suspicion from its dark corners. He had known from the first she was unique, one far above all others in more than royal heritage. He gave to her a smile of piercing sweetness.

Dazzling silver lights flared in green eyes and she rushed toward him, nearly flinging herself into his arms, tears of relief streaking her radiant face.

The ice layers built by repeated rejections of the many who deemed themselves superior for pure blood began to melt beneath the warmth of a queen's embrace. Strong arms wrapped about the delicate maid, tightening slowly as if subconsciously afraid he might yet frighten away the elusive treasure who only hours past he'd thought never to win.

Filled with happiness, Taine flowed against his long, hard body. Wrapped close and overwhelmed anew by his height and breadth, her old terrors dissipated in the heat of remembered pleasures, like morning mists subjected to the heat of the sun. She reveled in the growing strength of the hold binding her to him. The tension in powerful muscles changed and built, and she went hot all over, knowing herself once more a willing captive of the dragon's fire.

Her sweet wild-rose scent and soft warmth, come to Jorion's arms of her own choice, drove rational thought into the fog of steam rising from his simmering blood. One large hand moved gradually along her spine, urging her closer into the contours of his body as his mouth descended to drink the heady wine of hers. Under the warm crush of his lips, she moaned and arched up, arms lifting to twine about his neck and slender fingers tangling into golden strands glowing with firelight. She pulled him nearer, seeking more. Readily yielding to her unspoken demand, he deepened the kiss with a devastating slowness that sent wild shudders of sensation through her.

In past embraces he'd proven he could tempt her beyond her will's intent, but there she had learned a power of her own. Although sinking fast into the hazy smoke of desire, she clung to a determination to prove that no rejection, no disdain for him found home within her. Though wrapped in the bed's rich coverlet, held in place by tightly pressed bodies, she moved her sweet bounty sensuously against him. He released her mouth, head falling back as a low moan escaped from his arched throat. Taine smiled. Surrendering to a pleasure she'd thought ever forbidden, she rose on tiptoe to nuzzle between the laces of his front-closing tunic and rain teasing kisses over the wedge of bronze flesh thus revealed.

In effort to maintain some control, not frighten her again with the violence of his passion, Jorion stepped a hand-breadth away. Taine's only cover, once wound close, had loosened when her arms first lifted to him. It now slipped to rest precariously at the crest of her breasts. His breath caught and eyes burned on the uncertain hold.

Slender fingers took advantage of the space between to unfasten his laces and spear through wiry golden curls. Impatient with the restrictions of his wool tunic, Taine tugged at it. To no avail. Seduced by her exploring touch, Jorion stripped it off in one quick, smooth motion that sent muscles rippling. Her exquisite face was tense with desire, eyes wide and dark saying more of admiration than words ever could. Reaching out in silent praise, her hands wandered in fascination over the erotic combination of hard muscle and abrasive hair and moved up to slowly stroke the breadth of wide shoulders, feeling every line and curve burn beneath her touch. She loved the contact with his powerful body, the male scent of him, and her small pointed tongue ventured forth to taste.

Every particle of Jorion's being centered on her curious caresses. Passion blazed in his blood, rushing it through his veins like wildfire through the forest, uncontrollable and unstoppable. Heavy lids half-fell over smoldering eyes as Jorion joined the play. He urged the coverlet down to leave her high, full breasts only inadequately shielded by auburn curls. His hands followed the coverlet's fall and slid it over the impediment of gently flared hips.

Self-conscious nude before another, Taine stiffened but the golden fires in his eyes burned away embarrassment. He spread the fire by running his hands slowly up over the silky flesh of slender hips, through the luxurious mass of tangled hair to the intensely sensitive skin beneath her arms. Labored breathing caught on a cry of longing lodged in her throat. She arched slightly, seeking to press against him but gentle hands held her firmly a whisper from her goal. His palms swept in small circles, edging ever nearer soft mounds. At length he cupped their luscious weight while thumbs brushed over aching tips. Taine bit the deep rose of her lower lip to hold back another moan, but an aching sound escaped.

Jorion smiled as with his great strength he raised her until his adoring lips could nudge aside curls of living fire to uncover the perfect bounty of her flesh. Lightly they brushed over generous curves the velvet softness of rose petals.

The tantalizing caresses brought an ever-increasing longing until Taine buried her hands in golden hair and brought his teasing mouth to the center of the ache he had caused. The sweet suction was both achieved goal and kindling to hungry flames. He let her slowly slide down the length of his aroused body. Then, holding her back, he watched while he gradually buried rose tips in the golden hair covering his chest before brushing soft breasts back and forth against hard muscles. Palms flat, his hands swept over a satin back to grip a perfectly rounded derrière and press her to his urgent desire and move her against him.

Nearly overcome by a wall of fire, Taine trembled with

incredible sensations. Her knees would have failed her had Jorion not swept her up into his strong hold. Intoxicated by the sound of her soft little moans, Jorion yet restrained the blaze in his blood as he lowered her to the bed, determined she would share its madness before they found surcease. He laid her across the bed. Ridding himself of the last impediment to their touch of flesh to flesh, he looked down and the golden flames in dark depths scorched over the pale cream and tender rose of her slender body.

As if drawn by a temptation stronger than his will, he reached out to tenderly trace lush curves. Jorion intently watched as his deeply bronzed fingers moved against the nearly luminescent whiteness of her skin. The gentle rasp of hands hardened by sword grip burned Taine and she helplessly trembled beneath their caress. Pleasure heightened by her unrestrained response, he explored the textures with exquisite gentleness while stretching out at her side and lowering his mouth to kiss, nibble, savor soft skin.

"I could get drunk on the taste of you." His voice was deep and darkly textured.

Beneath the dragon's touch of fire, Taine helplessly moved, twisting sensuously against him. Feeling a strong shudder shake him at her response, she lifted toward him, pulled him to her and surrendered again to the dragon's fire. He eased over her and felt her arch under him, felt her hands on his hips urging him near and lost rational thought. Their bodies merged like two flames dancing in the fire's midst. They twined and surged together, stoking the need to an ever greater blaze, a conflagration of such intensity that, just as Taine thought she would perish in the scorching heat—die of the blaze's depthless hunger, they exploded in a burst of golden sparks.

Laying content on the smoldering coals of a fire banked but waiting to flare anew, Taine rubbed her cheek against the hard chest beneath. Jorion held his exquisite wife bound to his side, slowly smoothing her passion-tangled hair. Even the first day of their meeting, he'd recognized her as his fate, yet he'd expected that the same lack which had stolen mother, father, and the acceptance of others would steal away the one whose approval mattered most. He thanked the power that ruled all, more than willing to accept past and future disillusionments and rejections as payment for the sweet gift in his arms. Pray God he could keep her safe within.

Rousing from a state of blissful lassitude, Taine stroked the firm expanse of bronze skin beneath her hand, savoring with new appreciation the powerful contours. "Your golden skin is a fascination to me—so beautiful."

Jorion tensed, surprised by her praise of the clear mark of his unacceptable heritage, the skin tone that repelled so many. He found it a miracle that she could accept him, despite such betraying signs, and to hear her admiration was a wonder beyond measure.

Taine felt his reaction and misunderstood its source. "Aye, I know. Men are not beautiful—but you are." Again she stroked from throat down through the wedge of golden curls arrowing past his navel. "Gold and fire." She lifted up on her elbows to nuzzle the path of her hands. "I will pray every day that our sons are gifted with it."

Dark eyes closed in gratitude snapped open. Jorion was further amazed by this woman, this queen, who not only found joy in his appearance but wanted children who shared what he'd been taught to name shame. Here in her willingness to bear the children he'd been assured would be tainted by mixed blood was proof that she, without restraint, accepted him and all he was.

"I could be breeding even now." Suspending the nibbling excursion across his broad chest, with evident happiness for the possibility, she looked up to meet his black gaze. "Leastways, Halyse said 'tis true."

Jorion's arms crushed her against him, taking her mouth in a kiss already full of renewed passion. Banked embers ignited and flared anew, blazing into a passionate vortex the hotter for tenderness feeding its hungry flames.

When morning sent slivers of light into the chamber, Taine woke to an unaccustomed warmth against her back, fire come to bed, and a weight wrapped about her midriff. Memory seeped back with tantalizing scenes and Taine wiggled nearer to the heat's source with a smile of happiness on lips rose-red and slightly swollen from the play of night hours.

"My laggard wife awakens." A low, amused voice rumbled in her ear.

"Hmmm" was all she replied, snuggling tighter back against him. 'Twas a lie that the dragon's fire was consuming, for they had proven more than once that only did it scorch and build again.

"By the discretion of the people in my castle alone do we linger abed." He had lain wakeful since dawn but had given himself the luxury of holding his fire-sprite near and justified his sloth with the truth of his need to speak with her of private matters. "The sun has climbed more than halfway to the nooning hour, and when we at last show our faces below we'll be subject for many a ribald jest."

Taine showed no care for the talk of others but turned to face her husband, wrapping her arms about his neck and reaching up to lay soft kisses against his jawline before nuzzling his firm throat.

Jorion brushed his lips across the top of bright, tangled curls before speaking, choosing his words with care to assure she'd not take them amiss. "We have agreed to live here in peace, but to protect our safe harbor, I must learn all I can of the threats from your past."

Against the warm curve of his throat, Taine frowned. She did not want to let old hurts and lingering threats intrude on the sweet happiness of the present. Suddenly she remembered Morton's words of the night past, a menace unthinkable. Jorion was in as much danger as she, and that knowledge brought a willingness to share with him secrets no other knew. To ensure his safety she would tell him all. Yet as she looked up, intending to speak, it came to her that she could impart little more than what he must already have learned—her parentage, her long captivity, her escape. What more could she tell him that would be of use in ending the danger to them both—beyond his uncle's role in her past? And surely with Sir Thomas' visitors locked away and his men sworn to Jorion, he was a danger no more. She was loath to add to the antipathy between them, wanting to soothe, not irritate, Jorion's wounds.

Jorion saw her confusion, her renewed anxiety, and would give much to avoid the need to darken their bright hours with unpleasant memories. But to hold her safe, his first priority, there were things he must know. "Did you not realize that McLewell and Morton were your foes?" he questioned. "Had you not heard of them before?"

"Nay, I knew no names save Morag," Taine answered. A lifted golden brow asked explanation. "Morag was an elderly woman appointed my companion and gaoler. Too, I learned the given names of my rotating guards." Without need for Jorion's query, she explained, "They were changed twice a year, one group coming in the fall and one in the spring."

"But you knew it was the Baliols who held you?" Jorion asked, deeming it wise to define those responsible for her confinement.

"Aye, and that their bitter foes were the Bruces. In the first years of my stay, Morag talked extensively of her kinsman and rightful king, John Baliol. When her proud boasts ceased, I knew the shifting winds of conflict had swept in a new order, but knew not that he was deposed by King Edward until I heard talk among the guards."

"Did Bertwald not speak of it to you?" Bertwald's position in Taine's life was a puzzle to Jorion. The man had saved her from danger and released her from captivity. Surely he had kept her apprised of the political struggle tearing her country asunder.

"Only a serf bound to the castle and not privy to secret plots, Bertwald was my only friend for long years," Taine answered, aware that Jorion would find her disinterest in learning, nay, refusal to learn more a strange thing. "We never spoke of my past or the political battles filling the land with treachery and bloodshed. Rather, he told me marvelous tales of elfenfolk, of fairs and great feasts, and of heroes who save fair maidens. The dreams he gave me were my only escape from barren grey walls, and he never darkened them by speaking of the black deeds that had seen me imprisoned. At least, not until after he played shining knight, rescuing me from a vicious attack and spiriting me free of the dour castle and the wicked woman holding me there." Taine smiled at her description, which cast Bertwald in the mold of the handsome heroes of a minstrel's song.

Remembering Bertwald's statement that an oath to her

was as solemn as one to a sovereign, he urged her to continue by saying, "He knows who you are."

"My heritage, long imprisonment, and the gaolers who relentlessly pursued me he knows. He knows, too, my desire to leave it behind and has taken an oath to speak of them never."

"Know you nothing of the foes who still threaten you?" Jorion persisted.

"Clearly Bertwald has spoken to you of the two gaolers from whom I ran and who have long pursued me for fear of the punishment my escape would call down upon their heads." Jorion nodded but still looked at her steadily, compelling her to speak on. It seemed he would not allow her to protect him. She must reveal her final secret. "There is one more I know, one I fear will cause you pain."

"Sir Thomas?" Jorion questioned, nearly certain of the answer. The apprehensive looks he'd seen her give his uncle portended more than dislike of an overbearing man.

Taine took a deep breath and began. "I have only two clear memories of the time before I was trapped in a bleak castle on a rugged, stormy coast. My father, a man of silvery-blond hair and ice-blue eyes came to me the night before I was to sail away and put on my finger this 'cherish ring.'" She lifted her hand and stared at the twined metals curling about an emerald and gleaming in a lengthening patch of sunlight.

"And the other," he questioned, urging her onward.

Her head fell to his chest and fingers unconsciously tangled in the golden hair there as she continued. "On the ship I was not allowed out of my chamber for days. Then one stormy day my attendants wrapped me in a blanket, telling me 'twas a game which to win I must be especially quiet." Green eyes clouded with memories long suppressed. "I could feel myself lowered from ship to small boat and at length carried ashore. A cold wind pierced at my covering but my father had warned me not to struggle even if strange men took me from the ship." With a short mirthless laugh she added, "I even lay trusting when the horseman into whose care I'd been given set his steed into motion. But I was frightened when we fell to the ground and another pulled the blanket from me—your Uncle Thomas."

She looked into Jorion's face, seeking his reaction, but it was impassive as always. "By my ring he recognized me and I have lived in terror for what action he will take."

"Baliol allies held you, and Baliol allies pursued. Thus, so far as you know, all threats have come from that source?" Jorion's voice was flat, revealing none of his own misgivings.

Taine nodded in agreement, eyes unwavering. "So far as I know, 'tis true."

"My uncle's former supporters are now sworn to me," Jorion softly reminded her with a smile meant to comfort. "Moreover, the men I sent to follow your pursuers at the fair tell me they fled to McLewell, who lies powerless, his cohort at his side, in our dungeon. You are safe from them all." Jorion reassured her with words he did not completely believe, but he refused to frighten her more by speaking his own doubts about his uncle's part in the whole. Whatever it had been, surely the locking away of the others put paid to its name? There was no need to talk of the men who had tried to take Taine from her bed in Dunfermline. Though he was nearly certain they were not a part of the Baliol faction, their action had been taken in another country. They would scarce presume to invade the well-guarded castle of a much-feared lord. At least he prayed it would be so.

Jorion's words repeated what Taine had already decided, but his assurance was comforting nonetheless. Although he'd not revealed what he meant to do with McLewell and Morton, Taine felt safe now they were locked away and the spider's men sworn to her dragon. Presumed safety brought a relief which released the floodgates of her repressed past. She shared with him what she had told no other, the disappointment, loneliness, and despair of the monotonous future her prison had assured. Jorion held her in comfort and spoke of his own past with an openness not even Aleric had known. They did not descend the winding stone stairway until the nooning meal lay waiting, and people turned with teasing grins toward the tall lord and the shy lady standing in trust at his side.

Chapter 20

THE DULL ROAR OF a multitude of voices speaking at one time, punctuated by occasional laughter and near-constant clattering of mugs raised or lowered to tabletop, were the comfortable sounds of an evening repast well under way. Taine smiled with content. The mealtimes she'd dreaded only one week past were now an anticipated pleasure, a time she could be certain to spend in Jorion's company. Flickering flamelight from the scores of candles grouped on the three pyramid stands wove intricate patterns over bright hair and gilded thick lashes surrounding night-dark eyes. While Jorion talked quietly with Richard, who sat on her other side, she studied him. Delighting in the stunning contrasts of this man who was happiness to her, she welcomed his golden net of enthrallment.

The time since their coming together had been a joy never before known. With skies heavily overcast and air cold but dry, although his days were filled past measure with the duties of his demesne and his vassals' problems, he'd found time to fulfill a promise to her. Before foul weather descended in earnest, he had taken her to a meadow beyond sight of the castle and begun her lessons on sitting a horse.

In her pillion rides with him, she'd earlier overcome some of her apprehension of the large animals and with regular practice she was progressing well. However, no longer alarmed by closeness to the huge man once feared, she would now prefer to ride wrapped in his strength. She grinned at the impractical wish and, not wanting to explain its source, bent her head to stare at the table cover her slender fingers smoothed. To repress the image of foolery the notion brought, she turned her thoughts to other times they'd shared during the last sennight.

One cold but sunny day she'd accompanied him to the tiltyard, a long strip of barren land beyond the moat. The quintain, a straw-packed sack hung from a rod arm attached to center post, had been set on the far end, and earnest young squires with lances in hand waited their turn to ride toward it at speed. As they'd leaned against the tiltyard's split pole railing, Jorion explained their goal was to hit the quintain flat to point and move quickly away, avoiding the full swing round that would unhorse the unwary.

Seeing Sander intent on his imaginary adversary brought to Taine's mind another young lad longing to become knight. "Will you grant me a boon?" she impulsively asked, turning to the man towering behind.

Despite the slight cloud of suspicion in dark eyes, Jorion quickly answered, "If it be in my power."

"Stephen, my young friend from the forest flight, dreams of being a fierce knight like the Golden Dragon." Jorion frowned at mention of an unpleasant episode, but she fearlessly persisted. "It must surely be within your power to accept him for training as you've accepted these others." She waved toward the sizable group at practice.

"Aye," Jorion agreed, plainly reluctant. "It is within my power." He looked sharply away from her pleading eyes. "But 'twould be an experience far different from his shining dreams. Those you see here are of noble blood." He nodded toward the nervous group anxious to perform well before the famous warrior, who seldom had the time to personally attend to their training. His eyes were bleak as he continued. "Stephen is a serf and in all the years necessary to attain the skills for his goal he would be ever spurned." When she started to argue with him, his face closed into the hard mask of old as he flatly put an end to the matter. "I will not be the one to subject another boy to the painful rejections I have borne."

Upset with herself for inadvertently probing his wounds and bringing the first note of discord to their relationship since they'd found happiness, she dropped the issue. Although hoping to find some other means of helping the boy, she directed her full attention to the man doing his all to distract her from their cold exchange. He had taken the field and, even on a destrier less skilled than his own, thrilled both Taine and the gaping squires with demonstrations of his superior skill with lance and sword. And, more, he demonstrated his talent with the dual whirling blades of his ferocious Saracen weapons. A thing, he later told her, shown to none save on the field of battle since the day he, as a young boy, had horrified his grandfather and uncle. He was truly a warrior all others would do well to avoid. But not she. Taine gazed up at the man sitting at her side and still talking with Richard. Her smile deepened with admiration for the man she'd wed, proud of her powerful lord and secure within his hold.

Jorion glanced down and his face gentled with an expression of warmth. When first seen, this same look had surprised his people with its openness, a thing never shown by their dragon of power and aloofness. She was an addictive pleasure and only by strength of will, and the assurance that in the long hours of winter nights they would share delights untold, could he pull himself away to see to the duties of his position. Having taken his fiefdom's control into his own hands he must fulfill its demands. He had spent nearly the whole day in lengthy discussions of supplies he'd promised his people and the methods of distribution. A necessary but boring task. The meal's final course lay on the platter he was sharing with Taine, and he was impatient to escape with her to their chamber above.

Though Richard's question had gone unanswered, he beamed. Jorion's obvious captivity by the tender maid delighted him. Great court beauties had buzzed about the dragon only to be swatted away like so many pesky flies. Their enticing wiles had earned no more from him than annoyance hidden in remote politeness. Even the women of lesser station whom he'd taken to his bed had meant but a momentary diversion, a slaking of undeniable hunger. Now, even in the midst of a discussion on King Edward's battles and strategies, a subject once of paramount import to him, Jorion was prey to Taine's charms.

"When will the Edward return his attention to his own kingdom?" Richard patiently asked again.

Richard's question, barely heard by the man focused on the maid, demanded response. With difficulty, Jorion pulled himself from the crystal-green snare of Taine's eyes to answer. "Not, I think, until he has subdued his Scottish foes or—mayhap when winter snows threaten one year hence."

While Jorion looked back to Richard, Taine's gaze wandered to the top of a lower table. She heard Jorion's response but it was of little interest to her, and she grinned in amusement at Halyse, who appeared to be vehemently cautioning small Bryce against some mischievous deed. Dreams of a golden child filled her thoughts.

While Jorion spoke of Edward's planned victory over Scottish foes, he was aware of Taine's complete lack of interest. It still amazed him that she who held preeminent right to Scottish rule had rather live in peace, when there were many who would give all they possessed to obtain it. He glanced at Sir Thomas and found his uncle's eyes narrowed on Taine. Jorion's resolve to protect Taine hardened, and he reaffirmed his intent to watch over his treasure with the jealous zeal of a miser for his gold.

Sensitive to the sudden tension in Jorion, Taine looked up and followed his gaze. Once again, as many times in recent days, she found herself the subject of Sir Thomas' oddly calculating gaze. Driving back the uncomfortable feeling it brought, she unconsciously leaned closer to Jorion's strength and met it bravely.

A cold smile chilled Sir Thomas' ruddy visage when Taine met his stare. His nephew was watching, and he took pleasure in the discomfort thus given one so sure of himself, one who had shamed him by taking the only thing his greedy king had not—the allegiance of his followers.

"What plans have you for the morrow?" Sir Thomas questioned, his smile a sneer. "Do you travel to Burmley or do I go to stand in your stead as I have so oft in the past decade and more?"

Jorion's lips clamped into a straight line. This morn his uncle had first spoken of a promise made when he'd managed Radwyn, but only now remembered. To settle a dispute between two vassals, he'd arranged to meet them on the morrow in the small village of Burmley, a midway point.

"There was never any doubt, uncle," Jorion responded. "As Lord of Radwyn, I will sit in judgment on the matter." The judging of disputes among those residing on a fiefdom was a duty and right jealously guarded by all lords; but, often absent in support of his king, Jorion had chosen to delegate its exercise to his uncle. But with his recent experience of Thomas' unjust decisions it was a choice he deeply regretted. How many innocent children had he called to pay the price for another's misdeeds?

Sir Thomas nodded, contempt hiding his satisfaction in the decision. "If you can pull yourself from the clinging arms of your wife, I will be ready at dawn to lead the way."

Taine abruptly straightened away from Jorion, suddenly chilled flesh protesting the loss of his heat. Had she twined herself too closely about her husband, kept him from his duties? Basking in never-before-experienced contentment and welcome of another's company, had she asked too much? Her fingers tangled into the mulberry wool of her skirt as they'd found no reason to do in many days. It was true she had spent as much time as possible at his side, a deed he had seemed to gladly accept. That she had done, but she had not lingered near when he spoke on matters of management or defense with the men of his household and guard. Neither had she ridden out with him to oversee his demesne and talk with the serfs of his land. She grimaced with honesty, the last admittedly due more to lack of confidence in her horsemanship than lack of desire to be with him.

"Wait for me at the first portcullis and I will be there." Jorion's smile held all of the cold cynicism that had been absent the past week. He glanced toward the knights gathered at the top of a lower table, eyes settling on one who, aging and long ailing, he knew was feeling a lack of trust from his lord. To bolster his flagging spirits, Jorion chose him for this doubtless honorary task. "Sir James will accompany us." Though he would not travel abroad with so small an escort, here on his own lands there was surely no need for one larger. Looking back to his uncle, he deliberately wrapped his arm about the shoulders of the maid, self-consciously shrinking away, and pulled her near.

Reassured by his gesture, Taine willingly relaxed against his broad shoulder. With a look that pitied the overbearing spider, she let her soft form curve sweetly against the hard contour of Jorion's body from shoulder to hip.

Sir Thomas was irritated by the maid's pity but contained his ill humor and calmly told Jorion, "If we leave with the sun and follow the direct route I've found through the forest, we can be there, have done, and return by nightfall." Beneath his bland expression he comforted himself with a silent warning. Only wait, little queen, and see what such treatment earns you. He turned his attention to Jorion. And you, proud lord, see what folly there is in thinking you need only yourself and one other to travel in safety. He would feel neither remorse for the downfall of his mighty nephew nor sorrow for a widowed queen doomed to endure the monotony of life shut away from the world of light and happiness.

To break the strained silence that had settled on the high table, Taine leaned forward and spoke to Elspeth. "Did Richard take you to see the new foal I told you about?" Having found joy in her marriage, Taine had taken pains to thrust Richard and Elspeth together, hoping they would find the path to similar happiness.

Elspeth nodded, smiling warmly. "After the midday meal we had a lovely visit with the small animal." Her response was conventional, but the soft brown eyes spoke volumes for which there were no words. Richard's fury at his father's machinations to see them wed had seemed to Elspeth a clear statement of his lack of feeling for her. Her pride might have held her ever from him and left her to share cold nights with copious tears alone. But Taine had gently manipulated them into each other's company. A deed Elspeth appreciated and Richard seemed not loath to accept. They spent time together each day and Elspeth's only complaint was that

Richard again treated her as a child. Eager for his attention, she feared to jeopardize that joy by forcing him to treat her as a woman grown.

Today in the stable's dim reaches, she'd stared down at the newly arrived foal, all spindly legs and awkward grace. On turning suddenly she'd caught Richard looking at her, awareness in his vivid gaze. She'd unthinkingly leaned toward him, but he'd quickly turned away with some inane comment on the colt's coloring. Here at table Richard's blue eyes, serious for once, met hers unflinching. And why not, she inaudibly questioned with new-learned skepticism, he had the whole of a busy hall to protect him.

Richard felt himself nearly drowning in wells of brown velvet. After his own stupid error in approaching a bud so tender with a sweet embrace soured by foolish words and his father's unwelcome meddling, he'd nearly relinquished all hope of love shared. He'd sworn to praise the saints daily for Taine, who had restored what had surely been lost by providing a delicate bridge betwixt Elspeth and him. Though hesitant to risk their fragile bond by treating Elspeth as more than a well-loved child, once again hope had begun to grow in his heart. He was no prize for an heiress; but, with Jorion's recently acquired understanding of love's ways, he might agree to their union if he believed such feelings had grown between them.

Pleased with the clear emotion flowing between the other two, Taine looked up into surprised dark eyes. Golden brows rose in wordless query as Jorion tilted his head slightly toward first Elspeth and then Richard. Taine grinned and imperceptibly nodded. Jorion shook his head at these matters he'd plainly misunderstood.

The scarcely touched platter of fruit and deep yellow cheese that had been the meal's final course was removed from the table between Jorion and Taine. Small golden sparks began to flare in black eyes that turned to Taine. He would squander no more time on the problems of others, but lead his delicious bride to privacy above. The soft warmth of Taine's face proved her as anxious as he for time without the distractions of others. Jorion stood and formally offered his arm. It was yet the early hours of evening.

Others would linger long in gossip, games, and ale but he had no patience for such useless wastes of time and had grown impervious to the inevitable teasing looks and calls of others in the hall.

More than willing to accompany her husband, Taine laid her fingertips atop his forearm and rose. Once shy of the multitude in his home, she'd come to know most and had found no malice toward her in any—save the spider. Though she blushed at the ribald jests that followed their path, she did not resent their teasing. There was no harm in providing gossip to alleviate the boredom of people weather-bound in this castle with little else to occupy them.

After Jorion and Taine slipped away with, as Thomas felt, nearly indecent haste, he withdrew to his own chamber. There he waited with the patience born of years of practice. Some little time after the castle at last settled into the silence of night, at the darkest hour before dawn, he lifted both an unlit lantern and a small spark of light in one hand and eased his door open with the other. He peered cautiously up and down the hall. No one stirred. On bare feet he silently descended narrow, winding stairs. In the shadows beneath the arch opening into the great hall, he paused. Many slept on pallets randomly cast about the floor and benches. Even the serf detailed to stoke the great fireplace and keep it blazing through the night dozed.

Thomas reached around to stealthily unlock and open the massive, iron-bound door whose hinges he'd personally taken care to oil earlier. Leaving it slightly ajar, he stepped into the castle's lowest level and carefully moved into depths where no natural light would ever shine.

The dragon had erred. Sir Thomas' sinister smile could not be seen in the ominous dark. Assuming adequate restraint in locked cages and an escape route that meant a walk through his well-guarded hall, Jorion had posted no men in the damp, foul-smelling dungeon to watch his prisoners. He'd failed to consider the postern's well hidden escape route, meant as the family's last resort under siege, and a path whose secret Thomas shared. Cautiously feeling his way behind stacks of baskets filled with the apple harvest, Sir Thomas placed the metal lantern he carried on the packed dirt floor and felt blindly for its latch. Once opened, he lowered his small gleam, the smouldering end of a stick taken from his chamber's fire, into the oil reservoir. As it burst into light, Sir Thomas blinked against the sudden brightness. Squinting, he picked up the lantern and with firmer steps approached the corner cage where two men slept.

With the hard training of a warrior, McLewell immediately roused to the nearing glimmer. He stood to come forward and grip the bars.

Sir Thomas raised one finger of his free hand to his lips, cautioning silence, although it was unlikely any sound from these depths short of a scream could be heard above. He then motioned McLewell to wake Morton and bring him forward.

McLewell gave Sir Thomas a long, wary look but turned and moved to bend over Morton. Laying a hand across Morton's mouth, McLewell muffled the cry of one abruptly jerked awake.

When the two prisoners stood before Thomas, still locked bars between, Thomas whispered, "I have come to offer you escape."

Morton smiled his relief but McLewell's face was impassive. He knew this man well enough to believe him a wily creature unlikely to offer a thing without purpose.

"What must we do?" McLewell asked, restraining the smile that would be a sneer.

"No risk to you," Thomas hedged.

McLewell stood unmoving, eyes steady on the man he mistrusted.

Sir Thomas shifted uncomfortably. He and McLewell supported the Baliol cause but had little else in common. Moreover, he'd ever felt the other's dislike. "I will lead Jorion into the wood on the morrow. If a stray arrow pierces him, I can say poachers erred in their prey. Ever in his cursed black, he blends with forest shadows too well."

"And then we will be chased by the men of his guard and called to pay a higher price than imprisonment," argued Morton. His disgust with the bargain for freedom was so strong that his voice rose dangerously.

"Nay," Thomas responded immediately, frowning heavily at the other's lack of control. He had far rather have two less-seasoned men for this task, but he must use what providence provided. "By his own choice, Jorion will be accompanied by only one knight. A sign of his arrogance."

"In truth, then, we must kill two men," McLewell coldly restated the proposition. He was filled with disgust for the man who planned such treachery to one of his own blood. Since the early days of Jorion's arrival, McLewell, a boy himself, had known of Sir Thomas' disgust for his half-Saracen nephew. The mixed heritage had been enough to assure Thomas' dislike, but when the boy had turned into a fierce warrior and friend of the English king, even fighting beside him against the Scots, it blossomed into hate.

The other's clear disgust stiffened Thomas' back and he answered, "To earn your freedom—and a queen."

McLewell nodded once in silent acknowledgment. There were still dangers involved. When their escape was discovered, few would fail to believe they were the earl's murderers and they'd be left with only treacherous Sir Thomas to say the accusers nay.

Seeing the other hesitate in accepting his offer of freedom, Sir Thomas added an enticement. "To sweeten the pie, with her goes the one-half of Radwyn's wealth that Jorion swore to her, and such bounty will go far in furthering the battle for Baliol's throne."

"Open then the door," McLewell flatly said, "and lead us to the freedom you promise."

"In due time." McLewell's dislike of the plan was clear and Sir Thomas would not loose them so easily. He would demand assurances unbreakable. McLewell was a man of honor. One who would never break a solemn oath. "First, you must swear an oath on the Sacred Cross that you will do as I say."

"By the Sacred Cross," McLewell responded without pause, "I swear my oath to be waiting in the forest and fall upon your party, give aid to your mortal intent."

To be free of the close confines of darkness, Morton was willing to do near-anything that could be safely done and promptly swore a like oath.

Sir Thomas was surprised at McLewell's swift capitulation after his hesitation and distrust, but nonetheless congratulated himself on outwitting the prisoners and luring them with rich bribes. Still he did not open the door but laid out a devious plan, taking time to be certain the others understood each detail.

THE DRAGON'S FIRE

was arrayed at Malloesh's aunt Gruesome
after his beating and dashed out more choice thoughts
restrained himself by pretending the presence and looked
them with downcast. Still he dashed even the door but had
out a decisive plea, a last time to be outside the others
messaged each doubt.

❧ Chapter 21 ❧

A CREEPING CHILL PARTED the warm haze of Taine's dreams.
Lingering in a half-wakeful state and unwilling to rise
higher, she reached out one slender arm to seek the warmth
that would lull her back into happy dreams, but the hollow
where Jorion had lain, though still warm, was quickly losing
its heat. His absence provided the impetus to lift heavy
lashes. With his broad back to her, he stood, already dressed
in the rough homespun worn beneath mail.

Jorion sensed himself watched and turned to meet the
admiration in green eyes. A slow smile creased his face but
when she lifted inviting arms, he took a step back and firmly
shook his head, a motion that sent even weak predawn light
gleaming over golden hair.

"Jorion!" Taine called a clear invitation.

"Restrain your temptations, else all the cold water in our
precious well will not douse the dragon's fire."

"I pray not," Taine responded, sitting up and allowing the
bedcover to fall to her waist, no longer too inhibited with
him to reveal the rich bounty of her flesh.

"Heed your lord's command." Jorion laughed in mock
demand. Lifting the kirtle she'd hastily discarded the night

past, he tossed it about her enticing form. "I said at dawn I would meet my uncle and Sir James at the first portcullis and so I will—else I'll be damned as laggard of no will, completely beneath his wife's control."

As Jorion lifted his heavy, close-fitting mail shirt, Taine held the mulberry wool of her kirtle beneath her chin and lay down. Remembering the spider's comments of the night past, she nibbled at her lip in dismay.

Shining locks sliding through the close neck of the metal garment, Jorion saw her stricken look and cursed himself for assigning blame where there was none. She had never sought to force him to her will, not even for a crown that was hers, did she wish it. "Nay, sweetling," he reassured, coming down beside her on the bed. "That was not meant as you heard it. Merely did I tease for the fact that your presence and welcome of me entices me ever to tarry and turn from tasks that call, duties I must fulfill." Though placing his palms securely over the ends of the wool kirtle to hold it tight beneath her chin and shield him from temptation, he lightly kissed her cheek, brow, eyelids, and, at last, the soft petals of her mouth—a sweet communion of souls from which he rose again with deep regret.

Standing above her, he reached down to slowly pull the kirtle away and stare at the silken body that was such sweet torment and unknown satisfaction. "You are all and everything I dreamed of in a woman, a treasure more precious than life." Without another word he departed from the chamber, leaving Taine wondering what deed she had done to earn such rich reward.

Two men were mounted and waiting when Jorion arrived at the entrance to the drawbridge. Tugging on his gauntlets and clenching his hands a few times to loosen their stiff fit, he glanced at the flaming ball only half-revealed on the horizon and smiled. "Well, uncle, it's dawn and I'm here." Neither Uncle Thomas nor Sir James would ever know with what difficulty this fact had been achieved. A still drowsy Sander stepped forward and handed Apollo's reins to Jorion. He thanked that lad ever anxious to please, as he swung up onto the steed's wide back and motioned a start.

* * *

In the castle, Taine tarried only a little longer abed, for without Jorion's heat it was cold and unwelcoming. She rose and hastily donned the mulberry kirtle Jorion had playfully tossed to her from the chair where she'd left it the previous night. A rueful smile curled rose lips as she acknowledged their impatience had taught her to be careless of the fine new garments he'd provided. Nonetheless, she did not fool herself that matters were apt to improve, for she had no will to stall his ardor for such trivial tasks as neatly folding clothes.

Anxious for yet another glimpse before they were parted for one whole long day, on bare feet she dashed down the corridor to the tower. The chamber's glass windows looked down on the courtyard and meadows beyond the cliff's edge, but from an arrow-slit in the stairwell she would see the castle's approach and the forest beyond. Reaching her destination, she stood on tiptoe to peer out through the long narrow opening. She could see the three figures traveling away from the castle. The red hues of a nearly risen sun burned like flame over the embroidered dragon on Jorion's back. She smiled, so content it frightened her, for surely such happiness could not last. To shake away the disheartening thought, she tossed a glorious mane of auburn curls back to tumble past her waist in a cascade of dark fire.

It looked to be a fine day and welcome after the heavy clouds of days past. The old ones said snow would soon fall. A strong shiver shook her, and she wished she and Jorion could have just one more sunny day together. What strange imp had put such a gloomy notion into her head? Her silent query was more scold than question. They had all their lives and many happy days to share. She tried to shrug away the foreboding that had settled upon her as she watched Jorion riding toward the dark line of barren forest on the horizon. 'Twas simply that winter provided such bleak landscapes. That was all. Moreover, as spouse to a famous warrior, she must become accustomed to his absences, for he would oft be called to duty with his king and comfort herself with the knowledge that he was well able to defend himself. As she turned away from the window's bright light to the dim corridor where thick stone walls forbade the sun's rays to fall, she knew his vaunted martial skills were not solace enough, for even now her groundless fears grew stronger.

Chamber door closed behind her, she halted at the chest against the wall on one side. Her clothes had all been moved to this room. Wanting to look her best when Jorion returned, she rooted through its contents and settled on the special sea-foam green kirtle she'd last worn the morn following their wedding. She'd chosen it then for its unique loveliness and, quashing unwelcome memories of the chill that had followed, did so again. It was only cloth and thread, no more an omen portending evil than her small black cat who, though never venturing to the great hall where huge dogs resided, enjoyed free run of all upper rooms save the spider's.

Too impatient to wait for Mercia, she lifted the horsehair brush and swept it through softly tangled curls. She planned to visit Bertwald and Father Aleric. Preoccupied with shared happiness, she'd failed to earlier visit the two dear souls who had seen the facts far clearer than she, but today Taine meant to thank them for their attempted care. Much she owed Bertwald for his refusal to take her from this safe harbor despite her pleas.

By the time Mercia arrived, Taine was placing the last touches on hair once more plaited with silver-green ribbons and bound in coils at the base of her neck.

Standing in the door, eyes wide at finding her lady already prepared for the day, Mercia rushed to say, "Had I known you needed me earlier, milady, I'da come sooner." Since the earl and his lady had made peace, Mercia had become accustomed to their late rising.

"There was no need," Taine reassured her, amused at the younger girl's flustered reactions. "Lord Jorion was called to duties early this morn, and I chose not to linger in a cold bed alone." Mercia's cheeks went scarlet at the implied intimacy, and though Taine found herself surprised that she had said such a thing, she felt no shame, only regret for embarrassing the other.

Superstitious fancies aside, she was happy with her world and grinned, motioning the girl to join her in stepping out into the windowless corridor candlelit even in the hours of day. "Let us go and see what the morning meal offers."

As they walked down the winding steps, Mercia talked easily to the friendly lady she'd grown comfortable with. "They's two peddlers as came yestereve, and says they'll not show their wares to any here 'til the countess has seen them first."

Taine's brows rose at their audacity. Itinerant peddlers came and went constantly in any great lord's castle and Castle Dragonsward, known for its wealth, drew an overabundance. Well provided with more than she needed, Taine had found reason to view the goods of none.

"They must have rich items to offer for they've ever so many baskets and chests in their wagon and all in the castle are a-dyin' to see what they hold."

Clearly Mercia had been primed by other curious castle inhabitants to plead the cause. Taine glanced back at the plain girl's earnest face and smiled. "I will see them, but not until my other plans are complete."

Mercia's wide smile lent her unremarkable face a shining warmth finer than mere prettiness.

The waiting repast was strangely tasteless without Jorion to share it and Taine gave it little time. Once nourished, she set out for the small cottage beyond the inner bailey wall. Far from annoyed, as once she'd been, by the shadowy guard Jorion had commanded to follow her steps, she was warmed by Jorion's concern for her safety. She turned to the young knight surely no more than a year or two older than she.

"Come, walk with me rather than behind." The red tide that immediately glowed beneath his fair skin surprised her. She had not thought men could blush—save the spider, and his color was perpetual, deepening only with rage.

Sheepish at having been seen, still he came to her side.

"'Tis such a beautiful day, mayhap the last for some time, and I want to enjoy the sun while I can." The smile that had dazzled Sander had the same effect on the man at her side.

The guard was tongue-tied in the sweet beauty's presence, and for the rest of their walk the burden of conversation fell on Taine.

She spent but a short though happy time with Bertwald and Father Aleric, yet as she departed unexpected clouds were gathering ominously on the horizon. It seemed to her that the air itself had grown heavy with the same foreboding that had assailed her earlier when first she'd become uneasy for the dragon's safety. The one clear threat to their happiness was Sir Thomas, and he was with Jorion in the deep forest.

Her young guard saw the frown growing above deep-green eyes and was concerned. He was new to Radwyn and this his first task as one of the Golden Dragon's knights, a position he prized. "Have I done aught to displease you, milady?"

Taine looked at him in surprise but saw his clear anxiety and smiled reassuringly as she lightly shook her head. "Nay, only do I suffer a woman's fear for an absent husband."

The guard was relieved to learn her unhappiness sprang merely from a needless concern for the earl's journey. "What worry can there be when the dragon, known the length and breadth of this land as a valiant warrior, travels only through his own forest with his uncle and Sir James, a knight of great skill."

"Sir James?" Taine stopped mid-step. "Only Sir James goes with him?" She was dismayed and more to learn that Jorion had departed with only one aging knight as protection.

The guard stopped, too, and looked at her in surprise as he nodded his answer.

Taine smiled weakly and resumed her walk, talking again of unimportant matters that left her thoughts free to dwell on frightening possibilities. Her unease increased despite the rational denials she made, telling herself it was result only of the nebulous anxieties left from her superstitious fear of the lovely sea-foam gown and coming storm. After all, the spider's supporters had deserted him and his two friends were safely locked away. What could Sir Thomas do alone with two great knights. She had no fears of Jorion's ability to meet and defeat any fair-met foe, still—

Entering the castle's great hall, she found Halyse standing near the entrance, trying to contain her son's boisterous spirits. Halyse turned with a broad grin and invited, "Come, sit and talk with me awhile. You've been so busy with others of more import that I feel quite neglected."

Warmed by Halyse's never-failing friendship and merry

spirit, Taine's soft laugh bubbled out as she shook her head at the other's foolery.

Misunderstanding the action, Halyse reached out to take Taine's hand and tug her toward a bench near the fire's warmth. "Truly, I have missed our talks. Mayhap you've not noticed but no other of your knights has a wife, and I'm lonely for a woman to visit with."

Pleased by Halyse's desire for her company, Taine settled on the hard wood and turned to her friend. But, though ostensibly listening to Halyse chatter of mundane matters, which demanded no more than an occasional nod or smile, her eyes wandered again and again to the massive planks of the iron-bound and locked door to the dungeon. Her misgivings would not be denied by any but the proof of her own eyes. She stood abruptly, interrupting Halyse mid-sentence. Only by going into the dark caverns below and seeing the still-imprisoned men could she put ease to her tension.

"Where is Will?" she asked the woman staring up at her in surprise.

"He's in the metalsmith's shop, reviewing plans for the winter refurbishment of weapons and arms."

Taine turned immediately toward the door, but Halyse restrained her with a hand on her arm. "I'll fetch him, you stay here by the fire." Taine had been so distracted that Halyse could but think she was sickening and deemed it wiser to have her wait in the warmth.

Taine stood motionless, staring at the fearful door, until Halyse returned with Will at her side. Without turning, Taine asked, "As guard captain, have you the key to that door?" She nodded toward the subject of her long stare.

"Aye," Will nodded, "and to the larder, the metalsmith's shop, the—"

"'Tis the only one I need," Taine interrupted, walking toward the iron-bound door's forbidding strength.

Though his frown was heavy, Will followed her path, wondering what feminine foolishness had brought this demand. He fitted a key from the ring at his waist into the lock. The door swung noiselessly open, and Will froze, hands curling into fists. It had long ago developed a loud, scraping squeak, one deemed a wise defense against unwarranted use. Now he too dreaded what would or more properly would *not* be found below. He thrust out a restraining arm to hold Taine from the descent he would do alone, irrationally fearing desperate prisoners might yet wait below in ambush. Taine would not be denied, although she waited for him to lift the nearest firebrand from a wall-ring. By its light they traveled down the steep stairway and wound through stacks of produce to the cell in a far corner. It was empty, door still ajar.

Blood drained immediately from Taine's face. She felt dizzied by its quick leaving, but anger for this treachery and fear for her love gave strength to weak limbs. She turned to rush up the steps. Will was directly at her back. As she opened her lips to explain to the waiting Halyse, Will's loud battle cries urgently summoned all the men of the castle.

From the solar above, where he'd been talking with Elspeth, Richard flew down the steps two at a time. While fighting men gathered about Will to hear his commands, Richard moved to Taine's side. She looked like a ghost of herself, pale and lingering only by effort of will.

"What wickedness is here?" he quietly asked upon meeting pain-filled eyes nearly on a level with his. Green dropped from blue as he questioned again, "What purpose for this alarm?"

"The prisoners have escaped—" Taine answered, blindly watching fingers twisting into sea-foam green, "and Jorion rides into the forest nearly unguarded with one who, though kin, bears him no love." Trembling with fear for her dragon, she failed to consider Richard's relationship to the villain of her words until she looked up into anguish-darkened eyes.

Though leafless, the thick-grown oak, elm, and birch trees that towered overhead, branches intertwined, made the forest a dim and gloomy place. Following his uncle's lead over what seemed no path at all across the spongy ground, odorous with fallen leaves and dying undergrowth, Jorion shrugged his shoulders in effort to shake off the vague feeling of foreboding he began of a sudden to experience. If this was a more direct route, then they must be nearing their goal, for by the usual path they'd be fast approaching Burmley. Instead they seemed to be traveling ever deeper into the vast reaches of forest, farther and farther from human habitation. Riding single file behind Uncle Thomas, Jorion glanced over his shoulder and beyond Sir James to an oddly shaped birch trunk. He was nearly certain they'd passed this way more than once.

"Uncle," Jorion called to the man leading the way, "surely we are close to our destination?"

Looking straight ahead, Sir Thomas' irritation was hidden from his companions. "We've a bit farther to go, I fear. I took a wrong turn and we lost some time, but we're once again on the right track. Be patient." His own patience was growing thin. Where in sweet Mary's name were the cohorts freed to fulfill his plot?

The whistling zing of something speeding through the quiet came in answer to his silent question. With a stunned cry for the searing pain in his back, Sir James slumped forward and tumbled from his steed, unconscious before his body met the ground.

Reaching for the dual swords strapped to his back, Jorion whirled toward the sound. He had only long enough to take in the arrow protruding from his knight's back before a heavy weight dropped from above. Even on the downward fall, Jorion began struggling against his foe and when prone beneath the other's full weight he brought mighty arms up to hold him off, twisting to throw him to the side. Only when the sharp point of another's dagger appeared from behind and settled at the vulnerable base of his throat did he stop.

McLewell, breathing hard from the desperate struggle with the dragon, quickly passed a stout rope about Jorion's waist several times, tying it to bind strong arms powerless against his sides. He then scooted down to straddle the legs of the man with dagger point still at his throat and wound another length of rope there to hold them, too, in submission. The great warrior was now defenseless.

Coming from the shadows behind a massive oak, Sir Thomas snarled, "You failed to follow my plan. You did not kill him first," he waved in disgust at Jorion.

Still sitting astride Jorion's legs, McLewell wiped sweat from his brow with one sleeve and looked at the angry man coldly.

In full spate at the other's tampering with his careful plot, Sir Thomas let his wrath roll out in a tide of spite. "Why did you risk the possible miscarriage of an arrow loosed by a knight surely without training to archery?"

McLewell smiled derisively. "I choose my men for their particular talents, and a bow-propelled arrow is more certain to pierce chain mail from a distance than any thrown dagger."

"Then why did you not kill him?" Thomas demanded, waving at Jorion and fairly shaking with ire.

"'Tis your wish to see the dragon dead, not mine." Each word of McLewell's response was distinct and utterly emotionless.

"What?" Thomas' face was nearly purple with rage. "You made an oath, an oath on the Sacred Cross—and you will rot in hell for seeing it foresworn."

"I swore only to meet you here and give aid to your design, not to do the deed myself." McLewell smiled grimly at the man sputtering under the truth of his answer, then looked to the powerful man held immobile to their intent.

Jorion lay motionless but his black eyes glittered with gold malice. He was experienced enough in military strategies to know when he had lost and would boldly face death, even death at the hands of treachery rather than fair-fought battle, with eyes open and no whimper of fear.

In admiration McLewell watched the dragon face the inevitable with calm courage and prayed he would do as well when his moment came. He was sorry for such a foul end to so great a warrior. Yet had they met on the field of battle, he'd have done his all to strike him down—although against the dragon's skill it was more likely to end the other way about.

McLewell lifted his face again to Sir Thomas and said, "'Tis your wish and you must strike the blow." By forcing the motivator of the plot to carry it out, McLewell protected both himself and his knight. They two would be witnesses to the mortal action, and to assure their silence the doer would dare do naught else but support their defense.

Nearly overcome with fury, Sir Thomas' lips curled in a snarl as with both hands he lifted his fierce broadsword above the dragon's heart. A stray shaft of sunlight pierced the gloom to glitter on the sharp edge held threateningly above that goal, as he paused to speak with hate so thick his words were barely distinguishable. "I have planned this end to you since the first day you came to Castle Dragonsward. Without you it would have come to me, but your grandfather, addled by age, had rather see it pass to one who shared his name than one pure-blooded. Only my patience, my desire to see you wed to the heiress held me back. When that was lost, even then did I linger to see you wed her to my son. Her inheritance would have been another plum to add to the pudding I've simmered for long years. No matter now, you've obtained a richer prize, an escaped queen who foolishly trusts you to protect her."

For himself Jorion could face death without fear, but this reminder of the price his failure to protect the one he loved would force her to pay summoned from his depths a low growl of pain.

Thomas smiled evilly, pleased with the sign of agony he'd won. "Now, my patience is at an end." He flexed his muscles for a mighty downward stroke, but an unexpected action put end to his intent. He fell back beneath the force of a crossbow-shot arrow that found home deep within his chest.

Startled, McLewell's gaze lifted to the forest wall suddenly alive with the dragon's men. While Morton hesitated, fear-frozen, McLewell jumped to his feet and ran in the opposite direction. There more armed men stepped from the shadows to face him. Raising his sword to the ready, he glanced wildly about only to find himself surrounded. Once again he dropped his sword point in surrender to a superior foe.

"Praise the Saints we arrived in time," Will muttered as he bent to loose Jorion from his bonds. "And thank them, too, for the clear path left by three horses breaking through untouched forest ground."

"Aye, my uncle's more direct route was a fool's path laid down as we rode. But are you sure you did not linger for the moment of greatest effect?" Jorion asked wryly, sitting up to rub the flow of blood back into tightly bound arms. "One breath longer and you'd have had another body to carry to the castle."

"To forestall that heinous possibility, I've prayerfully beseeched every saint whose name I knew." Will ruefully spread his hands palm up. "In truth, I fear I created a few." His grin of relief slid away as he added, "I could not bear to watch your lady's fierce anguish—and blame—at a failure so great."

At mention of Taine, Jorion stilled. The thought of her in anguish sent a wave of renewed anger over him for the men who would have wreaked it upon her. Nonetheless, he defended her to his knight. "My lady would not blame you, Will, for the treachery of others."

"'Struth, she'd not blame me, but I fear she would never forgive herself."

Jorion looked sharply at Will, question for his meaning clear in black eyes.

"It was she who, without solid reason, insisted I unlock the door and allow her to descend into the dark below ground. I assumed her intent was to be reassured of our prisoners' secure holding," Will explained, shaking his head. "And I thought her a foolish woman of unreasonable fears, until the door opened soundlessly." He steadily met his lord's gaze and added, "You owe your life to her for, without her insistence, we'd not have known them gone until their meal was delivered in the evening hours—far too late for you."

Jorion slowly nodded. His life he owed to her—both its health and happiness. He quickly rose to his feet, anxious to return to the castle and relieve her obvious fears for his safety. Brushing away the pieces of crushed leaves and dead undergrowth that clung tenaciously, he glanced about the dim grove. Several of his guardsmen had taken the lengths of rope once restraining him and were trussing the two escaped men. Others knelt in the deep shadows beneath a massive oak where lay the badly wounded but yet living Sir James. Still others had spread his uncle's cloak atop the heavy brown vegetation in the space between two towering trees and were efficiently rolling his lifeless body in its folds.

After supervising the hoisting of his uncle's body across his steed's back, Jorion detailed several men to construct a litter to safely carry the wounded knight home. He then mounted his golden stallion and, with the majority of his guard, set out to escort the prisoners and what remained of his uncle back to the Castle Dragonsward.

In the privacy of the family solar, Taine paced impatiently from hearth to window. Leaning her head against its cool stone edge, for a long moment she stared out at winter-brown fields stretching toward the line of forest on the horizon. The storm that had earlier threatened now rolled overhead, while an eerie stillness reigned below. The clouds were so heavy it seemed twilight had come early and hung low, as if intent on smothering all light and joy from the earth beneath. Moving back to the hearth once more, she gazed blindly into the blaze. It was a pattern she'd repeated over and over again, but neither the fire's ever-changing flames nor the motionless scenery without could eradicate the mental image of a fat black spider mercilessly advancing on his trapped prey.

Halyse watched her lady in sympathy. Having been left behind many a time while Will rode to battle with the dragon, she knew the gnawing terror Taine suffered.

Starting the path back to the window, Taine wished for the hundredth time she'd not submitted to the arguments which had held her from accompanying Jorion's garrison as she'd first insisted. It was true that to the Baliols a widowed queen was a much greater danger than one married to a half-infidel. Richard's logic was sound in claiming that there was less danger to Jorion so long as she was free; but surely in the company of all Jorion's mighty army, there was little danger of her falling into hostile hands. Tightly gripping the edge of open shutters until their form was imprinted on her palms, she berated herself for allowing her strong will to be bent by fear—not for herself but for Jorion. Aye, she should have demanded the right to know what awaited rather than lingering behind, drowning in deep foreboding.

As Taine turned again from her useless glare across the unmoving countryside, Richard exchanged a worried glance with Elspeth. Taine's tension had grown so strong he feared she would snap like a longbow too tightly drawn. Determined to do something to break the vicious cycle, he stood and stepped into Taine's path, catching the distressed woman's slender shoulders in his hands and halting her. Knowing his unskilled military aid was little needed in a vast group of highly trained warriors, indeed would likely be more hindrance than help, he had stayed behind. He'd hoped to do more good by distracting the anxious bride, but thus far he'd had no success at that either. Desperate, he tried a new strategy.

"We will dance," he announced. The three women looked at him as if he'd gone truly witless, and he felt incredibly foolish himself. Yet it was the only thing further he could think of to lessen apprehensions. "Physical exertion is a great release," he explained with more conviction than he felt. Elspeth smiled and he grew more confident as he turned to Taine and added, "Your body knows that. 'Tis why you've nearly worn a trench between hearth and window."

Elspeth, ready to do whatever Richard asked, jumped to her feet as he moved to fetch his lute from the peg beside the hearth where it hung by the gay ribbons attached to its neck.

"Halyse," Richard called, motioning the orange-haired woman forward, "you and Elspeth demonstrate the steps. Then Taine can strive to duplicate them." Richard strummed a few chords of a tune whose rhythm demanded a most complicated dance. Turning to his cousin's nervous bride, he directed, "Taine, watch closely. The steps are intricate and will demand concentration until you're very familiar with them." He'd chosen this dance for that very reason and prayed it would take Taine's mind from her dread.

He set to playing the merry tune in earnest and his accomplices in distraction moved rapidly through the brisk, graceful steps, lifting their skirts high enough for Taine to see the movement of their feet. After they ended with an elegant curtsy, each to the other, Taine moved into place and with Elspeth attempted to repeat their steps.

Richard's ploy at distraction was so successful that the thin blade sliding through the crack between door and frame to slowly lift the bar from its mooring went unnoticed. Halyse stood several paces behind Richard, both with backs to the opened door through which two dark shapes appeared. Lips parting to laugh as the two female dancers nearly bumped heads, her merriment was cut short by the gag quickly wrapped about her mouth. Her struggle was silent and quickly restrained.

The hastily departing guard, Will in their lead, had not paused to order the bailey gates shut nor drawbridge raised. As their threat arose from a small group already in the forest, Richard had seen no harm in that. Yet, although he'd not demanded their closure, he'd herded the three wellborn women into the solar. Having personally barred the door in protection until the guard returned, Richard little expected the blow from behind that dropped him into dreamless sleep.

At the sudden cessation of music, the two dancers turned in puzzlement. Widened eyes traveled from fallen friends to two unfamiliar men approaching with unpleasant intent on their cold faces. Elspeth sank into a graceless heap at Taine's side.

❦ Chapter 22 ❦

JORION WAS WEARIED BY the day of treachery and death. But his spirit revived when he cleared the forest's edge and saw the massive fortress of Castle Dragonsward atop its steep crag, lifting fearless walls against a sky heavy with quickly gathering storm clouds. He spurred Apollo to increased speed, wanting both to end Taine's fears for his safety and seek solace in her arms. The sun still hovered above the horizon and both portcullises were yet opened to the day's traffic between outlying farms and villages and the castle's hub of commerce. Plainly, his hastily departing men had not paused to order them closed earlier than was their wont. Will knew the possible dangers in leaving a castle unguarded and open to attack, thus Jorion saw the depth of his guard captain's anxiety for him. Only great concern would drive such basic defense principles from the conscientious man, and Jorion had not the heart to reprimand him for it.

Once inside the courtyard, still humming with the daily activities of tradesmen, metalsmith, and castle-serfs, Jorion dismounted and threw Apollo's reins to Sander. By called greetings no more fervent than usual, Jorion realized the reason behind the garrison's sudden departure had not become commonly known and was relieved. It would be no good thing for his people to believe their lord and thus themselves in danger.

Quickly entering the great hall, he turned to the young boy stoking flames in the huge soot-darkened fireplace.

"Where is your lady?"

"I dunno for certain sure, milord," the boy stammered, nervously pushing lank brown hair aside with the swipe of a hand that left a streak of grey ash behind. He'd never before been addressed by the dragon, but under his slight frown rushed to add, "I heard as others say all the ladies be in the solar with Sir Richard."

Jorion had not meant to frighten the boy and gave him a reassuring smile, as well as his thanks, before looking over his shoulder to find Will behind him. He motioned the other man to join him in seeking their wives.

Neither Will nor the other knights commonly went to the family rooms above. Pleased by this demonstration of his lord's regard, he followed the earl up narrow, winding stairs.

Upon reaching the solar, Jorion threw the door open, but his smile of warm anticipation crashed into a dark scowl as heavy as the threatening storm clouds gathering in the skies above. Black eyes had quickly taken in the sorry scene: an unconscious Richard lying on the floor in an awkward heap, and a bound-and-gagged Halyse, whose eyes streamed with tears of frustration. Filled with a wrath that silently screamed an accusation of McLewell and Morton's hand in this vile deed, he spun and raced back to the stairs. He jumped down several steps with each leap and in moments had reached the dungeon doorway left open by guardsmen leading the prisoners back to their cell. With no thought to caution for safe footholds while descending unlit stairs, he reached the bottom and ran to the cell where the two he sought were again confined. The door had just been locked and a fine thing that was, or in his fury he might have strangled them before his questions had answers.

"What have you done with my wife?" he demanded, fingers gripping the bars so tightly his startled guardsmen thought it a wonder the iron rods did not bend.

McLewell's brows shot up at the words, but he almost immediately understood the deed behind them and jumped forward to grip the bars almost as strongly as Jorion. "She is gone?" he demanded.

"Aye, and I'll employ every agony known to Christian and Saracen upon you until you tell me where she's been taken." Jorion's words were as fierce as dragon flames.

McLewell was near as devastated as Jorion by the abduction, yet was quick to deny any involvement. "If I'd had supporters about, they'd have aided me in my distress."

"Not if you badly wanted my queen," Jorion instantly responded, "and there's no doubt that you do. Could be her imprisonment is more important than your freedom—or your life, which I surely will end for this handiwork." His intent was unmistakable in eyes where gold fires burned.

"Rethink your charge," McLewell quietly argued. "If your uncle had other cohorts about, why would he take the risk of setting us free before they had seen you dead?"

Knowing the absolute necessity for clear thinking in this matter above all others, Jorion struggled to contain the anger that fogged his reasoning.

To further his rebuttal, McLewell added, "There are others who would seek her as desperately as we." He bit out the words, as if he hated their meaning as badly as ever the dragon would.

It was McLewell's obvious fear of another gaining control of the queen that convinced Jorion of his innocence. Another, aye, but who? As he turned to climb the stairs again, Jorion methodically reviewed the options. Clearly there were others who would profit by taking Taine, others who coveted the crown. The most obvious was Edward, who had fought long, costly battles to bring it under his gauntleted fist. Jorion found that choice unbelievable, unacceptable. Had it not been Edward himself who told him that by marrying Taine he would keep her safe? So, if not Edward nor the Baliol faction, then who?

Jorion ran a distracted hand over his head, bringing disorder to golden hair. Could only be the Bruces. All other claims were paltry in comparison—except that any wellborn man wed to Taine could claim the throne in her name. But *only* after he was dead, and Jorion was still healthy and not an easy man to kill.

As he ascended the winding steps to the solar, he ran his

fingers through his hair again, more agitated than he'd ever been before. What use then could the Bruces have for Taine? The man who had met her in Edward's court had recently ceded the lairdship to his son, a man of nearly Jorion's age. Jorion paused mid-stride. A suddenly remembered fact, uninteresting at the time, was now of possible import. That man, the youngest Robert Bruce and grandson of the Competitor to the Scottish throne, had recently been widowed. Were he to wed Taine, he would have an unequaled claim to the crown—surely the goal of all Bruces. Doubtless once they had secured Taine, they'd have no difficulty or hesitation in bringing their vast resources to bear in seeing him the victim of some convenient accident. Oh, aye, when they stepped forward with his very useful widow the accident would be suspect, but it was unlikely any proof of mortal intent would ever be found.

When Jorion again entered the solar, Richard was sitting up, rubbing his palm over a sizable lump on the back of his head, and Will was holding Halyse close, whispering comfort in her ear as she sobbed. Although Jorion did not like to interrupt the couple, speed must be of highest import. "Will, call the men to prepare for a journey of a fortnight and longer, while these two tell me what they can of the attack and its doers."

Will gently put Halyse aside and stood to do his lord's bidding, but Richard demanded explanation. "Do you go to follow the path of those blackhearted toads?"

Jorion shook his head, motioning toward the long arrow-slit. Thick flakes were descending so fast the view was nearly a wall of white. "The falling snow has already obscured their path and will grow worse before we can set forth. I go to Edward in Dunfermline, for he is my only hope of finding the treasure stolen from me."

Richard looked clearly unconvinced, but Jorion was far better acquainted than he with Edward's extensive network of informants. They were the method by which the king seemed always to know firstly whatever mischief was afoot, one of the talents which made him such a powerful sovereign.

Seeing Jorion's determination, Richard jumped to his

feet, grimacing at the renewed pounding it brought to his head. "Aye, well, then I go too."

"You don't look to be in any condition to set out on a lengthy journey through foul weather," Jorion responded, well aware of Richard's distaste for any uncomfortable undertaking. He'd demonstrated oft enough his preference for lingering near fires to entertain the ladies, while other men rode into the cold to hunt or play mock games of war.

"'Twas by my lack of military prowess that this abduction succeeded, and I will be party to its foiling." Richard proudly claimed the right.

Wishing to spare his cousin needless blame, Jorion answered, "What good is military prowess when struck from behind? Sir James fell to sudden attack this morn, and I was subdued by one dropping from above." Of a sudden Jorion realized that in the midst of his own concerns he'd failed to tell Richard of his father's fate. Holding bitter disgust from his voice with difficulty, Jorion flatly added, "Nearly slain by your sire, I was saved only by the arrow that struck him down, doing to him what he'd intended for me."

Richard's eyes widened at the news, but it brought no sorrow, only sadness that the other's character had made it impossible for him to love the man who should have been the most important in his life. "He earned an unmourned grave, for he did no more to endear himself to me than to you." Others might expect him to stay behind and make a show of mourning his father, but Richard quickly put an end to that block in the path of his determined goal: "I suggest Father Aleric be requested to see his body committed to the earth; I'm certain his soul has already gone to the fiery reward he earned."

Jorion, not truly surprised by Richard's acceptance of his father's end, nodded agreement with the son's wishes for his father's burial. Turning his mind from the distasteful matter to preparations for the journey of overriding import, Jorion continued his arguments. He diligently strove to convince the cousin made vulnerable by lack of battle skills to remain safely in Castle Dragonsward.

Richard held firm until at last, because it was so seldom done, he shocked Jorion by losing his temper and yelling,

"Think you I have less right to risk my life in attempt to reclaim my love than have you?"

Caught off guard, for a moment Jorion misunderstood and his eyes flashed fierce gold at the incredible idea of Richard challenging him for Taine.

Richard read Jorion's expression as a denial of a philandering man's ability to care so deeply. Lifting his chin so high its pointed beard seemed to stab the opponent he squarely faced, he snapped, "I am as capable as you of loving a woman, of being as worried for Elspeth's safety as you are for Taine's."

Like a bolt of lightning from the day's already stormy sky, a flash of shame struck him. He'd long feared further attempts to abduct Taine, but never had he considered such actions against Elspeth. 'Twas reason but not excuse for his failure to earlier realize his ward as well as his wife was missing. Ashamed of both that lack and his earlier foolish interpretation of Richard's motives, he put his hand on the smaller man's shoulder and assured him, "I never questioned the depth of your heart and will not hold you from the quest it demands."

Relieved by Jorion's acceptance of his need, Richard smiled with warm affection for his cousin, although self-mockery tinged its curves as he scoffed, "You never know when a song might win a battle."

Jorion's amused smile faded into a curious frown. Tilting his head consideringly, he answered, "'Struth, Richard, and a finer tactician you are than ever you knew."

Richard looked at Jorion as if he suspected the day's pressures and treacheries had snarled normally sharp logic. Jorion grinned with returning hope. "Fetch your lute and pretty dagger," he directed, "then don your armor and be ready to ride."

While Richard rushed away to prepare for the journey, Jorion turned to Halyse, whose red eyes and flushed cheeks made her freckles even brighter. "Did you see the men who attacked you?"

"Oh, aye." Halyse nodded vigorously and her wiry orange hair, apparently loosened in her struggles with those she spoke of, shook as wildly as a tree's autumn-hued leaves in a strong wind. "And had seen them before."

Jorion frowned. "Before?" Did this mean the attack had been aided, even carried out, by one of Radwyn's own?

Holding her composure with great effort and despite a voice ragged and low, Halyse answered as coherently as she could, "They came as peddlers but a day past. I was in the courtyard looking for Bryce when they arrived. One short as Richard, but stocky, and one as tall as Will."

Jorion's first thought was of the bumbling men who had pursued Taine at the fair. Yet he couldn't believe those two capable of carrying off a scheme so smooth.

Halyse had paused to convulsively swallow back still-threatening tears, but with her next words she proved Jorion's disbelief justified.

"The tall one had a beard, dark brown but for a streak of white." She lifted a finger to indicate the position. Then, having imparted what little she could, she buried her face in her hands as deep sobs of frustration, anger, and fear began anew. "I failed to see them caught, but I tried!"

Jorion knelt beside her stool and drew her face against his shoulder as she let her burning and nearly unintelligible self-condemnation boil out.

"I tried to rouse the castle, yelled into the folds until my throat's raw, and thumped my feet till I thought there'd be naught left but battered stumps. But no one heard, no one came."

"You bear no more blame, indeed, far less than others of us," Jorion reassured, patting her back as he continued with irrefutable logic. "I should not have left the door to our prisoner's cell unguarded and should never have trusted my uncle, or followed where he led. Though forgotten in their fear for me, my departing garrison should not have left the gates open to easy traffic while mischief was afoot." Pulling a small distance away, Jorion smiled ruefully into a tear-soaked face near as bright as the hair that surrounded it. "Aye, there are so many things we should not have done, while you did everything you could."

Sniffing, Halyse looked into gentle black eyes, and forgave herself for a deed she'd had no part in, while her anger for the abduction and those behind it grew apace.

"Waste no time in wondering what you might have

done," Jorion added. "Simply pray that our attempt to bring them home will be successful."

"Our attempt?" Halyse asked, a smile trembling at the edge of her wide mouth. Perhaps this time they might not leave her behind to uselessly wait and worry.

Jorion nodded. "I ask but will not demand your aid in my plan. 'Tis only that women and children will lessen suspicion."

Women—and children? Halyse immediately answered: "For myself, I will gladly join you, but Bryce I cannot risk."

"Bryce?" Jorion was horrified that he'd worded his proposal so poorly it had been easily misunderstood. "I would never take a child so young into even the limited danger you will see, and Bryce least of all. Only will we take Sander— and, mayhap, one other as we pass by his home on our journey."

The trip to Dunfermline, long in the best of weather, was lengthened by continually falling snow. By the time they arrived at the white-mantled meadow of the fair where Jorion had met Taine, his famous iron nerve was worn nearly clean through. On this last day of their journey, the sun had reappeared, although it was now slipping over the steep hills behind the town, giving them golden outlines against the cloth of a deep-rose sky.

Jorion ordered his company to make camp among the sparse trees through which he and Taine had first ridden. As Will assigned men to various tasks and fires were built, Jorion leaned against the trunk of a towering elm on the wood's edge. Staring at the glittering lights of city fires, he pondered his best course of action. Recognizing subtlety as his best weapon, in the fast-deepening gloom he remounted his steed and set out alone.

Circling the base of the steep hill crowned by the old wooden fortress that was his king's winter court, Jorion moved unseen through moonless night. Eyes accustomed to the dark, in the back he picked out the small garden where once he had walked with Edward. He left Apollo in the dim reaches beneath a stand of trees, where no light would penetrate to reveal golden hide. Black cloak rendering him nearly invisible, Jorion climbed the nearly barren incline.

An outmoded wall surrounded the fortress. Far, far shorter than a castle palisade, indeed no more than one level high, it was still obstruction to his goal. Yet, with the aid of ivy vines thick-grown and sturdy, he agilely scaled its height.

Dropping lightly over the top, he paused to study the structure's dark silhouette, only blade-thin strips of light proving it occupied, and wondered what step to take next. Risk entering the king's private chamber uninvited? Sneak into the antechamber and bribe a servant to summon him? The opening door rendered such actions unneedful. Edward stepped out, yawning and stretching wide as Jorion moved into the light spilling out through the open door.

Edward's face revealed no surprise as his gaze drifted over the travel-weary Jorion. He turned to quietly shut the door before descending shallow wooden stairs.

Jorion met him at their bottom and without preliminary said, "My *wife* and ward have been taken from me by vile trickery."

Thick white hair fell across Edward's forehead when he nodded an acknowledgment of Jorion's stress of the maid's new status. "Do you know who is responsible?"

"I know who is not," Jorion answered. "The Baliol faction, led by my uncle and aided by McLewell, made an attempt on my life, doubtless intended to end in claiming my bride—at nearly the same moment others stole her away."

"What befell your Baliol opponents?" Edward immediately asked.

Irritated by this useless talk of a matter already resolved while greater dangers threatened, Jorion answered briefly, "My uncle is dead, and McLewell and his man are secure in my dungeon."

Again Edward nodded, before leading the way deeper into the garden's shadows. "Castle Cregel is held by the Bruces, vassals of mine just as are you."

Although to any listening ears it might have seemed the king had exercised his right to speak never of matters he would rather avoid, Jorion took his meaning immediately. Those he sought were held in Castle Cregel, but Edward could not openly support a fight between two of his vassals. Indeed, as Jorion had expected, the king was telling him there must be no certain fight between them. What had been taken quickly, anonymously, must be reclaimed by like means.

Edward looked hard at Jorion, plainly waiting to see if his message had been understood. A stray gleam of light had escaped the chamber's shutters and pierced the gloom to glow on golden hair, as Jorion slowly nodded.

"No doubt," Jorion spoke at last, "with Christmastide fast approaching, Castle Cregel will appreciate a band of mummers and minstrels to entertain the revelers."

Edward smiled broadly and agreed. He bore a strong affection for this intelligent man and, happy with his own young wife, was glad to see Jorion anxious to reclaim an obviously precious bride.

Jorion had taken the few steps needed to reach the wall and grasped the mass of vines to aid his ascent when Edward softly called to him once more. Motion stilled, Jorion looked over his shoulder toward his sovereign's shadowy form.

"When next your wife is with you, I would deem it a favor if you would bring her again to me. This season of peace I have a gift for her, one she will appreciate."

Now knowing where Taine was held, Jorion felt a welcome confidence in his ability to recover his priceless treasure. He smiled at his sovereign's generosity and quickly nodded his agreement. From Castle Cregel he would bring Taine to the small house still awaiting him in Dunfermline and from thence to Edward's court.

Still steadily looking at Jorion, the king added, "Safety is a gift more precious than any other." With those final words, he turned his back and reentered the bright-lit chamber.

❦ Chapter 23 ❧

"AND SO YOU SEE, ladies," Sir Godwin Hurlwitt said, clasping his pudgy, ring-laden fingers together, "your abductors merely took advantage of the foolish arrogance of Radwyn defenders." A small hiss of contempt prefaced his next words: "Who but overconfident swaggerts would leave gates open to common traffic and manned only by gate guards who fail to question the coming or going of peddlers."

Who, Taine rephrased his rhetorical query, but men fearful for their lord's well-being would make such unfortunate errors? She forced her lips into the stiff shape of the smile she'd learned to adopt when their gaoler made his daily visit. Painting himself as merely their temporary host, the short and slightly overweight Sir Godwin was talkative in the extreme and babbled on again and again about the ease of their taking and the fine opportunity it had afforded the Bruce's men. He made no secret that this remote place of confinement, Castle Cregel, was one of the Bruce's minor holdings and he its trusted castellan.

"Pray tell me if there is aught I can do to make your days more pleasant," he said in his most solicitous tone. "Any pastimes for which I can provide?" Taine shook her head, and he turned his brightest smile on Elspeth. "Cloth, needles, and thread for embroidery?" he enticed, leaning closer to the plump maid. "Have you made use of the chess board and pieces I brought?"

Already he had made sure to inform them of his unwed state, and it had become ever more plain that he found the pretty heiress of great interest. Taine's worth to their captors was clear, yet their abduction of Elspeth had surprised her. It seemed greedy men could not let pass any opportunity to claim the profits of a woman's inheritance. Although Sir Godwin was not one of the original abductors, Taine found it increasingly difficult to bear his smooth company, slick like a wet flagstone floor which, when moved across too quickly, nearly always resulted in a painful fall. Her fingers twisted into the skirt of the brown kirtle he'd borrowed from the wife of one of the castle's knights. He'd brought several for the use of his two forced visitors, so they need not dress always in the same gowns they'd worn when abducted.

Sir Godwin looked back to Taine, letting his eyes run over her before his smile turned coy. Copying Jorion's talent at holding expression devoid of emotion, Taine carefully blanked her face. The arch look and leer were the same as those he'd given her when letting fall the gossipy tidbit that she, though already wed, was destined to another. She wanted to attack him and demand he speak, for she feared he had news of Jorion that he did not share. Bound, gagged, and confined in large baskets, she and Elspeth had been hustled from Radwyn lands without word of what end had come to the forest conflict. The tension of not knowing whether her beloved husband had lived or died was a terror that burned in her heart, destroying her from the inside out.

When their "host" returned his fulsome attentions to Elspeth, Taine sought to block near-overpowering apprehension, as she had a hundred times before, by taking note of each luxury afforded them here in this comfortable prison. Although there were no deep carpets, the floor rushes were fresh and sprinkled with sweet-scented herbs. Their fire ever blazed to drive cold before it, and the furnishings were of delicately carved wood and luxurious cloth. The bed's mattress and pillows were of goose-down and blankets of soft, thick wool. Aye, 'twas a soft prison, but for all the joy it brought Taine, it might as well have been the cold and dour fortress on a rocky shore where she had lived so long. How could she appreciate physical comforts or even her own safety when she did not know if her love lived?

She had once thought warm memories of joy in Jorion's arms and happiness in his company would be more comfort than minstrel's songs or Bertwald's tales, were she again to fall to captivity. Instead, they were a source of bittersweet pain, nearly unbearable. A sudden shiver shook her, and she wrapped her arms tightly about herself.

Having caught her action, Sir Godwin jumped to his feet. "Ah, sweet lady, come, sit here closer to the fire. You must not catch a chill."

Green eyes narrowed on the man who sounded like a mother hen clucking over one of her chicks. Was his concern for her health or his own? Surely he would be blamed if any harm befell the "guests" under his care. Nonetheless, she left her perch on the side of the bed to take his vacated chair beside the fire, hoping its loss would speed his leavetaking.

Elspeth smiled reassuringly as the delicate beauty moved nearer. All color had drained from Taine's silky cheeks. Living on nerves alone, she seldom took more than a bite or two of the rich delicacies served them and was so slender she looked as if even a gentle spring breeze would snap her in two.

Finding neither of the ladies listening, Sir Godwin paused in his effusive descriptions of one of the Bruce's great castles. Standing before the fire with hands clasped behind his back, he rocked on his toes for a moment until Elspeth's gentle brown eyes returned to him, polite interest and no more in their depths. Slightly annoyed, he curtly made his excuses and departed.

Once the door had snapped shut, Elspeth leaned earnestly toward the other woman. "Jorion *will* come, Taine." She restated a reassurance repeated time and time before, but earned no greater belief.

Taine smiled her appreciation for the other's attempted

encouragement but lowered her eyes to hide the increased pain it brought. How could a man injured—or killed—come to rescue them? Nonetheless, Taine was thankful for Elspeth's surprisingly positive reaction to their plight. Beyond her swoon at the first threatening danger, Elspeth had seemed to find in her soul an unexpected fiber of quiet courage. She had borne the rigors of their journey without visible fear and nary a tear, her own peril overshadowed by concern over Richard's injury, Jorion's danger, and Taine's sorrows.

"I can see you don't believe me," Elspeth continued, a touch of exasperation creeping into her voice, "but he will. The Golden Dragon has withstood far greater dangers than any offered by two escaped prisoners and a treacherous old man. Why, it's said he can defeat a whole company with his two foreign blades alone."

Taine's eyes lifted, and her smile deepened at the maid's simple faith in the tales of traveling minstrels and mummers. The sort of tales that had brightened the bleak days of her confinement, a confinement culminating in the accursed deceits that had cost her easy trust. She believed her dragon well able to face and defeat any honestly met foe, but treachery and deceit could lay low even the bravest and most skilled warrior.

In addition to her fears for Jorion, Taine carried a deep guilt for the fall of so innocent a maid into the snares of the intrigues ever swirling about herself. Once delivered to this small castle nearly surrounded by thick forests, feeling Elspeth deserved some explanation of their abduction, Taine had revealed her identity and her secret past. Elspeth's eyes had widened with the knowledge that her companion was a queen, but her sweet temperament had not changed nor had her simple faith in the dragon been shaken. From the first she had comforted Taine with the certainty that he would come and see them freed. Having experienced far more of the unkindness of fate that Jorion talked of, Taine was unable to attain Elspeth's quiet trust. The good things of life had been snatched from her hands before, and she found no easy faith in a different ending to this accursed plot.

* * *

Sir Godwin was irked by the limited appreciation his "lady-guests" offered for the care he'd given them, treatment far exceeding the honorable supervision commanded. The one was intended for his liege lord, but the younger lady, well-rounded and sweet, he hoped to claim for himself. The abduction and stealthy wedding of heiresses was not uncommon, and she'd been taken with the queen on assumption that the claim of another woman of wealth would not go amiss in the Bruce's plans. Surely so long as the Bruce had use of the greater share of the maid's wealth, her husband would retain use of a generous part—far more than Sir Godwin would elsewhere see. Yet there would be many anxious for the same easy riches, and he had counted on building with the maid an emotional attachment that might swing the decision in his favor.

Fairly stewing at her limited response to his overtures, but ever one to appreciate comfort, he relaxed in the padded ease of the large chair holding preeminent position on the dais. He peevishly watched the approach of a group of traveling players. From the cluster of less than clean people, all garbed in bright though tattered clothes, a small, slender man stepped forward. Doffing his bright red cap, he swept a low bow. Beneath such toadying, Sir Godwin's sour expression eased to a condescending smile. It soothed his ruffled pride.

"I am Richard the Minstrel," the new arrival said, clasping the ragged cap tightly to his chest with both hands. "We pray your lordship will allow us to offer yuletide entertainment in this great and fine fortress."

Sir Godwin's smile deepened to thinly disguised contempt for the flowery overstatement, a trait ever exhibited by those of lesser intellect. Nonetheless, the prospect of new entertainments for the merry season pleased him. Though he indulged himself by paying the too-high expense for keeping resident entertainers, he was bored by the minstrel whose songs were as tired and oft-repeated as the jester's jokes. Still, he hesitated. Entrusted with such valuable charges, dare he allow strangers access to his domain? Had he not just reminded the women again of the dangers in welcoming strangers?

The growing scowl on the castellan's face boded ill for the

waiting group. Rubbing the tender flesh of a recently shaven chin, Richard mentally cast about for some argument and found one that would also ease their plot. "Gentle lord, lest you fear harm of even so harmless a group as we"—he waved the limp cap toward his companions—"we will happily camp on the far edge of the village outside your mighty fortress walls."

Through narrowed eyes, Sir Godwin studied the group that contained at least one woman, a young boy, and a child. What harm could such a sorry group offer him, his two knights, and a garrison that, though small, outnumbered the band? Willing to be convinced of the rightness in a choice he'd already made, he commanded, "Prove your talents fine enough to warrant my hospitality."

Richard pulled the thick cloth cover from the lute slung by a hide strap across his shoulder and in his unusually sweet, clear voice began to sing an old song of love lost and found.

The two women in the chamber directly above were engaged, at Elspeth's insistence, in a game of chess. They both froze as the sweet voice from below rose to them clearly.

The first tears in weeks welled in brown eyes, and Elspeth buried her face in her hands. Here was proof her love had recovered from the blow she'd seen delivered. Here was the first step in a delivery that under Taine's disbelief she herself had begun to doubt.

While the haunting tune floated about them, Taine knelt beside the younger girl. She pulled the plump frame into her arms and, though these were tears of relief, returned the comfort the other had given. A small gleam of hope glowed in Taine's heart. There was no proof that Jorion was a part of this rescue party or that he had survived the forest attack. But the fact that others had come was heartening, for it seemed unlikely they would face such risks without his leadership.

Below, the last note held and echoed into the hall's silence. All activity had ceased in deference to an exceptional voice. Richard prayed none here had visited and heard him sing in Edward's court. He'd feared someone might recognize his face and thus had shaved it smooth. Moreover, he'd adopted the fawning manner of an ambitious servant, had affected a slightly effeminate stance and tone of voice, but he'd not considered that his distinctive singing voice might betray the whole.

"Have you sung for me before?" Sir Godwin asked, brow furrowed in puzzlement. "Your voice is familiar."

"Not here in your hall," Richard responded with a false smile meant to show pleasure in the other's recognition. Then, bolstering his courage, he added, "But I've sung in many others. I have even performed for His Majesty, King Edward." He puffed his chest in exaggerated pride. "Perhaps you heard me there?"

Sir Godwin sneered at the common man's preening. "Perhaps so." Never one to overtax himself with matters of small import, like the possibility of having heard an insignificant minstrel before, he coldly continued, "You are welcome to take meals in this hall. Then, in appreciation for my bounty, after the last you will perform. Once done you will leave to make camp where you offered, while the gates are closed and locked at your back." Surely the only dangers a motley group like this could wreak must need be accomplished in the dark hours while all others slumbered, and by this restriction such trouble was prevented.

"Thank you, gentle lord," Richard bent low, once more pressing the cap to his chest in assumed humbleness and appreciation. "Your generosity is exceeded only by your kindness."

"One thing further, Richard the Minstrel," Sir Godwin called out, halting the party which had turned to withdraw. "I demand your best and expect you to contrive original entertainments as I've grown weary of those repeated over and over in every hall."

"Fear not," Richard responded immediately, bowing low again to hide the amusement in sparkling blue eyes. "The entertainments we offer will be exciting and unlike any you have seen before!"

Taine and Elspeth waited for the evening meal with a hitherto absent anticipation. Its deliverer left their chamber with a message for Sir Godwin, prettily phrased, begging a moment of his company.

An impatient Sir Godwin came, still a little vexed with them and anxious to return to the hall before the entertainment began. He came only to the door. Seated with assumed calm on chairs drawn near the fire, the two women smiled at the man in the doorway who clearly meant to enter no further. They watched as their gaoler smoothed his velvet tunic over a rounded belly. It was deep yellow, a hue unkind to his sallow complexion. As he waited to hear the reason for their summons, his irritation was plain and not a little daunting. Nonetheless, for so important a purpose they were willing to chance much and set their well-rehearsed ploy into motion.

"This morning you offered to provide distraction to our tedious days," Elspeth reminded Sir Godwin as she moved to his side, smiling sweetly.

Eyes that seemed even smaller in a pudgy face widened at her flirtatious manner, but he nodded acknowledgment of his offer.

"Not long after you left, a most wondrous song floated to us." With seemingly innocent wiles, she reached out to clasp his arm in both of her small hands.

"As if a tunesmith from the faerie realm had opened a secret door to us," Taine said with a touch of awe in her tone.

Sir Godwin smiled indulgently at such feminine fancies.

"If it be of human origin, then we beg you let its singer perform for us," Elspeth earnestly pleaded.

"We would both deem it a great favor," Taine added, "for, in truth, it grows monotonous here in one room."

The prospect of so easily earning the gratitude of a queen pleased Sir Godwin.

"And if he will consent to teach us a song or two," Elspeth further enticed, "we can entertain ourselves for no little time to come."

Added to a queen's gratitude, the pleasure in finding the heiress at last warming to him convinced Sir Godwin that there was no harm in fulfilling their request, particularly not if it warmed the heiress even more. Besides, what danger could there be in one effete little man?

"Tomorrow, once the noontide meal is done, I'll lead him

to you." His promise was given with the smug satisfaction of one who sees his goals in sight.

"Not tonight?" Elspeth pouted coyly.

Sir Godwin laughed and with one beringed finger lightly tapped the luscious lip protruding. "Nay, not tonight, for he will be occupied entertaining those in the hall below, but doubtless your 'faerie door' will open and you will hear some of what he sings."

After a quick glance at Taine, who slightly shook her head, Elspeth shrugged in mock disappointment and stepped back. Sir Godwin withdrew and hastily closed the door behind himself as the chords of Richard's first song drifted to them.

The same hope that brightened their outlook affixed leaden weights to each hour that followed, and they dragged by with all the speed of a particularly slow snail. The night was not restful and the following morning even less so as the appointed midday hour finally came—and passed. Platters of food that neither woman had found hunger enough to more than nibble at had been removed.

Tension had grown so strong that to Taine the small chamber seemed filled with the heaviness which precedes a storm. She sat on a small stool near the fire nervously pleating the crimson skirt of her borrowed gown into an extravagant design; Elspeth leaned against the hearth and nearly drove holes into fire-warmed stone with her drumming fingers. At last the chamber door opened.

Sir Godwin stood in its frame, grinning in expectation of profuse thanks. "I promised I'd bring him, and he's here." His wide frame stepped aside to reveal the smaller man first hidden by his girth.

While Sir Godwin turned his back to pull a chair from the table on one side of the room, blue eyes ran over Elspeth as if testing for damage and then met brown. In that timeless instant, hearts spoke what words had yet to say. Elspeth's smile would have melted even a strong heart, and Richard's was already potter's clay in her dimpled hands.

Feeling unable to withstand another tense moment when the answer to her fearful question stood so near, Taine rose, breath caught in her throat with apprehension of what she might learn. Richard's attention was caught by the motion and, while Sir Godwin continued to struggle with one chair apparently tangled with the legs of another, met the unspoken question in fear-filled sea-mist eyes. Smiling, he nodded the silent answer she'd prayed for long and fervently. The spirit imprisoned by the possible success of vicious treachery now broke free and soared. She suddenly felt she could free herself by stepping from the window so high above ground and floating down on a pillow of happiness.

"Here, Richard the Minstrel," Sir Godwin said gaily, hiding his impatience with the chair as he settled the uncooperative item in the midst of the room and looked into the minstrel's carefully blanked face. "Sit and sing for these fine ladies. Something gay and light, I think."

A glossy brown curl fell across Richard's forehead as he nodded to the other man before sitting down with a flourish to draw his lute into position and strum a few chords. He sang first a joyful tune and next a merry song of silly matters. Then he paused to suggest, "Pray let me sing a tale about one of King Arthur's knights who saved his lady-fair from a tower not unlike this one." He waved his hand in a limp sweep about the chamber.

Both women understood his meaning but by neither look nor word gave sign to alert the still-beaming Sir Godwin, who was clearly pleased with his own generosity and the aid to his courtship that it surely portended.

As Richard began he gave Elspeth a look full of meaning. The tune was the one always used when they played their song-story games. As the verse came to an end, Elspeth clapped her hands in apparent pleasure. "Oh, I know that song! A very dear friend used to sing it to me."

Sir Godwin smiled benignly at her joy as she sang what seemed the following verse, stumbling a little as if seeking the words in a distant corner of memory. By the time Richard had returned the next, Taine had learned the rhythm of the important game and answered with another. Richard sang the last and by its end a daring plan had been laid clear despite hidden meanings.

Wrapped in the concealing folds of a pure black cloak, without the embroidered dragon on its back, Jorion stood at the camp's edge. His impatience he held tightly in check while staring through dense forest at the horizon, nearly willing the last gleams of daylight to fade into night. Unreined thoughts traveled back, as so oft in past days, to the moment he'd entered his castle's hall to meet his carefully chosen party and set out on this rescue attempt. His attention had been caught by forest-green cloth draped over a stool before the fire. Left, Halyse had told him, by one wrapped in fearful worriment as she moved to the dungeon door with Will. Lifting Taine's cloak, he'd buried his face in the velvet and a trace of her wild-rose scent had washed over him with anguish. His determination had increased fourfold to find the villains who had taken her without even its warmth for a cold winter's journey.

Thus far his plan had gone exceedingly well. The presence of Halyse, Sander, and Stephen had initially allayed the castellan's discomfort, just as a sennight's enjoyable but uneventful entertainment had smothered any lingering doubts. Richard had played his part to perfection, and for tonight had promised the castle inhabitants a special pageant written only for them. As hoped, Sir Godwin's pride in the honor backed by carefully built trust had killed suspicion when for the performance Richard demanded total darkness. It was necessary, he'd said, for the dramatic scene to be lit only by the torches carried by mummers.

Aye, all was proceeding smoothly, yet Jorion found only temporary comfort in the plan that had sent Richard to Elspeth but held him from Taine. A man of action, used to controlling his own destiny, he found it difficult to stay behind while others carried out the plan he had devised. But he, by his height and coloring alone, was far too distinctive, too easily recognizable to participate in its early stages. Still, only by exercise of cool reason had he restrained the compulsion to accompany Richard. Such foolish action, he'd reminded himself, would risk his plot before it had begun and see Taine ever held by another.

That same cool reason had provided no solace for his aching heart. He could near feel Taine curled in his arms, basking in the warm content of their banked fire and stroking his bronzed skin with appreciation. Another image rose in his mind—Taine smiling seductively, lifting her arms to him with intent to yield all without demand of any price. Firelight glinted on a golden head as Jorion shook it to clear away fantasies and enter the final scene with the sharp thinking and concentration demanded by possible battle.

Only a dim rose glow faintly outlined the distant horizon. By now the castle inhabitants were surely eating their meal with no question for the lack of their entertainers. Richard had told them he and his mummers would not appear until the meal was done and all lights extinguished. The time had finally come to see to the right doing of the final details for his plan's ending before setting it in motion.

Jorion turned to the group behind. Guarded all round from peeping eyes, fantastic figures loomed in their campfire's wavering light. Some were clothed half in a black which blended into darkness and half in luminous white. Others were dressed all in black so that only their extravagant white headdresses were clearly visible. Still others wore a shiny red which seemed to burn in torchlight like demons spat out from the depths. And each voluminous costume concealed a fully armed and mail-clad warrior. Jorion's eye was caught by Halyse's struggle to secure a wig of horsehair, hennaed to match her own wiry locks, atop a slight man obviously disgusted with the process. Neither Halyse nor the young ones would enter the castle this night.

Watching the continuing preparations without seeing, he felt nearly crushed beneath the weight of an emotion he'd not experienced until Taine arrived in his life. He, the much-lauded warrior who frightened most, had never before felt such terrible fear. But neither had he cared for another more than himself, and this fear which clung to him like a multitude of pricking thistles was not for himself but for Taine. He could not bear to think of her bright flame muffled by a drab existence or doused by another's command to a life she would deny. He flexed powerful shoulders to ease their tension, comforting himself with the assurance, half-certainty and half-plea, that the fire-sprite was fated to be his.

Jorion gave his attention again to the small army making final adjustments to their garb. Garb for which he owed unending thanks to Lady Du Marchand. Once he'd said they were intended to aid in the rescue of his lady from danger, without question she'd seen to their hasty preparation. The shroud of a moonless night fully enveloped them and he turned to watch as the castle's lights were doused. At Richard's request even the dull glow of the great hall's fire was to be masked behind tall screens.

As Jorion lifted his arm to motion his companions forward his cloak flared out, a silhouette against their fire's light like a dragon flexing his wing. The sight reaffirmed his followers' belief in their dragon's power and gave them courage to fulfill their hopefully peaceful but possibly dangerous deed. 'Twas a deed strange to fighting men used to expected battles fought on daylit fields rather than this night-shielded stealth.

A firebrand in the hands of every other man dressed half in white and half in black, they crossed the lowered drawbridge. The courtyard of packed snow, muddied in places by constant use, had been deserted by Christmastide merrymakers intent on the promised entertainment.

Richard entered the dense gloom of the castle's unlit great hall first and in sepulchral tones bade everyone watch. "See the struggle for power between the forces of light and dark, good and evil." His voice sank to a sinister cackle on the last word and the widened eyes of every viewer followed the movements of red-garbed demons whirling into the middle of a circle of light formed by firebrands.

Beyond checking to be certain no eye turned his way, Jorion wasted no time. His black garb blended with the shadows as he slipped up the stairs, following Richard's directions to the two women they'd come to reclaim. A guard disgruntled by being chosen to miss the entertainment stood at the top of the staircase, craning his neck to catch a glimpse of the antics below. So intent on his goal was he that he failed to note the shadow moving up the steps and afterward could not say what had struck sense from him.

Guard slumped in his arms, Jorion lightly kicked at the door. It sprang open immediately. He deposited the guard on the floor in one corner and turned to catch the woman who fairly flew into his arms.

"Praise God you are alive!" Taine whispered fervently

into black folds across a powerful chest. This time his habit of appearing in doorways had been more welcome than any treasure. "I feared—I feared—" Her voice faltered away. Seeking further reassurance of his health, proof that he was more than a phantom born of longing, she reached up and thrust back his hood to twine her fingers into his golden hair and pull his mouth to hers for a soul-binding kiss.

After long moments Jorion drew back only far enough to lay adoring kisses across her eyelids and cheeks, to nuzzle her ear and murmur, "I feared too—for you. If they'd succeeded in stealing you from me forever, I'd be near-ready to do my uncle's deed for him." Arms full of a pleasure he'd feared never to hold again, Jorion lifted her feet from the floor in an embrace likely to crush her ribs. She did not protest but wound her arms about him and returned the passionate fire.

"Uhrmm," a voice interrupted. "I am sorry to interrupt so tender a scene," Elspeth whispered, "but mayhap you've forgotten the small matter of our unsecured freedom."

Summoned back to reality, Jorion set his love on her feet. Cursing himself for allowing distractions, no matter how sweet, to waste even one precious moment. Well he knew that in a battle, whether one of arms or one of words, such momentary inattention could be fatal. From beneath his voluminous cloak, he pulled two cloaks half black, half white and urged the women to hastily don them. The play below was likely drawing near its conclusion and they must join the final dance and outward march.

"Take care to keep your white side to the wall as we descend," he instructed, "and immediately join whatever action others dressed as you are performing." Reaching out, he tucked an errant dark-fire curl back under the hood he then pulled forward to hide Taine's trusting face.

Certain of their success now that Jorion had come, Taine was anxious to see the deed done and stepped first into the corridor beyond the door. She waited impatiently to be joined by Elspeth and Jorion, who quietly pulled the chamber door closed behind them. He led the way and Taine followed, silently acknowledging her willingness to follow him anywhere, even into hell. Moving cautiously down the steps, she nearly thought she had. Taking pains that the folds of her cloak's white half would be visible to none, she was startled by the strange scene below.

In the limited light of torches held high, small white forms like angels seemed to dance above red demons who writhed on the floor. Beneath her hood's shielding cover, Taine blinked repeatedly to see if the forms would disappear. Only as Jorion nudged her forward to join the circle of black and white forms surrounding the scene did she realize the angelic host actually consisted of black-garbed figures wearing curious headdresses. For the purpose of easing the tension of standing still amidst their foes, she studied the headdresses carefully—solid forms draped in thin, luminous cloth which floated in mock flight with the wearer's each movement. Given other surroundings, she would have enjoyed examining them more closely.

"And, by God's will, good defeats evil," Richard's low voice intoned before he struck a chord on his lute to begin a song of victory and turned to lead the way from the hall. Beneath the mock prodding of the heavenly hosts, cowed demons rose and followed, each with an angel to accompany him. The half-black, half-white figures fell next into line.

Jorion waited till the last and Taine refused to leave before him, despite his signals and small jabs. She could feel his anger at her stubbornness, yet refused to go without him. She'd once allowed herself to be held back from his peril, but not this time. Were he to fall to danger, she had rather be with him than exist in a terror of worriment without answer. And, without drawing the attention they must not, what action could he take to force her into the path she denied?

In truth, Jorion, caught between irritation and pleasure for the obvious care in her foolhardy refusal, was limited by that very restraint.

Sir Godwin had been entranced by the pageant, although he would rather it had been a common lighthearted farce. Yet he had demanded unique entertainment and it had certainly been that. Still, by the time it had come to an end, his unease in allowing total darkness to reign had grown to an uncomfortable level. As the players began their outward march, he trod quietly up the stairs, expecting to find his nebulous fears groundless.

As, unbeknownst to Taine, Sir Godwin climbed upward, Taine at last fell into step at the end of the line with only Jorion behind her. Once they had cleared the hall's door and the bright burning torches on either side of the lowered drawbridge were in sight, Taine nearly shouted with joy. Richard stood beside the gate guard near the portcullis' chain and winch that controlled it. He continued his song while demons and angels filed by, passing through the arch opening in a thick stone wall and over the rough plank bridge. One small figure in black and white fell out of line and went to his side. Taine grinned. Clearly, Elspeth, too, was unwilling to be separated from her love in hazardous times.

The sound of a raised alarm reverberated across the nearly emptied courtyard, sending chills of terror down Taine's spine. Before her stunned eyes, in a flash the vicious iron jaws of the portcullis came crashing down as the gate guard responded immediately to the sound.

It was the dreadful event that Taine had feared when first entering Jorion's castle. Momentarily nerve-frozen, she had only one rational thought—praise be none had been caught beneath the deadly iron jaw.

With well-honed reflexes, Jorion whipped the voluminous cloak from his shoulders and pulled the dual blades from his back. He dispatched the gate guard to his reward with ease and in a moment more had taken stock of his resources. Only he, Richard, and one other man remained inside—with the two stubborn women they'd come to rescue.

Will threw aside the restraint of his costume and moved to Jorion's side to meet the additional battlement guards running to confront them. Taine fell back several paces and watched in terror the deadly dance of shadows and glinting blades.

While Jorion and Will battled other men, Richard struggled mightily to turn the portcullis winch. It normally took two brawny men to move the massive iron gate, but with the strength of desperation he raised it nearly the breadth of himself.

"Roll under, Elspeth," he demanded, voice guttural with the strain of throat muscles clenched as tight as all others.

"No," she refused, terror in her eyes, "not without you."

"Get out!" he groaned. "With you safe I'll be free to find my own escape."

Glancing again at the fierce battle, she saw Jorion's blades end one threat and turn to another. Richard had no such skill in battle. Thus, he must quickly find freedom. Not wanting to be the hindrance to so important a need, she dropped to her stomach and rolled beneath vicious iron teeth that tore her clothing and scratched her flesh.

Still Richard held the chain tight, arms shaking with fatigue. "Now you, Taine."

Only the rasped anguish of the words broke Taine's horrified visual bond with her dragon's broad back. She glared at the narrow opening, shaking her head and backing away—into the powerful figure towering above her. Startled, she looked up into black eyes.

"Go!" Jorion commanded, taking slender shoulders into powerful hands and shoving her forward. He and Will had defeated the few foes already in the courtyard when the alarm sounded, but doubtless many more would spill from the castle in moments. Will had bent to aid Richard's task, and he must get Taine out before the additional defenders arrived.

Taine twisted and wrapped her fingers about his arms in refusal.

"Lady, don't you ken?"

Both Taine and Jorion looked down in shock to find Stephen beside them. He twisted grimy hands into her skirts and pulled hard. "You stay and he be ever looking for your safety and not careful of his own."

Taine looked up quickly into Jorion's eyes and read the truth in them.

"You saved my life, now give me the right to save you from one you would deny," he quietly demanded.

The courtyard was quickly filling with men still struggling to don mail over fine clothes and buckle swords to their waists. She wasted not a moment longer but followed Elspeth's example and rolled beneath the menacing iron jaw. Will had been forced to fight off one advancing foe intent on seeing the grating lowered sooner, and the moment Taine was free the winch slipped from Richard's weakened grasp. The portcullis slammed down, and he slumped over the handle, bathed in sweat.

While both warriors were engaged in mortal combat, Stephen scrambled to loose one of the firebrands placed to light the now-barred gate. With it he ran toward the stables, a wooden structure leaning against the wall nearby. Dashing to the forger's room in its farthest reaches, he gathered up a covered jug of liquid. Opening it, he took a deep whiff and grinned. Stoppering the jug once more, he moved to the nearest stall and set the straw alight. It flared and he moved quickly forward to do the same to the next and the next. By the time he'd run free, the stable was a burning inferno where horses snorted and lashed in maddened fury.

When the stable first began to burn, Richard had dragged himself up the stone steps to the battlements. From its vantage he watched Jorion and Will meeting ill-prepared defenders. But, though ill-prepared, the opposition had the advantage of superior numbers. It was at the moment when he'd nearly given in to the inevitability of defeat that his eye was caught by a small boy. He watched in amazement as Stephen tossed the contents of a crockery jug through the portcullis' fearsome bars, firebrand next. The wooden drawbridge exploded with flames.

With the blazing stable lighting even distant shadows, Richard next saw Stephen run to a wooden ladder leaning against the far wall, a convenient way for guards doing duty in the back to reach their post. In the heat of battle it had apparently been forgot. Even as the boy scrambled up the ladder, Richard rushed over the battlements' narrow ledge to help him draw the awkward structure up.

Both Will and Jorion had purposely backed toward the narrow stone steps ascending to the battlements, a place where a crowd of men could not follow. Fighting valiantly, one foe and then another fell before their might. But tiring under the onslaught of many, they'd been forced ever upward toward the encircling ledge.

Opposition scattering to fight both fire and foe, from the corner of his eye Jorion saw Richard and Stephen struggling to carry a ladder to a point behind him. He smiled in grim admiration for their resourcefulness and, above the fierce clash of sword blades and the cries of wounded men, called a heavily engaged Will to join him on the battlements.

Richard leaned through a notch in the wall's edge to yell directions to those anxiously waiting on the moat's far side. After a short but seemingly endless wait, he carefully maneuvered the ladder over the wall into the hands of a man standing in the waterway, which in winter months was narrow and shallow. Swords wielded in violent contest gleamed in the firelight while the lowered ladder's bottom rung was carried to the moat's solid edge and steadied by waiting hands.

"Stephen"—Jorion risked a quick glance behind—"go down."

Stephen did not argue with a direct order and, with Richard's aid, his tousled head immediately disappeared below the wall. The ladder was now angled from battlement to moat's far side and the boy had been lowered to its first step.

"Now you, Richard," Jorion ordered, without looking as fresh foes demanded his full attention.

Without hesitation Richard did as he was commanded. His dagger was useless in such battles as this, and he was wise enough to know it. A dagger once thrown in the midst of a fight was not easily retrieved and left a man without defense; a dagger in hand was no match for the long, deadly length of a broadsword.

The narrow stairway was filled with castle defenders, and Jorion had begun to tire beneath their unending onslaught. Will, engaged in a lengthy battle with a skilled foe, had already stepped back onto the battlement ledge. Holding two others off, Jorion failed to stop another from leaping past. Lifting a rock, part of the rubble that filled the wide space between stone walls, the man smashed it down toward the figure halfway to the ground. Struck a glancing blow on the side of his head, Richard fell.

In fury, Jorion finished his foes and jumped to the ledge. After driving one of his blades through the culprit, he set his foreign weapons aside and lifted the lifeless body. He threw it down the stairway, knocking those quickly ascending into a tangled heap at its base. Standing behind Will's opponent, he jerked the sword from his hand, threw it into the flames licking the wall nearby, and picked up the panic-stricken man. A few hardy men had surmounted the confused mass at the stairway's bottom and begun to climb. Jorion heaved the second burden at them and they all tumbled onto others already at the bottom of the steps. With such soft landing it was unlikely any further mortal injury was sustained.

"Now you, Will," Jorion directed his exhausted knight. "I will follow."

Will started the descent, leaving Jorion alone on battlements bathed in the blazing fury of the stable's leaping flames. Jorion raised his two curved blades and crossed them over his head. Flamelight burned equally on vicious, blood-stained blades and golden hair. To the faces now turned toward him in terror he warned, "Beware the Dragon's fire!"

The men on the courtyard floor shrank back, knowing the minstrel's songs were true. With his twin blades, he was truly able to defeat a whole garrison nearly alone. In an eye-blink, the dragon disappeared over the wall.

Having no idea of the depth of the water's below, on his steady descent Jorion anxiously searched for some sign of his cousin in the moat, but the placid surface and its perfect reflection of the orange light above proved Richard not within. When he reached the ground, still grasping the ladder's parallel poles of smoothed wood, he swung the ladder free to crash into the moat. Turning, he found his party already mounted on the swift steeds he prized and which had been held in a secluded forest glade, hidden until now. Though his face betrayed no emotion, his eyes quickly scanned the group and stopped on Richard, also ahorse.

Richard smiled ruefully and pointed to the makeshift bandage wound about his head. "It throbs like a b—" He paused and glanced to the two women. "And I hope you ensured the vile oaf who inflicted it upon my harmless self will feel an equal pain."

Jorion grinned his relief but shook his head. "Nay, I fear

my blow ended all human pain, and you must only pray the tortures of what comes after will be recompense enough."

"Ah, well," Richard sighed with mock disappointment, "at least I was rescued from mud-fouled waters and a sweet angel sacrificed her surcote to bind my injury." His smile turned tender as he looked into Elspeth's adoring eyes.

"Aye, and you are fortunate, too, that dry clothes were near to hand," Jorion dryly added as he swung up onto his golden steed. "It is seldom that men go into battle with such advantages."

From her viewpoint so far beneath, Taine had helplessly watched when the conflict moved to the wall's high ledge. Both heartbeat and breath had seemed to freeze with fear until Jorion stood in solitary splendor. Then her heart pounded with pride as, against a dark sky, flamelight from below had outlined his magnificent form with gold. His warning to beware the dragon's fire had called from her not fear but anticipation.

Jorion felt the caress of another's eyes and immediately looked to his wife, sitting with ease on the mare he had promised her. Reaching out instinctively, he brushed his fingers lightly across her cheek as if reconfirming her whole and healthy. The hard lines of his face softened as they would for no other. He silently scolded himself for allowing even a moment's doubt for their success. She was his fate and treasured. No evil would be allowed to again take her from him.

Despite the warmth of his touch, a strong shiver shook Taine's delicate form. She'd been abducted without warming cloak and had now been rescued with the same lack, for the thin cloth of her costume was no defense against winter-chilled air.

Irritated with himself for his heedless lack of care, Jorion pulled a tightly rolled bundle from the same position where Taine had found his cloak the day their adventure together began. He shook out her fur-lined cloak, draped it carefully about slender shoulders and pulled its hood up over thick auburn curls.

A slow, sweet smile curved Taine's lips and melted deep-green into sea-mist. Even in moments of stress, Jorion had thoughtfully planned for her comfort. His deed, joined with the gentle touch of his powerful hands, did more to ease her cold than the forest-green cloak, for it warmed from the inside out.

Eyes whose depths burned with golden flames stroked fire over the woman who was his tender fate. Breath caught and heart pounding so loudly he felt certain others must hear it, Jorion forced his gaze away. It fell upon Stephen, riding pillion behind Will and looking back in pride at the flames that lit the night sky.

Richard, filled with euphoria for their night's work despite his pounding head, saw the new focus of Jorion's interest. "'Twas our Stephen who set light to the stable and destroyed the drawbridge," he informed the dragon.

Golden brows rose in surprise. "I saw only your joint effort with the means of our delivery."

"Aye," Richard agreed, "and that, too, was his notion."

Jorion was impressed. One small boy had managed not only to provide escape but to bedevil and waylay pursuit. Deep, rich laughter echoed against the stone wall so near which, though built in defense from those without, had become foe, holding all within as unwilling prisoners. Even after the inhabitants of Castle Cregel managed to raise the portcullis, a mechanism designed to fall with far more haste than ever it could be lifted, they'd have no easy way to follow. What steeds survived would take long hours to calm and their drawbridge even longer to repair from the inside out! Though the moat was narrow and shallow, the drop from the raised portcullis was steep and dangerous.

"I can see, Stephen"—Jorion's voice was still filled with amusement—"if ever your military prowess is as fine as your strategy, you'll be a fearsome enemy. Thus, having strategic talents of my own, I realize I'd best have you on my side."

With pleasure at the unexpected praise from the great warrior and his hero, Stephen's cheeks burned so bright they nearly glowed.

"In truth, for bravery demonstrated alone you've earned the right for knighthood, and when we return to Castle Dragonsward, you will join the other pages for the first level of your training."

As the meaning of the dragon's words sank through his confusion, Stephen's grin grew and grew until it was so broad it nearly swallowed his face. Taine's laughter rose clear and free on crisp air. Warmed by the happiness of those about him, Jorion joined the laughter as he lifted his hand to signal a start to their journey.

✌ Chapter 24 ✌

TAINE'S CHILLED CHEEKS AND lowered chin were buried in the fur lining of her cloak's close-drawn hood, but the happy smile hidden in softness sparkled in green eyes when she caught sight of the house allotted for Jorion's use in Dunfermline. Their entourage approached the town from the direction opposite the path of the weeks-past departure for Radwyn and came to the house from the back. It was indeed small in comparison to Jorion's great stone castle but still a welcome sight. From both of the hall's chimneys, smoke curled in lazy invitation against the pale sky of late afternoon. A heavy overcast and intermittent snow had plagued previous days, but as this one had matured the clouds drifted away, a seeming reflection of the group's happiness to reach this first destination.

Although they had traveled all through the first night, this journey that in fine weather could be accomplished in one day had taken two. Slowed by deep white drifts that demanded precious time to navigate, when darkness had fallen the night past, a full day's journey still lay ahead. Exhausted by long and arduous travels, they stopped at a crofter's hut, who, overawed by his grand guests, welcomed

348

the three wellborn couples into his humble abode. The ladies were to share the coarse homespun pallet filled with straw and vacated by the crofter and his wife, while the men slept wrapped in their cloaks near the open fire pit in the hut's center. The rest of Jorion's companions found shelter in a crude structure with the farm's half-starved animals.

They rose early the next morn and were generously fed with provisions the family could clearly ill afford. When Jorion gave the man a golden coin for kindnesses rendered, widened eyes and hands hesitant to accept so great a reward proved it a wealth never before seen and even less possessed. To Taine, unaccustomed to such prolonged union with a horse's back, this day seemed longer than the one preceding, although in truth 'twas much shorter. But at last they were nearing their destination.

With indulgent eyes, Taine took in every detail of the rustic stable, two walls and a roof, built against Jorion's house. As the sun slid below the horizon, she followed Jorion's lead and rode straight into its dim interior, ducking her head to accommodate the low ceiling. Jorion dismounted and reached to lift her down. She came happily into the claim of strong hands, welcome in her heart.

Despite his anxiety to reach the court and have done with the visit he'd promised Edward, Jorion lowered her slowly, enjoying the brush of her tantalizing form against the full length of him—a foretaste of delights to come once their duty to the king was finished. Then they would return to the seclusion of their chamber for the private reunion so far denied them.

Taine wrapped her arms about Jorion. For long, aching moments she snuggled closer, loving the feel of his big, hard body before looking up to fall willingly into fathomless black depths with no thought spared to the other weary travelers about them.

Near drowning in sensations that demanded what this was neither the time nor place to share, Jorion gently unwound enticing arms. "Come, wife." His smile held a touch of the old half-tilted mockery, but tiny gold flames had begun to burn in his eyes. "We've a command visit to perform." Curling his arm about Taine's shoulders to bind her near, he led her into the soft shades of twilight, following a moonglow path across an ice crystal carpet, which crunched beneath their feet.

"Once that chore is complete, lady fair"—he bent to whisper in her ear—"you can thank me properly for rescuing you as the minstrels' tales claim is the rightful task of all good knights."

"Minstrels' tales?" Taine looked up at him, delicate brows raised in apparent surprise. "I fear we must rewrite their words, for in them 'tis the handsome knight who rescues the maiden from the dragon's hold—not the other way about." At that moment the door of the house was thrown open and a patch of warm light fell across the couple on snow-packed steps. It gilded blond hair and bronzed skin, as precious to Taine as the golden coin to the crofter. "No matter," Taine softly added, gentle sea-mist eyes caressing her beloved dragon. "You are both while I am a maiden no more."

The meltingly sweet smile that was Jorion's response called Taine nearer and she curved closer to his side as they entered.

Behind the self-involved couple, Halyse exchanged a glance full of meaning with Will. Never before Taine's coming had they seen their lord smile so often or with such happiness. Following Halyse and Will's path, Elspeth was too preoccupied with a weakened Richard, and he with her, to notice another's ways.

Anxious to waste no time in reaching the court, concluding their business, and returning here, Jorion led Taine up wooden stairs to the chamber above, while for all his haste a slight smile played at the corners of his lips. A surprise awaited. When Lady Du Marchand had agreed to make the mummers' costumes, he'd asked her also to prepare clothes suitable to a court visit for both him and Taine.

Below, Elspeth ordered aid to see Richard carefully ensconced in his bed. Between loss of blood and the necessary rigors of the journey, Richard had grown light-headed and unsteady. But even had he possessed the strength, he'd not have protested when Elspeth insisted on sitting beside him on the bed to tenderly apply compresses formed of cloth immersed in water chilled by icicles. The lump on his head was of a shape and hue to lend an odd, lopsided look.

Elspeth blessed him with a gentle, reassuring smile as she carefully dipped the cloth again into the basin, keeping it frigid to ensure the greatest benefit, before laying it against his injury once more. Thank sweet Mary and all the saints that although his wound had bled copiously at the start, the red flow had soon eased to a halt. "You shouldn't have come to Castle Cregel," she softly remonstrated. It was the first time since their escape that they'd had opportunity for private words.

One eye closed against the compress' trailing cloth cover, Richard gave her a look of disgust.

She continued, "You know you hate the fighting and noise of battle. And you must have known Jorion would come for us."

Richard stiffened and glared.

"Nonetheless, I thank you, kind sir." Although the words were primly said, brown eyes gleamed as she paused to turn the compress over. "You were very brave, leading the way into the enemy's camp! Only now you've been hit twice on the head; and if you'd not gone witless from the first, 'tis sure to be the price for the courageous deed that brought the second."

Pleasure for her admiration of a bravery he'd been surprised to find in himself, no matter how lightly spoken, went far to restore Richard's merry spirit, and a short laugh escaped him. "I did the thing for you."

Elspeth looked suspiciously into sparkling blue eyes.

"Yes, both blows. With your soft heart, ever bruised by an injury to some fortunate wild creature or hapless wretch, I decided the clearest path to your undivided attention was to join their ranks."

"Hah!" Elspeth responded, letting the water-heavy cloth drop from her grasp to the pillow by his head and freeing her hands to be planted as small fists on well-rounded hips. "Whenever you turned my way, and that seldom enough, I have always welcomed you, always been willing to give you my every moment. 'Twas you who had so many admirers demanding your time that little was left for me. And when you were about, you never noticed me."

Sitting up abruptly and flinching at the renewed fierce throbbing which was price for the inadvisable action, Richard retorted, "What I noticed was your impending betrothal to Jorion! Why then should I not seek solace elsewhere?"

"Jorion needed me." Elspeth felt as if she'd sustained a foul blow, one that deflated her proud defense and drove irritation out. She had planned to wed another—before she admitted the hopeless truth buried in her heart. Her shoulders slowly drooped, and her defending words wavered for all their heat. "A thing you have never."

"Not need you?" Richard asked, gentleness lowering his voice to a purr as he reached out to tug at an ebony ringlet resting on a flushed cheek. "You have always been necessary to me. Why did you think I kept coming back to Castle Dragonsward? For the sake of my loving sire?" Having the soul, if not the talents, of a poet, he continued, "Know you not that 'tis you who makes my sun shine on a rainy day and a nightingale sing on a winter's eve?"

Drawing in a strangled sob, Elspeth collapsed against Richard. All practiced wiles fleeing in the face of deep emotion, Richard patted her back in awkward solace as he whispered nonsensical endearments interspersed with tender kisses.

Elspeth pulled a breath away and looked up into suspiciously damp blue eyes, wherein lay a wealth of love to match her own. She unhesitatingly wrapped her arms about his neck, laying her head on his shoulder as their souls twined in love.

Above stairs, Taine stepped from the bath into the hearth-warmed towel held open by Mercia. Jorion had brought the girl with the party to Dunfermline when he came to consult Edward, but had left her safely behind when they'd set out for Castle Cregel. Of Taine's particular friends it seemed only Father Aleric and Bertwald had been left behind. Father Aleric was too infirm to easily travel such distances, while Bertwald, once in the employ of Baliol supporters, would likely have been recognized by someone in Castle Cregel. It was nearly certain that at least one or two of the rotating guards from her castle-prison were posted therein.

Wrapping the towel closer, sat down on the stool
beside the fire, ready for Mercia ish her hair dry before
the flames' heat, a long but sooth Jorion had left her
to bathe in privacy, saying if he sta ey'd likely not see
Edward for a week to come. Luxuriat a warm comfort
she'd not felt for several days, Taine ga thought to her
serious lack of garb until her hair was d shining and
the evening well-advanced. Then, as she dress, the
realization came to her that the sea-foam go 'd worn
for two days was unworthy of a court visit, ere it
clean and fresh, which it assuredly was not.

"Did the earl bring my court gown here?" she as
little hope. A frown clouded her eyes. She'd not for
the fault-finding eyes of the king's company and w
rather go dressed in her best.

"Nay, milady," Mercia responded but her lips purse
with a grin restrained.

Worried by the answer she'd expected, Taine turned
toward the travel-stained gown spread across a chest near
the bed and failed to see the poorly hidden anticipation on
the open face of the girl unaccustomed to subterfuge. "Then
we've a deal of toil before us," she finally sighed, lifting the
gown with a curl of distaste to her lips.

"Nay, milady," Mercia responded again but with a wide
grin.

Surprised by the unexpected answer from one always
meek, Taine looked up. Seeming to flow from Mercia's
fingertips was a gown of dazzling beauty. Uniquely hued,
the hemline's bright yellow subtly darkened as it rose until
at neckline 'twas near the shade of her hair.

Taine was almost afraid to don the delicate satin kirtle,
but Mercia had no such apprehension and dropped it over
her head. As the girl gently drew and tied the back lacings,
Taine gazed down at the wondrous gown that seemed to
glow. There followed a surcote, whose very deep armholes
revealed more than they hid but whose golden embroidery,
though dainty, nearly obscured the deep red cloth beneath.

"You fair look a queen," Mercia breathed in awe.

Taine smiled. Pray God the gentle girl would never know
the truth in her compliment. Still, in appreciation for the
innocent praise, Taine sank into a deep curtsy.

THE ith pleasure for her lady's action,
Pale cheeks gone pᵣ the chamber.
the shy girl slippeᵣ ne watched her skirt float gracefully
Twirling slowl gown truly held an unearthly beauty.
about her toeᵣely, she spied a small detail, one that
Examining ;ᵣnent would be treasured above all others.
ensured tʰʳcote's intricate golden stitches, so cleverly
Among ᵣg flowers and leaves that casual eyes would fail
meldeᵣiny dragons.
to sᵣheard familiar footsteps in the hall and whirled
ᵣ the opening door intending to thank the gown's
ᵣder. But when Jorion stepped in, the words were
ᵣven away by amazement. Her husband, the man garbed
ᵣver in black—save for their wedding day—was arrayed as
magnificently as she. Dressed all in deep red velvet, a color
which alone would catch every eye, he was overwhelming.
She walked slowly about him, examining each detail. Across
his chest, emphasizing its powerful breadth, lay the heavy
gold chain he'd worn the day she met him. There was not a
touch of black to his attire, but green eyes narrowed on the
gold-embroidered bands edging his tunic. She smiled. Tiny
golden dragons lay there, too.

Jorion was accustomed to stares and had long ago learned
to freeze them from his consciousness. It was a reaction he
could never bend to her, and like some untried lad he could
feel his cheeks warming beneath her prolonged appraisal.

"When Lady Du Marchand agreed to make the mummers' costumes," Jorion quietly explained, "I asked her also
to prepare clothes suitable to a court visit for us both."

"And did she choose the cloth—and hues?" Taine halted
a handbreadth from him and tilted her head to one side,
aiding the escape of more irrepressible ringlets from the
confines of her gold net crespine. She was curious to know if
his new coloration was by his choice or another's.

"Black and gold are my colors," Jorion stated. "And I've
seldom found joy worthy of brighter."

Taine nodded and hid a small ache of disappointment.

"Only on the day of our wedding rites, when hope
demanded light, did black seem purely wrong." Jorion met
Taine's soft smile and reached out to let an auburn curl
wrap about one gentle finger. "Aye, black and gold are my

colors, but red is plainly yours. And in planning for this visit I prayed would come to be, I joined your red to the gold of mine—a talisman of hope."

His words were the hope she'd hidden even from herself, and rose petal lips curved invitingly. Jorion remembered too well their nectar sweetness and again cursed the promise to his king that prevented his yielding to mutual desire. Instead he stepped away and opened the chamber door once more.

"Shall we parade our splendor before others?" he asked, moving forward to offer his arm to her.

Taine laid her fingers lightly atop red velvet and moved toward the stairs with him.

Halted once more before the castle housing Edward's crowded court, Taine studied its massive silhouette, black against the star-speckled background, with newfound confidence. When first she'd come, she'd feared the English king as a foe and had been alarmed by so many critical eyes. She returned with a husband who accepted her desire to be free of her past, indeed had saved her repeatedly from those who would force it upon her. Aye, this time she would place her faith in him and walk in confidence, able to face down a thousand supercilious foes. As Jorion lifted her down from the mount she'd grown accustomed to in the last two days, she smiled lovingly into dark velvet eyes soft with concern for her.

Jorion worried that this repeat of an experience clearly distressing might overwhelm one who had already been called to withstand many fearful deeds. Yet her trusting smile and clear crystal eyes showed her undaunted by the visit. Without thought to the two knights who had accompanied them, Jorion hugged her close.

Smoothing her hands over the surcote whose sideless style she no longer found offensive, Taine inwardly smiled. Even here, facing a situation that in the first instance had brought tension in great measure, she felt no urge to twine her fingers into her garment's rich texture. Jorion offered his arm and Taine formally placed her fingers atop, turning to face the door with tilted chin and a smile of happiness.

Jorion had sent a message to inform his sovereign of their

coming, and as the pair entered the hall they were met by the king's chamberlain and immediately led through the curious crowd, which again parted for their passage. But this night, instead of finding the watching people a threat, Taine was filled with pride in the man at her side, certain the rising tide of whispers was in response to his unexpected garb.

When the door closed behind them, she was surprised to find the room brightly lit only near the fire and apparently occupied by only their host. He moved toward them, a broad smile warming the face beneath a mane of thick white hair. "I am most pleased to find you *both* returned to my court."

Jorion sank to his knee in honor of his liege lord and Taine swept a deep curtsy. Rising, she steadily met Edward's piercing blue gaze. Apprehensions of him relieved by his support of her dragon's rescue, Taine noted for the first time that although he yet stood tall and strong, the cares of many years had worn grooves into his cheeks and forehead, and lines of disappointment creased the corners of his eyes. He was a man like others, aging and grown weary from continuing battles with foes as stubbornly unyielding as he.

Jorion had told her that by her ring this man had almost assuredly known her nearly the moment they'd met. Before their earlier meeting she'd acknowledged him her great-uncle but had failed to consider the likelihood of his recognizing the ring first worn by Margaret, Queen of Scotland, his sister, and her grandmother. Still, she no longer berated herself for not tossing the betraying circlet into the tarn's deep waters. It had brought unwelcome recognition from some, but had also led her dragon to the truth and had given him the knowledge to protect her. Unconsciously, her thumb caressed the band and when she realized Edward's eyes had dropped to it, she glanced down at the two bands now twined as if meant to be one and blessed with a sparkling green gem. With a warm smile she looked up again, and Edward nodded toward her hand. "'Tis a lovely piece and strengthened by its mate."

Taine's smile deepened in acknowledgment of his allusion.

"And I have a small gift I hope will not seem paltry by comparison." She had known aforehand they'd come to receive a special Yuletide gift, but had rather been given the night in peace with Jorion, the first alone since before her abduction. But they could not refuse a kingly gift nor a sovereign's summons. She glanced adoringly at Jorion and when she looked back found blue eyes alight with amusement.

"I apologize for this hindrance to plans more inviting, but my gift for you, Lady Taine, is one I believe will compensate for lost moments." Taine's cheeks went hot with a rosy color that deepened the king's smile.

Only as Edward turned his wide back to move toward a table before the fire did Taine notice two other figures standing in the shadows of a far corner. Green eyes narrowed as she tried to make out their features. She could not, yet they were both familiar. A small shiver of dread shook the golden bubble of her happiness. She tried to drive it back as the king turned to face them, several pieces of parchment in his hands.

"First I must introduce the two men who have contributed to this gift that I pray you will treasure." He waved the shadowy figures forward into the light.

Standing scarce a breath from Jorion, she felt him tense. One revealed shadow was Robert Bruce, the man she'd met at her last court visit and almost certainly the force behind her recent captivity. But, although he was an unwelcome sight, he at least could be expected in this fortress. The other they had thought locked in the dungeon cell of Castle Dragonsward. Both McLewell and the Bruce nodded, but neither Taine nor Jorion responded. After their violent schemes and plots there seemed no need for courtesies.

"Yes, Jorion," Edward said, waving his hand toward McLewell but keeping his eyes on the golden-haired lord. "You told me he was bound in your castle and by royal writ I had him transported—as Baliol's representative 'twas necessary he be here."

Although his lips were tightly compressed, Jorion nodded his acceptance, for there was no other choice for a loyal subject.

"Lady Taine, you have kept your secret long and well, but

now is the time for truth bared—once and never again." His eyes on hers were commanding. Taine shrank back from a deed she'd so often refused, but without waiting for her agreement he began a succinct narrative of her antecedents and ironclad claim to the Scottish crown. "Granddaughter of King Alexander III of Scotland, daughter of King Erik of Norway, small Margaret known to the masses as the Maid of Norway and to all as the rightful queen of Scotland."

Facts spoken in Edward's strong, clear voice felt like blows to suddenly revealed, tender flesh. They were her but a person she did not know. She was queen, but of a land unwelcoming and nearly unknown.

He continued with an outline of the part each of the three had played in the Maid of Norway's life, and she shrank from words which stripped the protective layers from her life, forced light on memories willfully buried in the hidden corners of her mind. Caught in a tangled maze of bitter emotions and hurtful scenes from her past, she heard no more than a few disjointed phrases of the king's speech that followed.

"I betrothed my son and heir to you, a marriage that would have given me and my heirs the throne of Scotland without all the bloodshed and desecration that, for their stubborn refusal of my rule, have since befallen it." He shot an accusing look at the two men just come from the shadows. Though both were ostensibly sworn to Edward, their eyes fought a battle with piercing blue as fierce as the conflict that still sundered the land.

"I summoned the child-queen, but the Bruce"—he lifted his hand in a sharp gesture toward the man of whom he spoke—"thought to steal the Maid and see her wed to his own son, securing the crown to his family." He gave a wry smile. "'Twas a fine plan, my plan. But the Baliol faction wanted her threat to their claim removed and so stole her from the Bruces who stole her from me.

"Have I stated it clearly, objectively enough for us all?" He looked about the group, one white brow lifted, seeming to become a part of his crown of white hair. "'Tis a tangled plot yet one surely we all understand as we've each played a pivotal part in the whole. Still, it seems, although the Baliols could abduct their rightful queen, they balked at murdering her. Doubtless they realized that if caught it would be a stain never removed and a sure and certain loss of support. Instead, they imprisoned her in a remote stronghold where they planned to keep her the length of her days."

In the quiet that followed Edward's accusing words, Robert Bruce stepped forward and spoke quietly to Taine: "Your father was wed to my daughter and that makes us kin—of a sort."

Pulled back from the bleak cavern of her thoughts, Taine responded in a voice sharp and cold. "I had no father." Filled again with the pain from her past and unwilling to face this sharpest wound—the treachery of her own father —she took a quick step back. In support, Jorion wrapped his arm about her and glared at the Bruce.

Gaze never leaving the anguished woman's face, the other man paid no attention to the dragon. "You did have a father," he softly responded, head shaking in sorrow for her discomfort in the deed. "A strong father who loved you very much."

"Loving father?" Taine sneered. "What loving father would send his child into a cold, dreary exile and claim her dead to the world?"

"An honorable father who truly believed his beloved child gone," came the immediate answer. It was just as quickly clear that Taine did not accept his words as truth, and he explained: "We of the Covenant would not have you wed the English prince and by the child of your union bind us Scots to the English forever. Your father understood our need for he, too, would have suffered much to preserve his land's independence from foreign rule—'tis a king's duty!"

Learning that her father had fulfilled his royal duty did not ease Taine's pain in his betrayal, and she shrank closer against Jorion.

Jorion curled his arm about Taine's shoulders and held her tightly shielded in his strength. Edward had claimed the intent of bestowing a treasured gift, yet thus far he'd given Taine only unhappiness and hurtful reminders of a dismal past. In defense of his love, black eyes dared to glare at a king. Edward only smiled and lifted his hand to motion for patience.

"I promised my own daughter in marriage to your father

to seal the pact by which you would have been held in peace and comfort until of an age to wed my heir." With this further fact the Bruce sought to prove his honorable intent to the skeptical beauty.

Taine still looked disbelieving, for her prison had held none of the comfort he claimed.

"We told all on the boat you had died in the crossing and asked a stop in the Orkney Isles to send message to Edward. I carried you from the boat myself and gave you to one I trusted. A boat was to meet him and carry you to a secluded fortress where you were to await marriage to my son." He cast a disgusted look back to McLewell. "After my man rode from sight with you in his arms, Baliol supporters killed him and stole you away. When the boat sent for you went unmet, a party was sent out and found our man's lifeless body and the bloodied blanket in which you'd been wrapped. Both I and your father truly thought you dead. Yet I gave my daughter to him in marriage to ease the grief in so hideous a miscarriage of our plan."

His sorrow seemed so sincere Taine could almost believe it true.

Edward broke into the narrative. "But when you saw her ring here in my court so short a time past and discovered the queen yet living, your plan was reborn. Your son is a widower and, once again, through marriage to her, the Bruces had opportunity to win undisputed right to a crown. 'Struth?"

The Bruce's pleasant face soured as he gave a disgruntled nod.

This reminder of so recent an attack ended Taine's sympathy.

"So," Edward continued, "you plotted to steal her away, hoping you'd be quick enough to take her before vows were said. But for the sake of a crown, once you learned yourself too late meant not to hesitate in disposing of the impediment to your goal."

Silver flared in green eyes with the vicious defense of dagger blows at the one who had seemed to offer sympathy but had intended harm to her love. Aye, he and another for two here there were who would have seen Jorion dead. Taine's fierce gaze shifted to McLewell.

With a heavy sigh, Edward turned to lift three sheets of parchment from the table. Facing them again, he stated, "These are legal writs by which Margaret, daughter of King Erik of Norway and the granddaughter of King Alexander III of Scotland, resigns all rights to the crown of Scotland." He lifted them a fraction higher, then laid them carefully on the table in a neat row and motioned Taine forward.

Seeing the end she had prayed for in sight, without a moment's hesitation Taine took the quill held toward her. She was thankful that before sailing from Norway her father's indulgent cleric had taught her the pattern of her name. Although in the long days of her confinement she'd learned no more of writing or reading, she'd practiced tracing the pattern in dust and with charcoal on hearth stones. Dipping into a small bronze pot, she signed first one and then the next and the next. Here, as she'd once told Jorion she willingly would, she foreswore the crown and, of more import, kept Jorion safe from the schemes that had oozed around her like witches' brew all her life. When she had finished the last, she tossed the quill down and stepped back, meeting the eyes of McLewell and the Bruce defiantly.

Jorion laid his hands on slender shoulders and drew her back against the protection of his powerful form. He had seen her eyes flash at the threat to him. The sight of his fire-sprite blazing in his defense brought the warmth of assurance in the love she bore him, even as he coldly met the eyes of his opponents.

As Edward bent to add his name as witness, Taine settled into Jorion's hold, welcoming the arms of the man who had saved her time and time again to claim her his own. Edward finished and handed the quill to the Bruce, who added his signature and left room for McLewell, who signed as representative of John Baliol.

"These three I will close with the royal seal," Edward informed them. "One I will keep and give one to each of you." First nodding toward McLewell and Robert Bruce, he bent and suited action to words.

Inside Taine the joy of freedom, begun as a small bird pecking its way free of a restraining shell, now soared into flight as Edward commanded the other two to join him in an oath to hold these documents in trust, make them public only if she, her spouse, or her heirs were to seek the crown of Scotland. Taine nearly laughed aloud at the ingenuity of it all. This English king, this great-uncle of hers had given her the thing she prized above all (save Jorion), a life without fear, without threats from her past. Any advantage sought by one faction in manipulating her would result in the other two factions wielding this irrefutable weapon of denial.

"We all shared a part in destroying her life—and now will share in restoring it to her, born anew," Edward said as, one in each hand, he gave sealed writs to the Bruce and McLewell. The beneficiary of his actions fairly glowed with happiness, and it pleased him. The priests said 'twas a fine thing to do good deeds for others. That it was a deed aiding himself as well by removing a potential threat to his endeavors only made it the finer. Moreover, Jorion was a good man, a fine and mighty warrior, whose loyalty he would do much to hold.

Taine sank to her knees before Edward and lifted his hand, dropping her forehead on its back in honor as she fervently said, "Thank you, sire, for a gift truly beyond price."

Turning his sword-callused palm up, Edward helped her rise again, then turned once more to the table where candles of various height were grouped on a silver salver. The soft yellow light they cast warmed the drab parchment of his copy to a creamy hue and laid dark shadows in back of the wine flask and goblets standing behind. After pouring a measure of deep-red liquid carefully into five golden vessels, he passed one to each of the waiting four. Lifting the last, he spoke: "A toast of sorrow for the passing of Margaret, granddaughter of Alexander III." It was solemnly drunk to. Again Edward lifted his glass. "And a toast of health and long life to Martaine, Countess of Radwyn!"

Outside the court's bright-lit hall the two knights who had accompanied them were waiting with their horses when Jorion and Taine stepped into crisp night air. While Jorion moved forward to mount, anxious to reach home, Taine held back. Puzzled dark eyes turned to her. Too oft the brunt of rejection, insidious doubts snaked around the wall of his confidence. Now sure of her freedom from seekers for the crown, did she no longer have need of him? Would she renew her struggle for release? The possibility drove a painful lance thrust into his heart.

"No, Jorion." Seeing handsome features harden, Taine read his misgivings and immediately reached out to wrap her hands about both strong arms as she rushed to explain. "Only was I thinking of the first time we rode through Dunfermline—together."

Relieved by her reassurance, still Jorion did not understand her reason for wasting time talking of the past.

Taine gave up on oblique hints. Running her hands lightly up and down his muscular arms, she said, "I want to ride with you as I did then."

Jorion failed to see her purpose, but found the idea not unwelcome. Traveling in this manner, he could cradle her close even before they came again to his house. Pretending not to see the man's knowing grin, Jorion directed one of his knights to lead her horse home before quickly mounting and holding his arm down to her.

She clasped it and reveled in the strength that pulled her up to sit across Apollo. Following her lonely time in Castle Cregel, she'd spent the two days of their journey surrounded by others, but watching Jorion on Apollo and wishing she were riding again in his arms. Those first times she'd been too frightened to appreciate or enjoy the experience. Now, as Countess of Radwyn, she'd be expected to ride her own mare. This was a rare opportunity to indulge in such pleasures and she would claim it.

As Jorion set their steed into motion, she settled back into her husband's embrace and softly told him, "When you carried me from the fair, I was terrified by your strength, but fascinated too. I could not stop staring at you and that only frightened me more. Like a victim of the legendary Golden Dragon, I fell prey to your unique attractions, snared by enthrallment's net."

Jorion looked down into her delicate, adoring face and answered, "Nay, 'tis you who have beguiled me until in support of you I would have defied my sovereign and fought to regain for you the kingdom he wants. If you flew from me now, as you sought to do when last we rode these streets ahorse together, I would enter the next battle without intent to survive."

Taine would never again let him fear rejection from her. "This time," Taine assured him, "I will not grab hold of a mane to keep from falling too near you." To prove her words, she curved close against his powerful chest. Laying one hand atop one broad shoulder and arching up, she gently brushed her lips across his.

Caught unprepared by her sudden sweet caress, Jorion returned it full measure, stealing her breath and invading her senses with a smoldering pleasure which threatened to flare out of control. Only the barking of a dog disturbed in his slumbers recalled Jorion to their surroundings, and he forced his head back despite the mouth that clung, unwilling to forgo such delights. He held his kiss from her, but could not prevent his gaze from tracing her each enticing curve.

Feeling bereft, Taine lifted toward him, but strong hands held her back. She looked questioningly into a crooked smile without mockery and eyes that burned with golden fires. "Your temptations are a welcome pleasure and willingly would I surrender to their call, but now is not the time and here is not the place." He tilted his head back to the two shadows following at a discreet distance.

Taine buried hot cheeks in the curve of his throat. She'd not paused to consider the end she offered with such solace. For some time they quietly wound through dark streets until, at length, luxuriating in her husband's mighty arms, Taine peeked up. A few gleams escaped from between cracks in drawn shutters and pierced the velvet night surrounding them to gild blond hair and burnish bronze features.

Although his eyes were steady on the route ahead, Jorion felt the green-fire gaze stroking him with a touch that scorched and set his blood to boiling. Mayhap it was not such a fine notion to carry her in his arms, when she was clearly willing but the place so wrong. He turned her fully against him, crushing her soft breasts against his broad chest as he urged his golden steed to greater speed.

Focused on the man who held her near, sending tingles of pleasure trembling through her, she barely noted the bunching of Apollo's powerful muscles or the wild dash through narrow streets which followed.

Leaving their knights far behind, they reached the house on the town's outer boundary in an incredibly short time, reaffirming Jorion's value of his Saracen breed's fleetness. Sander jumped to his feet from the post he'd taken near the door to await their return. Jorion swung down, threw him the reins, and reached for Taine all in the same motion.

Breathless from more than the wild ride, Taine slid into his arms, but a grubby face peering around the edge of the door caught her attention. She leaned back from an impatient Jorion to motion Stephen from his hideaway. Impervious to the dragon's frown, Stephen scampered forward at Taine's bidding.

"You should be abed," she scolded, without heat.

Stephen diffidently shrugged away the words. "I only wanted to be sure you came safely home."

Bright hair gleamed as Jorion shook his head in mock disgust. "And you deemed it possible I might fail to see her protected without your aid?"

Stephen did not respond, merely looked at Jorion suspiciously from beneath frowning brows.

"Best you tread with care, young sir, else I may take back my promise of training to knighthood."

This threat widened Stephen's eyes and he immediately stammered, "Oh, nay, milord—I—I—"

Jorion relented in the face of such consternation and reached out to ruffle an already untidy thatch. "Do not worry, I ever hold to my promises. Besides, anyone with as much audacity as you deserves to train and by the doing learn his own limitations."

As Taine watched the teasing, she remembered the plan she'd devised to aid the boy while seeking distraction from fear in Castle Cregel. Jorion had spoken true when he said as serf Stephen would find acceptance hard to earn from others all of noble blood.

"Sander," she called, turning her winning smile to the squire still lingering near, "as boon to me, I beg you will take my young friend, Stephen, teach him how to behave and comfortably join the other pages in Castle Dragonsward. Stand him as friend among strangers."

Sander gave Stephen a doubtful look but nodded compliance with his lady's request. Her sweet smile warmed him again and was reward enough to earn what she asked.

Taine was pleased. As squire to the dragon, Sander was the leader among the squires and pages of Radwyn. Were he seen to accept the boy, likely the others would follow his lead. She turned back to Jorion and met eyes gleaming with understanding of her deed. Giving her his arm, he led her into the house and straight to their private chamber where a fresh stocked fire burned, but not nearly so hot or bright as the pyre of pleasure they built.

Enclosed in the warm, dark cavern of a heavily draped and shared bed, Jorion was too filled with joy to sleep. Once more he silently acknowledged that all the disappointments and rejections of his past were small price for the priceless burden lying half across his chest. He'd survived his penance and fate had delivered the prize. Taine was his with no lingering threat to steal her away. Moreover, she offered herself willingly, welcomed his embrace, and accepted, even delighted in, the things that made him different from other men.

He reached out to tug the draperies slightly apart and let hearthlight dance like fire in the riot of curls beneath his chin. As Edward had told him when first he'd taken Taine to him, her safety would be assured by bearing his sons. Inconceivable as it would seem, the three parchments with royal seal could be stolen and destroyed. Greed for a prize as rich as a throne could inspire miraculous deeds. But their part-Saracen children would be his heirs as well as hers, and none would be anxious to see one of them on the Scottish throne. In the end, as the ultimate source of peace and safety for the woman he loved, his disdained and long-cursed bloodline had become a blessing.

A strong hand lightly caressed Taine's back from nape down the length of her spine. The gentle touch and soft glow of dwindling firelight nudged sleep from her. Yet, still filled with the lassitude of contentment, she lingered in sweet dreams where pleasure and fire joined. As she arched against her living pillow to nuzzle passion-swollen lips into the curve of Jorion's throat, happiness wrapped its shimmering cloak about her. She was free to love where she would, free to share and enjoy a life without threat. Rising up on one elbow and letting the weight of her thick curls fall over her shoulder into a satin pool on his chest, she traced his dark-gold brows, straight nose, and firm lips with a gentle finger. "I love you." The whispered words ached with the same wealth of emotion that glowed in crystal-green eyes.

"And I love you, my fire-sprite, my treasured fate." Jorion's low voice of rich, dark velvet smoothed over Taine like a caress, before he drew her mouth slowly to his, kindling to a renewed blaze.

❧ Epilogue ❧

Spring of 1305

THE PIPER'S GAY NOTES danced round and through the trimbel's steady rhythm, just as the colorfully garbed acrobats jumped and rolled through the laughing crowd. What seemed a lifetime ago, Taine had escaped Bertwald's watchful eye to find a fair and here in brightly striped tents, merry spectators, and excited children it was. Turning slowly, she absorbed each detail—the appetizing aroma of fresh honeysweet pastries, the amazing dexterity of jugglers, and the tradesmen enticing fairgoers with unique wares. It had been a lifetime past. A dark and dreary life of bitterness and hunted flight replaced by one of happiness, trust, and love. Most of all love.

Taine looked up into the laughing face of the tall man at her side. Strong sunlight glowed gold on his hair and she thanked the fate he'd once spoken of for, in her moment of despair, drawing her eyes to the beacon of his hair at that Scottish gathering, which had disappointed her in being no fair at all—merely her saving. Her face went still with the memory of all he had risked for her.

"Worried for little Edward?" Jorion asked, misunderstanding her serious look and shaking his head ruefully.

"I've never journeyed away from the castle without him before." Taine willingly turned her thoughts to his topic, not wanting to raise past and near-forgotten threats on this glad day.

"'Tis hardly a journey of note," he said, waving his arm around the meadow stretching beyond the fair's tents. "We're barely beyond the outer bailey wall. Indeed"—he pointed over her shoulder—"look there and you'll see our home still stands all of a piece and near invincible."

Taine glanced back where he indicated. Castle Dragonsward's towers, newly whitewashed, glistened in the sun and her husband's standard rippled from the highest point—a golden dragon rampant, dancing on the breeze. She grinned. The sight was reassuring for it seemed a symbol of the protection that had brought her to safety and would easily hold their small son protected.

"You are as bad or worse than Elspeth. You should see her hover over her tiny daughter. Richard has even written a song about his wife and their wee one." Jorion shook his head in mock disgust.

"I wish I could have seen all three," Taine responded. Jorion had recently stopped at their home on Elspeth's hereditary lands, as he returned from his last foray into Scotland with King Edward. Their sovereign had claimed victory and begun the process of organizing government, ordering the community of Scotland to meet at Perth and choose representatives to come to his parliament and treat for the secure custody of Scotland. Jorion doubted 'twould be a lasting peace, but Taine did not wish to think on it more. Yet, if he were called again to war, she would accept the need calmly, as she had no doubt but that Jorion was well able to defeat any fair-met foe on the field of battle.

Unaware of the turn Taine's thoughts had taken, Jorion continued his arguments on the matter of their son's care. "If Halyse can manage that young terror of hers, she can easily watch our toddling for a few hours."

"Aye," Taine grinned, "Bryce is a dreadfully mischievous child. Isn't it a fine thing that her new daughter is so dark and quiet?"

"A son like the mother and a daughter like the father—seems only just," Jorion responded.

"Then what of our family? Edward has your golden skin and hair, but my eyes. What then of this wee one I carry?"

Black eyes settled on his wife's gently rounded shape and softened to velvet. "Well, then, I guess our daughter must have your hair and my eyes." He wrapped his arm about Taine and turned her toward the mummers' play about to begin. She leaned back against him, snuggling closer in trust as the players appeared. He nestled his chin on dark-fire ringlets and closed his eyes, savoring the warm feel of her soft form and fresh rose scent. He had been blessed.